O9-BUC-064

PRAISE FOR DESTINY SORIA'S

IRON CAST

★ "Energetic and original, this alternative history, fantasy, and mystery mashup with its pair of smart, resourceful, flawed but engaging heroines never disappoints."
—*Kirkus Reviews*, starred review

★ "Hand this entrancing historical fantasy to fans of Libba Bray's Diviners series or anyone who likes their magic on the seamier side."
—*Booklist*, starred review

★ "Stories of the diverse cast of flawed and complicated characters striving to do better complement the solid female friendship at the core of this absorbing novel . . . Mystery and fantasy blend well in this witty title filled with twists and fast-paced action."
—*School Library Journal*, starred review

"Destiny Soria's debut is without a doubt one of the best of the year."
—*YA Books Central*

For Isaac and Bryson. If words are weapons, you're the reason I fight.

Library of Congress Cataloging-in-Publication Data

Names: Soria, Destiny, author.
Title: Beneath the citadel / by Destiny Soria.
Description: New York: Amulet Books, 2018. | Summary: Cassa, the orphaned daughter of rebels, and friends Alys, Evander, and Newt, fight back against the high council of Eldra, which has ruled for centuries based solely on ancient prophesies.
Identifiers: LCCN 2018001836 | ISBN 9781419731464 (hardcover with jacket)
Subjects: | CYAC: Prophecies—Fiction. | Revolutions—Fiction. | Orphans—Fiction. | Fantasy.
Classification: LCC PZ7.1.S678 Be 2018 | DDC [Fic]—dc23

Book design by Siobhán Gallagher

Printed and bound in U.S.A.
11 10 9 8 7 6 5 4 3 2

BENEATH THE CITADEL

BY DESTINY SORIA

AMULET BOOKS
NEW YORK

ONE

THE CHANCELLOR

FOUR people were supposed to die at sunrise. The four members of the council sat in the Judgment Hall, prepared to declare the prisoners' fate. The high chancellor himself oversaw the proceedings, as was customary in trials for treason. Deep beneath the citadel, the executioner was waiting.

The chancellor was a very old man. On days like this, he felt it in his bones. The last execution of rebels had been several years ago, but the chancellor hadn't held his position then. His predecessor had been a younger man, better suited for the rigors of the office. Better suited for the heavily embroidered, smothering ceremonial robes. Better suited for hours of standing on the dais with only a table stacked with documents for support.

Better suited for realizing how very *young* the first prisoner was when the two guards led her into the hall. She was of true Teruvian stock, her fine black hair chopped short around her shoulders, her bronze skin muddied from the dungeons and showing faint purple bruising on her arms and under one eye. The gray dress they had put her in hung sacklike on her thin, boyish frame. The chancellor felt momentarily ill. Sixteen years looked different on paper than it did in real life. She was a child.

A child who had knowingly committed treason. Or attempted to, anyway. Unfortunately, the law didn't allow for the distinction.

"Cassandra Valera," the chancellor read from the paper in front of him, frowning at the surname.

"Present and accounted for," she replied. "The name is Cassa though."

The chancellor looked at her, surprised at her light tone. The two guards had stepped to the side, leaving her alone in the center of the room. Her stance was relaxed, almost casual. She lifted her manacled hands absently to scratch her cheek as she stared around the room in open curiosity.

"Do you know why you're here?" the chancellor asked.

"I'd be pretty dim if I didn't," she said, finally casting her gaze in his direction. "I mean, even more than I was in getting caught."

"So you don't deny your crimes?" The chancellor looked at the other council members, at a loss. They seemed just as perplexed as he was. He'd been expecting terror and pleading or hatred and vitriol. It had never occurred to him to expect this.

"Why would I deny successfully infiltrating the Central Keep with nothing but some barrels and a pry bar? I'm really quite proud of myself."

One of the council members cleared their throat pointedly, and the chancellor looked back at the parchment in front of him. Her name, her age, her crimes. What a strange, inadequate summary of a life.

"In accordance with the evidence against you—and your own confession—this council will now pronounce its judgment."

Each council member stood and spoke their verdict. The prisoner was declared guilty four times over. She didn't seem overly concerned. She was looking around the Judgment Hall again, squinting at the mosaics of the elder seers on the great domed ceiling.

The chancellor paused a moment, awkwardly. He took the cue from his fellow councilor and cleared his throat. Still her attention did not return to him. The men and women of the council were starting to fidget.

"In accordance with the judgment of this council," the chancellor finally said, "you are found guilty of high treason and sentenced to death in the customary manner."

It was the first time he had ever officially sentenced someone to death. He had imagined it would carry more weight, when the time came, but it was hard to take even himself seriously when Cassa Valera was still admiring the decor.

"Do you think the elder seers saw everything?" she asked, giving no indication that she'd even heard the ruling.

The chancellor hesitated, looking to the councilors, but again their expressions mirrored his own confusion. He had a feeling he was supposed to order the guards to escort her back to her cell now.

"What do you mean?" he asked instead.

"I mean, do you think they saw the entire future, every moment of every decade to come?"

There was a certain innocence to the question. It reminded him so much of his niece—she was about Cassa's age—and how she would ask similar questions of philosophy and history, her face screwed up in concentration.

"The teachings laid down by Teruvia's forefathers tell us that the elder seers saw every thread of the tapestry that is our present and future."

"So a few hundred years ago, some old bearded man somewhere fell asleep and dreamed about a girl standing beneath a hideous mosaic of his face while another old bearded man sentenced her to die?"

Her tone and expression had not changed at all, but her innocence had melded into mockery. The chancellor's neck grew warm.

"The elder seers understood the world differently than we do," he said. "It is not something we in the present can comprehend."

She nodded slowly.

"That's probably for the best. I, for one, would not care to have a vivid dream every time a baby somewhere soiled itself."

A low rumbling among the councilors.

"Do you think it wise to mock our sacred traditions on the eve of your death?" Councilor Barwick snapped, red-faced, even though the chancellor alone was supposed to address the prisoner.

"I imagine that would be very unwise," she said. She was still looking at the chancellor. "But I don't intend to die."

A wry chuckle escaped the chancellor before he could catch himself.

"Ever?" he asked.

Cassa shrugged. The metal around her wrists jangled softly.

"Alys keeps telling me I'm not immortal, but that's never actually been proven, has it?"

"I suppose tomorrow we'll see."

"I suppose we shall."

The chancellor could feel the discontent among the councilors like a thick cloud. He waved at the guards, and they stepped forward to lead the prisoner away. She cast one glance over her shoulder at the threshold, but she didn't look toward the dais. She was surveying the mosaic dome one last time, a strand of dark hair falling over her dark eyes. The door shut with a reverberating sound.

The second prisoner was more demure than the first. Newt Dalton stood quite still and stared at his feet while the chancellor read the charges, and he had nothing to say in his own defense. Between the two guards, he seemed a small and fragile thing. He had the white skin of northern ancestry, flushed a rosy, timid pink. Dishwater blond hair curling at the nape of his neck. Narrow shoulders. Bony arms. He was barely fifteen years old.

The chancellor scanned the parchment in front of him a second time but saw no indication of the boy's role in the plot, only that he had been apprehended with the others.

"What is your trade, boy?" the chancellor asked, not unkindly. It was mostly curiosity. The judgment would be passed presently. His fate was all but sealed.

"My father was a cooper, sir." His voice was tenuous but respectful.

"And you learned the trade from him?"

"I learned a great deal from him, sir."

"And how did you get mixed up in this business then, if you've a father who loves you enough to teach you a useful skill like barrel-making?"

The boy's shoulders hunched slightly, and he ducked his head a little lower. A proper show of shame.

"Cassa and the others can be very . . . persuasive," he muttered.

"I am sorry that you found yourself among such bad company," the chancellor said, and he truly meant it. The boy was so young. "This council will now pronounce its judgment."

The verdict of "guilty" came dutifully from four mouths. Newt didn't cringe at the word, but he didn't look up either. His head was still hung when the chancellor spoke his sentence and the guards led him away.

The third prisoner gave the chancellor a headache before the proceedings were even under way. Evander Sera, sixteen years old. Practically a man by society's standards, despite his boyish mannerisms. He shifted restlessly from one foot to the other, fingers tapping a staccato rhythm on his iron cuff. His short, dark hair was disheveled and powdered with dust. His skin was the light tawny brown that came from old Teruvian blood, with an odd grayish streak on his right forearm. A scar?

Evander didn't stand still long enough for the chancellor to figure it out. He cast his gaze over the assembled councilors but discerned quickly who was in charge and addressed the chancellor directly.

"Did she say it was my fault?"

The chancellor, who had still been trying in vain to get a good look at the mark on the prisoner's arm, blinked.

"Excuse me?"

"Cassa? Did she say it was my fault?"

The chancellor frowned and looked down at the parchment before him.

"You stand here before the high council faced with charges of—"

"Of course she did! As usual. Do you know that I'm the one who told her that the barrels were a bad idea? But that won't be the way she tells it."

"Charges of high treason and—"

"Listen to me, Your Chancellorness. If you ever get an offer from a mysterious girl to join a rebellion, do yourself a favor and take up bare-knuckle street fighting instead. It'll be less painful in the long run. You can have that advice free of charge."

The chancellor stared at him for a second, wavering between disbelief and annoyance.

"Is that all?" he asked after a few seconds of silence.

"I can tell your fortune too, if you like," said Evander. "Costs a silver to read the silver though." He raised his bound hands. A shiny coin flashed between his slender fingers.

Several of the councilors recoiled as if he'd just pulled a weapon. From their reactions, the chancellor realized suddenly what the mark on Evander's arm must be and felt foolish. Of course that's what it was. The words were scrawled just beneath his name on the document, a caution: *Bloodbond. Silver.*

"Guards," he snapped, but the guards had already raced forward, grabbing at the prisoner's hands.

Evander gave up the coin without a fight, smiling serenely at the pistols pointed in his direction. Satisfied that the threat was in hand, the chancellor took a deep breath and glared between the two guards.

"How did he get that past you?"

The two men exchanged a nervous look, caught in a silent battle of wills as to who would reply.

"I don't know, sir," said the apparent loser, his voice cracking.

"Don't blame them," said Evander. "Silver's such a tricky metal, when it's in the right hands."

As he spoke, there was another flash between his fingers. The second coin rolled across his knuckles, inciting uproar as it went. The guards practically tackled him in an effort to wrench it away. The council members were demanding that the chancellor do something. A couple stood up to leave. Coins might seem harmless, but the chancellor had seen people with bloodbonds cause damage with less. With a bloodbond's complete control over a particular metal, any number of everyday items could become weapons—and there was no telling what other silver implements the boy had managed to smuggle past the guards.

"Take him back to the dungeon," the chancellor shouted over the panicked din. "Evander Sera, you are found guilty of high treason and are sentenced to death in the customary manner."

Perhaps the prisoner did not hear his fate, because he was laughing as the guards dragged him out of the chamber.

The fourth prisoner didn't look much like her brother. Alys Sera was shorter and quieter than Evander. Fat with a heart-shaped face and big bright eyes. Only the nose was the same, straight and sharp. Unlike her brother and other companions, she hardly looked worse for wear, with a clean face and black, silky hair in a perfect braid over her left shoulder. Her brows arched when the chancellor asked her if she had anything to say in her defense.

"Just pass your judgment and be done with it," she said, a touch of irritation in her tone. “I’ve got better things to do than stand around watching old people hem and haw over my choices.”

The chancellor’s first urge was to ask her what better things she had to do, considering the rest of her short life would be spent in a cell. But she was staring at him with such unblinking, uncompromising displeasure that the words died in his throat.

“This council will now pronounce its judgment,” he said.

She eyed each council member in turn as they spoke, and then her gaze swiveled back to the chancellor expectantly. He cleared his throat. Why did he feel like a schoolboy again? For seers’ sake, she was only seventeen.

“In accordance with the judgment of this council, you are found guilty of high treason and sentenced to death in the customary manner.”

Alys sighed, and it sounded absurdly like relief.

“Finally,” she said. “Maybe in the future you should consider a more efficient means of sentencing people to death. Surely there are better uses of the council’s time than all this pomp and circumstance.”

Before the chancellor could say another word, she had turned on her heel to go. The guards rushed to her side in a vain attempt to make it seem that they were escorting her and not the other way around.

two

Evander

EVANDER hated the dark. He wasn't exactly scared of it. He just hated the uncertainty it brought. The fumbling blindness. The chaos of his other senses trying to compensate.

A few years ago, he'd started having nightmares about being lost in a dark cavern. The tunnels twisting and endless. The stone slick beneath his fingers, giving him nothing to grasp. A pit with no bottom, jagged rocks on all sides like teeth in a gaping maw. Sometimes he fell, sometimes he didn't.

His sister, only a year older but always decades wiser, had told him that nightmares were the mind's way of exploring subconscious fears. He knew that a clinical explanation was Alys's idea of comfort. As long as he could remember, she'd been collecting facts and assembling logic like armor and weaponry. She told him that the reason she never used her skill at divining was that the future was shifting and unreliable. Logic never was. Evander knew that wasn't the real reason, but he'd never told her that.

The future wasn't his area of expertise anyway. He couldn't even manage a simple divination, to his mother's mostly well-hidden dismay. Evander had found ways around his lack of gifts during the last days of the rebellion, when his family was daily on the brink of starvation. People were happy to pay silver to a charming street diviner. They liked his tricks with the coins, and they liked being told what they wanted to hear—whether or not it would really come to pass. And then of course there had been the Blacksmith. But Evander didn't remember much about that day beyond the events leading up to it: the sudden, forceful decision and that long, dusty road outside the city. Knocking on the front door. Being afraid that he wouldn't be able to go through with it. Being afraid of what might happen to his family if he didn't. After that, his memory was only a bright spot of impossible pain.

In a place like this, it was easy to get lost in those memories. In dreams of dark places.

The citadel's dungeons were precisely what dungeons were supposed to be. All gray sweating stone and thick oaken doors and iron bars. When he made himself listen, he could hear the sounds of other prisoners—whimpering, chattering manically. The skittering of rodents. The dripping of condensation. The only light came from the eye-level iron grate in the door of his cell: a tenuous golden glow from the lantern hanging in the corridor.

If he closed his eyes, he was in the cavern of his nightmares, lost in the fathomless dark.

But no, the cell wasn't fathomless. Maybe three paces wide in every direction, with a bed of rotting straw and a putrid bucket in one corner. Evander didn't mind any of that. His eyes were on the light. He had realized a few hours ago, before they had taken him in front of the council, that the golden gleam shone also in a thin line beneath the door. The gap was too narrow for a rodent or even a finger but plenty wide enough for a coin.

Evander's cell was near the head of the corridor. Straining to peer through the grating, he had seen them leading Cassa and Newt back from their sentencing before they'd come for him. And after they'd deposited him back in his cell, he'd seen the same two guards leading Alys up the stairs.

He hadn't bothered calling out. The four of them knew they were down here together, and he didn't want to bring any unnecessary attention to himself. He'd already earned a few bruises during the interrogation. It wasn't supposed to be a painful process, but the sentient who was reading his memories hadn't appreciated his sense of humor and had called in a burly guard to impart the wisdom of keeping his mouth shut. Lesson learned, although the display in the Judgment Hall was necessary. Luckily, all his bones were still intact, and he was in possession of all his fingers and toes. He intended to keep it that way.

Once the footsteps of Alys and the guards had faded and the door at the top of the stairs had slammed shut with a distant thud, Evander focused on the stationary guard in the alcove at the base of the stairwell. From his vantage point, Evander could see only half of the table where the guard sat devouring his evening meal. Though the light outside his cell was golden, a different light suffused the alcove, pale blue and altogether eerie. He personally had never understood the appeal of ghost globes as a source of illumination, regardless of how alchemically advanced Alys insisted they were. Pressing the side of his face against the iron, Evander studied the back of the guard's left shoulder, the knife in his hand sawing at a tough piece of meat, the tin mug beside his plate. Evander smiled.

Without stepping back from the door, he twitched his fingers at his side. A silver coin rolled from beneath the straw in the corner, dipping with the grooves in the floor until it fell onto its side beside Evander's bare foot. He was careful not to let it touch his skin. Even the brief contact with the two coins in the Judgment Hall had made him dizzy. He wasn't used to being so cautious with silver. Usually the metal was his comfort. His saving grace.

But these particular coins had been coated in a very particular poison, and Alys was especially skilled at her trade.

Another twitch of his fingers, and the coin shot under the door. Then came the tricky part. He couldn't see the coin, only where he needed it to go. The silver line on his right forearm burned with his concentration. It didn't hurt, but the insistent heat throbbed noticeably just below his skin. He could feel the silver like an extension of himself, moving farther and farther away, the connection weakening more and more. At some point, when he guessed the coin was still a few yards from its target, he lost it.

Evander cursed under his breath and redoubled his concentration. The mark on his skin burned ever hotter. It was a curiously painless sensation, but he couldn't shake the ridiculous notion that if he touched his arm to the wooden door, he would scorch it black. Finally, he felt the silver again.

"Come on," he coaxed in a whisper. It was like trying to move his foot after it had fallen asleep, awkward and ungainly.

Impatient, he pressed harder against the door, straining to see a flash of the coin on the floor, pushing vigorously with his mind. He felt the coin shoot into the air before he saw it. Once he caught a glimpse of silver, he was able to regain control. He stopped it in midair, a few inches from the back of the guard's head.

Evander hissed a breath through his teeth. Cassa never would have let him live *that* down. He let the coin hover where it was rather than risk losing sight of it again. He wasn't sure what he was waiting for. He just hoped whatever it was would happen soon.

The guard continued his meal for five more minutes, oblivious to the coin floating just behind his head. Every second dragged on excruciatingly for Evander. He was sweating by now from the heat in his arm and the effort of his concentration. He was focused so completely on the silver that when the guard dropped his fork and bent to retrieve it, Evander almost missed his chance.

He dropped the coin into the mug a split second before the guard straightened. He breathed a heavy sigh and sagged against the door. More than anything, he wanted to curl up on the floor and go to sleep, but he had to be sure. He watched until the guard took a long pull from the mug, and then he smiled. If Alys was right—and she always was—the poison on the coin would take effect soon.

Summoning his dwindling strength, he licked his lips and let out a long, piercing whistle.

One down.

THREE

Newt

NOT that he would ever admit it to the others, but Newt hadn't expected the dungeons to smell this bad. He kept thinking he would get used to the stench of his own waste mingled with mildew and sweat and whatever other invisible odors past prisoners had left behind in the tiny cell, but so far he still gagged every time he accidentally breathed too deeply.

When they returned him from his sentencing, the brief reprieve above made the smell seem ten times fouler in the citadel's underbelly. It took him almost five minutes to convince the meager contents of his stomach to remain where they were. The guards thought he was upset about the judgment and were surprisingly sympathetic. Newt knew it was because of how young he looked. He'd spent his whole life trying and failing to convince people of his age. It was even worse now that he'd thrown his lot in with Cassa, Evander, and Alys.

Evander was already tall, and his perpetual frenetic twitching only made him take up more space. He had an easy confidence about him that usually made people assume he was older than sixteen.

Cassa matched Newt in height and Evander in outward confidence, though hers was charged more with sheer determination. Most people couldn't keep up with her, much less make assumptions about her age.

Alys was the shortest of the group, and she was a perfectly balanced mixture of caution, logic, and acerbic wit. She'd always scared Newt a little bit, although that was something else he would never admit. People usually didn't ask how old Alys was.

Newt was short, spindly, and mousy. People usually thought he was at least three years younger than he was. At the moment he didn't mind seeming weak and waifish, because the guards left him alone for the most part. He'd witnessed Evander and Cassa take a few extra cuffs courtesy of their smart mouths, and Newt didn't feel a need to assert himself to those ends.

The only need Newt had felt recently with any conviction was the need to vomit, but he wasn't about to add to the stench of his cell, so he gritted his teeth and composed himself. Besides, he had other concerns at the moment.

It had been ten minutes since the guard on patrol had passed his cell. If the man kept to the same pattern, then he would be returning down the corridor any minute. Newt sat down cross-legged, with his back to the door and his manacled hands resting in his lap. He'd been waiting as long as possible, afraid that the stationary guard by the stairwell would randomly decide to check on the prisoners. But he couldn't put it off any longer.

Newt breathed in deeply through his mouth and, with a wince, popped his left thumb out of its socket. It didn't hurt, but he'd never grown used to the uncanny sensation. With his thumb bent flat over the top of his hand, he maneuvered himself free of the cuff. He pushed his thumb back into place and repeated the process with his right hand. In less than a minute, the manacles were on the floor, and he was rubbing his chafed wrists with no small sense of satisfaction. The hard part wasn't over yet though.

He tucked one of the cuffs into his waistband and stood up. He eyed the distance between the top of the door and the ceiling (less than three feet) and the distance between the walls on either side (six feet, maybe less). A few hours ago, when he'd settled on his plan, not knowing when or if the others would be able to escape, the distances had seemed ideal. He wasn't sure anymore, but he was also running out of time. He could hear cursing and jeering from the prisoners down the hall who had yet to resign themselves to quiet contemplation of their sins. The patrol guard was on his way.

Newt swiped his hands over his thighs to dry his palms and placed them against the wall adjacent to the door. He walked his feet backward and up the opposing wall until he was stretched horizontally across the door, several feet off the ground. To his chagrin, his arms were already starting to burn, and his lungs tightened with the exertion. He hadn't exactly had time to fully rest and recover from the absurdity that was Cassa's plan to infiltrate the citadel. From the beginning, he had never been convinced that her plan for uncovering the council's involvement in the mysterious disappearances throughout the city was going to work at all, but there was no way he was going to tell Cassa that. In all fairness, her plan to get into the citadel *had* worked. It was getting out again that had proved to be the problem.

The guard was getting closer. Newt could hear his distant footfalls, thudding on stone. Ignoring his aching muscles, Newt alternated moving his hands and feet until he was suspended over the top of the doorframe. His breath came in short, tight gasps, but the hard part still wasn't over yet. In the back of his mind, buried beneath the protests of his body and the ever-nearing footsteps of the patrol, he registered the sound of a single, reverberating whistle.

Maybe he'd imagined it. He really hoped he hadn't. He also really hoped he wasn't about to die.

Painstakingly, Newt moved his right hand across the wall, centering it with his shoulders, and then removed his left hand and pulled the manacles from his waistband. He only had one shot at this. He wasn't even sure it would work, but he didn't have any other ideas. He didn't have Alys's brains or Evander's gift or—well, he actually didn't know how Cassa would break free. Possibly irritate the guard into releasing her.

Newt only had his body, which he'd learned as a child how to bend where others would break, how to hold steady where others would fall. A lesson from his father.

When the footsteps were even with the cell door, Newt flung the manacles against the back wall. Iron clattered on stone, echoing tremendously. Newt held his breath, listening. Sweat trickled down his forehead, tickling his nose, dripping to the floor. He imagined he could hear the droplets as they landed, the breathing of the guard as he considered the source of the sound. The footsteps stilled.

"What's going on in there, kid?" The guard rapped on the metal grating in the door.

Though his muscles trembled and went into spasm, Newt didn't move. Didn't break. Didn't fall.

The cell was illuminated slightly by the guard's lantern as he pressed it against the grating, trying to get a better look inside. Could he see the manacles? Would he just fetch more guards?

"Come on, kid," the guard groaned. "I'm half an hour from the end of my shift. Couldn't you figure out how to slip your cuffs on the next guy's watch?"

Newt remained still and silent. There was no way the guard could see him. He probably assumed Newt was sitting right against the door. It was the cell's only blind spot—or the only one the guard knew about.

"Just move to the back wall so I can get in there." The guard was starting to sound peeved.

Silence, silence. Newt was good at silence. Another lesson from his father.

"For seers' sake, kid. I don't have time for whatever you're playing at."

The whisper-hiss of steel against leather. He'd pulled his dagger. There was a brief rattling as he secured the lantern to the hook on the wall. The lock clunked heavily under the key. Newt's life wasn't flashing before his eyes, and he was grateful for that, but he was pretty sure he was about to die.

He'd rather it be here and now than tomorrow in the catacombs below the citadel. He wouldn't go quietly to the executioner, to have his memories stripped away by the death rites before meeting whatever gruesome demise awaited him. He wouldn't give them that.

The door flew open with surprising force. The guard—who had

assumed he'd be pushing Newt's weight as well—stumbled after it, off-balance. Newt didn't wait, didn't think. He dropped to the floor, kicked at the back of the guard's knee, then threw his shoulder into the small of the man's back. Without the slightest pause to even ascertain if the man was going to fall or if a blade would soon be buried in his back, Newt dove for the corridor, yanking the door as he went. It latched behind him, shuddering almost immediately with the guard's weight as he shouted profanities at Newt.

Newt didn't stop to reflect on his success. He grabbed the lantern from the wall and ran. And as he ran, he let out two short, shrill whistles.

Two down, two to go.

FOUR

ALYS

ALYS'S problem with the escape plan was that there wasn't an actual escape plan at all. None of them had expected to get caught. Alys had, of course, mentioned to Cassa the wisdom in making provisions for the worst-case scenario. The high council was served by the best seers and diviners in the city. There was a good chance that someone was going to see them coming. Cassa had, of course, dismissed her out of hand. She didn't take kindly to being reminded that her actions might be foretold.

Vesper and Evander had sided with Cassa, as always, and Newt had refused to take a side, as always. So really, Alys should have known from the beginning that she couldn't win. That didn't stop her from being prepared though.

As always.

As they neared the bottom of the dungeon steps, she could tell that the two guards escorting her were moving more sluggishly than they had on the way to the Judgment Hall. She wasn't exactly sure about the timing of the sleeping poison she'd doused Evander's coins with, especially since she had no idea how much contact the guards had had with the silver when they had taken Evander before the council. Evander would have had no trouble getting the coins confiscated, but he couldn't have controlled any variables beyond that. She'd been terrified they would both drop unconscious right at the high chancellor's feet. That would've put an abrupt end to her semblance of an escape plan.

Now that they were safely in the dungeons, she had relaxed somewhat. When they reached the bottom of the steps and she saw the man in the alcove slumped over his dinner, snoring soundly, she relaxed even more. Her escorts both laughed at the sight of their fellow guard.

"After ten years on the job, you'd think he'd be able to hold his liquor," said one of the guards as the other went to smack his dozing comrade on the back.

"Come on, you oaf, wake up," he said.

When the man didn't stir, the guard shook him harder. When that didn't work, he picked up the tin mug by the man's left hand and took a whiff.

"Something's wrong." He slammed the cup back onto the table. "This is just coffee."

But by then the guard at Alys's elbow had already slid to the ground, unconscious. Somewhere down the corridor came two whistles. Alys allowed herself the luxury of believing this might actually work.

"Witch," snarled the last standing guard. He drew his pistol. The light from the ghost globe glimmered on the steel, on the brassy rows of buttons on his dark blue uniform, on the white of his bared teeth.

"Apothecary, actually," said Alys, backing away from him. But there wasn't anywhere for her to go. He was blocking the corridor, and she couldn't exactly run up the steps and back into the Central Keep.

It occurred to her that he probably hadn't handled a coin long enough for the poison to take effect. It occurred to her that the miscalculation was going to cost her her life. It also occurred to her, very forcefully and with no small amount of indignation, that this was all Cassa's fault.

She didn't see Newt until he was only a few feet away from the guard and was swinging something—a lantern—in a high arc toward the back of the man's head. There was a terrific thump, followed by another thump as the man fell to the floor, his gun clattering beside him. Alys met Newt's eyes over the man's limp form. He was flushed bright red and trembling but looked no worse for wear.

"Good timing." It was all she could think to say.

Newt just nodded.

"Get his keys." Alys gestured toward the guard at the table, then pointed to the second door down the corridor. "Evander is there."

Newt nodded again and did as she said. Alys knelt down and searched the bodies of the two guards on the floor until she found the key to her manacles. She freed herself and cuffed the guard that Newt had knocked unconscious, just in case.

Newt and Evander were coming back by then.

"Aren't you going to get these off me too?" Evander asked when he realized he was the only one still manacled.

"Depends on how attached you are to your hand bones," Newt said.

"On second thought, I think I'll keep them. You know as soon as I take them off, they'll come into fashion."

"I have the key." Alys stood up and tossed it to her brother. "Does anyone know where Cassa's cell is?"

"Do we know where the deepest, darkest part of the dungeon is?" Evander asked, fiddling with the lock. "I imagine that's where they shoved her."

"We don't have a lot of time." Newt glanced nervously toward the stairwell. "The patrol guard's shift change is in half an hour."

"Maybe we should split up," Evander said.

Alys stared down the long corridor lined with cells. From where she stood, she could tell that farther down it branched into more and more corridors. She wondered, briefly, if any of the rebels from the failed insurrection were still rotting down here, then shook the thought away. If they wanted to survive this, there wasn't time for mercy missions. She wasn't even sure there was time for Cassa.

"We should stay together," she said. "We can't risk losing each other again. And take the ghost globe. It will last longer than the lanterns."

Neither Newt nor Evander protested. The globe, which was a little less than a foot in diameter, was suspended from the ceiling of the alcove, netted in thin rope. The swirling, unnatural blue of the Alchemist's Flame, trapped mid-combustion inside the glass orb, was rumored to be eternal—although of course there was no way to prove that. Evander took a knife from one of the unconscious guards and hopped onto the table. He sliced the rope as high as he could reach, so that they could tie it into a makeshift handle. With the crisp light illuminating their path, they started together into the maze of cells. Alys tried not to linger on the question that kept crawling into her head. If leaving now was the only way to escape, would Cassa want them to go without her?

She didn't know the answer to that. And she didn't know what it meant that the thought had even occurred to her at all.

FIVE

CASSA

REBELLION was in Cassa's blood. She'd been born a rebel, rocked in a cradle while her parents whispered treasonous plans by firelight. Low voices and locked doors were her childhood. She'd learned how to keep a secret before she knew how to spell her own name. She learned loyalty with her letters, lost timidity with her baby teeth. She'd had a fire in her belly for sixteen years, and last night was supposed to be the moment it finally meant something.

The worst part about it was that her plan *had* worked. The kitchen workers had unknowingly smuggled all four of them into the basement storerooms in barrels of beer that were only half full. Cassa hadn't minded the journey as much as she'd expected, although if she never took another sip of beer in her life, she would be happy. She'd amused herself by reciting as many of the elder seers' fifty infallible prophecies as she could remember, over and over again in her head. Her father, who hated the seers as much as any man could, had made her memorize all of them when she was young. He insisted it was the only way she could understand what was missing.

He'd died before he could tell her exactly what that was.

It was Newt who had freed them from the barrels at the muffled clanging of seven bells. He was the only one who could maneuver enough in the wooden confines to kick his lid off. Then he'd used a pry bar to remove the other lids. They'd brought fresh clothes in tightly bundled oilcloth sacks. At that point, Cassa had no reason to think anything was wrong. Even when Vesper had backed out at the last minute, Cassa knew her plan was solid.

Most of the citadel's inhabitants would be at the monthly council session, where any new prophecies were discussed and the fulfillment of old prophecies was speculated on. Cassa had been to one when she was very young, before her parents had been outed as rebel spies. Mostly what she remembered about it was the incessant droning and how little everyone who was crammed into the massive but stuffy hall had seemed to care about it. The prophecies kept the council in power, but their day-to-day minutiae held little interest for the citadel's elite—even though they were the ones who benefited most from the seers' influence.

Cassa didn't care about the prophecies. She didn't believe they dictated her life any more than the rebellion had believed they should be able to dictate the city. "If they own your future, then they own you," her mother had murmured into her ear while the chancellor went on and on. Her lithe fingers brushed through Cassa's hair softly, a wordless sort of lullaby. "Never let that happen."

Cassa had never been sure how to steer clear of prophecies in a city that subsisted on them, but ever since that day, she'd done her best. There had been fewer and fewer prophecies coming out of the citadel in recent years anyway, though not so few that the council's purpose was in question. The council, headed by the chancellor, had been established several centuries ago by the king and charged with protecting the seers and rooks born in the city of Eldra, as well as the diviners and sentients, whose gifts were weaker but nonetheless important. It was the council's duty to keep a record of all the seers' prophetic dreams and to ensure that no rooks ever abused their power to take memories from a person's mind. The councilors interpreted the prophecies of seers and diviners, using them to give Teruvia advantage over its neighboring countries. They trained sentients and rooks as interrogators, ensuring that criminals' guilt could never be hidden.

Maybe all those centuries ago the council had actually served the citizens as intended, but that wasn't the case anymore. Now the prophecies were twisted to justify the council's seizing land and raising taxes on the lower wards to fund their lifestyles and buy loyalty from the nobles at the expense of ordinary citizens. Diviners were hired to warn the council of impending plots, and sentients were hired to identify dissenters. Rooks administered the council's justice, devouring the memories of the condemned under the guise of death rites. The executioner, who was rumored to wait beneath the citadel for his victims, was supposedly a rook, though Cassa wasn't sure how true those rumors were, and she certainly had no intention of meeting the executioner to find out.

What Cassa did know for sure was that the council was hiding something worse than its usual corruption. In the past few months, people who visited the citadel, either to plead some case before the council or to attend one of the open memorial services for the Slain God, were going missing. It had just been gossip at first, but then a well-known baker from the lower ward had gone into the citadel and never come back out. The guards refused access to his family, who wanted to look for him, claiming there was no record that he had ever entered the citadel.

There were other rumors too, of people in the citadel collapsing suddenly, crying out in pain before falling unconscious. Maybe it was some kind of illness. Maybe it was something worse. Either way, the council denied all knowledge, which meant they were somehow complicit. The rebellion might be over, and all the real firebrands might be gone, but Cassa wasn't ready to just leave the city to its fate—not when her parents had died defending it.

Her plan to break into the citadel was foolproof, though her plan on how they were going to find evidence of what the council was hiding was a little shakier. She knew after they made it past the walls she would figure something out. She always did.

But she never got the chance. They barely made it out of the storeroom before the guards surrounded them. Guards who should have been stationed near the Great Hall to keep eyes on the citizens streaming into the council session. More guards than should ever have been charged with the safety of a storage basement.

The process had been faster than Cassa could have anticipated. They'd been captured, interrogated, and put on trial in less than twenty-four hours. Alys probably approved of the efficiency, but Cassa refused to admit that their plan had been foretold. There was more to it than that. She felt it in her gut.

She jumped to her feet and began to pace the cell, twisting her wrists against the cuffs in absent rhythms, trying to make sense of her own instinct. The bruises on her arms where they'd grabbed her had stopped hurting, but the one under her eye, from insulting the interrogating sentient too many times, still hurt when she blinked. Now that the sentencing was over, she knew that time was running out. She should have come up with a way to escape the cell by now. She was the one in charge after all.

"A whistle for each guard you take down," she had whispered to the others right before they were dragged away. "We'll find each other. We'll get out."

It was less a promise and more a directive. There hadn't been time after their capture to formulate an actual plan. But they knew each other well enough to depend on certain facts. Like that each of them would be able to figure out how many guards were in the dungeons at any given time—four—and that each of them would be able to devise a way out of their cell. But perhaps she had been a little too optimistic on that front.

Cassa also hadn't considered the possibility that her cell would be so far from the others. She'd heard plenty of cursing and crying and dirty ditties over the past day, but no whistles. Maybe none of them was going to get out of here.

If that was the case, she hoped she didn't have to see them before she died. She didn't want to see their faces when they realized she'd let them down. And she certainly didn't want Alys's "I told you so" to be the last thing she ever heard.

She'd tried every form of bribery and deceit on the guards, but her usual bag of tricks had failed her. The quelled rebellion was still fresh in the minds of the public. The council wasn't going to miss a chance to execute dissenters, especially considering who Cassa's parents were.

At the sound of footsteps in the corridor, she paused. An unwelcome surge of panic rose in her chest. More interrogations? Surely in the time they had spent together, the sentient had laid bare every detail of her past, but maybe the council wanted to be sure. The chancellor wanted quick executions, probably hoping their swift justice would overshadow the fact that rebels had managed to break into the citadel in the first place. But there were several hours until dawn.

A face appeared at the iron grating, indistinct in the shadows. Cassa stood firm, unwilling to back away. Then came the voice.

"Wait a minute, are you telling me that the great and mighty Cassandra Valera was the only one of us who didn't manage to break herself out?"

The panic bubbling in her chest dissipated so suddenly that she felt dizzy. Cassa had never been more relieved to hear Evander's voice in her life. Not even when she'd gotten trapped a few years ago for almost two weeks while exploring the caverns under Aurelia Valley and he'd been the one to find her, his lantern a blinding beacon after so much darkness.

Cassa couldn't help but smile.

"Why would I waste the effort when I knew one of you would be coming along to do it for me?"

"Your quick wit isn't going to distract us from your laughable incompetence."

"Just open the damn door."

The other prisoners in the dungeon had caught on to what was happening and were starting to raise a din. Cassa vaguely considered releasing as many as they could, to slow down the guards, but there was no telling how many of these people were imprisoned for actual crimes. She didn't fancy being responsible for murderers and rapists being let loose in the city.

She let the others lead the way back to the alcove at the base of the stairs. Her mind was racing almost too fast to keep up. There was no way they could escape through the Central Keep. She knew she needed to mention as much, but there was also something she needed from the alcove where, aside from the table and chairs and padlocked weapons cabinet, there was a small, dusty writing desk, presumably used for record-keeping.

One of the three unconscious guards was stirring, and Evander helped Alys pour some coffee down his throat. Seemed counterproductive, but Cassa was intent on searching the desk. It took her only a few seconds to find what she was looking for. Everyone else would assume the council had foreseen their coming, but Cassa knew otherwise. The real truth was a terrible, wrenching pain in her chest, but she wouldn't let it go.

"What are you doing?" Newt asked in a nervous whisper.

Cassa smoothed out the scrap of parchment as best she could and shook the ink pen.

"Didn't your mother ever teach you it's polite to leave a note when you're breaking out of someone's dungeons?" she asked as she wrote.

Newt shook his head. Possibly an answer but more likely an expression of disbelief. It was hard to tell with him sometimes.

A creak and thud at the top of the stairs. The door.

"The shift change," Newt whispered.

"We have to fight him," Evander said. "That's our only way out."

Cassa finished her note and folded it into her palm.

"If only you knew someone who had another way out of here." She stooped down to snag one of the unconscious guard's pistols from his belt. Just in case.

Her friends were all staring at her. Cassa smiled again—she was having fun now—and began to run back the way they'd come. She knew they would follow. They always did.

SIX

THE CHANCELLOR

FOUR people were supposed to die at sunrise. The council had passed judgment. The high chancellor had looked them each in the eye and informed them of their fate. Beneath the citadel, even deeper than the dungeons, the executioner waited. But by midnight, the only trace of the condemned was four empty cells.

And a single scrap of paper.

The guards had found it in one of the girl's cells. Cassandra-called-Cassa. The one who thought she was immortal. The chancellor had to admit: She still had not been proven wrong.

High Chancellor Ansel Dane sat down behind the oak desk in his study, which was warmed by a large hearth. He was as far away from the dank despair of the dungeons and the cold justice of the Judgment Hall as he could be. He'd already ordered the stablemaster to prepare his carriage, but he wasn't in a hurry. It wouldn't take long to reach his destination. The chancellor was an old man, less suited than his predecessors to the rigors of his office, but he knew how to play the long game. How else did a nobody from the countryside, the son and grandson of farmers, become a high chancellor of Teruvia?

He unfolded the paper carefully. The parchment was ragged and stained with what he hoped was mud. The ink was blotchy and smeared, penned in a rush, but each word was legible.

Vesper—

I know it was you. I should have let you burn.

Ansel stared in silence for a long while, listening to the crackle and hiss of the fireplace. Finally he stood up, his bones creaking with the effort. He shuffled to the hearth, rested one hand on the mantel to steady himself, and fed the paper to the flames.

SEVEN

VESPER

THE darkness in the chapel was absolute. Vesper knew her head was supposed to be bowed in reverence, but since no one could see her anyway, she kept her eyes wide open, straining instinctively for a glimpse of light. She'd been attending memorials for the Slain God since she'd been old enough to not cry in the darkness, but every service still felt new. Because she was staring forward, where the ornate marble altar sat atop the dais, she saw the first tiny flame spark to life. A pinprick of gold in a sea of black.

The choir began to sing a gentle, haunting requiem in Teruvia's dead language. The tale of the god who had once cradled Teruvia, protecting it from those who, in envy and greed, would do her harm. As the disembodied voices rose and fell, two more candles were lit on either side of the first. These seemed brighter. The song built in a slow fury, reaching its crescendo. The tale of the god's brothers and sisters, equal in power but racked with jealousy over Teruvia's devotion. Three rows of candles sprang to life in quick succession, like a river of fire running across the altar.

The voices rose to a terrible height, fierce and staccato. The tale of their god, set upon by his own kin and the devastating monsters they'd created for the gruesome purpose. The tale of a battle that rocked the heavens and the earth and all that lay below. The candles that lined the walls of the apse were lit all at once. Vesper blinked at the influx of light and stared upward at the mirrors built into the shadowy recesses of the ceiling, which refracted the new light in a thousand directions. Mirrors lined the walls as well, creating endless echoes of flame. For the space of a breath she was eleven years old again, trapped in a chapel just like this one while fire danced in her vision and smoke filled her lungs.

Vesper forced the memory away with practiced ease. With a final, roaring note, the choir cut off. For a split second, all was glorious light and breathless silence. Then the lights went out. The suddenness caught in Vesper's throat, though she knew it was coming. She'd never managed to discover the mechanics behind the theatrics. Maybe she would ask Alys for her opinion.

The thought was accompanied by a pang in her chest, the biting truth of what she'd done. She'd made the only choice she could, but her friends wouldn't understand. She might not even have a chance to explain herself. She might never see them again. This memory wasn't one she could so easily push away.

Her thoughts were thankfully interrupted by a single, lovely voice lifting in the new darkness. The aria was plaintive and elegiac. The tale of their dying god, who used the last of his strength to scatter his omniscience across Teruvia, a gift for the chosen devout few. The ability to see the boundless future in dreams, to take and give memories with a touch.

Gifts to be passed down through the bloodlines for centuries, fading eventually to the skill of divining the near future in objects and reading the past in faces.

Vesper had heard the requiem for the Slain God so many times that it felt like a part of her. She couldn't believe the story with the same unquestioning innocence she had in her youth, but the weight of tradition felt so enormous, it brought tears to her eyes all the same. As the lonely voice's last echoes died away, a single candle on the altar flickered to life once more, a guiding star in the perfect dark.

Then came the screaming.

At first Vesper thought it was a frightened child, but after a few seconds she realized it wasn't a child's cry. People were murmuring and shifting in their seats. Someone called for light. Slowly the chapel came into hazy view as acolytes in dark robes scurried along the walls, igniting the gaslights. Vesper stepped into the aisle and saw the huddle of figures near the last row. Through the staggering motion of the crowd, she saw a woman on her back—the source of the screams. A man clutched her tightly, desperately, crying out for help as the woman flailed against him, clutching her head. Her shrieks were almost inhuman.

A few guards raced into the room, pushing people aside, shouting in decidedly uncalm voices for everyone to stay calm. Then the screams stopped, and the woman fell limp.

"Not again," murmured the man next to Vesper.

She didn't wait to see more. She stumbled through the crowd toward the altar, slipping through the intricate maze of puddling wax. She knocked over a short candelabra with her skirt but didn't slow down. She went through the door at the back of the nave and into the cool, dark corridors beyond.

She wound her way through the maze of hallways until she emerged into the crisp air. The sky was velvet black, with only a smattering of stars visible through the clouds. Memorials for the Slain God were always held in the middle of the night, although Vesper had never been entirely sure why. Something about the importance of keeping a vigil, although she suspected the priests and acolytes were probably just guessing on that front. The religion of the Slain God had begun to fade. During the century-long rebellion, the upkeep of many traditions was lost. No one had time to mourn a dead god when hunger and violence stalked the door.

The memorial service was in the Mirror Keep, which was named not for the surplus of mirrors in its chapel but for its having been built as an exact replica of the keep that was gutted by fire two hundred years past. *The left arm of the citadel will burn on the night of the equinox, in the spring that the crops fail to yield.* The twenty-second infallible prophecy, and one of the few that dealt directly with the city of Eldra. A year of drought, a negligible harvest, and an unquenchable flame.

Sometimes Vesper wondered if, in the face of their loss, the citizens had been comforted by the knowledge that the elder seers had foreseen it all. That there was nothing they could have done to prevent it.

The citadel felt both crowded and vast as she headed for the clerks' dormitory in the Anchor Keep. The paved streets were arrow-straight, unlike the winding paths of Eldra's tiered wards, which belted the citadel in concentric circles like a bull's-eye. The gray stone edifices cast everything in shadow, while their windows caught the dazzling sparks of the street lamps. The streets around the Central Keep, hemmed at four corners by the other keeps, were the oldest parts of the citadel. They had been built even before the fortified walls that separated the five keeps from the rest of Eldra.

Because it was a memorial night, chapels all over the citadel had been hosting crowds of the reverent. So, despite the hour, the streets were inundated with citizens in their mourning garb, though there was nothing drab about the assortment of black silk and velvet, darkly glinting gemstones, and delicate lace fans that surrounded Vesper as she walked. Most of the elite only visited for the memorial and would soon return to their feather beds in the upper echelon to sleep the day away. Mingled with them were the working citizens of the citadel. An alchemist scurried past in his stained green smock and gloves, muttering to himself. Clerks in their typical black attire, with leather sleeve-protectors and ink-stained fingertips. She passed a couple of senior clerks she recognized and kept her head down. She doubted they had been talking about her, but they definitely fell silent when they saw her. She'd gotten used to it a long time ago. People tended to keep a tight tongue around her. She couldn't blame them.

Strictly speaking, she should have gone through a couple of years of training before she was qualified to wear the clerk's uniform. Children typically started when they were thirteen, their positions bought or traded by families rich or ambitious enough to do so. But Vesper was better connected than most.

A knot of people made their way toward her, boisterous and laughing. Three women and two men, all dressed simply but expensively. Vesper recognized them before she could make out the gold pins on their lapels designating their skills. The men and one of the women were diviners. The other women were sentients. All were employed by the council, and all ignored her as they neared. She stepped aside to let them pass, eyeing their carefree demeanor with a touch of envy. Then she walked on.

The castellated roof of the Central Keep was coming into view, a dark fortress against the darker sky. The gas lamps lining the streets winked orange and blue, bathing Vesper in a faint glow. A breeze played across the back of her neck, and she shivered. She'd left her wrap in the chapel. Would they have moved the woman yet? Would they let her husband stay with her?

It was the first time Vesper had seen someone in that state. She'd heard the rumors, of course, and her uncle had confirmed them for her after the fourth person was struck down. But it was different to hear the screams for herself. To realize how easily it could have been her. Vesper shivered again and walked a little faster.

EIGHT

EVANDER

THE first problem with being underground was that you never quite knew where you stood. Literally. Evander had lost track of how far they had come and what direction they were going. Fortunately, the tunnel, which sloped gently downward, offered no options but forward or back. They had only been running for about ten minutes, but he hadn't had a proper meal or more than a few gulps of water in the past day. He was so exhausted, the minutes were starting to feel like hours.

Cassa hadn't said anything about the purpose of the tunnel, which was behind a heavy oak door deep in the dungeons. It was just wide enough for two people to stand side by side and low enough for Evander to touch the ceiling without stretching. He had no idea how Cassa knew about it or where it was supposed to lead. He couldn't afford to expend energy on anything but moving forward. The only breaks in his strict rhythm of left foot, right foot, breathe in, breathe out were when Cassa handed him the ghost globe or took it back from him. The glass was hollow, but it was already becoming unbearably heavy. Both his shoulders ached so badly that he was close to convincing himself it would be worth it to ditch the globe and continue in the dark. He'd noticed that Cassa's last turn was much shorter than his, no doubt unconsciously on her part. On another day he would have mocked her relentlessly for that, but tonight it seemed a waste of breath. He kept thinking how stubborn he and Cassa both were for not just asking Newt or Alys to take a turn. He wondered if she was thinking that too. Neither of them said anything.

The second problem with being underground was that there was no telling what was around the next bend. Cassa was in the lead when the tunnel turned at a sharp angle, and suddenly they weren't in a tunnel anymore. Cassa skidded to a stop at the edge of a precipice. Evander was so immersed in his contemplation of their joint stubbornness that he barely stopped himself from running into her. Newt wasn't as quick. He barreled into Evander, who knocked into Cassa, who flew forward. She threw out a hand and caught herself on the wall right before she tumbled down what Evander now saw wasn't a precipice but a steep flight of stone steps. Cassa kept her grip on the pistol, but the globe crashed to the ground and rolled down a few steps before losing momentum.

"Sorry," Newt mumbled, peeling himself off Evander's back.

"Seriously, Evander?" Cassa snapped as she recovered her balance. "The kid's half your size."

Even in the blue light, Evander could see that Newt was bright pink. Their eyes met, and Newt quickly looked down, brushing off the knees of his ratty prison-issued trousers as if all they needed to be clean again was a light dusting. Alys, who alone had managed to retain her dignity, moved between them.

"Be careful with it," she said, stepping down to retrieve the ghost globe. She was breathing heavily and trying to hide it. "If it breaks, the alchemical reaction with the air can be dangerous."

"Dangerous how?" Cassa asked, taking it from her and observing it with new interest. There were no visible cracks in the glass, and the mystifying flame still whirled.

"It would blind us for starters—maybe only temporarily. Maybe not," Alys said, slipping into the clinical tone that sounded so much like their mother. "The process to ignite an Alchemist's Flame can take months, and the combustion is so volatile that only someone who has a bloodbond with glass can capture it in the globe."

She looked like their mother too, pretty and plump but with eyes that could gut anyone with a glance, though at the moment they were as bright as the Alchemist's Flame. She never could resist the chance to explain something.

"I didn't know a bloodbond with glass was even possible," Newt said. Bloodbonds typically only worked with pure, liquid elements—usually metals that could be melted down.

"It's possible," Alys said. "Just not very viable."

"What does that mean?" Newt asked.

"It means the person usually dies." Evander scratched absently at the scar on his arm.

"If we lose the light, the alchemical reaction won't be our biggest problem," Cassa said. She had already drifted away from the conversation and was descending the steps slowly, holding the globe over her head. The stairs were hewn painstakingly into the bedrock, and though they were cracked and crumbling at the edges, they seemed sturdy enough. The steps curved away from them, into the inky darkness beyond the blue light, and Evander realized it was a spiral winding down a massive central pillar.

He followed Cassa down, with Alys and Newt close behind him. As they descended, the cavern opened up around them, a vast, echoing chamber of shadow and stone. Evander ran his fingertips along the wall to his left. It was smooth but patterned with intricate designs carved deeply into the stone. Whorls and arrows like a forgotten language.

Deeper and deeper they went, until the ceiling of the cavern was lost in darkness above them. The steps were too steep to risk running, which Evander's lungs and legs were grateful for, but his ears were pricked for sounds of pursuit. Surely it wouldn't take long for the guards to realize where they had gone. And if this path led out of the dungeons, shouldn't they be going up, not down? He stared at the back of Cassa's head and had the thought, not entirely unprecedented, that she had no idea where she was leading them.

Finally the stairs ended at another tunnel, but this one felt different than the other. As soon as they entered, the hairs on the back of Evander's neck and arms stood on end. The ghost globe's eerie light cast their shadows in distorted shapes against the walls and low ceiling. The walls were composed of stacked slabs, all roughly the same dimension, like building blocks. Evander stopped in front of one and studied it. More strange engravings, delicate and mesmerizing but altogether incomprehensible. The longer he stared, the more he was certain they weren't just decoration.

"That's the language of the first seers." Alys came up beside him, frowning as she traced a finger along one of the swirling lines.

"Looks like scribbles to me," Cassa said. She was waiting impatiently farther down the tunnel. Evander couldn't help but notice the edge of worry in her tone. Judging from the way Alys had just turned to glare at her, he had a feeling it wasn't concern about the guards catching up.

"These are the crypts." Alys's voice was sharp and resonant against the stone.

A chill ran down Evander's back. The crypts beneath the citadel were where the elder seers were buried. He eyed the stacked rows of slabs stretching into blackness. Not building blocks. Tombs.

"Shit," he muttered under his breath, taking a step back. He knocked elbows with Newt, who was peering at the walls with more puzzlement than horror.

"Of course we're in the crypts," Cassa said. "Where else did you think a tunnel in the dungeons would lead? A wine cellar?"

"You might have mentioned it," Newt said, not sounding nearly as irritated as he should have at Cassa's convenient omission.

"It was the only way out." There was no hint of apology in her voice.

"Your idea of an escape from our executions was to take us straight to the place where the executions happen?" Evander asked. "Were you just hoping to save time?"

"If we make it through the crypts, there's a path that leads out of the caverns and into Aurelia Valley," Cassa said.

"And you know this how?" Alys demanded.

"Have I ever let you down?"

"I'm not sure we have time for me to make a list," Alys said coolly.

Evander winced. Behind Alys, Newt took a tiny step backward. A hare shying from a confrontation between wolves. He probably had the right idea.

Cassa was quiet for a few seconds, her dark eyes unyielding. The light washed over her face in waves of blue. With her puckered lower lip, her snub nose, and the faint splash of freckles over her cheeks, she didn't look particularly fierce. That was an assumption that only people who'd never met her could make though.

"Unless you want to take your chances in the citadel, this is the only way out," she said at last.

"The crypts are a maze," Alys said, unappeased. "We could get lost in there for days. They won't have to execute us, just drag our bodies out."

"That's the spirit," Cassa said with a grim smile. "Now let's go."

"Shouldn't we at least talk about this?" Evander asked.

"Talk about it all you want," Cassa said, "but I'm going this way, and I'm going now." Without another word, she took off down the passage, taking the ghost globe with her.

"Insufferable," Alys muttered into the growing dark.

"I guess we should follow her," Newt said.

"She would come back if we just stayed here," Alys said.

"She would," said Evander, "but we should follow her."

Alys sighed but didn't argue further. The three of them followed the light, which hadn't slowed at all, as if Cassa really didn't care what they decided to do. Or she just knew they would decide to follow. Soon enough the passage split into multiple passages. Every direction looked the same to Evander, but Cassa studied the corners one by one until finally she tapped her finger triumphantly against one of the carvings. Three arrows stacked, all indicating the same direction.

"It's only a maze if you don't know the way," she said with no small hint of self-satisfaction. Evander tried to think of a pithy reply, but before he could, Cassa had launched into a jog. He groaned, then started jogging too. They'd lost too much time to keep walking. There was no telling how far behind them the guards were, unless maybe the guards had decided that there was no way they'd escape the crypts anyway and weren't giving chase—an oddly comforting but likely vain hope.

The tombs passed by in a gray blur. Cassa paused only briefly at each fork in the passage to determine the way. Evander was struggling to keep his breathing even, and a stitch was forming in his side. He kept pace with Cassa, though he stayed a few feet behind her. If she was so smug about her possession of the ghost globe, then she could damn well carry it herself for a while. Strangely enough, the feeling of self-righteousness fueled his pace much better than his fear of being dragged back to the dungeons. He was beginning to understand why his sister subsisted on it.

They navigated the maze in silence for at least another ten minutes. Bare feet slapping on stone and their wheezing were the only sounds in the crypts. Up ahead the passage split left and right. Cassa stopped and studied the walls. Evander dropped his hands to his knees and gulped in a few breaths. The stitch in his side was just starting to fade when he realized how long they had been standing there. He looked to find Cassa still staring at the walls. It didn't take him long to see what the problem was. The walls of both passages, as far as the light reached, were smooth and bare. No carvings, no arrows.

"Shit," Evander said, helpfully.

NINE

ALYS

BY the time they stopped, Alys was having trouble remembering what was so terrible about a noble execution. Surely it would be better than being skewered in the back as they ran, with no death rites, covered in sweat and muck and too winded to even catch a proper final breath. Ever since they'd entered the crypts, Cassa and Evander had set the pace, flagging only to check the symbols on the walls. Behind them, Newt's arms and legs pumped at an infuriatingly steady speed. Alys lagged several yards behind Newt, far enough that when they took a left or right turn, she would lose sight of them and be plunged into darkness for a few terrible seconds.

Finally, they reached a split in the passage that gave Cassa pause. Alys knew she should probably be concerned, especially when Evander cursed and Cassa shot him the same glare she always did when she didn't know what to do and someone had dared to notice. But Alys decided that since Cassa never listened to anyone but herself anyway, she might as well rest. She collapsed flat on her back, even though Newt told her she would have an easier time catching her breath if she were upright. After a few gasping minutes, she finally managed to pull herself into a seated position, her back against the stone wall. It was slick with condensation, and she turned her head to the side, pressing her hot cheek against the blessed coolness. Her inner thighs had begun to chafe annoyingly, and the shapeless, calf-length dress they had given her pinched under her arms, but she didn't have the energy to adjust it.

Evander, abandoning Cassa to her contemplation, sat down beside her. He looked tired but not exhausted. Alys wondered if maybe Cassa wasn't really stuck and they had stopped just for Alys's own benefit. It wouldn't be the first time. She was an apothecary—or at least she was trying to be one. She'd spent her life behind a workbench, measuring and mixing and studying. She wasn't meant for this business of hiding in beer barrels and facing down armed guards and descending barefoot into the bowels of the earth. That world was for Cassa, Evander, and Newt. It always had been.

She closed her eyes, trying to return her breathing to normal, determined to convince everyone that she could keep up. If she couldn't, they would have to leave her behind. The guards would find her. The sentient would read the truth in her features. Her friends would be betrayed. Maybe it would be better if she just died before they caught up. Maybe it would be better if she died now. Maybe it would be better. Maybe it would.

Round and round, the familiar, dizzying maelstrom, tossing her back and forth inside her head. Her lungs were constricting again, her chest aching with a new, sharp pain. She was light-headed. Weightless. The stone against her cheek was gone. She couldn't feel her fingers. This couldn't be happening. Not now not now not now not—

"Alys." Her brother's voice. Soft. Steady. "Alys, open your eyes."

She was afraid to open her eyes because sometimes in the middle of the maelstrom everything was hazy and dreamlike, and what if one day she couldn't find her way back to the waking world? But Evander said her name again, softer this time, or maybe she had withdrawn too far into herself to hear him. She didn't know what else to do. She opened her eyes.

His face sprang into focus. A little blurry but mostly not. Mostly he was just Evander. Brown eyes, darker than hers, almost black. His jet hair shiny with sweat. His eyebrows drawn together in concern. The ghost light cast shadows across the planes of his face. Sometimes he looked so much like their father, it made her want to cry.

"Is there any way we survive this?" she asked. Her voice came out sounding hollow and all wrong.

Evander studied her for a few seconds. His lips quirked slightly.

"Truth or lie?" he asked.

She might have smiled if she'd had the strength. The question was a familiar one, stretching back to their early childhood. For a long time it had been a guessing game. One of them would tell a story or state a fact and then ask, "Truth or lie?" Evander was a better liar than she was, but she'd always been better at seeing the truth. Then, after that harrowing night eight years ago, when their family had lost everything, the game had changed. The question meant something different now. *What do you need to hear?*

"Truth," Alys said, even though the word caught in her throat.

"We'll find a way," he told her. "We're going to make it."

Slowly, Alys pressed her fingernails into her palms, harder and harder until finally she could feel the pinpricks of pain. She squeezed until the anxiety faded, until her lungs loosened, until there were purple half-moons embedded in her palms. She took a deep, slow breath and nodded at Evander. He nodded back, the creases in his forehead fading.

"I almost forgot," she said to Evander, as she pulled three coins from the pocket in her dress. "Here. I cleaned them off as well as I could. They're probably safe."

"Probably?" Evander echoed, a little dryly. But he was smiling when he took them from her.

Alys watched the silver roll one by one across his knuckles and disappear. When they were younger, she loved to watch him practice, memorizing the motions, making suggestions when he couldn't get a trick just right. She loved being a part of the process, sharing in the thrill of success.

That had been before he went to see the Blacksmith, of course. Alys's eyes were drawn involuntarily to Evander's forearm. In the dusky light, the scar was a dull gray. Alys looked away before he noticed.

"Well, I have good news and bad news," Cassa said, turning to face them.

"What's the bad news?" Evander asked.

"I don't actually have any good news."

"We're lost," Alys said flatly.

"We're not lost," Cassa said. She turned back to stare at the smooth wall and did not offer any alternatives.

"They're going to catch up," Newt said. There was a definite break in his usually calm exterior, though his voice betrayed nothing.

"They're not going to catch up," Cassa said. Again, no justification. Just that baseless, infuriating confidence.

"We shouldn't have come," Alys said. She wasn't sure if she meant into the crypts or into the citadel in the first place. She knew people had been falling ill and disappearing, and she knew the council was probably involved, but she didn't think that made it their job to take on the whole citadel by themselves.

"The route is supposed to be marked." Cassa ran a hand through her shoulder-length hair, leaving streaks of grime. "Vesper said—"

She cut herself off. Alys closed her eyes for a few seconds, trying to keep her focus. Their group felt off-balance without Vesper here, like a house with a cracked foundation. She was the only one who could keep Cassa in check, the only one who always made Alys feel like she was a necessary part of the team rather than a hindrance or someone who needed to be saved. She'd made Alys feel that way from the very first day they met. "Between the two of us," she'd said, with a conspiratorial smile, "we might just manage to keep Cassa alive." Those words had been more than a welcome; they were a promise. *We* meant together. *We* meant friends.

But Vesper was gone now. They were alone down here. She didn't want to believe that Vesper had betrayed them to the council—surely it made more sense that a diviner in the citadel had foreseen their plot. But from the moment that Vesper had backed out of their plan, there had been a seed of doubt in the pit of Alys's stomach. Now when she looked at Cassa's face, she knew that she wasn't the only one.

"We could split up," Newt said softly. "See where each path leads and meet back here."

"The guards will catch up by then." Evander climbed begrudgingly to his feet. "We need to pick a path and take our chances, together."

"We could always flip a coin," Alys said, her voice dripping with more disdain than she'd intended. Her exhaustion and looming mortality were wearing down her self-control.

"Actually . . ." Cassa began.

"Cassa, *no*." They all three spoke at once.

Cassa blinked at them, then rolled her eyes. "I was going to say, there's a way to know for sure." She looked pointedly at Alys.

Alys stared back at her, uncomprehending. Then she realized.

"No," she said, scrambling to her feet. "You know I don't read the coins anymore."

"It can't hurt anything," Cassa insisted.

"It can if I read them wrong and we—and we—" The words caught in her throat. Red-hot iron. Searing screams. She'd seen it all, and she hadn't stopped it.

"Alys, you have to try."

"She doesn't have to do anything," Evander said, stepping up beside her.

"It's either that or flip a coin," Cassa said, crossing her arms, though the severity of her expression had begun to soften. "What's the use of being a diviner if she never even tries to see the future?"

"She said no."

"Stop talking about me like I'm not here," Alys snapped. She could feel the familiar tightness in her chest, the dizzying spin of her thoughts. Not now, not now, not now. There was a sharp light at the edges of her vision, colorless and painful. They were trapped down here, surrounded by bones and stone. Trapped unless she read the coins. Trapped because she *couldn't* read the coins. Stone and bones and iron and screams. They were all watching her, and that only made the maelstrom in her mind worse. Not now, not now, not *now*.

"Give me the coins," she said. It came out more like a gasp. Her lungs felt clenched like fists. Her heart was thudding in her ears.

"Alys," Evander began. Why did he always look at her like she were about to shatter into a thousand pieces? Why did he always act like it was his job to protect her, when he was her younger brother, when it should have been the other way around? "You don't have to—"

"Give them to me." Alys held out her hand. She knew it was shaking. Let it shake. She wouldn't be the reason they died down here among the bones and stones.

Evander hesitated, then dropped the coins into her palm. They were warm from his pocket. For some reason she thought of the first coins she'd ever earned from helping the rebels, the day she had met Cassa—how accomplished she had felt. How unstoppable.

That was a long time ago now. Alys dropped to her knees, clutching the silver in her hand. Her breaths still came short and sharp, but the spiral of her thoughts was slowing. Maybe she was trapped and helpless, but she had the blood of the elder seers in her veins. That had to count for something.

She opened her hand and let the coins fall to the ground.

The future felt like a half-remembered poem, like glimpsing someone else's foggy memories. Diviners could never see farther than a week or two, a month at most. The far-flung future was only for the seers to know. Alys's mother had begun to teach her the moment it became evident she had the gift. There weren't a lot of diviners and sentients born outside the citadel and upper echelon, and rooks and seers were almost nonexistent in the lower wards—not because the gifts had anything to do with nobility, but because across generations the council had brought as many rooks, seers, sentients, and diviners into their employ as possible. The gift ran through bloodlines, though it wasn't unusual for it to skip a generation or even several.

If they'd wanted to, Alys or her mother could have gone to the citadel, been confirmed as diviners, and received lifelong employment. The possibility had never been tempting before, when the family apothecary shop had been thriving, but then her parents were caught helping a dying rebel and branded traitors. Red-hot iron, searing screams, and the possibility was lost. Alys didn't really care about the missed opportunity. The thought of working for the council turned her stomach, not that she was any good at divining anyway. Alys had never been slow to learn anything, but her gift proved to be difficult for her. She was used to precise measurements and structured formulas, not the haphazard scattering of coins or runes. The hazy, shifting future was not something she could dissect and study, and so she was always a little afraid of it.

She felt she had a right to be. If she were a better diviner, she might have saved her parents from the council's punishment.

Those memories wouldn't help her now though. She cleared her mind as best she could and concentrated on the coins. Some diviners worked better with more natural markers, like rune stones or tea leaves. She'd met a woman once who could read flower petals as they were plucked. For Alys the coins were the easiest. They were practical and uniform, and Evander always had some in his pocket. The future took shape for her in their distinct pattern and in the number that fell with the citadel's seal face up. The discrete, minute details all served as markers, and in her mind's eye she could see them all connecting like puzzle pieces. There was never just one future though; there were dozens, sometimes hundreds, and the longer she studied the coins, the more the variations began to crowd her mind. Her mother had told her to think of every future as a piece of thin paper, and when they were all stacked together and held to the light, the patterns that overlapped the most, that were bolder than the rest, formed the most likely future. Nothing was certain in divination, and the future could always change, but a talented and experienced diviner could be accurate more often than not.

Alys was neither talented nor experienced, but as she read the coins, she thought she could pick out some clear patterns. Water. A boat. A bargain. Moonlight. Before she could make sense of them, the images began to fall away from her, as if they were being pulled. She focused harder, but every time she thought she saw something, she lost it. Was she falling into another maelstrom?

No, it wasn't that. Her mind felt quiet, but it also felt like a sieve.

And then, so faint and so delicate that she knew she was just imagining it, there was a voice, coming from nowhere and everywhere.

Left. Go left.

She started and whipped her head around. There was only stillness beyond the ghost globe's steady blue glow. The others were staring at her in confusion. They hadn't heard the voice. She wasn't even sure *she* had heard the voice. She wasn't an expert diviner—she was barely even a novice diviner. Could the future manifest as a whisper? She looked back down at the coins, but she'd lost whatever she'd seen in them. Water and a boat. That didn't mean anything. Moonlight might mean the way out, but by itself the image was useless. They were still trapped down here. They were still going to die down here, and it was her fault, because she couldn't read the coins. Not again, not again, not again. Not now, not now, not—*Now. Go left. They're coming.*

She stood up so fast, she felt dizzy. She didn't know what was happening. She just knew that she couldn't bear to fail again.

"We have to go left," she said. "Hurry. I think the guards are coming."

Evander flicked his wrist, and the coins spun into the air and slipped one by one into his pocket. Cassa was eyeing her, not like she didn't believe her but like she could tell there was more going on in Alys's head than a simple divination. Before she could say anything, there was a faint, echoing sound. Footsteps.

"I guess we go left," Cassa said, sprinting into the tunnel. Newt and Evander went after her, and Alys followed them, driving her nails into her palms, trying to anchor herself to the stinging pain.

The footsteps weren't close yet, but they were getting closer. The citadel guards would know the maze well. They had led countless condemned souls through these crypts to meet their fate at the hands of the executioner.

More wrenching, useless panic. Maybe Vesper had been right to abandon them. Maybe none of this mattered anyway. Maybe the future was already decided, and they were never meant to make it out of here alive.

The thought was vaguely comforting, and that terrified her.

TEN

NEWT

AS they raced breakneck through the passage, Newt did not feel nearly as alarmed as he would have expected. Fear tightened his chest as he struggled to breathe, but it was muted. Alys knew what she was doing. She insisted she was a terrible diviner, but for as long as Newt had known her, Alys had never been truly terrible at anything.

As if in answer to his optimism, the tunnel widened, ending in an archway carved with the elaborate symbols of a long-forgotten language. Beyond the archway was a vast, empty darkness that the four of them hurtled into without hesitating. The cavern beyond the crypts felt boundless. Cassa held the ghost globe over her head, but the light still didn't dispel the shadows above. As they walked, rows of stalagmites came into view, gleaming wetly around them. Some were only a couple of feet tall; others were twice as tall as Evander. A strange stone forest interwoven with a natural path. They hadn't walked for very long when suddenly the cavern opened up, and the light reflected across smooth water.

It took Newt a few seconds to understand what he was looking at. A lake. He could glimpse only a fraction of it, but it was the most bizarrely beautiful thing that he had ever seen. The clear water glowed blue in the light, so still that it might have been glass. A forgotten enchantment amid the forgotten dead.

A few seconds later, he realized what else the lake was. A dead end.

Cassa turned to Alys, but before she could say a word, Alys snapped, "I don't know. I told you I didn't want to read the coins."

"Did you see this?" Cassa waved a hand toward the lake, which could have extended past the edge of the light a few feet or a few thousand feet.

"I—maybe. It's not that simple. It's not like reading a book."

"It's not your fault," Evander said to his sister, shooting Cassa a glare that Cassa very pointedly ignored.

"I'm not saying it's her fault," she said. "I'm just trying to figure out what she saw."

"I—I thought we were supposed to go left," Alys said. Her consternation was clear, even with her face half obscured in shadow.

Newt left them to their discussion and wandered down the edge of the shore. The archway they had just come through hadn't ended up there by accident. The sheer time and effort that must have gone into its architecture felt like a sign that they hadn't reached the end of the path.

Behind him, Alys and Cassa's argument increased in heat and volume while Evander tried in vain to mediate. Without Vesper here to buffer, Alys and Cassa's relationship was less like a good-natured contest of wills and more like a powder keg. Newt ignored them and looked down. The floor of the cavern was relatively smooth and a dull charcoal gray, except for some odd pale streaks that extended toward the shadowy recesses of the cave wall. Newt toed one of the lines thoughtfully, then returned to the others.

"Let me have the light," he said to Cassa, interrupting what was probably going to be a very long diatribe about how she was the one who'd figured out how to get them *into* the citadel and *out* of the dungeons, so shouldn't someone else take a turn?

Cassa blinked at him but handed him the globe. He headed back toward the scuff marks he'd seen on the ground. They were concentrated in a narrow area from the lake's edge to the wall.

"What is it?" Evander's voice, suddenly close, made Newt jump.

"It doesn't make any sense to build an elaborate archway to a lake that can't be crossed," he said, pleased at the evenness of his tone. As if escaping ancient tunnels while death closed in behind them was a regular pastime of his. As if being this close to Evander didn't send his heart into a thundering stampede.

"I'll be damned," Evander said, as the light spilled over wood. A rowboat with two oars stacked inside was tucked beneath a rocky outcropping.

Newt set the globe into the boat, curled his fingers over the bow, and tugged. It wasn't as heavy as it looked, but the strain still registered in his shoulders. A dull, familiar ache held the threat of something worse than sore muscles. He ignored it and pulled harder. The boat slid out a few inches, scraping loudly on the stone.

Beside him, Evander grabbed the edge, and together they dragged it the rest of the way to the shore.

"I'm not getting in that," Alys said. "It looks like it's a hundred years old."

"Someone's kept it in good repair," Newt said, running his fingers along the tarred sides.

"We don't even know what's on the other side of the lake."

"Our only other option is to go back to the fork and take the other passage," Evander said.

"We don't have time for that," Cassa said.

"If we take the boat, at least we know that no one can follow us," Newt said.

Alys frowned across the lake, but Newt could see the resignation settling into her face. She looked as if she wanted to say something else but paused. They all heard the sound at the same time, a faint echo, almost impossible to pinpoint as it ricocheted around them.

Rapid footsteps.

"That solves that dilemma. Get in." Cassa handed Alys the pistol.

Alys hopped in and pulled the ghost globe into her lap. Newt grabbed an oar and clambered in beside her, nearly capsizing the boat in his haste. Evander and Cassa pushed them off and swung in from each side, nearly capsizing it again. Newt tossed Evander the other oar, and they began to paddle in tandem, pushing them farther away from the shore.

Three guards came into view, shouting so furiously that their words were just chaos in his ears. They were lifting their guns.

"Duck," Alys gasped, trying to hide the light and throw off their aim.

Newt's gut told him it was too late. The guards were too close, and they had four targets. They wouldn't miss.

And yet there were no gunshots.

Newt squinted toward the shore as he struggled to keep pace with

Evander. All three of the men had stopped moving, one with his finger on the trigger, the others with their guns only half-raised, staring forward. Newt looked around but couldn't see what they were looking at. The lake only extended into further darkness. He looked back toward the shore, just in time to see one of the men collapse. His gun slid from his hand, at the edge of the water. The other men collapsed moments after. They rocked on the ground, moaning and holding their heads. One of them let out a ghastly shriek of pain. Then one by one they fell silent, fell limp. All else on the rapidly receding shore was perfectly, impossibly still.

The Night Cassa Met Vesper

CASSA was inside the citadel for only the second time in her life. Tonight there was no throng of people to gawk at in the streets, no droning of a councilor in the Great Hall. Tonight there was only silence, the schooling of her own breath, the tension in her muscles from being poised for so long. She was watching and waiting. It was almost midnight. And on the twelfth bell, they were going to burn down the chapel.

Her lookout position was atop the roof of the stables across the street. She could see the chapel clearly, as well as all the paths leading toward it. It was built of gray stone, meant to be sturdy rather than beautiful, like most things behind the citadel walls. Like all chapels of the Slain God, there was a small alcove inset above the doors, encased in glass, for the eternal flame. Alchemist's Fire, blue and swirling and lovely. Very distantly, she could hear shouting. That was the distraction—her mother's task. She had sneaked past the citadel walls first, through a sewer drain. It was her job to provoke the guards on patrol routes near the chapel into a chase.

"Don't worry, she's very provoking," her father had said on the night this plan had taken shape, his eyes glinting in the lamplight of their cramped kitchen.

Their fellow compatriots had chuckled, but her mother only smiled. She had a clever smile. A knowing smile. Her amusement was always the sort that left the rest of the world on the outside, wishing to be let in.

"True enough," she'd said.

Cassa had watched her mother's hand slip under table, where it found her husband's with familiar ease. When other couples held hands, it was tender and romantic. When her parents held hands, it was a reminder of how unbreakable they were together. How untouchable.

Her father was in charge of leading the rest of them to the chapel. They weren't going to the main chapel in the Mirror Keep but to a smaller one attached to the western wall. The fire wasn't about damaging the citadel. They wanted to send a message to the council. Their walls couldn't keep them safe anymore. The end was coming.

They had chosen midnight because it was hours after the last acolyte had left the chapel and hours before the first would arrive in the morning. Chapels of the Slain God were left unlocked for the reverent at all hours, but reverence was hard to come by in the middle of the night. No one would get hurt, but the message would be clear. The council would feel its sting.

Cassa wasn't the only lookout, but she was the only one small enough to climb through one of the stable's windows and take the ladder to the loft and then onto the roof. She was on her stomach, peering over the edge of the gutter. There was a tilt to the roof, and her head hurt from all the blood flowing to it, but there were only a few minutes left.

A whistle sounded to her left, quick enough to be a bird call. Cassa eyed the murky streets for a bit longer, then licked her lips and whistled the all clear. After a few moments, there was another whistle somewhere to her right.

The closer they got to midnight, the faster Cassa's heart raced. She'd helped the rebels before in small ways. She'd carried clandestine messages across the city and lugged provisions from one safe house to another. This was the first time she'd persuaded her parents to let her do something meaningful. She refused to let herself be afraid. She couldn't let them down.

She took deep breaths until her heart maintained a steadier rhythm. The bells in the clock tower began to ring. Because she knew what to look for, she saw three shadows detach from the wall and slip across the cobblestones to surround the chapel. They were going to set a fire just inside each of the three entrances simultaneously, to ensure that it wouldn't be easily put out. The exterior of the chapel was mostly stone, but the interior was wood paneling and pews and old tapestries. With the help of a little lamp oil, it would burn quickly.

Even in the darkness, she could pick the shape of her father out of the shadows. He wasn't the tallest or the broadest, but he had a way to his movements. He wasn't cautious and creeping like the others. He strode straight to the main entrance as if he were the high chancellor himself. Her father wasn't afraid of being caught. He was only ever afraid that the mission wouldn't be complete.

Cassa tore her eyes away from the motion at the chapel to keep an eye on the streets. Now were the most precarious moments of the entire enterprise. Her father and the others were totally exposed. The streets remained empty. The only light came from the Alchemist's Fire. This side of the citadel was mostly storage buildings and stables and a few shops. There shouldn't be anyone nearby at this hour.

She heard the crackling of flames and looked back to the chapel in time to see the front windows glimmer orange as the fire roared to life within. Three shadows flitted away from the chapel and melded back into the wall. It was done then. So quickly. So quietly.

Cassa watched the figures of the other two lookouts drop from their posts and disappear into the night. She was supposed to climb back down the way she'd come and meet her father and the others in the sewer drain. She started to shimmy across the roof toward the little access door that led into the loft, but then she heard something that made her heart skip a beat.

A scream.

She hesitated, then crawled back to the edge of the roof, searching the night for the source of the sound. The area was growing brighter with every passing second as the fire blazed. Another cry. Someone was repeatedly calling for help. She thought someone must have noticed the fire, but the streets were empty. Then she realized the cries were coming from inside the chapel.

Her blood ran cold.

The flames had already consumed the front of the chapel, and she had no doubt the two side entrances were engulfed as well. She scanned the area, hoping one of the others had heard the plea, had come back to help. But they were already gone.

No one was supposed to get hurt.

Without letting herself think about it, Cassa gripped the edge of the roof and swung down. She dangled from her arms for a second, then dropped the rest of the way into the pile of hay below. The landing hurt worse than she'd expected, but she rolled with the impact as her mother had taught her and started running. She vaulted over the low fence surrounding the stable. All the horses were inside for the night, but she could hear a few start to whinny nervously.

She ran to the chapel, aware that she was in the open now and vulnerable. Her father would be furious if he knew the risk she was taking. She couldn't stop though. They had chosen this spot because the chances of anyone noticing the fire before it had already consumed the chapel were slim. She was the only one who could hear the screams. She couldn't just leave a person to die.

The front of the chapel was a wall of flame. She circled to the right, coughing in the smoke that was already drifting into the cool night air. There was a tremendous crash inside the chapel. The screaming had stopped. The newer chapels to the Slain God didn't have many windows, but this one still had the old, stained glass archways that reached almost from the ground to the roof. Cassa finally found a window near the back that wasn't glowing orange. She picked up two fist-size stones from the little flower garden that ran along the chapel's exterior and flung them both through the glass. Then she slipped out of her jacket and wrapped it around her hand. She punched at the jagged remaining pieces of the window until she thought she could fit through.

Smoke billowed into her face. She held her breath and climbed inside. There were cutting stings on her arm and leg, but she didn't slow down. Her heart was pounding so fast that it was just a steady hum inside her chest. In a distant part of her mind, she recognized the absurdity of what she was doing. She wasn't big or strong. If this person was unconscious, there was no way she'd be able to drag them out. That was assuming they were even alive.

That was assuming she'd be able to stay alive long enough to find them.

She made her way to the center of the chapel, where the smoke wasn't as thick. Flames danced at the corner of her vision, but they weren't close enough to hurt her yet. The smoke was a different story.

She stood in the center aisle, still holding her breath, and blinked against her burning tears as she searched the chapel for any sign of movement. Her lungs had begun to ache, and she had almost decided to give up the fool's errand when she heard a weak, coughing cry. She ran for the altar.

Flames had reached the ceiling of the apse, and one of the wooden crossbeams had already fallen down. It had splintered on the wide stone altar where the Slain God's candles were lit during services. Beyond that, at the rear of the apse, a girl was clutching at one of the thick, faded tapestries. A long red braid fell down her back, streaked gray with ash, and her dress was the fine, flouncing attire of nobility. Cassa half ran, half stumbled up the steps and around the altar. She grabbed the girl's arm. The girl whirled around. She had to be around the same age as Cassa. A litany of emotions flashed through her wide eyes. Shock. Confusion. Relief.

Then she coughed out one word: "Help."

Cassa's lungs felt ready to burst, and she sucked in a short breath that felt more like smoke than oxygen. The girl was clambering at the tapestry again. Maybe her head was jumbled from the lack of air. Cassa tugged at her arm.

"This way," she managed to spit out. "The window."

She pointed, but at that moment another ceiling beam roared to the ground just behind them, showering them with embers. The girl let out a little shriek and redoubled her incomprehensible efforts with the tapestry. Cassa wiped her arm across her face. Her vision was so blurred with smoke and tears, she couldn't see the altar anymore, even though it was less than a hundred feet away. Everywhere she looked, the smoke was tinged orange now. The way she'd come was probably already swallowed in flame.

Her parents would never have found themselves in this situation. They never would have charged in without a plan. She wondered vaguely if they'd even know what had happened to her.

Then came a smack on her shoulder, and she shook herself free of the wandering thoughts. The girl was staring at her, this time with purpose.

"Help me with the latch," she said. Her voice was low and ragged but clear enough.

Cassa frowned and looked at the girl's hands. She realized the girl wasn't tugging on the tapestry but on a sliding wooden latch behind it. Cassa grabbed the edge of the cloth and yanked it back. There was another door.

She didn't waste any more time. She needed to breathe, and there wasn't any air left in the chapel. The heat had grown unbearable. The roar of flame was deafening. She gripped the latch beside the girl, and together they pulled. With both their weak efforts combined, the stubborn wood slid free, and Cassa yanked the door open. She was greeted by a blast of cool air so invigorating that she realized she was grinning. The girl tugged her by the arm, and together they ran into the dark tunnel beyond the door. After a few feet, the tunnel split into two narrower passages. The girl hesitated a moment and then pulled her to the left. They stumbled single file through the dark until they reached a dead end. The girl groped across the wall, and Cassa heard a rattling sound. A doorknob. To a door that was obviously locked.

Cassa's heart sank, but the girl only turned and slid past her. Cassa pressed up against the wall, feeling the heavy brush of far too many layers of skirt against her legs.

"Wrong way," said the girl, running back the way they'd come. "Come on."

"Where are we?" Cassa asked through her scratchy throat.

"Inside the wall."

They passed through the fuming smoke from the chapel door and kept running down the opposite passage. They didn't have much farther to go before reaching another dead end. From the fiery glow emanating from the chapel a few yards behind them, Cassa could see another wooden door, set into the passage wall on their left. It was only a few feet tall and wide. They worked together to open the two stubborn latches, and finally the door swung open into the free night air. The girl crawled out first, then Cassa.

They were on damp grass. Cassa flipped over to rest on her elbows and gazed in awe at the massive height of stone rising above her. They were in the upper echelon, outside the citadel wall. They were alive.

Beside her the girl was coughing wildly. Cassa looked around, and in the distance she could see the light of lanterns moving toward them. Guards.

Her heart leapt into her throat, and she dragged herself to her feet. Her knees were wobbly. A few coughs forced their way out of her chest.

"Go," the girl said weakly. She was struggling to stand. "Before they see you."

The offer caught Cassa by surprise, and she scrutinized the girl. Her pale skin was flushed red and dusted with ash, and her hair was a frizzy mess, but in that voluminous satin gown, there was no mistaking her for anything but a blueblood. Had she guessed that Cassa had something to do with the fire?

"You don't even know who I am," Cassa said, even as her legs were itching to escape.

"You don't know who I am either," said the girl, meeting Cassa's eyes.

Cassa hesitated, and then, because she was certain she would never see the girl again, she said, "I'm Cassa."

"I'm Vesper."

Cassa smiled at her tentatively, and Vesper smiled too. Cassa broke into a run toward the heart of the city, away from the guards. She didn't look back. She never slowed down.

ELEVEN

ALYS

ALYS was determined to keep a measure of how long they spent paddling across the lake, to create in her mind some kind of picture of how wide it actually was. But it proved an impossible task, with only the rhythmic splashes of the paddles and the unsteady hammering of her pulse to mark time. Her thoughts too were a distraction. In this vast cavern, with the blue of their globe being swallowed in darkness only a few yards in all directions, it was easy to turn her thoughts inward, taking stock of her own fears. And her mind was racing backward too, to the shore they'd left behind, to the citadel guards who were probably still lying there. Were they dead?

There was no ready answer. Only the movement of the paddles, the beating of her heart.

She sat at the prow of the boat, facing the boys and Cassa. None of them had spoken since watching the guards fall. Alys held the globe in her lap, hating the way the ghastly blue light shone on Evander's and Newt's faces, casting deep shadows, making them seem half-skeletal, half-gone. She shied away from that thought and turned her attention over the side of the boat. She held the light just above the surface, delighted by how it rippled outward, magnified by the crystal water. The lake was so clear that she could see fish swimming, ugly, mottled things but amazing nonetheless. How could anything live down here, so far from any hope of sunlight?

Despite the clarity of the water, she couldn't judge the lake's depth. Her own light was reflected back at her too vividly. It could have been a few feet or a few leagues. From the corner of her eye, just at the edge of the light, she thought she saw a dark shape in the water, much too large to be a fish, much too quick for her to discern anything else. She settled back on her seat, hugging the globe to her lap, thinking of the sorts of creatures utter darkness could create.

It was Cassa who spoke first, naturally. Always.

"I don't know what happened back there, but I vote we take credit for it when the time comes for the bards to sing of our wondrous deeds. Agreed?"

Alys smiled, and the boys both huffed a little in laughter. A nervous release more than anything. She knew that's what Cassa was aiming for. Cassa could be devastatingly clever, but she wasn't always reckless with it. Sometimes she was extremely calculating. Alys had learned to see that over the past couple of years, to respect it.

"I'm not sure we get a say in what the bards sing about us," Alys said, keeping her tone dry. She wasn't in the mood to be contrary, but Cassa needed the challenge to keep her jest going. Alys could be calculating too, although she was fairly certain Cassa had never learned to appreciate that.

"We'll get a whole tavern drunk one night and spread the rumor,"

Cassa said, turning in her seat to face them. "The legendary tale of the firebrands who felled three citadel guards without ever touching them."

"You have to start earlier than that for it to be a proper tale," Evander said. "With the seers foretelling our births."

"Under auspicious stars," Newt added. "There are always auspicious stars in those old songs."

"We don't need seers in our song," Cassa insisted. "Only the four of us, making our own way. That's what we'll be remembered for."

Alys opened her mouth with a sarcastic comment about how well their own way was working out for them so far, but then she saw the look in Cassa's eye, in Newt's and Evander's, and she stayed silent. There were certain things that needed to be said—believed—while they rowed ever closer to the distant shore where the unknown awaited them. And certain things that didn't.

They weren't really firebrands. At least not anymore. But she couldn't help but feel sometimes that the weight of all those who had come before them was resting on their shoulders. The rebellion had started nearly a century earlier, so long ago that the first rebels were already immortalized in legend. It wasn't a glorious start to a glorious revolution though. The rebellion had been birthed in blood and flames.

There had been unrest about the council's rule for a long time leading up to that grisly night. Bitterness had been brewing in the lower wards for years as the council trotted out prophecy after prophecy that only ever seemed to benefit the city's elite. When there was a food shortage predicted in the vague future, it was the farmers who had to give up a percentage of their crops to be stored in the upper echelon. When a seer dreamed that the river was rising, the walls to the higher wards were shored up and the gates locked tight, leaving everyone else to fend for themselves. Whenever anyone spoke out against one of the councilors or accused them of a crime, their sentients would somehow never find any evidence to support the claims.

Those injustices were only the tinder. The spark came when the council received a new prophecy, one that painted a disturbing image of an uprising in the lower ward. The council didn't investigate, didn't send guards to question citizens or search for stockpiled weapons. Why should they? The seers were almost never wrong.

Half the lower ward was devoured in flames before the night was over. Hundreds of innocent citizens were murdered by citadel guards in the streets, in the taverns, in their beds. The council sought to stop a brutal uprising, but unwittingly they started a rebellion that would burn for generations.

The firebrands were all dead now. Four years ago, their last stand had been crushed by the citadel. But Cassa had never given up, and though Alys wasn't convinced that any of this was their responsibility, she hadn't given up either. She wasn't much of a rebel, but the council had taken everything from her family for no reason other than her parents' compassion. She'd spent years helping her family get back what they had lost, and now she wanted them to have justice.

The four of them might not be remembered in story and song, but maybe there was still something they could do to honor all that sacrifice.

They reached the shore after a few more minutes of silent rowing. This side of the lake didn't seem very different from the other, from what she could see. Intricate rock formations reaching from the ground and stretching from the ceiling, gleaming with the moisture that had shaped them so elegantly over centuries. There was a path of sorts, leading away from the lake. The ceiling and the walls grew closer as they walked, until they were once again in a tunnel. Alys stayed by Evander as Cassa forged ahead, holding up the globe as if light was all she needed to protect them. Newt trailed behind, quiet as usual.

"I shouldn't have read the coins," she said quietly. "What if we're going the wrong way?"

Evander glanced at her, his eyes unreadable in the dim light.

"Well, think about it this way," he said. "Even if we all die a slow, miserable death down here, you'll at least have the satisfaction of blaming it on Cassa. It's her fault after all."

"I heard that," Cassa called over her shoulder, though she didn't slow down.

Evander flashed a grin at Alys, but she didn't find it funny. Didn't see how he could either. There were certain things about her brother that she'd probably never understand.

"Do you really think we're going to die down here?" She hadn't intended to ask it so bluntly, but the question had been building inside of her since the citadel door had first shut behind them.

Evander hesitated, the smile drifting from his face as effortlessly as it had come. And because there were certain things about her brother that Alys understood very well, she knew what he was going to say next.

"Truth or lie?" he asked.

The old game. An answer in itself. Alys barely knew what she wanted.

"Lie," she said at last. What good would the truth do, when it was too late to turn back?

"I think we're going to come through this just fine," he said, the smile curling tentatively at his lips again, "with some exciting stories to tell and a few moral lessons about life and friendship and the virtues of rowboats."

It wasn't much of a comfort after all, but Alys accepted it anyway. She would take what she could get, down here.

When the tunnel finally opened into a new cavern, Alys wasn't prepared for the sight before them. Even Cassa stopped dead in her tracks. There was too much to take in all at once. Fires burned in large bowls set atop white pillars, spaced at regular intervals so that the whole cavern—easily as vast as three Great Halls together—was warm and bright. Raised pathways ran in intricate, almost mazelike patterns, above narrow channels of darkly glimmering water. Along the walls of the cavern were giant statues, carved so that they appeared to be emerging from the stone. Men and women, all with serene visages, all depicted with their eyes closed. The elder seers.

Cassa had already stepped onto the path, and Alys followed hesitantly. Clearly this direction was leading somewhere—but where? This place felt just as ancient as the crypts, but she'd never heard about it before.

"Why would these fires be lit?" Newt asked.

No one had an answer. Alys stared at the dancing flames, and she couldn't stop thinking about the voice in her head when she had been reading the coins, so faint and insistent. She hadn't told the others yet. She wasn't sure how to explain it. She also didn't know how to explain the twisting, growing certainty that *somehow*, they were expected.

TWELVE

CASSA

CASSA was scared. It wasn't an overwhelming fear, but it was palpable. A weight on her chest, a sick taste in the back of her throat. She tightened her grip on the pistol. There was something wrong with this place. She'd grown up exploring the cave system beneath Aurelia Valley. To her, the world of twisting stone passages, glistening rock formations, and mirror-still pools of water was home. But the deeper they went, the more convinced Cassa was that this wasn't the world she knew so well. There was something darker here. Something waiting.

Cassa gripped the ghost globe tighter and reminded herself that she wasn't superstitious and there wasn't anything dangerous or powerful about the crypts that held the elder seers, whose vivid dreams of the future had carved the city of Eldra's place in history. That was hundreds upon hundreds of years ago. The crypts held nothing but bones and dust now. These days, true seers were few and far between, guarded jealously by the council. Diviners like Alys were a little more common, the power in their blood weakened through generations until they could read only the near future.

Cassa had seen the confusion in Alys's face as she studied the coins, the hesitation when she said they had to go left. Cassa had always assumed that, like most things, Alys was better at divining than she thought. Now she wasn't so sure. When Vesper had told her about the way out of the crypts, she hadn't mentioned a lake or this chamber of statues and flame. Then again, there were obviously a lot of things Vesper hadn't bothered to mention. Like how instead of helping them infiltrate the citadel she was going to warn the council about their plan. Like how after seven years of friendship, after seven years of fighting back, she was willing to just give them up, to let them die down here in the dark.

Cassa pushed away the gnawing, helpless anger that accompanied all thoughts of Vesper. Now wasn't the time for helplessness. She'd gotten her friends into this, and it was her job to get them out.

They left behind the seers' chamber and filed into a narrow passage less perfectly hewn than the others. She was just starting to think that maybe they were going to find a dead end after all when ahead she saw a faint but unmistakable golden light.

"Daylight?" Newt asked from behind her, though he didn't sound particularly hopeful.

"It's still the middle of the night," Cassa said. She stared hard at the distant light, but it was stationary, not bobbing like a lantern. They had to be at least a mile underground. The only light that should be down here was their own. This place was all wrong. She glanced back at Alys, whose tight-lipped expression didn't inspire much confidence that she'd seen any of this in her divination.

Cassa opened her mouth to ask her again exactly what she'd seen, but Evander, as usual, guessed what she was about to say and preempted her.

"It doesn't matter," he said. "It's not like we can go back now."

If it was something that was going to kill them, something that was responsible for the instinctual dread that had gripped her since they'd gone left, then it most certainly did matter. But Cassa didn't feel like arguing, and she didn't feel like running anymore. She kind of felt like shooting something.

"I guess you're right," she said, and she forged ahead with Evander hard on her heels.

As she neared, the light resolved itself into a narrow rectangle, almost like a doorway. Fear still burned in the pit of her stomach, but that had never stopped her before. She stepped into the light, pistol leveled, blinking away involuntary tears as her eyes adjusted.

They were standing in a bizarre sanctuary of civilization. A cavern a little larger than a sitting parlor had been painstakingly decorated to look like one. She couldn't make sense of anything she was seeing. There were two matching armchairs, a sofa, and a fainting couch with elaborately carved wooden legs and hideously florid patterns that had been in fashion decades ago. A brass cart with glass panes held a silver tea service. Ghost globes were strung along the rock formations at the edges of the room, but instead of blue, the swirl of light in them was brightly golden, like a fire in a hearth.

"You can shoot me if you like, but I fear it won't do any good." The voice, silk and honey, snapped her out of her reverie. When she saw the man standing in the center of the room, it was like she was seeing him for the first time, but surely he had been standing there all along. His appearance immediately sharpened her dread into a razor's edge. There was nothing frightening about him, but there wasn't anything firm about him either. He was an old man with gray hair and a gray beard, his eyes deep-set in wrinkles, but then he also looked young, as young as any of them, with round, waifish eyes and shaggy hair. He wasn't changing exactly; he just wasn't staying the same.

Cassa's head had started to hurt. She didn't lower the pistol.

"I was afraid you wouldn't make it," the man said, his hands raised in innocent surrender. He wore robes that resembled the ceremonial garb of the council, but his were much simpler and threadbare. As he spoke, he glanced briefly over Cassa's shoulder before meeting her eyes again.

Cassa tried to say something, but no words would come. A rare, uncomfortable phenomenon.

"Sorry to disturb you," Evander said with an impossibly casual air. He had stepped up beside her. "We're a bit lost. If you'd be kind enough to point us in the direction of the nearest exit, we'll be on our way."

The man might have smiled, but it was hard to tell with his wavering features.

"I've known for a while that you would be coming." He held out a hand. Cupped in his palm were what looked like tiny white stones, all different shapes and marked with black symbols. "I saw it in the runes."

Bone runes, Cassa realized, and shuddered. Another diviner.

"Who are you?" Alys's voice was strained and thin.

His hands were still lifted, and he frowned in thought, like the question perplexed him.

"My name, when I had one, was Solan Tavish. It doesn't get much use down here though." He took a step back and gestured toward the couch and chairs. "Won't you take a seat? I promise, the guards won't find you here."

Cassa stiffened.

"How did you—" But her eyes were drawn again to the runes in his hand. "What else do you know about us?"

This time there was no mistaking the smile on his face. It was a sad smile though. Heartbreakingly so.

"Everything," he said. "I've been waiting for you a very long time."

Cassa just stared at him. The rest of the caverns felt faraway and fading, and the world above hadn't felt real for a long time. Was that her own mind playing tricks, or was there something in the air down here? Finally, because she couldn't think of any other options, she moved to sit gingerly in one of the armchairs. It smelled terrible. When she looked a little closer, she saw that the furniture and dishware had not fared well in the dank depths of the cavern. The upholstery was mildewed, the wood rotting, the silver tarnished almost to black. How long had all this been down here?

Alys, Newt, and Evander followed her lead and sat on the sofa, each of their faces drawn tight with caution and uncertainty. The man—Solan—went to the little cart and started to pour the tea. Everything had taken on a surreal tinge. Not long ago they had been running for their lives from the citadel guards. Now a strange man was serving them tea in an underground parlor.

When everyone had a steaming cup, Solan sat down in the armchair beside Cassa. He was so close that she could feel his shifting, unnatural presence. It made her feel seasick. What was wrong with him?

"I'm aware you must have some questions." He took a sip of tea. No one else did.

"What do you mean, you've been waiting for us?" Cassa asked.

"You're down here for the same reason I am. You want the council to be held accountable for their crimes."

"Not an answer," Evander said.

"You broke into the citadel because you knew they were hiding something. You've been hearing rumors of a sickness that strikes people suddenly, and within minutes they've lost all speech and thought, drained of everything they are until they are merely shells. I can assure you, they aren't just rumors."

Cassa's breath caught in her throat. She'd known the council was somehow responsible, that there had to be some truth to the gossip. Too many people who went inside the citadel walls had never come back out again. That's how it had been a few years ago, in the final days of the rebellion, when the council was closing in and no one knew whom to trust. One day someone would be there, and the next day they'd be gone without a trace. Cassa's parents hadn't been able to stand idly by, and neither could she.

"What do you know?" she asked Solan. The unsettling mystery of this place and this man no longer seemed important. Not when there were finally answers to be had.

"Their memories are being stolen." He leaned back in his chair, swirling the dark liquid in his cup.

"By who?" Evander asked.

"By me."

Silence. Cassa had forgotten how truly silent the world below could be, when there were no heaving breaths and racing hearts and pounding feet to fill the void.

"You're the executioner." Newt's voice was quiet, a bare ripple in the stillness.

Solan nodded. Cassa's fingers tightened instinctively on the pistol, though she left it in her lap. The executioner was something of a legend in the city, shrouded in secrecy and fear. Though she was Teruvian born and raised, Cassa didn't know much about the Slain God's religion. It was the oldest in the country but had begun to fall into obscurity just as the elder seers' bloodline started to fade out. To most citizens nowadays, the death rites were a tradition based more on familiarity than on faith. Her own parents hadn't subscribed to it at all. She did know that the devouring of memories was meant to be a cleansing of sorts, a final penitence in honor of the Slain God. Not that Cassa believed in that sort of thing.

Traditional rites were a peaceful affair. Supposedly the offering of death rites to prisoners was evidence of the council's mercy, but to Cassa there was something horrifying about the thought of every part of yourself being ripped away before you were executed, alone in the dark, so far away from everyone you knew and loved. That wasn't how her parents had died, and sometimes despite the tangle of fury and grief that lived in her heart, she managed to feel grateful for that at least.

"You said you were a diviner," Alys said. "How can you be the executioner?"

"I am a diviner," Solan said. "But that's not all I am."

"You're a rook too?" Newt asked. His face was screwed up in confusion.

Cassa had heard of people being born with more than one skill, though it was rare. Diviners were descendants of seers—their ability to read small fortunes and near futures was a trickle-down effect through weakening bloodlines. Rooks were almost as rare as seers and could give and take memories with a touch. Sentients descended from rook bloodlines and were able to read the past—and sometimes thoughts—in people's faces. It was possible, if someone had rook and seer blood in them, for a person to manifest with more than one skill.

"To my knowledge," Solan said, "there has never been anyone else like me."

"I like the confidence," Evander said.

Another possible smile from Solan.

"I was born a rook and a seer," he told them. "Over time, I developed the skills of a diviner and a sentient as well."

Silence.

"That's impossible," Alys said at last, but she didn't sound certain. That was uncharacteristic enough that Cassa began to feel nervous, though she wasn't sure why.

The rook-seer-diviner-sentient shrugged.

"You don't have to believe me," he said. "I know how strange it all sounds."

"Wait," Cassa said, her mind finally catching up to the conversation. "You said you've been stealing people's memories. Not just prisoners'. Why?" And why was he admitting it to them?

"Do you think that the threat to the council's power ended with the rebellion? It's only been four years since the last rebel was executed. The wealthy and entitled in the citadel might have cloistered themselves away from the fight, but they are very aware of the council's lingering vulnerability. The councilors surround themselves with the most talented diviners and sentients in the city. The moment a member of the nobility—or anyone at all—starts to contemplate that vulnerability, the council knows, and they are swift to act. Though, of course, they are also careful to keep their hands clean of it." Solan stirred, a faint expression of sorrow and regret flickering across his face. "Not every condemned in the citadel receives a trial, and I am the citadel's executioner."

"Why?" Cassa asked again. She cast her eyes around the room again, around the trappings of civilization that had been so carefully collected. She was beginning to feel a new sense of unease. "Why are you helping them? Why are you down here?"

Solan hesitated. He set his cup down on the table between them and folded his hands in his lap.

"I'll tell you the story," he said. "I can't promise you'll believe me, but I promise it's all true."

Cassa swept a glance over her friends. They were all staring at Solan with varying expressions of suspicion and uncertainty. None of them replied.

"I told you I was born a rook and a seer," Solan said. "When my powers became evident, I was still a young man. Foolish. I stole some memories. Not always on purpose. You have to understand how difficult it was for me—I was the only one of my kind. At night I dreamed the future, and by day I felt people's thoughts like thick webbing, closing around me. I was only trying to gain some control." He sighed and shifted in his seat.

"When I was discovered, the council had me arrested. Even then they were corrupt, desperate to keep the power that prophecies gave them. When they realized what I was capable of, they wanted to use me. They knew the number of seers and rooks were dwindling with every generation, and now they had someone who was both—someone completely under their control. As my punishment, they locked me down here, told everyone I loved that I was dead. In the past a different rook was chosen for each execution, but now I'm the only executioner. Another punishment. But it was my prophecies they really wanted. They know that without genuine prophecies, they'll lose their hold on the city. At first I resisted, but soon I was so desperate down here in the dark that I started trading dreams for comfort." He looked around at the shabby furniture and ornamentation surrounding them—a useless attempt at turning a prison into a home. "I'd already done so much evil for them, I couldn't bring myself to care about what they would do with the prophecies once they had them."

"Why haven't you tried to escape?" Newt asked, nodding in the direction they had come.

Solan looked down at his hands.

"Over the years, all the memories I've been forced to take have grown unbearable. The council provides an elixir." He gestured toward a dark shadow on the ceiling, across the room. Cassa squinted and realized it was a hole carved into the rock, only a couple of feet wide. "They lower it through there, and I have to take it every four hours to maintain my faculties. Without it my mind breaks apart. I become little more than a slavering, helpless animal, with no thoughts or feelings but pain."

He spoke with a gentle cadence that belied the horror in his words.

"Mirasma," Alys said. "They give you mirasma to suppress all the memories you've absorbed."

Solan nodded gravely. Cassa had heard of mirasma before, though she wasn't entirely sure how it worked. A long time ago, Vesper had explained to her that rooks could give and take other people's memories but not their own. Once they took a memory, even if they gave it back, they still remembered it themselves. Over time those memories from other lives could grow overwhelming. The capacity of the human mind was vast, but it wasn't limitless. Mirasma was an artificial element that the citadel's alchemists had developed centuries ago as a remedy, though it wasn't a cure.

"I've tried to leave before," Solan said. "Many years ago, when I couldn't bear this prison a moment longer. I made it across the valley and into Eldrin Wood before they found me. I'd lost all control by then. All I remember is the chaos of it. The boundless pain of my mind being shredded to pieces, of being consumed by every memory I'd ever consumed. They tell me it took almost a dozen guards to finally subdue me. Everyone who came near me found their memories draining away. I never meant to hurt anyone. I was just trying to be free."

"Rooks have to touch people to take their memories," Alys said, as if the only thing she'd taken from the miserable tale was the factual inconsistency.

"That was true for me once, a long time ago." Solan picked up his teacup, then set it back down. The story had taken a toll on him. There was no hint of a smile in his features anymore, only a grim despair. "But I've had a lot of practice through the years."

"The people in the citadel whose memories you take," Newt said slowly. "The council doesn't even have to bring them down here, do they?"

Solan shook his head gravely. Cassa's breath hitched. If that was true, if he could really steal all of a person's memories without even laying eyes on them . . .

"It's why I can't risk leaving here again," he said. "At least not until I find a way to cure my dependence on the mirasma. If I lose control again, I don't know how much damage I might inadvertently do to the people above."

Cassa's unease was growing steadily into anger—at what, exactly, she wasn't sure. As if summoned, there was a light scraping sound from the hole in the ceiling and a wooden tray came into view, fitted perfectly to the hole and suspended by four ropes. Smoothly, it was lowered to the ground. Atop it sat a clear, corked bottle. The effervescent blue-green contents seemed to swirl like liquid Alchemist's Fire.

She wasn't sure she believed Solan Tavish, though everything he'd said about the council matched the cruelty and corruption she'd always known was hiding behind their fancy robes and fake smiles. Nothing he'd said explained the way his features rippled agelessly, like he was somehow outside of time, like he wasn't entirely human. He definitely wasn't telling them everything, but did that mean he was lying?

She realized Solan was watching her, his eyes flickering between the elixir and the gun in her lap, as if he expected her to shoot him the moment he turned his back. Without really knowing why, Cassa set the pistol on the side table, a tentative truce.

Solan smiled at her, but it was that sad smile again.

"Cassandra Valera," he said, a little wistfully. "The daughter of greatness."

It took Cassa a few seconds under the strange intensity of his gaze to realize that if he was a sentient, he could intuit her past in her features. She turned her face away, scalded by the thought of her history laid bare.

"I'm sorry," he said with faint mortification. "I have been down here alone for such a long time that I fear I've lost touch with common courtesy." Letting out a long breath, he crossed the room to the tray. He drank down the mirasma in four gulps and set the bottle back down with a shudder of relief. When he returned to his seat, he sat a little straighter.

"You led us here," Alys said suddenly. Her voice was tremulous. "I heard you inside my head."

Cassa blinked and looked at her. Newt and Evander were staring at her with equal shock.

"I did," Solan said softly. "I can speak into any mind that's near enough, but it's easier when they have rook or seers' blood, like you do."

"You said you saw the way in the coins," Cassa said to Alys, unable to keep the accusation from her voice.

Alys crossed her arms and refused to meet her eye.

"I never said that, and anyway, I didn't know what was happening at the time. I thought maybe it *was* the coins."

“Coins don’t talk,” Cassa snapped. “For seers’ sake, are you telling me that you led us down that tunnel because a strange voice in your head told you to?”

“Cassa,” Evander said warningly, but his sister cut him off.

“You’re the one who put me in that position,” Alys said, leveling a glare at Cassa.

“Because it was the only way.”

“Because you couldn’t be bothered with an escape plan!”

“Stop it,” Newt said, with such uncharacteristic force that Cassa and Alys both stopped and looked at him. He seemed genuinely surprised that they had listened and unsure of what to do now that he had their attention. “There’s no point in arguing about whose fault it is.”

Cassa wanted to reply that he was right, there was no point in arguing, because it was clearly Alys’s fault, but Evander, who always seemed to know when she was about to say something unwise, was giving her a look. Begrudgingly, she held her tongue.

“There is one thing I haven’t told you,” Solan said into the awkward silence that followed. “The reason I’ve been waiting for you. Four years ago, only days after the last rebel was brought down here to die, I dreamt a prophecy. It came to me so vividly, in such detail, that I knew—I *knew*—it was infallible.”

Cassa’s mouth went dry. A fifty-first infallible prophecy. There hadn’t been a new one for hundreds of years.

“What was it?” she asked, when Solan didn’t go on.

He looked at each of them carefully. It was a keenly discerning look, as if he’d known them their whole lives.

"It was the four of you," he said. "It was the way to my freedom. And it was the council's downfall."

Solan looked Cassa full in the face. Perhaps he was mining her history again, studying pieces of her past. She wouldn't look away, wouldn't let herself drop her gaze. It felt important somehow, in this moment of all moments. Her heart was pounding so hard in her chest that she was certain everyone could hear it. Maybe this was what her father had meant all those years ago, when he told her she had to know each of the infallible prophecies by heart because it was the only way she could see what was missing. Maybe was what missing was an ending.

Suddenly she didn't care if they could trust Solan Tavish. She didn't care what he was hiding from them, if only this one thing could be true. She'd been born a rebel. She'd carried a fire inside her for sixteen years. Now was when it finally meant something. Briefly, Solan's shifting features stilled, and Cassa felt she was seeing his true self. A man who had weathered years of solitude and torment to stand against the council. A man who had been waiting for them to come.

THIRTEEN

EVANDER

WHILE Solan was promising the council's demise, Evander couldn't look away from Cassa. Her joy was incandescent, as if each of Solan's words were feeding something ravenous inside her.

Evander had never seen her this way.

"You want our help," Cassa said.

"I *need* your help," Solan said. "After all those years I had given up hope. I reached a point where I would rather die than go on serving the council's agenda. But then I saw the prophecy, and I saw what you have done to make it this far, and I knew that if I gave up now, without helping you dismantle the council once and for all, then all those years would have been a waste."

Evander's breath hitched in his chest. He couldn't help it. If they could succeed where the rebellion had failed, then maybe all those who'd died, all the years his family had suffered, all the sacrifices they had made to get this far—maybe it would be finally worth it.

"You want us to help you escape?" he asked, still a little breathless.

"After a fashion." Solan glanced at the empty bottle on the tray. "While I am dependent on the mirasma, I cannot leave here."

"There are ways to get it in the city," Cassa said. "If we had enough money."

Solan shook his head.

"Only the council has access to the doses I need to stay in control of my mind." He paused and glanced at Cassa. "And they keep their store too well-guarded for anyone to steal."

Judging from the look on Cassa's face, Solan had plucked that last thought straight from her head. Maybe he was telling the truth about being a sentient, which meant maybe he was telling the truth about the rest. Even if he wasn't—even if there was no infallible prophecy—having someone on their side with knowledge of both the past and the future could be invaluable. They would no longer be fighting uselessly against the council's near-omniscience. Their attempt to uncover the council's secrets had been disastrous, but now Solan Tavish was giving them the answers they needed—and a chance to overthrow the council for good.

"If you really are both a diviner and a seer," said Evander, "I'm guessing you already know a way to escape."

A smile was briefly visible in Solan's shifting features.

"I need to visit the Blacksmith."

Evander stared at Solan, trying to work his mind around what he was saying.

"A bloodbond?" he asked. "With what?" The Blacksmith could forge a bond between a person and a liquefied element—usually metal, like

Evander's bond with silver—which gave them control over that element. But what good could any bloodbond possibly do Solan?

Alys, as always, had the answer.

"With the mirasma," she said. "You think if you're bonded with it, you won't need the regular doses."

"It may very well be impossible," said Solan, leaning back in his chair. "But I have to trust the prophecy. It's all I can do."

Evander looked to Alys. Cassa and Newt were eyeing her too, waiting for her opinion. Her face was screwed in concentration.

"It is a pure element," she said. "There's no reason why the Blacksmith couldn't use it the same as iron or silver or any other metal. It's probably even more likely to work than a bond with glass. And if the mirasma was bonded with your blood, theoretically its effects would be permanent in your brain."

"Just because the Blacksmith can do it doesn't mean he will," Evander said. If they showed up at his cottage with Solan in tow, he was fairly certain the Blacksmith would turn them in to the council—he was in their employ after all. Or maybe he would just shoot them.

"We could talk to him first," said Cassa. "Maybe we could convince him."

Which Evander took to mean that she expected *him* to do the convincing. Unlikely. It was true that the Blacksmith didn't always need official papers. Sometimes all it took was the right price—or in Evander's case, the right debt. His fingers drifted absently to the scar on his arm. The debt was paid now. He didn't have any more favors to call in.

"None of this matters if we can't escape the guards," Newt said. "They're probably swarming the tunnels by now."

Solan nodded sagely, as if he'd been anticipating the concern. Evander had the unsettling thought that maybe he'd foreseen this entire conversation. Maybe he already knew if they would help him or not. If so, did they ever have a choice in the first place? He could feel a headache coming on.

"You don't have much time," Solan said. He scattered his bone runes across the table at his elbow and studied them for a few moments. "The guards will be leaving the city by now, trying to cut you off in the valley. If you go now, you can still make it."

He climbed to his feet and moved across the room to a ratty tapestry with a design that was faded past recognition. He pulled it aside, and beyond there was another dark passage. A way out.

"So if we help you, you'll let us leave?" Alys asked, her voice tight.

Solan might have frowned. His vacillating features were impossible to read.

"I'm not keeping you here," he said. "I only ask that you'll consider all that I've said. If you decide to help, you know where to find me."

"That's it?" The words spilled out before Evander could stop them. "You're just going to let us go?"

Solan stared at him for a long moment before nodding.

"I have been a prisoner down here long enough that I would never force it on another," he said. He gestured toward the tunnel. "I've made my plea. The decision is yours."

Evander rose to his feet. Deciding whether or not to commit treason again was a conversation they could have later, away from the insufferable closeness of this decaying sanctuary.

"We'll think about it," he said.

Cassa did finally break her gaze away from Solan, if only to shoot Evander a resentful glance. She was used to being the one to answer for everyone. He wasn't sure he trusted her to do that right now, not with the way she had been watching Solan. She might very well offer up all their firstborn children if she thought it would hurt the council. After all she'd been through, Evander couldn't blame her for her tunnel-visioned tenacity, but a part of him had always worried that one day she might go too far. It was better to get aboveground first, to weigh their choices without the citadel looming over their heads. Evander tried to avoid the lurking suspicion that the choice wasn't really theirs. Solan was eerily calm about the fact that his freedom rested in the hands of four people he'd never met before. Maybe that was because he already knew what they would decide.

Newt and Alys stood up on either side of him, and the tense muscles in his shoulders relaxed at their silent support.

"Right," Cassa said, her calculating gaze sweeping across them. She climbed to her feet. "We'll think about it."

"I will say this." Solan's voice was even and unhurried. "If you go into the city tonight, you'll discover the truth of all I've told you, but once you do, there will be no turning back."

Evander wanted to demand why he was being so damn cryptic, but he also didn't want to be here another second. Apparently the others were in agreement. Cassa still had the ghost globe, so she went first, unhesitatingly, into the blackness. Evander let Alys and Newt go ahead of him. Before he could follow, Solan stuck out a hand across his chest, stalling him and fixing him with a somber gaze. His eyes weren't a real color—not blue or green or brown or gray. Like the rest of him, they were inexplicable.

"I've seen something else," he said softly. "There's a way to save your parents, but it's not by giving in to the chancellor's demands."

"What's that supposed to mean? Save my parents from what?" The words had rattled him, but he kept his voice steady.

Solan was still watching him with those strange, keen eyes. He dropped his hand to let Evander pass. He bowed his head.

"Divining is rarely clear and never exact," he murmured. "I'm sorry, I don't know what else to tell you."

Evander opened his mouth to reply, but Alys was calling for him farther down the tunnel. Once again, they were running out of time. Evander left the warm glow of Solan's prison and followed the others. He could worry about cryptic prophecies later. The future didn't matter if they couldn't make it out of here alive.

FOURTEEN

Newt

AS Solan Tavish had promised, the tunnel led them away from the citadel and into the vaulted caverns beneath Aurelia Valley. From there, Cassa knew the way. Newt had no idea how Cassa could tell where they were exactly, but he trusted her. She knew the Aurelia caverns better than anyone. These clear, rippling pools and strange rock formations, glistening in the light like white cathedrals, were her home away from home.

Newt had never really felt the need to explore the caves. He didn't like the darkness and the damp air and the tingling certainty that the narrow tunnels were slowly closing in around him. It reminded him too much of the crawl space beneath his father's house. He felt more at home in the grasslands just over their heads. Aurelia Valley stretched for miles on the eastern edge of Eldra. The land was owned by the high council and had been kept vacant for centuries, as it featured heavily in one of the elder seers' fifty infallible prophecies.

Newt had never managed to learn all the prophecies, but he liked the valley the way it was. An ocean of swaying grass, brushed purple in the summer with blooming heather. When he was a child, he would creep into the field while his father was away and watch the passing clouds. Those were the days he learned how to hide his passage through the grass, how to lie so still that the rabbits forgot he was there, and how to leave the world exactly how he had found it, as if he had never been there at all. He'd met Evander for the first time on one of those days.

When they were finally free and in the blessed night air, he let himself begin to hope that they might actually make it to safety. As Solan had promised, there was still no sign of the guards pursuing them. Newt knew better than to hope this would last though.

Once they were aboveground, they took a few precious moments to breathe, sheltered by the massive boulders that broke the earth around the cavern entrance. Newt sat on a flat slab of stone and tried to examine the state of his bare feet in the mingled glow of the moon and the ghost globe. The thin trousers they had given him were too long, and the hems were nearly shredded. He couldn't tell if the wetness on his soles was mud or blood. Thanks to the night's escapades, his joints had begun to wobble with a familiar ache. The guards who arrested them had stripped him of the adhesive bandages he used to brace his knees, wrists, and ankles.

"You okay?" Evander dropped down next to him on the slab, stretching out his long legs. His trousers were a little too short.

"I'll live," Newt said, then bit his lip. The joke seemed in poor taste at the moment.

Evander just nodded absently and yawned. If they rested here any longer, he'd probably flop down and go straight to sleep—an uncanny ability of his that Newt had never understood. Carefully, Newt rolled both his aching ankles, trying to decide how much further he could push himself. Evander was side-eyeing him as he massaged his wrists. The others had noticed, of course, that he usually bandaged his joints. They probably thought it was precautionary, since he tended to be the one scaling walls and wriggling into tight places. He'd never told them about the alarming frequency of sprains when he didn't use the braces, that while he could bend his body in fantastic fashion, it came at a price. He'd never told them that one day he might finally break, irrevocably, and that this thought haunted his nightmares.

"Where do we go from here?" Alys asked, her voice heavy with exhaustion. She hadn't said much since they'd left Solan, since she'd admitted it was Solan and not her divination that had led them down the other tunnel. As unsettling as the idea was, Newt couldn't really blame her. He had barely a layman's knowledge of what divination entailed, and in her place, if a mysterious voice had started giving him advice, he had a feeling he probably would have listened too. Neither she nor Evander talked much about the night their parents were branded as traitors, but Newt knew that she blamed herself for not seeing it coming.

"The forest might be a good place to hide," Newt said, when no one else replied. He glanced south, toward the sprawling silhouette of Eldrin Wood in the distance. "I know it pretty well."

"Maybe," Cassa said, but she was staring west, where Eldra's walls abutted the night sky. "We might stand a better chance in the city. They won't expect us to go back."

"Please tell me you're not serious." Alys glared at Cassa from where she was slumped on the ground, her back against a boulder. Cassa paced between them but didn't say more.

"You think Solan was telling the truth," Evander said flatly.

"I don't know if he was or not." Cassa didn't quite meet his eyes. "But he said in the city we'd find the truth."

"He also said there would be no turning back."

"And why should we?" Cassa demanded, whirling to face them. "We broke into the citadel to find out why people were getting sick and disappearing, and now that we have an answer, you want to run? You want to let the council get away with it?"

"Solan is the one stealing the memories." Alys climbed to her feet, wincing with the effort. "He said so himself."

"Because the council is forcing him."

"So he says."

"At least in the city there's a chance we can know for sure."

"There's a bigger chance we'll be arrested and executed," Evander said. "I doubt your half-assed escape plan would work a second time."

"It was *my* escape plan," Alys muttered.

"Cassa is right," Newt said. He was caught off guard by his own conviction. "If we run now, we can never stop running. Everything we did will be for nothing."

For the second time tonight, they were all staring at him with mild shock. Cassa most of all. He and Cassa had never been close. It was difficult for them to find common ground, when her parents had been two of the most famous heroes of the rebellion and his father one of the most infamous traitors.

"Exactly." Cassa couldn't disguise the wariness in her voice, as if she suspected this might be some sort of trap.

"Do you really think this is a good idea?" Evander tilted his head toward Newt. The light from the ghost globe flecked his dark eyes with silver.

"I think it's a terrible idea," Newt said, ignoring the erratic rhythm of his heart, "but I don't want to spend the rest of my life on the run. I'd rather stay and fight."

Evander's eyebrows twitched, and he searched Newt's face for a few, interminable seconds. Then he shrugged.

"Fine." He stood and stretched his arms over his head, suppressing another yawn. "Let's go back to the city."

Alys made a few more protests in the name of logic, but they were half-hearted. She was outnumbered, and she followed them without further complaint as they started the long walk across the valley to the Merchants' Bridge. The six beacon lights burning on its spires were like stars against the black sky. To avoid drawing unnecessary attention, they had to leave the ghost globe behind, hidden inside the cave mouth.

No one spoke as they crept across the broad, cobblestone bridge toward the city gates. During the day, Merchants' Bridge was pure chaos, with people entering and leaving the city and bargaining with the vendors who set up shop along its full length. At this late hour, the only signs of movement were the canvas flaps of market stalls stirring in the breeze. Newt knew of several ways to get into the city without using a gate, but he doubted the others would be as comfortable as he was scaling stone walls or worming through drainage pipes barely three feet in diameter. The bridge was much faster anyway. The sooner they could disappear into the anonymity of Eldra, the better.

When they neared the front gate, a man with a lantern came out of the guardhouse, yawning loudly. Without a word, Evander flicked three coins into the air, and their descent, while too slow to be natural, was just slow enough for the guard to catch on and extend his palm. He examined the silver in the light of his lantern and then unbarred the door. He went back into the guardhouse without giving them a second glance.

"We have to stay in the lower ward until morning," Cassa said. "We can't risk more guards seeing our faces."

"You're the one who insisted we come here," Alys said. "Where do you suggest we go?"

"I got us this far," Cassa said, throwing out her arms in exasperation. "Isn't it someone else's turn?"

Alys began to rub her temples but didn't argue further. She must really be exhausted, Newt thought. Of course she was. They all were. It felt strange, standing in the city where they had all been born and raised and having nowhere to go. The council had all their papers. They would know that Alys and Evander lived with their parents above their apothecary shop, only a five-minute walk from the main gate. They would know that Newt lived with his father in the third ward, as near to the citadel as anyone could without having been born into wealth and favor. They would know that Cassa didn't have a real home, not since her parents had been killed and their house seized as property of the council.

"I know where we can go," Newt said. "At least for the night."

No one had the strength to even ask him where. Newt led the way west along the thoroughfare. The stalls for the meat vendors and beer sellers were shuttered tightly, and the only sounds were the scratching of stray animals and occasional raucous laughter from taverns. The lower ward was short on refinement and proper sewer drainage, but there had always been plenty of taverns.

A figure in the street ahead made Newt's heart skip a few beats, until he realized it was just a statue. The woman, cast in copper and just a little larger than life, was depicted in a flowing ceremonial robe, her hair twisted at the nape of her neck. In the moonlight it was hard to make out details, but Newt knew the statue had taken on a greenish hue over the years and that the woman's eyes were shut. The elder seers were always shown with closed eyes, to represent their prophetic dreams.

As they passed, he caught a glimpse of the inscription in the base of the statue. *In the year of the storm, the grassland tribes will prevail.* The first of the fifty infallible prophecies. Almost a hundred years ago, in the same year that a hurricane devastated the southern coast, the horsemen who ruled the grasslands of a distant northern country claimed victory after years of bitter conflict with a neighboring kingdom. Newt didn't even know the name of the kingdom or the tribes. They were too far away to have any real effect on Teruvia. The fifty infallible prophecies weren't important because they impacted the country or even the citadel—most of them didn't. They were important because all of them had come to pass, specific enough to be indisputable proof of the elder seers' ancient gifts. Other prophecies were vague and didn't always come to pass. Circumstances could shift. People could change their minds. Infallible prophecies were different. They were clear and detailed, and they always happened exactly as the seer predicted. A seer with an infallible prophecy had absolute knowledge of the absolute future.

The citadel's power in Teruvia had been rooted in those prophecies for centuries. Though Teruvia's capital city was much farther south, the high council ruled Eldra with almost complete autonomy, free to nurture the gifts of the remaining seers. The statues had been gifted to the city by the king himself, several hundred years ago. The statues were scattered throughout the city and within the walls of the citadel in the city's heart. One for every infallible prophecy. Of course, that show of the king's favor had been before the seer bloodline began to weaken, before the last infallible prophecy passed and the citadel lost all relevance to the rest of Teruvia. In some ways, it was comforting to know that the current queen didn't care what happened in the secluded city in the northern reaches of her domain. It meant that if the council was ever overthrown, there might not be an army of royal soldiers sent to help them.

Solan had told them he'd seen the council's downfall in an infallible prophecy. He'd said *they* were the ones responsible for it. Newt had been very careful not to think too hard about the night's events, careful not to let hope creep in where there was none, but the thought of their destiny being assured—everything they'd worked toward for years—was tantalizing. He couldn't blame Cassa for the glimmer of excitement in her eyes when Solan had laid out their part.

Past the statue, they took a street headed north that narrowed as the shops became actual brick buildings, stacked so tall that when Newt tilted his head back, he felt certain they were leaning inward, just a strong breeze away from crushing them all. The sliver of sky between the eaves was coal black, studded with stars behind thin wisps of clouds.

Newt turned into a winding alley between buildings, which felt more incidental than planned. His father had moved them to the comfort of the third ward a long time ago, after he'd struck his treacherous deal with the council, but Newt still knew the lower ward like the back of his hand. This was where the rebellion had sparked a hundred years ago, and it was here that Cassa kept the embers burning for the rest of them.

Newt's feet were so cold and sore that he barely felt the cobblestones and the murky puddles of what he hoped was rainwater. They were in the last days of winter, and the warmth of spring had only barely begun to take hold. He pushed aside some rotting crates stacked against the rear of a brick building, revealing a small wooden door.

"It's the basement of the carpenter's shop," he explained as he yanked the door open on protesting hinges. "He knows my father. He lets me sleep here sometimes when I'm too late coming back into the city."

"Oh, good," said Evander. "I was hoping we'd get to spend more time belowground tonight."

"I'm sorry." Newt felt his cheeks flush, and he rubbed the back of his head.

"Don't apologize to him." Alys gave Evander a light shove toward the doorway.

"I was just kidding," Evander protested as he stooped to enter.

Alys and Cassa followed, but Newt waited a little longer, casting a few final glances down the alleyway, searching for prying eyes. Everything was still and quiet. Maybe they could finally have some peace.

FIFTEEN

EVANDER

THE carpenter's basement was dry and cool and pitch-black, and for a few heart-stuttering moments Evander was back in the dungeons, iron on his wrists, reminding himself that he wasn't afraid of the dark. Not really.

There was the scrape of a match, then the features of the basement leapt into sharp relief, bathed in a golden glow. The space was cramped with various half-finished pieces of furniture and stacks of wood. Newt fiddled with the lantern for a few seconds, then left it hanging by the steps that led up to the shop. He glanced over his shoulder at Evander, the light glinting on his sweat-damp curls, in the blue of his eyes.

Alys and Cassa came down the steps behind him, and Evander flopped onto the uneven wood floor, lying on his back with his arms under his head. Newt was dragging a cot from a corner.

"This is what I sleep on when I'm here," he said. "Sorry, there aren't any blankets."

Cassa had already dropped onto her stomach beside Evander, burying her face in the crook of her elbow. Newt gestured wordlessly to Alys, who took the cot without argument. She wasn't one to be polite for form's sake. Evander eyed her when he was certain she wasn't looking. Other than her obvious exhaustion, she seemed fine. Hands loose, face lax. None of the telltale signs of a panic attack.

She'd been experiencing the episodes since they were kids, triggered by moments of high stress or sometimes by things that Evander couldn't understand. He'd learned to recognize the onset of what Alys called her "maelstroms," even though he wasn't always sure how to help.

"You don't need to help," Alys had told him once. "Just be there."

It still didn't feel like enough, but he tried.

Once they were settled, Newt retrieved the lantern from the wall and doused it. Evander blinked against the sudden darkness, listening to the small, comforting noises of his friends and his sister. The cot creaked and shifted as Alys tried to get comfortable. Cassa's breaths had already evened. It felt strange being this close to her but decidedly apart. They had broken off their romance six months ago. It had been a mutual decision and very amicable, but you don't just forget almost a year of your life being so closely intertwined with another person's.

On Evander's other side, Newt lay down almost soundlessly.

"We did pretty good tonight," he said, his voice so soft that Evander wasn't sure if he was talking to everyone or just to him.

"We did," Evander said, turning his head slightly. He couldn't tell how close Newt was in the dark, and it was disorienting. He had a strange, overwhelming desire to reach out and touch him, to see if Newt's blond hair was as soft as he sometimes caught himself imagining. Evander had figured out he was bisexual around the same time he'd figured out what sex was. But

Newt held a strange fascination for him, ever since their first chance meeting years ago. After his split with Cassa, Evander had found himself spending more and more time with Newt, and slowly that fascination had begun to evolve into something else entirely—something Evander was afraid to examine too closely when the rest of the world was falling apart around them.

"Dammit," Cassa said suddenly, her voice so sharp that Evander sat upright, his blood surging.

"What?" He blinked uselessly in the dark.

"I left my pistol on Solan's table."

Alys let out a groan.

"Well, maybe you should go back and get it, and let the rest of us sleep in peace."

"I would if I thought you could last the night without me."

Alys let out another frustrated noise. Evander tried to think of a retort, but he was too tired. If Vesper were here, she wouldn't have let the comment slide. He could always count on her to counterbalance Cassa's exhausting overconfidence. Sometimes he felt like Cassa had counted on her for that too.

He remembered a time when they were all just kids trying to find their place in a city simmering with rebellion. His sister, who had somehow managed to work for the firebrands for months without him or their parents noticing, was the one to introduce him to Vesper and Cassa. There were a lot of secrets between him and Alys in those days, but fewer after he met her new friends. He hadn't thought much of Cassa at first. She was short and loud and excessively rude. He'd changed his mind a few days later when she scaled the clock tower to paint the symbol of the firebrands in red on the bell. Her parents—the leaders of the rebellion—were furious with her and the risk she'd taken.

"She just did it to impress you, you know," Vesper had told him, while they waited outside for the Valeras to finish castigating their daughter.

"Why would she want to do that?" he asked, a little pleased with the idea despite himself.

"Because she can't stand for anyone not to be impressed by her."

"You don't seem impressed."

"We're best friends," she said with a shrug. "I'm the only person who doesn't have to be."

Vesper and Cassa were inseparable back then. Vesper wasn't officially a spy, but she brought news from the citadel to the Valeras. Her help, however small, was a major coup for the firebrands. Once whispers spread around the lower ward that the high chancellor's own niece was on their side, their ranks began to swell. For maybe the first time since the rebellion's first spark a century prior, there was real hope that it might succeed.

Not that it did them any good in the end. Only a month after that conversation with Vesper, all the rebels were dead, without even the symbol on the clock tower remaining to mark their empty sacrifice.

Evander lay back down and closed his eyes, willing sleep to come. His entire body ached for rest. He counted his breaths, in and out, but even after he lost count in the hundreds, his mind was still skipping across thoughts and memories, across the events of the night, and beyond that, to all the events that had led them here. Maybe for him it had all started when he watched Cassa climb that tower, secretly in awe. Maybe that was the real point there was no turning back.

After almost an hour, when he was sure that everyone else was asleep, Evander climbed to his feet. He felt his way around the edge of the room to the stairs that led to street level. They creaked deafeningly beneath his weight, and he had to wrench the warped door open, but no one stirred behind him. He stepped into the alley and shut the door as quietly as he could. The night felt cooler than he remembered, with a light breeze playing across his skin. He shivered.

He retraced their steps to the main road and the statue of the elder seer. The oxidized copper shone jade in the moonlight. For a brief moment, he wished that when he'd gone to see the Blacksmith he'd brought pure copper with him instead of silver. The statues were scattered throughout the entire city, large and solid enough that he'd probably be able to feel most of them no matter where he was. He couldn't fathom the rush of all that copper pulsating in his veins, connected to every part of the city as if he were its beating heart.

Copper was all but worthless though. It was silver that Evander had needed to pull his family from the gutter. He didn't have to depend on the pennies earned from fake divinations when people's silver would slide freely from their pockets into his. From a crowd of five or ten, he could pull twenty coins easily without anyone ever noticing. It added up fast. Between his work in the upper echelon and Alys's work with the rebels, their parents had been able to afford a new shop less than a year after his trip to the Blacksmith.

Of course, it was because of people like Evander that the high council was so selective about who was allowed to bloodbond with metal. Usually they allowed only talented craftsmen with skills useful to the council, and only those who might be strong enough to survive the process. Bloodbonding had been introduced in Teruvia only recently, brought here by a mysterious foreigner they called the Blacksmith. More people died than lived.

Evander had met only a few other people with bloodbonds in his life. The most recent was Captain Marsh, the captain of the citadel guard who had overseen their arrest. He was somewhat famous for his bloodbond with iron—one of the more difficult metals to bond with—and his skill with the iron chain he kept looped at his side like a whip. Fortunately, he hadn't felt the need to exercise his skill on any of them.

Evander rounded the statue of the elder seer and headed west along the empty street. Even the sounds from the taverns had begun to die down. He couldn't see the clock tower from where he was, but it had to be nearing dawn.

"Evander." The voice startled him, and he whirled around. It was Alys.

Shit.

"What are you doing?" she demanded, though she kept her voice quiet. She was hugging herself against the chill air.

"They need to know we're all right," he said.

"It's too dangerous."

"Alys, you know rumors have already started. Our parents probably think we're dead. They don't deserve that." He half expected her not to buy in to his reasoning. He only barely believed it himself. Solan's divination was still rattling in his head. Save his parents from what?

Alys regarded him in silence for a few seconds. In the thin, silvery moonlight, her features were soft and indistinct.

"Fine," she said. "But only for a few minutes. We have to get back before Newt and Cassa wake up."

Evander nodded and started west again. Alys fell into step beside him, limping a little. Begrudgingly, he slowed his gait. They walked in silence the rest of the way home.

The Day Newt Met Evander

SUMMER. The air was thick with buzzing insects. Overhead, the sky was relentlessly blue, relentlessly bright. The world smelled like the color gold. There was no breeze, and Newt's skin was damp with sweat, sticking to the dirt and grass beneath him. He could feel the prickle of flies on his bare arms and neck. There was a rock just beneath his shoulder blades, pressing insistently against bone. Salt trickled into his eye, and he blinked, but that was the only movement about him. He was just a part of the landscape, fading gently into periphery.

Then came the crashing of footsteps, labored panting, brush crackling, birds in flight. Newt was debating whether he should sit up and determine the source when the source tripped over his midsection and sprawled onto the ground.

"Shit," said the tangle of long limbs and shock of dark hair. "Shit." With grunting effort, he rolled onto his back and sat up, spitting out a mouthful of dirt.

Warily, Newt pushed onto his elbows. The boy looked vaguely familiar, but Newt couldn't place him. He was too distracted by the way the boy's sweat-soaked shirt clung to his chest.

"Hey," said the boy.

"Hey," said Newt, meeting his eyes. He was glad that his face was already flushed from the heat, because he could feel a blush burning up his neck and cheeks.

"I thought you were dead."

"Oh," said Newt. "Well . . . I'm not."

"What are you doing out here?"

"I—"

"Hold that thought." The boy was craning his neck, his eyes scanning the field around them.

Newt sat up the rest of the way and looked around as well, but he didn't see anything except for the city in the distance, Merchants' Bridge spanning the river, and to the south, the towering trees of Eldrin Wood.

"I don't suppose you know any good places to hide around here?" asked the boy.

"Are you in trouble?" Newt asked.

"Only if Cassa finds me. We were exploring that cave over there, the one with the weird name, and I might have pushed her into a reservoir."

"Why?"

He shrugged.

"She said she'd like to know how deep it ran." He was grinning now, his eyes bright with mischief. "I'm Evander, by the way. Evander Sera."

He stuck out his hand, and Newt took it self-consciously.

"Newt."

"Shit." Evander jumped suddenly to his feet. "Looks like my time is up. Tell my family I—"

He didn't get a chance to finish the sentiment because he was tackled quite effectively to the ground by a girl who was six inches shorter than him and soaking wet.

"Dammit, Cassa," coughed Evander. "You could have broken something."

He didn't sound too upset though. Cassa was straddling him, her palms pressed into his shoulders.

"You're lucky I don't break a lot of somethings," she said. "I only brought you along because you promised to behave."

"Is that the only reason?" His lips curved into a smile.

"You're the worst," Cassa said, then leaned down and kissed him.

Newt, only a few feet away, couldn't recall ever feeling this uncomfortable in his life, even including the time his father had insisted he spend the night in the crawl space under their house because hardship bred courage and courage bred strength. He started to stand up. Evander made a sound against Cassa's mouth and broke from the kiss.

"We're being rude," he told her, struggling onto his elbows. "Newt, this is Cassa."

Cassa sighed and slid off Evander to sit next to him. She eyed Newt, somehow managing to keep her disdain to a minimum.

"We've met," she said.

Newt's face burned hotter. Even if they hadn't met, it wasn't as if Cassandra Valera needed an introduction. Her parents were bastions of the rebellion. They had given their lives trying to free imprisoned firebrands from the citadel. His father's infamy was of a different sort. Betraying fellow rebels in exchange for clemency was the kind of cowardice that people didn't forget or forgive.

"Great," said Evander, looking between them curiously.

"I should go," Newt said.

"No, wait," Evander said. "We're the ones who interrupted your—whatever you were doing out here."

"I wasn't doing anything," Newt said, suddenly feeling defensive. "I was just about to head back to the city."

"We'll walk with you." Evander jumped to his feet, pulling Cassa up beside him. "We have to get Cassa dried off. She has a delicate constitution."

Cassa snorted and punched his arm, but there was unmistakable affection in the way she looked at him. Evander extended a hand toward Newt. There was a residual smile on his face, slightly lopsided. Newt had never known anyone to look so earnest and so roguish at the same time. He took the hand and stood up, and for a split second, with their hands still clasped, their eyes met, and Newt could sense the world around them in perfect clarity—the buzzing insects, the sun on his skin, the smell of dirt and stone and heather. It all spun around him in a symphony of colors and sounds and sensations. It was as if he and Evander were the only fixed points in a universe of motion.

Then he dropped Evander's hand, stepped away, and turned his gaze toward the city. There was a thrill of new energy inside him, a tingling in his fingertips, and the dawning certainty that one day he was going to fall in love with Evander Sera. He wasn't sure how to escape it. Or if he wanted to.

SIXTEEN

ALYS

THE apothecary shop of the lower ward was situated between a bakery and a tailor who had closed his doors months before. Even though her family had been living here for three years, it still didn't feel like home to Alys. She'd been born and raised in the fourth ward. Her parents hadn't been wealthy, but they had been important. There were several families in the upper echelon and even in the citadel itself who would special order her father's tinctures or ask her mother's advice on treatments. That was before the night the citadel guards came though. The night they lost everything. No one wanted anything to do with her parents once they had been marked as traitors by the council for aiding rebels.

When Alys thought about that night, what was clearest in her memories wasn't the way her father clutched her mother or the way her mother had screamed at the guards not to touch her children. It wasn't even the sickening whistle of the red-hot brand.

What shone so brightly in her mind were the coins on the kitchen table, left in a careless heap. And how a day before, in those same coins, she'd seen her father's face, her mother screaming, and the painful bright glow of the brand—and she hadn't understood the divination until it was too late to warn them.

That was when she gave up on divination. Maybe there were some things better left unknown. Her failed attempt tonight only shored up her resolve.

The apothecary's wooden sign, depicting a mortar and pestle, hung over the whitewashed door. It creaked slightly in the breeze. The windows upstairs were all dark. Neither of them had a key, so Evander reached up and tugged the cord dangling from the lintel. The muffled clattering of the bell inside the store seemed deafening in the silence of the street. Alys glanced around them nervously, but there was no one else in sight.

Evander had to ring twice more before the door finally swung open. Golden light spilled over them. Alys had expected her parents to be asleep, but Lenore Sera was fully dressed in her usual work attire of loose brown trousers and a white collared shirt with the sleeves pushed up around her elbows. Her tan apron was stained with a rainbow of spilled ingredients and smudged powders.

When she saw them, Alys could have sworn her face fell. Was it a trick of the light? Her mother's dark hair was piled into a messy bun, and she pushed some loose strands from her face. The X-shaped scar on her right cheek was puckered and ugly on her otherwise smooth skin. Her hand was shaking.

"You shouldn't have come," she said.

Alys's heart skipped a beat, and she looked around. Where seconds ago the street had been empty, now there were two citadel guards on either side of them, closing in fast. Evander swore, and Alys saw his hand drift uselessly toward his pocket. Even if he had his coins, they wouldn't help.

Lenore pulled the door open wider.

"You'd better come in," she said softly. "There's nothing for it now."

When they didn't move, Lenore reached out and took Evander's wrist. She tugged him gently into a quick embrace. Feeling numb, Alys stepped inside as well. She could hear the guards behind her, very near but not approaching the shop. Her mother hugged her too, wordlessly. Alys eyed the interior of the shop. Everything appeared to be in order. The long wooden counter was tidy, with only a couple of bottles not put away. The floor glistened like it had been recently mopped, and it looked like someone had dusted and reorganized the books on the broad shelf behind the counter. Her father tended to clean things when he was anxious.

She didn't see him in the main shop, but there were more lights farther down the hall to the right, where the kitchen was. When they entered, Alys saw him first. Her heart settled a tiny bit at the sight. Edric Sera was stooped slightly in the shoulders, with gray streaks through his black hair and a pair of thin wire spectacles that always sat crooked on his nose. After his first shop had been seized by the council, he grew a bushy beard that Alys always thought looked wrong on his angular face. She wasn't sure if he'd just given up on shaving every day or if he thought it would somehow distract from the scar burned into his cheek. She'd never gotten up the courage to ask.

Edric pushed his spectacles up when he saw his two children. His dark, bushy eyebrows were knitted in a frown.

"Ah," he said. A useless, helpless, hopeless sound. "Ah."

The man seated across from her father at the table stood up slowly, his chair scraping against the wood floor. At first, Alys didn't recognize him. She'd only seen Chancellor Dane up close once before, and the man had been a different sight then, bedecked in ceremonial robes, pronouncing death from the high dais. Here, in her family kitchen, wearing a gentleman's jacket and a black silk tie, he looked more like a blueblood from the upper echelon who'd gotten terribly lost than the arbitrator and administrator of the seers' prophecies.

"Excellent," he said. He retrieved a silver watch from the pocket of his pinstriped waistcoat and checked it. "Right on time."

For a brief moment, Alys felt outside herself. She felt as if she was looking at the city, at her entire world, from a distant height. She felt she could see all the choices that had led them this far, all the threads of the past. And she wondered why they had ever thought they stood a chance against a regime that held the very future in its hands.

Her head had started to spin lazily, and she drove her fingernails into her palms until she was back in her parents' kitchen, standing face-to-face with the high chancellor. Her thoughts stilled, and the maelstrom was quiet, for now.

"That's a pity," said Evander. "We were hoping to be fashionably late, but what can you do."

He shrugged and slumped into the empty chair beside their father. Arms crossed, features arranged into an expression of vague boredom, he was the picture of nonchalance. Alys wondered if there was any way the chancellor would be fooled. She certainly wasn't, but she could read her brother like a book.

Alys didn't have any witticisms. She sat down in the chair opposite her brother, careful to keep her chin high and her hands hidden from sight. They had begun to tremble.

Lenore waited in the doorway, eyeing them with frowning concern. Her mother had never been one for fluttering nerves or anxious energy. Chancellor Dane gestured wordlessly to the seat he had just vacated, and she took it without looking at him.

"You have a beautiful family," said Dane, though it wasn't clear to whom he was speaking. He remained standing at the corner of the table, between Lenore and Evander.

Alys waited for a threat to follow, but none did.

"I don't personally enjoy the cloak-and-dagger act, but it was unfortunately necessary in this case," he went on, interlacing his fingers over his stomach. "The council will have your children back in custody soon, so I took it upon myself to intercept them first."

He was looking between her and Evander now. She was more confused by his expression than anything. Impossibly earnest. His words didn't make much sense either. None of this did. Why weren't they being dragged away in chains?

"I need your help," said the high chancellor to Alys and Evander. "You and your friends."

Alys blinked at him. She looked at Evander, but he was staring at the chancellor, mouth slightly open. Her mother's lips were pursed, her gaze locked on the tabletop. Her father had dropped his head into his hands.

"What do you mean?" Alys asked finally. Beneath the table, she gripped handfuls of her skirt in her fists, willing herself to stay calm, to stay present.

"I'm afraid it's difficult to explain," he said, hesitating. "Perhaps it's best if you fetch your friends first."

A spark of hope. Alys met Evander's eyes across the table, sensing he was thinking the same thing.

"Maybe you should fetch them yourself," Evander said. "Unless you don't know where they are?"

The chancellor's lips twitched in a small, sad smile.

"My niece told me you were a clever lot," he said. "I suppose I can't complain. That's what I'm counting on."

Alys had a hundred questions suddenly, but she bit them back. Evander leaned forward in his chair. "We aren't going to help you," he said. "We'd rather die."

Alys felt a surge of panic at his words, but she was careful to school her features. There were things that had to be said, in moments like these. Her father made a strangled noise and lifted his head. Her mother stiffened.

"For seers' sake, son," pleaded Edric. "Just listen to the man."

The chancellor raised his hand gently. "It's all right," he said. "I understand this is all very . . . unorthodox."

"That's one word for it," Evander muttered.

"Your friends are in the basement of the carpenter's shop on Wellis Lane," said the chancellor. His tone was mild. A tone for pleasantries and casual observations about the weather.

Alys's heart plummeted. Evander's eyes flickered toward hers, but she didn't have any reassurance to give.

"The rebellion is over," the chancellor said. "You aren't firebrands; you're just children playing with fire. You can all go to your deaths—a wasteful end to your wasted lives—or you can listen to my proposition."

It occurred to Alys that the chancellor might already know what their answer would be. With talented enough diviners at his disposal, he could know the most likely course of the entire night. He could have known how they were going to escape before they did. Which, of course, begged the question: Why did he let them?

"We'll listen to what you have to say," Alys said. "That's all."

"But we reserve the right to die wastefully," Evander added.

Cassa would have appreciated the remark, but to Alys the levity felt hollow rather than brave. What good was posturing when they were at a perpetual disadvantage? What was the point of everything they had done if their fates were already foretold?

SEVENTEEN

CASSA

THE high chancellor didn't look evil enough to be the villain that Cassa knew he was. He looked like someone's grandfather. He insisted on helping Lenore with the tea and spread of cold meats, cheese, and apples she was laying out on the table. When Evander had come to fetch her and Newt, Cassa had been certain that the chancellor's tale about needing their help was just a way to lure them into a trap, but the guards stayed peculiarly unobtrusive as she and the others devoured the food and two pots of tea. She kept one eye on the chancellor though. He was sitting in an extra chair someone had brought in, hands folded in his lap. Occasionally he would check his pocket watch and nod to himself.

As she finished her third cup of tea, Cassa couldn't tell if the uneasiness in the pit of her stomach was dread or indigestion. Possibly both.

Once all the food was gone, Chancellor Dane quietly asked Lenore and Edric to give them a few moments of privacy. They obeyed, but with the citadel guards hovering in the doorway, they didn't really have a choice.

Dane checked his watch again, then stood. He paced slowly, ponderously, from one end of the kitchen to the other. His gaze flickered around the table, considering each of the teens in turn. Cassa felt hemmed in, trapped. It made her blood surge hot in her veins.

When the chancellor finally spoke, his voice was measured and careful. "Before we go any further, I need to know how you made it out of the crypts."

"Easily," Cassa said.

The chancellor frowned faintly at her, unamused, though not nearly as irritated as Cassa would have liked.

"We followed the arrows," Evander said, shrugging away the glare Cassa shot him. "If you wanted a difficult maze, maybe don't mark the way out."

"The arrows only lead halfway," said Dane. "How did you navigate the rest of the tunnels?" There was something shrewd in his gaze, like he was fishing for an answer to a question he wasn't asking.

Cassa caught Evander's eye across the table and saw that he was intuiting the same thing. The chancellor was less concerned with how they escaped the crypts and more concerned with whom they might have met while down there. She glanced at the others, willing them to stay silent about their not-so-chance encounter in the caverns. Newt was staring into his teacup, lips pursed tightly. Alys was watching Dane closely, as if she could unpack all his secrets.

"I used Evander's coins to divine," Alys said. "That's how we knew the way."

The chancellor stopped his pacing to consider her answer. Cassa's breath caught in her throat, but Alys was unflinching under Dane's scrutiny. Finally he nodded and clasped his hands behind his back.

"Here is the deal I am willing to make. Your lives in exchange for one task." He took a long breath, as if the offer was a physical strain. "There is a monster beneath the citadel. I need you to kill it."

Cassa's hands twitched, and she dropped them into her lap. *If you go into the city tonight, you'll discover the truth of all I've told you.* Was this what Solan meant? Was this what he had foreseen?

"What are you talking about?" she managed.

"Just what I said." The chancellor resumed his pacing. "The monster has been imprisoned in the crypts beneath the citadel for a long time. The council has reason to keep him—it—alive, but I know that if we don't act soon, then Eldra will suffer dearly for it. More than it already has."

He clamped his lips tightly over the last words, as if he'd said more than he intended. Cassa wasn't sure anyone else noticed. She opened her mouth to ask what he meant, but Alys spoke suddenly.

"You're talking about the executioner."

Cassa bit her lip, but the chancellor just nodded. The existence of the executioner wasn't exactly a secret after all.

A chill danced along Cassa's spine. The truth. Could Solan have possibly been telling the truth? Could the council's demise really be within their grasp?

"You want us to kill him?" Evander asked, his brow furrowed slightly.

The chancellor nodded again but, infuriatingly, he did not offer further explanation.

"Why us?" Newt's gaze moved tentatively to the chancellor.

"The last prisoner to escape the dungeons also used the tunnels," Dane said. “It was before my time. They found his wasted body three weeks later in the depths of the caverns. The poor wretch had gotten lost.”

“So you need our excellent sense of direction?” Cassa asked dryly.

“I need people who succeed where others fail.” He’d crossed his arms, bony fingers tapping on his sleeve. “There are more dangers than getting lost in those crypts.”

The simple way he said it, not like he wanted to scare them but as if he was stating a fact, made Cassa wonder whether Chancellor Dane had ever been below the citadel or if he’d just been told secrets of the crypts. It was strange to imagine him down there in that world of shadows and sweating stone. He might scuff his perfectly polished shoes.

“If he’s so dangerous, why has the council kept him alive?” Cassa asked.

“It’s a little more complicated than that,” Dane said. He eyed them for a moment, then checked his watch and nodded again. “I’ll give you the short version. A long time ago, before I was even born, there was a man of noble birth named Solan Tavish. A rook and an alchemist, and very skilled at both. He was also a member of the council, until they discovered that he was stealing memories. He had grown so powerful that he didn’t even have to touch a person to take their memories. Just being in the same room with them was enough. The council sought to punish him for his transgressions, but because he hadn’t killed anyone, they spared his life—perhaps to their detriment. He was imprisoned in the catacombs, there to suffer the burden of the death rites for the rest of his days.”

It was mostly the same story that Solan had told, minus the fact that he was also a seer and plus the claim that he had been an alchemist and a member of the council. If all of it was true, then Solan Tavish had been a very busy man. It took a moment for the most salient detail of the chancellor's story to sink in. Alys was the first one to notice, of course.

"I don't understand," Alys said. "If he was on the council before you were born, then how is he possibly still alive today?"

If the chancellor recognized the insinuation about his advanced years, he didn't show it.

"I told you he was a skilled alchemist," he said. "Before he was caught stealing memories, he did some sort of experiment on himself. He achieved something . . . impossible."

"Are you trying to say he uncovered the secret to eternal life?" Alys asked, skepticism bleeding through her tone.

"No man can judge eternity," he said lightly. "But I have laid eyes on him myself, and though he does not eat, does not drink, and has not seen the sun in nearly two hundred years, he is still very much living."

The room fell silent. Cassa could hear the restless thrumming of Evander's fingers on the table and the creaking leather of the guard's holster as he shifted in the doorway.

"You called him a monster," Newt said at last, his voice quiet but not faint.

"The years have warped him," said Dane. "He is no longer a man. It is his duty to devour the sins of the condemned, to send them pure to their deaths while he carries their entire existence inside of him. How could that not drive a person out of their humanity?"

Cassa checked her breathing. She couldn't help but remember the way that Solan's features had shifted perpetually between young and old. The sense of dread that suffused the air beneath the citadel. She didn't trust the chancellor, but she couldn't help but think he was right about Solan Tavish no longer being entirely human.

"So you've created a monster, and now you want us to slay it for you?" she asked. Her pulse drummed in her ears.

The chancellor looked at her but said nothing.

"How's he supposed to be dangerous?" Evander asked. "He's been down there this long without anyone being the wiser."

"He's growing stronger," Dane said. He averted his gaze. "I think it's the influx of memories he's been fed in the past decade."

Cassa's heart began to pound more vigorously. He was talking about all the rebels who had been executed. All those lives. An *influx*.

"You didn't really answer the question," Alys said, pushing a strand of hair behind her ear. Cassa caught sight of the red indents in her palm where her nails had been digging in. "Why are you so desperate to kill him now, after so many years?"

The chancellor sighed, a slow, sad sound.

"Solan is stealing people's memories again—all their memories. So far, it seems he can only reach the citadel, but there have been three victims in the past week alone. Every moment we delay, people are at risk."

Cassa's breath caught in her throat. Finally, an admission, and with it, a kind of vindication. She'd been right to lead the others into the citadel. She'd been right to think the council was hiding something deadly.

"So the rumors are true," Cassa said, "and the council hasn't done anything to stop him."

"The council needs the executioner," Dane said. "They'll do anything to make sure no one finds out. That's why I need you."

"Why do they need him so badly?" Evander asked. "Any rook could do the death rites." His voice was mild, but Cassa could see the contempt darkening his eyes. That same contempt was unfurling in her chest, thorny and creeping.

Dane's lips wavered as if he couldn't decide on the right words. Cassa was almost amused at how carefully he was shaping his story, with no idea that they already knew everything he wasn't telling them. The council didn't need a rook under their control as badly as they needed a seer. Solan's ability to assassinate their enemies with only his mind was just an added bonus to the prophecies he fed them.

"It doesn't matter why," the chancellor said finally. "What matters is that we stop him."

"Sorry, I'm confused about where the 'we' comes into this." Evander glared up at the chancellor. The only movement about him was his right pointer finger, which tapped a steady, driving rhythm on the tabletop.

"You'd all be dead by now if it weren't for me," said Dane. The control in his tone never wavered, but Cassa suspected they'd finally rattled him.

"Your backstabbing niece is the only reason we were caught in the first place," she said.

He flinched at that, and she smiled tightly. Dane stared at her for a few seconds, his keen eyes unreadable. He didn't disagree.

"For a century, the rebels tried to bring down the council," he said softly. "For a century, they claimed to fight for Eldra, for its people. If you truly want to follow in their footsteps, then protect the city now. The executioner will only get stronger, and his reach will only grow."

Something inside her stirred at his words, but she tamped it down. He wasn't offering them a chance to save the city, a chance to make all these years of struggle *mean* something. He wasn't offering them a choice at all. They were pawns to be sacrificed in whatever power game he was playing with the council.

"You can save the inspirational speeches," she told him. "You aren't fooling anyone."

The chancellor met her eyes. She wondered if he could feel the hate dripping off her, viscous and acidic. If he could, it didn't show in his calm features.

"How do you expect us to kill him anyway," Newt asked, "if he really is immortal?"

The chancellor retrieved something from inside his jacket and set it on the table. A vial of liquid, black as ink but glimmering with strange iridescence. "It took my alchemists a year to make this poison. It's all we have, but they think it's strong enough to kill him."

"Are we supposed to just . . . ask him if he'd like a nice poisoned cup of tea?" Evander asked, bewildered.

"Frankly, for a master plan this sounds a little weak," Cassa said.

"You'll enter the caverns through the valley and retrace your steps to the fork in the tunnels where the arrows ended. Take the other route, and you'll find a lake and a boat. Solan lives on the other side."

"Does he observe teatime?" Cassa asked. She tried to reconstruct a map of the crypts in her head. The way Dane was talking, there was another way out of the caverns—one they would have found if they'd gone right instead of left. One that led straight to freedom instead of into the lair of a man who may or may not also be a monster. She considered being annoyed at Alys again but found that she couldn't. Solan's words were a spark in her heart. He had been waiting for them. He had seen the council's downfall.

Chancellor Dane went on as if she hadn't spoken.

"Because of all the memories he's consumed over the decades, he has to drink an elixir of mirasma every four hours. If you leave tomorrow, you can reach him before he receives the dose at the fifth evening bell."

"Wouldn't it be easier to poison the elixir before it's given to him?" Evander asked with an earnestness that made Cassa's stomach clench. Surely he wasn't actually considering going along with Dane's scheme.

"I've tried." The chancellor shook his head. "The council's alchemists formulate the mirasma just before each dose, and then it's guarded closely until the moment it's lowered into the cavern. The council chooses their lackeys well. They can't be bribed or threatened. This is the only way to succeed without the council knowing I'm involved."

"So we somehow manage to poison his mirasma, and then what?" Newt asked. "Spend the rest of our lives as fugitives?"

"I'll have pardons for each of you, signed and sealed, as soon as you complete the task."

Complete the task. What a delicate way to phrase the nature of what he was asking them to do. As Cassa stared at the chancellor, it occurred to her that such honeyed speech must come to him naturally. He probably didn't even realize he was doing it.

"We haven't agreed to anything yet," she said, mostly to be stubborn but also to see how he would react.

He wasn't perturbed.

"You can either accept the deal I'm offering you or accept the council's verdict. Your chance to escape was lost the moment you stepped foot in the lower ward. Whether you agree to help or not, you'll find yourselves in the catacombs, facing the executioner. It's your choice whether you will be equipped to survive or not."

Again, not really a choice at all. Cassa did her best to ignore Alys's pointed glance. Coming back into the city had seemed the best course of action at the time—how was she supposed to know the chancellor himself would be here waiting for them? *There will be no turning back.*

"We need time to talk about this," Cassa said.

"Please, take all the time you need," he said, then checked his watch. "But not longer than ten minutes, if you please. I'm on a tight schedule. My diviners are quite insistent that I must return before the sixth morning bell if I want my absence to remain undetected."

He left them then, crooking his finger at the guards, who followed him out of the dining room. Cassa could hear murmured voices from the front of the shop, but they were alone for now. She looked at the others and realized with some bemusement that they actually seemed conflicted.

"Please don't tell me you believe his noble hero act."

"Of course not," Evander said, "but you have to admit that it's just as likely as Solan's suffering-victim act."

"Except that the council wanted to execute us, and Solan is the one who helped us escape." Cassa pushed her chair back and stood up, feeling cramped all of a sudden. She walked to the door, peeking into the shop beyond. The chancellor was talking to the Seras. She wondered if he was promising proper rites when their children inevitably died horribly in the crypts.

"The chancellor is working against the council though," Alys said into the uneasy quiet. "Maybe he—"

"Maybe he *what*?" Cassa whirled around, and Alys flinched. Cassa lowered her voice with difficulty. The thorns in her chest had begun to constrict her lungs, making it difficult to breathe. "Maybe he just wants what's best for us? Maybe he just wants to make the world a better place? Maybe four years ago, when he ordered his soldiers to slaughter *thousands* of people, it was just an honest mistake?"

He could distance himself from the council all he wanted, but it had been Ansel Dane who'd crushed the firebrands in their final stand. After almost a hundred years of fighting back, after generations of sacrifice and determination, the rebellion had ended in a brutal defeat beneath the noonday sun. Nearly three thousand people massacred just inside the citadel walls. Nearly everyone Cassa had ever known and loved. That was the day she'd lost her parents. The day that Chancellor Dane had taken them from her.

Alys stared hard at her hands, folded on the tabletop. Newt and Evander both avoided Cassa's gaze as well. She realized her breaths were coming in short gasps. Her heart ached so badly, she thought it would burst.

"I'm not saying we should trust Solan Tavish," she said, once she'd regained some semblance of control, "but if keeping him imprisoned and using his prophecies is the only way the council has stayed in power, then maybe freeing him is the only way to stop them."

"And if he's lying?" Evander asked, finally meeting her gaze. He looked so much older than he had a year ago, when all of Cassa's grand schemes to overthrow the council had still been fantasy, when their reality had been late nights and late mornings, waking up with their bodies still pressed together as if there was no reason to ever be apart, whispering about tomorrow as if it could be anything but what it was—a relentless battle against an enemy with all of the past and all of the future at its disposal. Maybe Evander really had hoped for a different kind of tomorrow. Maybe she was the one who had taken it from him. She didn't like to think about it.

"Solan hates the council," Cassa said. "That much is true at least. With his help, we finally stand a chance."

"You've never put any stock in prophecies before," Evander said.

"There's never been a prophecy in our favor before."

One of Evander's eyebrows arched, but he just gave a small shrug. Cassa looked at Alys and Newt, but they still hadn't looked up.

"You all know what I want," Cassa said at last, hating how vulnerable she felt in that moment. "But we're in this together. We decide together."

A century of struggle. All those people dead, fighting against the corruption infecting their city. She and Evander and Alys and Newt hadn't started this war, but they were the only ones still fighting. She had to believe that mattered. They couldn't quit now.

"We don't have to decide now," Newt said softly, though he still didn't look up. "Either way we have to tell the chancellor we're going to help him."

Evander regarded Newt for a few seconds. Cassa couldn't help but notice the way his eyes had begun to linger on Newt when he thought no one was looking, the quiet captivation that had once felt so familiar. Something else she didn't like to think about. Evander was nodding slowly.

"He's right," he said. "Lie now, decide later."

"I agree," said Alys, after a pause.

It wasn't what Cassa wanted to hear, but it was a small hope. Through the doorway, she could see the chancellor and his guards making their way back toward the kitchen. Even if she convinced her friends, she wasn't sure *how* they were going to help Solan, but she had no doubt something would occur to her. Something always did.

"Have you made a decision?" Chancellor Dane asked, eyeing Cassa for a moment and then glancing over her shoulder at the others.

"We'll help you," Cassa said, "but we are *not* on your side."

He fingered his pocket watch idly while he studied her face.

"I understand. And I hope you'll understand that there is one . . . precaution that I had to take. I always trust my diviners' advice in these situations." The chancellor's expression was one of mournful regret.

"What are you talking about?" Cassa asked, then she heard the front door of the shop slam. She swore and pushed past him. There was a guard stationing himself in front of the door, glaring at her with arms crossed. Another two guards near the windows. Lenore and Edric Sera were gone.

"Where are they?" Alys cried, stumbling out of the kitchen behind Cassa.

"It's only a precaution," the chancellor said, stepping smoothly aside as Newt and Evander ran into the shop as well. "I promise they'll be perfectly safe and released as soon as Solan Tavish is dead."

Outside the door was the muffled sound of another door slamming and then carriage wheels on cobblestone. Cassa barely registered what was happening as Evander charged past her and collided with the guard at the door. He kneed the man in the gut and got one hand on the doorknob before the guard recovered and flung him backward into the counter. Cassa rushed forward instinctively, but a strong hand caught the back of her dress. She whirled, her palm angled upward toward the other guard's nose, but he caught her wrist. She tried to twist free, but he jerked her around so that he had her arm bent painfully behind her back. She felt the cold barrel of a gun against her neck.

Evander recovered and launched once more at the guard in front of him but was sent flying again, this time to the floor. Alys cried out, but Evander's eyes immediately found Cassa's and then the gun pressed beneath her chin. His chest was heaving, and Cassa saw the glint of silver rising from behind the counter, too long and slender to be a coin.

Do it, she mouthed.

And Evander sent the letter opener flying, not at any of the guards but straight at the chancellor.

"Evander, stop!" Newt's voice rang out the instant the razor-sharp silver flashed in its unnatural arc.

And an instant later the blade froze in midair, hovering a couple of inches from Chancellor Dane's right eye.

"Just wait," Newt pleaded. "It won't help your parents."

Cassa strained against the grip on her arm, tears flooding her eyes at the ripple of pain. She wanted to shout at Evander to do it, to end it right here and now. But even as the words rose in her chest like a battle cry, she knew that Newt was right. This wasn't the way.

The shop was achingly silent except for everyone's labored breathing and the thrum of her own pulse in her ears. Evander held Newt's gaze for a brief eternity, his face flushed, his dark eyes made darker with desperation. Then came a soft *plink* as the letter opener fell to the floor.

"Thank you," said the chancellor, though it wasn't clear whom he was thanking. He had never for a moment dropped his air of utter equanimity, which impressed Cassa, entirely against her will. He gestured to the guard who held Cassa and the other two who had their pistols aimed at Evander. Immediately they all holstered their weapons. The chancellor straightened his jacket and checked his watch one last time. "As I said, your parents won't be harmed, as long as you keep up your end of the bargain. I harbor no illusions that you'll ever be on my side, but I'll do anything to protect this city from the monster that's trying to destroy it."

"But who will protect the city from you?" Cassa asked quietly.

The chancellor met her glare without flinching, his expression once again softened with regret.

"Good night, children," he said, heading for the front door. The guards filed after him. Cassa had to resist the urge to punch the one who had been holding her as soon as he loosened his grip. Alys crossed the room and forcefully pushed the door shut behind them, like she couldn't bear to see them for even a moment longer.

Evander ignored the hand that Newt extended and pulled himself up with a wince, using the counter for support. He was looking at Cassa, his eyes so hard that for an uncomfortable second he was unrecognizable.

"I want to help Solan," he said.

Cassa blinked. It was the opposite of what she'd expected to hear.

"What?" Alys demanded, turning from the door. "Evander, they have our *parents*."

"And they aren't going to get away with it," he snapped. "Not again."

Alys stared at him, mouth agape. She was trembling. Evander stalked toward the stairs without another word.

The Day Alys Met Cassa

SHE was going to see the Dream Merchant. She didn't know his real name, or if he even had one, but she had a scrap of paper with scribbled directions to his shop. She'd been told he paid good money for good dreams. She still held a few of those in her memory, despite the piling misery of the past several years. She'd also been told he was dangerous. A thief. A traitor. A cutthroat.

That didn't stop her from slipping out of their filthy tenement, clutching the directions close even though she'd memorized them days ago. She'd been putting off the visit, trying to convince herself that it wasn't necessary. But the night before, she'd overheard her parents whispering when they thought she was asleep. The landlord was coming to collect on their debt—three months' worth of rent. If they didn't have it, they'd be out on the street.

She couldn't do that again. The huddling in dank alleyways. The scrounging for any kind of shelter, any modicum of dignity. Their tenement was vile no matter how much she tried to scrub it clean, but at least it had four walls and a roof. She wasn't going to lose that.

Evander had been gone for two days now, which wasn't unusual lately. He would leave for long stretches, ranging the city, and return with a pocketful of coppers, sometimes even a silver or two. He never said much about what he was doing, never asked Alys to come along.

She'd followed him once, on a day when she felt particularly curious, particularly daring. She'd watched him roll a silver coin across his knuckles for a small crowd of onlookers, flick it out of sight, retrieve it from behind a toddler's ear, from the flower in a woman's hat, from the empty air. He was only twelve years old, but she'd watched him charm them all with his easy smile, his twinkling eyes, and his quick wit. Then he offered to divine someone's future in the coins. "Costs a silver to read the silver," he'd said.

Alys knew that Evander didn't have a smidgen of divining ability, but she'd found herself believing his predictions, so earnest and confident he was. The lady with the hat was going to find something she'd lost. A man in a fine black suit was going to have a run of good luck. Alys left before the crowd dispersed. She doubted that any of them could see the tightness in her brother's expression, the tinge of sadness in his false smiles. He looked so tired.

She never told Evander she'd followed him that day. It was one of the few secrets she'd kept from him. She had an aching feeling that it wouldn't be the last.

Her parents had left before dawn as usual, off to find work where they could. She knew that whatever work they found, it wouldn't be enough. With his weak lungs, her father wasn't well-suited to hard labor, and her mother was a middling seamstress at best. They were both apothecaries. They knew the medicinal properties of any plant, the obscurest remedies, the latest cures. Their lives were meant for a different path.

Whenever Evander came back with his ill-gotten gains, their mother would toss the coins onto the rotting tabletop. She'd study them with her tired, bloodshot eyes, as if there were any hope for a future that could save them. But Alys knew divination wasn't an answer.

So that morning she'd tugged a threadbare cap onto her head to hide the hack job that had been done to her hair. She'd sold it a couple months ago for a few coppers. Her mother had shouted at her for ten minutes while her father sat in a corner and rubbed his temples. Evander had been away again. Alys didn't care about her hair. It would grow back, though not fast enough to help them.

She followed the directions to the north side of the lower ward, along streets she wasn't familiar with and among people she didn't recognize. The roads were flooded inches deep with rain and sewage. She could feel it seeping into her battered shoes. She tried not to care.

The Dream Merchant's shop was a shack near the end of a row of other identical shacks. The only thing setting it apart was the large window opened at the front with a narrow board nailed into place as a countertop. The sign dangling above had a symbol carved into it that she didn't recognize.

"It's the rook's mark," came a voice, and she jumped. A man had appeared at the window, resting his hands on the sill and eyeing her appraisingly. Just the sight of him made her uneasy. He was wearing an odd assortment of gentleman's attire that had seen better days. A jacket with patched elbows, yellowed shirtsleeves, a limp blue tie, and a mismatched waistcoat. He was balding on top, his black hair slicked back with too much oil. When he smiled at her, she caught sight of a mouthful of cracked, rotting teeth.

His eyes were what troubled her though. Too keen and darting. This was a man who always knew more than you told him.

"All the rooks in the citadel wear the mark," he went on when she said nothing. "The diviners and sentients and seers have one as well. Though in the citadel they prefer gold." He tapped his lapel and chuckled like he'd made a joke.

"I've come to sell a dream," Alys said before she could lose her nerve.

"'Course you have." He plopped down in the chair behind the counter and lounged back, interlacing his fingers behind his head. He looked her up and down. "I only pay for quality merchandise. I'm not sure how pleasant a guttersnipe's dreams can be."

Heat rushed down Alys's back, and she clenched a fist.

"If the upper echelon's dreams were so wonderful, they wouldn't be buying them off guttersnipes," she replied.

He chuckled again.

"True," he said. "Let me have a look. If I like what I see, you get a silver a dream." He leaned forward and beckoned her with tobacco-stained fingers.

Alys hesitated at the thought of those fingers touching her skin, but she couldn't turn back. Dreams were worthless after all. Yet this man was going to pay handsomely for hers. She closed the gap between them, careful to breathe through her mouth as he leaned so close she could see the whites of his eyes—and the unnatural blue-green of the bulging blood vessels. She'd heard about the condition before, though she'd never seen it herself. Addiction to mirasma was common in rooks.

The Dream Merchant reached out with both hands to touch her temples but was interrupted by a voice behind Alys.

"If I were you, I wouldn't let him anywhere near me. At least not until he's washed his hands."

Alys jerked back instinctively and turned to face the newcomer. It was a girl around her age with messy hair and a streak of mud across her forehead. She was dressed like a beggar, but she didn't look anywhere near starving.

"Get out of here," snapped the Dream Merchant. "This is none of your business, you little bitch."

"Gaz Ritter, is that any way to greet an old friend?" The girl pressed her hand against her heart with mock dismay.

"Come here and I'll give you a greeting you won't soon forget." Gaz reached below the counter and slammed a knife onto it.

Alys stumbled a few steps back, but the girl didn't move. She was actually smiling.

"I almost want you to try," she said, cocking her head to the side. "I can only imagine what my parents would do in return. My father might be happy just taking your eyes, but I think my mother would be more creative."

Gaz blanched at that, though he didn't remove the knife.

"I'm Cassa Valera," the girl said, turning to Alys and extending her hand. "I've been looking everywhere for you."

"For me?" Alys shook her hand reflexively, though she still hadn't figured out what was going on. The name sounded familiar, even though she was certain she'd never met Cassa before.

"You *are* Alys Sera, right?"

Alys nodded.

"Good, let's go." Cassa tightened her grip on Alys's hand and tried to lead her away, but Alys pulled away from her.

"I can't," she said, glancing back toward Gaz. Her heart was racing like a jackrabbit. She didn't want to stay, but she couldn't leave empty-handed.

Gaz flashed his disgusting grin and leaned back in his chair again, the picture of leisure.

"You heard the lady," he said to Cassa. "Why don't you run along? Miss Sera has business with the Dream Merchant."

"If you're a merchant, then I'm the queen of Teruvia," Cassa snapped. She looked at Alys. "He doesn't trade fair. He buys dreams for a silver and then turns around and sells them to bluebloods for twenty silvers each."

"Man's gotta make a living," said Gaz.

"Except I hear you also skim a few memories off the top." Cassa stalked forward a few steps, even though that knife still gleamed between them. "Then you sell them to the council if you find anything worth their while."

"You hear that from your scum parents?"

Cassa ignored him and pointed over Gaz's head, toward the sign with the rook symbol.

"See the smaller symbol there?" she asked Alys. Alys squinted and saw that there was another symbol on the sign, carved roughly into the wood. An X with an extra horizontal line through the center. "It's a warning. Means he can't be trusted." Cassa crossed her arms.

Gaz scowled at her.

"You filthy firebrands deserve everything you get," he said. "I ought to rip down that sign and burn it."

"Try it," Cassa shot back. "We'll carve the next one into your forehead."

Alys was just remembering where she'd heard the name Valera before. Cassa's brash confidence, despite her age and Gaz's knife, was starting to make more sense. But why had Cassa Valera been looking for *her*?

Gaz had risen to his feet, resting his hand on the knife's hilt. Alys touched Cassa's shoulder.

"Let's go." She didn't want things to escalate further, even though she had a strange feeling that Cassa would be able to hold her own.

"Finally," Cassa said. "The stink around here is giving me a headache. I can smell the mirasma from here. Hitting it a little heavy these days, aren't we, Gaz?"

"I'll hit as much as I like. I can afford it," Gaz replied, his lips suddenly curving into a smile. "The council pays prettily for the things I know." He tapped his temple.

"In that case, it's a wonder you didn't starve to death years ago."

"Oh, I know quite a lot about what goes on around here." He was still smiling. "I see all sorts of folk come and go. Like a certain little redhead who doesn't like to be seen but isn't very good at hiding. I wonder how much the council would pay to know the company the high chancellor's niece has been keeping."

"Bastard." Cassa surged forward, and Alys instinctively caught her arm. "If you so much as breathe her name, I'm going to ram that knife down your throat."

The sudden fury that twisted her voice made Alys's hair stand on end.

She believed that Cassa meant every word. She knew she should just leave them to their feud and escape while she was still an innocent bystander. Instead, she found herself grabbing Cassa by both shoulders and propelling her down the street, away from Gaz Ritter and his shop.

Once they were a couple of streets away and Cassa's stormy expression had calmed somewhat, Alys cleared her throat.

"Why were you looking for me?" She hoped her tone was passably nonchalant. Inside, her mind was roiling. What could the rebellion possibly want with her?

"You're an apothecary, right?"

"I'm thirteen."

"Good to know. Not what I asked."

"My parents are apothecaries."

"I hear you're pretty handy at it too." Cassa shot her a sideways glance.

Alys gnawed her lip for a few seconds.

"So?"

"So, if you want to earn some real coin, I've got a job for you."

"My parents—" Alys cut off, thinking about the scars burned into her parents' faces, the mark the council gave rebels whose crimes didn't warrant a death sentence. But her parents weren't rebels, and they never had been. Their only crime had been giving a dying man comfort. For that, the council had taken everything.

Maybe Cassa knew what she was thinking, because she stopped walking and tugged Alys to face her.

"Your parents have done enough," she said, her brown eyes solemn. "Don't you think it's your turn now?"

Alys stared down at her wet, filthy shoes. Her parents were wasting away—she could see it in their sunken cheeks and their tired eyes. Her brother was far gone and going further every day. It occurred to her that maybe she didn't have much of a choice. Her chest had constricted so tightly that she could barely breathe, but she looked Cassa Valera in the eye and nodded.

EIGHTEEN

VESPER

AFTER a few hours of restless sleep, filled with visions of infinite burning candles and the sound of that woman's screams, Vesper pulled herself out of bed and into her clerk's uniform. The black pants, collared shirt, and buttoned vest were crisp and neat but comfortable. By the time she'd laced on her leather sleeve-guards and pulled on her light half-cape, she felt more like herself than she had all night.

She left the clerks' barracks and made her way through the citadel streets, which were much quieter now, at dawn, though workers still scurried about their duties. All the wealthy patrons of the chapels had returned to the upper echelon, where most of them had probably just finished drinking themselves unconscious. Memorial services for the Slain God were as good a reason as any to celebrate in excess.

Vesper had just turned onto the main street that ran past the Central Keep when she heard the rumble of hooves and wheels from the direction of the front gates. She stopped and waited for the slick black carriage to near. When the driver saw her, he eased the horses to a halt. Almost immediately, the carriage door popped open and the high chancellor stepped down. He moved more slowly these days, but he still had a spryness about him, as if he were a much younger man trapped in an aged body.

"Ah, Vesper," he said, squinting at his pocket watch. "Right on time."

Vesper hadn't intended to meet him, but apparently she was meant to anyway. Her uncle Ansel had access to the best diviners in the city. She had long since grown accustomed to him knowing where she was headed before even she did. There were very few secrets in the citadel—that was part of the reason her uncle had hired her.

"Did you find—did everything go well?" she asked. The passersby gave the chancellor and his clerk a wide berth out of respect, but that didn't mean their ears weren't perked.

Ansel probably had the same thought, because he shook his head.

"Not here." He gestured toward the keep and dismissed his driver. Vesper walked beside him in silence, wishing she'd at least had time for breakfast before the day's intrigue began.

"How was the service?" asked her uncle, his face a pleasant mask. There might be very few secrets in the citadel, but she and her uncle had mastered the art of keeping them. It was especially dire now, as they reached the crux of their carefully laid plans.

"There was another incident," she said.

"What? Who?" He looked at her, and the frown lines were sharp in his face, eviscerating the mask.

"I didn't recognize her," Vesper said. "A lady. Her husband was there. I'm sorry, I should have stayed and found out their names."

She had been so eager to escape the chapel that she'd forgotten how important it was to her uncle to have every possible scrap of information. Vesper felt most like herself in her uniform, but the truth was that she wasn't really a clerk at all. Her appointment was a smokescreen. Her uncle didn't need a clerk; he needed an extra pair of eyes and ears. He needed someone he could trust in the shifting sands of the citadel's politics. Filling the role of clerk just assuaged any suspicion—from his enemies in the citadel and from Vesper's parents, who lived in the upper echelon and were exceedingly pleased that their daughter had received such a high placement, nepotism or no. In her clerk's uniform, she had access to areas of the citadel that most people didn't, and as the clerk to the high chancellor, there were very few places she couldn't go, as long as she could invent a good enough reason for being there.

Ansel looked ahead again as they passed through the gate into the outer courtyard of the keep. A man in a fine gray suit on his way out traded brief pleasantries with him. Crispin Cavar. He was one of the more well-established sentients in the citadel, and his services were utilized by several council members. Vesper averted her eyes in what she hoped was a demure fashion. Ansel scratched his forehead during the exchange. A casual enough gesture. She wondered if the sentient had noticed. Surely people often tried to conceal their full faces from his unnaturally discerning gaze.

Technically it was illegal for sentients to read people without their consent, though there was no easy way to prove it. Laws governing rooks were even stricter. Any rook caught taking someone's memories against their will received an automatic death sentence, which Vesper had always found morbidly ironic, considering that the traditional death rites of the Slain God depended on a rook taking all of a person's memories. Context was everything, especially in the citadel. Sentients and rooks working for the council never seemed to find themselves on the wrong side of the law.

"The attacks are getting more frequent," Vesper said, once they had cleared the courtyard and were winding their way through the great halls of the Central Keep. Ansel just nodded.

Though the rest of Eldra had progressed with the times, the decor in the citadel's keeps was as it had ever been. Immense, fading tapestries hung from the stone walls, depicting various prophecies and scenes from the Slain God's history. Gaslights were mounted at intervals, casting wavering light and shadow. The richly colored rugs, once plush velvet, were threadbare under Vesper's feet. A century of stalemate with the rebellion had drained the citadel's resources to almost nothing, trapping it in time. That was part of the reason fewer and fewer citizens were allowed past the walls. The council didn't want the public catching on to the fact that their steadily rising taxes were barely keeping the citadel solvent. That, and the fact that more and more people were collapsing in agony within the walls, waking up utterly senseless, if they even woke up at all.

She glanced at Ansel's profile and could see the careful concentration there as they walked. She didn't speak again until they had reached the southeast tower—the chancellor's private quarters. They mounted the steps past his sitting room and study doors, past his bedchamber, all the way to the top of the battlement. Vesper was used to the climb, but her uncle needed to stop and rest periodically.

The sunrise was breaking across the horizon by the time they were in the open air. The chill was more pronounced above the narrow confines of the streets. Their vantage point was higher even than the citadel walls, and Vesper could see all of Eldra stretched out, bathed in the burgeoning sunlight. There was the pristine brick and whitewash of the upper echelon, where the nobility lived alongside the wealthier merchants and families of council members. The next tier down held the finest establishments the city had to offer, the museums and public gardens and gambling halls for people with money to lose. Next were the more prominent tradesmen with their modest shops and the people who were neither wealthy nor poor.

On and on it went, each class neatly divided from the others, with few exceptions. From Vesper's bird's-eye view, it was deceptively neat and simple. Beyond the curved city walls was the great glistening ribbon of the river, the bright spires of the Merchants' Bridge, the golden expanse of Aurelia Valley, and the dark green smudge that was Eldrin Wood. If she squinted, she could make out a lazy stream of smoke from a clearing in the wood, where the Blacksmith lived. The mountains beyond were shrouded in a murky mist.

They were safe nestled in their far corner of Teruvia, distant from the machinations of the world, but they were also trapped in a future that had been handed to them hundreds of years before. Trapped with the monster that lurked beneath the citadel. A monster of their own making.

"I think your friends will help us," Ansel said into the silence.

Vesper's heart clenched in her chest, though she knew she should be relieved.

"Were they—did they seem—" Vesper swallowed her words, uncertain of exactly what she wanted to ask.

Ansel smiled at her, a soft, sad smile.

"They were as well as could be expected. No broken bones at least."

Vesper didn't ask what she really wanted to know. They wouldn't have asked about her. In the days of the rebellion, traitors to the cause were killed and their bodies burned—the same fate that the council dealt captured rebels. But though rebels were granted death rites by the council, albeit at the hands of the executioner beneath the citadel, the rebels didn't extend the same courtesy to their enemies. Traitors to the rebellion were granted no good-byes, no death rites. They died with the poison of their guilt still inside them, their ashes given to the wind and forgotten.

The others might have believed that a diviner saw their plan and warned the council, but Vesper knew how Cassa's mind worked. Cassa would know the truth. And though the rebellion was over, Cassa had never left it behind.

Vesper had betrayed their plans to her uncle because she thought it was the only way to save them in the end. There was so much more at stake than even she had ever imagined. They wouldn't understand though. They wouldn't forgive. Maybe her friends hadn't asked about her because she was already forgotten. Ashes in their memories.

"I think it's time," her uncle said into her silence. "You can see the rest for yourself."

"Already?" Vesper asked.

"I have to meet with the council within the hour," he said. "We can't risk anything. Not now."

Vesper nodded, wishing she felt more like the capable clerk that everyone else saw, like the clever confidante her uncle thought she was.

Less like a girl still clinging to the simplicities of childhood faith while she grew more and more lost in the world that faith had forged.

"Should we go inside?" she asked.

"No, here is better," he said. "It's the only place we can be sure we're alone."

Vesper nodded again. She was shivering with the cold. The sunlight was still timid and new. Ansel's features were pockets of shadow as he turned to face her. She was shorter than him, but they were more closely matched now than they had been the first time she'd ever done this.

"Vesper," he said gravely, "some of the memories I have to give you, they're . . . well, they're not memories I would wish on anyone else. I can't take any chances though. I'm sorry."

Vesper had a feeling she knew at least one of the memories he meant. The grief lining his face was impossible to miss. She'd grown used to it over the years. Some days she didn't even notice it at all. But it was always there. In reply, she lifted her hands and pressed her fingers against his temples. He closed his eyes, but she kept hers open.

"Take good care of them for me," he said, a ghost of a laugh in his tone.

Vesper knew her face was set in a grimace. She concentrated on the cold of her fingertips and the warmth of his head, then drove her focus deeper. She saw his proffered memories in her mind's eye, erratic and dreamlike. The streets of the lower ward, rolling past. The interior of the Seras' apothecary shop. Lenore Sera arguing, her cheeks in high color. Edric Sera shaking his head, a mournful look in his eyes. Then Evander was there, smirking. Alys clutched a teacup, not quite hiding the shaking of her hands. Newt, ever watchful, ever careful. Cassa said something, her eyes hard with anger, but Vesper couldn't make it out, not yet. Seeing them all so near made her stomach somersault, but she kept her focus. If she'd wanted, she could have reached further back. She could have seen anything the high chancellor remembered, but she would never do that to him.

Ansel offered the relevant memories, and she reached out to take them. Then she pulled. They were thin threads, dangling from her fingertips like gossamer webs, iridescent even in the dim light. Rooks had to be patient and gentle, so very gentle. Memories were fragile. They could be torn or teased out too thin. With methodical movements, she drew the threads in, wrapping them around her fingers. Some were frayed or nearly invisible. Others were thick and bright, wrapped with smaller threads like vines around a tree. If her uncle had opened his eyes, he would have seen nothing out of the ordinary, but for Vesper the morning was aglow.

Once she'd found her rhythm, the memories flowed more freely. They twined up her arms and around her torso, shimmering and humming softly with music only she could hear. When she was sure she had the last of them—every memory her uncle had of their scheme and a few other key memories he had entrusted—she broke off the last threads. Instantly the cocoon tightened. For a brief moment, she felt the warmth of it on her skin, deliciously delicate. Then the light died away, the threads melded into her body, and the memories were her own.

NINETEEN

Newt

NEWT'S dreams were a horrifying stream of panic, frustration, and mortification, though neither the citadel dungeons nor the labyrinthine crypts made an appearance. He dreamed he was home again, sitting at the kitchen table. His mother wasn't there; but then, she never was in these dreams. His father sat across from him, twisting a piece of steel in his hands like putty. *We bend, but we don't break,* he said. *We never break.* Then the metal was a dagger, and he thrust it into Newt's hand, pinning his flesh to the wood.

Newt woke with a start, his heart racing. His shoulder had rolled out of joint again. He eased it back into place, wincing at the stab of pain. The bed in the Seras' spare room was comfortable enough, but sleep had done nothing to relax his aching muscles, and his ankles and wrists protested every slight movement. He'd pushed himself too hard. He was lucky he hadn't sprained an ankle or worse.

We bend, but we don't break.

The daylight streaming past the curtains was weak and gray with the vestiges of night, but Newt climbed out of bed anyway. He bit his lip against the pain and made his way across the room. There was a roll of bandages in the top drawer of the rickety pine dresser. Last year, when he'd started spending less and less time in his father's house and more and more time anywhere else, Lenore Sera had made up the guest bed for him a few times, when he'd been here late with Alys and Evander. In the past few months, without ever really discussing it, she'd started keeping the bed ready all the time. She'd tucked some towels, extra blankets, and bandages in the drawers, and she'd told Newt to leave some spare clothes too. It was easy to see where Alys had gotten her brisk practicality.

Newt didn't know if he had Evander and Alys to thank for the hospitality, and he'd never mustered up the courage to ask. He knew the Seras were aware of who his father was and what he had done. They had never technically been rebels, but they certainly had no love for the council or the chancellor. There were plenty of people who had never technically been rebels who still spat at the mention of his father's name. The rebellion had waxed and waned over time, but all told it had lasted almost a hundred years. Firebrands were legends, especially in the lower wards, where most of them had been born and bred.

What made it worse was that Newt's parents had been firebrands once too. Though not quite legendary, they had done their part tirelessly for years. Then, when he was nine years old, his mother fell ill and never recovered. Almost a year to the day after her funeral, his father packed up their belongings and moved them both to a beautiful brick house in the third ward.

The thought of home made Newt's head ache, and suddenly the spare room felt cramped and warm. With practiced speed, he braced his wrists, ankles, and knees with the bandages, then pulled on some fresh clothes and boots. He peeked out the door into the corridor, but the second floor was still dark and silent. He'd had enough of the dark for a lifetime. Without really thinking about it, he went to the window and pushed it open. Once he'd climbed onto the narrow ledge, it was surprisingly easy to find purchase in the old, uneven brick, grip the edge of the roof, and pull himself up, though his muscles and bones screamed with the effort.

It was worth it though, when he got a full breath of the fresh morning air. The first magnificent colors of dawn were spilling over the city walls and across the lower ward. He sat still for a long time, letting them wash over him, letting them clear away the shadows of the dungeons and the world below the citadel that clung to him like cobwebs.

A sound from below caught his attention. He peered over the edge of the roof and watched with bemusement as Cassa descended from another open window to the street. She wasn't particularly graceful about it, but she did manage to land on her feet, which was impressive. He was curious about where she was going but not enough to call out or risk following her. It didn't even occur to him to be suspicious. Cassa was nothing if not fiercely, uncompromisingly loyal. It's why she'd taken almost a year to warm up to Newt, even after Evander and then Alys and Vesper had welcomed him into the fold, even after Newt had proven himself useful in tight spots.

Newt couldn't really blame her. He had never been ignorant of his father's crimes. After their sudden move to the third ward, it had taken him only a couple of days to figure out the reason for their sudden good fortune. The illustrious Valeras—then-leaders of the rebellion and practically gods in their own right—came to that beautiful brick house in the dead of night and called his father a traitor. They told him that the only reason he was still alive was for Newt's sake, but if he ever set one foot outside the third ward, they would gut him in the street. Newt wasn't supposed to be awake, wasn't even supposed to know they were there, but even back then he was good at being invisible. Caris Valera, her hair glinting in the firelight, leaning against the doorframe with a smile as sharp as the knife she toyed with. Luc Valera, so quiet that Newt had to strain to hear him, but every word a precise blow.

The Valeras were dead now. His father still never left the third ward. He'd always been a hard, exacting man, but over the years that drive decayed into something bitter and broken. On bad nights, he would rant about the rebellion, how he hadn't defected because he was a coward but because he could see the rebels were losing and he had to make sure Newt was provided for. The house and the garden and the cushy stipend from the council in exchange for all the information he had on the rebellion—those were for Newt.

Newt could understand perfectly well everything his father wasn't saying. The vitriol he received from rebel sympathizers, the accusations of cowardice, the death threats that would sometimes be left on the door—those were Newt's fault.

"All I want," his father would say, "is for you to make something of yourself."

Newt's father had a lot of ideas about how to make something of his son, to teach him to bend without breaking. Newt learned how to twist his way out of rope and iron bindings if he wanted to eat. He learned how to dangle from just his fingertips if he wanted to save his bare feet from the glass shards below. He learned how to lie perfectly still in the crawl space below the house if he didn't want the spiders and rats to notice him. He learned how to hold his breath for minutes at a time if he didn't want to drown in a bucket of water.

He learned how to hold a world of hatred inside him without a single crack in his exterior calm. Sometimes he felt that that was his greatest accomplishment. And sometimes he wished the Valeras hadn't done him the favor of letting his father live.

Newt flexed his left hand, scratching at the three scars on the back of it. Cassa had vanished into the city, but the quiet was broken by the ringing of the sixth morning bell. The lower ward was starting to stir. Newt remained still, unwilling to leave behind the ripening daylight and the crisp breeze. If he closed his eyes, it was almost like being in the valley again on a clear summer day, a fixed point while the rest of the world moved around him.

His reverie was interrupted a second time, now by the sound of someone cursing repeatedly under their breath. Newt leaned over the edge of the roof just as Evander's face popped into view.

"How do you always make this seem so easy?" he demanded breathlessly.

"I think you just make it seem hard." Newt tried and failed to stop the smile tugging at his lips. "Need some help?"

"Shit," Evander replied. He'd managed to get his forearms onto the roof and was struggling to get a leg up. "Shit. Shit. Shit."

He finally pulled himself up enough to flop the rest of the way over like a struggling fish. Newt scooted over to give him some room, biting back a laugh at the absurdity of everything in that moment. Evander took a few seconds to catch his breath and then pushed onto his elbows, his eyes flicking appreciatively over the view. His black hair, pushed back from his forehead, was still mussed from sleep. Newt almost asked why he had climbed up here, but he swallowed the question at the last second and looked out at the city again. Evander made it about five seconds before coaxing a coin from his pocket to fiddle with, balancing it on each of his fingertips in turn. He'd never been one for idle hands.

With Evander so close that their arms were almost touching, with the dawn light slowly turning golden around them, Newt couldn't help but remember a day two years ago in the middle of Aurelia Valley. It had been clear like today but warm and humid. He remembered the stickiness of the heat, the ridges of the uneven ground against his back, the shivery sensation every time Evander shifted and brushed against his elbow.

Evander had wanted to know why Newt spent so much time in the valley, so Newt tried to show him. Considering Evander couldn't remain perfectly still to save his life, Newt wasn't sure he really understood what was so appealing about the ritual. It didn't matter though. They'd talked about Evander's parents, about the caves that honeycombed beneath them, about Newt's father. Evander was easy to talk to, even about that. It wasn't just his natural charisma; it was the way he listened, like there was nothing else worth hearing, like everything he heard he'd take to the grave.

Newt wasn't sure if Evander remembered that day. If he did, it probably wasn't in the same way Newt did. He knew Evander was bisexual, but that didn't mean Evander would ever think of him as anything other than a friend. Why would he, when he could charm almost anyone with a single smile, when he was impossibly confident and clever and kind, when Newt was just . . . Newt?

"So was there a particular reason you climbed up here?" Newt asked, as the silence he usually loved grew unbearable.

"Probably," Evander said, as the coin spun lazily on the tip of his thumb, "but I can't remember. It's too early in the morning for coherent thought."

Newt hesitated.

"What you said last night—do you really think we should help Solan?"

Evander looked at him over the impossibly balanced silver. The glibness had faded from his expression.

"Before we left the caverns, Solan told me he'd seen something else in the runes. He said there was a way to save my parents, but not by giving in to the chancellor. I didn't know what he meant then—I don't even think he did. But now it makes sense."

Newt wanted to point out that if Solan was trying to manipulate them into helping him, then a convenient divination was just as effective as the chancellor's blackmail. He didn't say anything though. He had a feeling Evander already knew and that he just didn't care. The council had taken everything from the Seras, and Evander and Alys had given up their childhoods to earn it all back. Now the chancellor was threatening to take even more.

"I'm with you," Newt said. *Always*, he didn't say.

"Thank you." Evander palmed the coin, and a second later it had disappeared. "And thank you for . . . last night."

Newt swallowed hard, remembering the look in Evander's eyes when he'd sent the blade flying. It wasn't the unfamiliarity of the look that had frightened him—it was how chillingly familiar it actually was. A world of hatred locked inside.

"It's not a big deal," he said, trying to keep his voice light.

Evander glanced at him but didn't say anything more. For a long time, they just sat quietly, listening to the sounds of the city waking up.

"I guess we'll have to figure out how to convince Alys," Evander said finally.

"She'll come around." Newt lay back on the roof. The wooden tiles were uneven and splintery but pleasantly cool against his flushed skin. He closed his eyes against the brightening sky. Despite the trials looming over them, another smile curved his lips. "Although a more pressing problem might be how you plan on getting yourself off this roof."

A beat.

"Shit," said Evander.

twenty

Alys

ALYS woke to the sight of Cassa tumbling through her open bedroom window. For a few seconds, she considered burying her face back in her pillow and ignoring the incident for the sake of her own sanity. But Cassa made a ridiculous ruckus latching the window, divesting herself of her shoes and the loose jacket she'd probably stolen from Evander, and splashing her face with water from the basin. Alys dragged herself into a sitting position against the headboard with a shiver. It was early enough that the room retained the night's chill.

"Is it even worth it to ask what on earth you're doing?" Alys asked, a yawn chasing her words.

"Ask me anything you like. I'm an open book." Cassa flopped onto the bed at Alys's feet, her legs dangling off the side and her head propped against the wall despite the fact that Alys had made her a perfectly comfortable pallet on the floor. It was messy enough that Alys knew she must have gotten at least a few hours' sleep.

"How long have you been gone?"

"An hour or so."

Alys hadn't even heard her get up. Heavy sleeping was not particularly conducive to survival, but she would have to worry about that later.

"Where did you go?"

Cassa shrugged—a difficult maneuver from her current position.

"Nowhere special. I was just curious what rumors are circulating about us, and I wanted to see if there was any word on the streets about your parents."

Alys's stomach twisted as the realities of the night before crashed around her. In the sweet place between dreaming and waking, she'd been able to forget the dread that clamped down on her like a vise, thinking about her parents at the chancellor's mercy, their lives dependent on her and the others. It was enough to start the maelstrom spinning in her mind. She clenched her hands into fists and tried to breathe.

"Anything?" she managed to ask, when Cassa didn't go on.

"No." Cassa hesitated, her eyes flicking to Alys. "I'm really sorry they got dragged into this. I wish there had been another way."

An apology from Cassa was a rare enough occurrence that Alys was temporarily distracted from her worry. She squeezed her eyes shut for a few seconds, concentrating on the crisp cotton of her nightclothes against her skin, the raspy sound of her own breath, the scent of the outdoors that Cassa had brought in with her. She opened her eyes to find her friend watching her with a faint frown of concern.

"Any good rumors about us?" Alys forced a wryness into her tone that she didn't necessarily feel, but pretending she was fine helped her believe that she really could be.

"The most prominent one is that we were caught and executed

immediately." Cassa made a face and scratched her nose absently. In the stark morning light that spilled through the window, her dusting of freckles stood out on her flushed cheeks. "There is one going around I'm partial to—that we set diseased rats loose in the Judgment Hall and two councilors fainted right out of their chairs."

"Did you start that one?"

"Obviously."

"And was there a reason you couldn't use our front door like a normal person?" Alys tried to pull the blankets up to her shoulders, but they were bunched under Cassa. She kicked her shoulder lightly. Cassa swatted at her foot and didn't budge. Alys kicked harder.

"I didn't want anyone to know we were here, in case someone recognized me," Cassa said, begrudgingly rolling enough to the side for Alys to free the blankets.

"You could have stayed inside."

"Then who would make sure that proper rumors are being started about our heroic feats?" Cassa flashed a grin and stretched her arms above her head with a wince. She closed her eyes against the sunlight slanting across her face. "Your window is trickier than Evander's. There's no drainpipe handy."

Alys wasn't sure why her stomach flipped at that. Neither Cassa nor Evander were prone to secrets. They had never been tight-lipped about their relationship—except for exactly why they had ended things. Still, Alys had to take a moment to compose herself before replying with forced lightness.

"Then maybe you should have used his window."

"Considered it," Cassa said, giving no indication that she'd noticed Alys's discomfort. "But I thought it might be unwise, given the circumstances."

Alys told herself to drop it. She should get out of bed and get dressed. It was so cold outside the blankets though.

"Which circumstances?" she asked. "That we're currently fugitives or that you two aren't together anymore?"

Cassa's eyes sprang open, and she squinted thoughtfully at Alys, as if she had just realized what conversation they were having. She licked her chapped lips.

"Both."

Alys dropped her gaze and fiddled with a lock of hair. Cassa let out a sigh, struggled up to her elbows, then rested her back against the wall.

"You might as well ask what you really want to ask," she said, "especially if we're all going to die soon."

Alys flinched, although she knew that wasn't Cassa's intention. She still couldn't bring herself to meet her eyes.

"Are you two really done?" she asked.

"Yes."

Their romance hadn't surprised Alys. Her brother and Cassa were cut from the same cloth, kindred spirits in almost every regard. A part of her had suspected it was inevitable ever since she'd first introduced them four years ago. But the sudden end to the romance *had* surprised her. As far as she could tell, there hadn't been a fight or another person or anything of the kind. They had just called it quits. There had been an initial few months of awkwardness, when Cassa suddenly had renewed interest in planning an infiltration of the citadel and Evander suddenly had renewed interest in exploring the valley with Newt or irritating Alys while she tried to help their parents with apothecary business. Now they were friends again, still close but in a different way. Alys was relieved that they'd been able to move past it. Even though she told herself it was because she didn't like having her bored brother underfoot in the workroom, she knew deep down that she hadn't been ready for Cassa to drift out of her life.

But she still didn't understand why. Alys hated mysteries. She decided that if there had ever been an opportunity to learn, it was now.

"Why?"

"He was terrible in bed."

Alys flinched, though she could tell from Cassa's smirk that it had definitely been her intention this time. Cassa laughed and stretched her arms in front of her, lacing her fingers together and arching her back.

"Lighten up, Alys. I'm just kidding," she said. "He was perfectly adequate in bed."

Alys kicked her in the knee and then again for good measure. Cassa just laughed louder.

"Forget I asked," Alys said, pulling up her blankets higher, as if that could protect her from more unwelcome information. "I'm never talking to you again."

"What do you want me to say?" Cassa asked, still chuckling. "There's not some big, scandalous reason. We were just always better as friends."

"That simple?" Alys was unconvinced.

Cassa shrugged.

"That simple." She blew some hair from her face and cast a sideways glance at Alys. "I do second-guess our decision sometimes, if that's what you're asking. There's this look he has, when he's flipping those ridiculous coins around and saying something he thinks is clever, and—I don't know. I just miss him. I miss us."

Alys couldn't remember the last time she'd seen Cassa so serious, without her usual acerbic tone, except for maybe the morning before they broke into the citadel, when Cassa had told them that Vesper wasn't coming after all. That was different though. Or maybe it wasn't. Alys wasn't sure how to reply, and so she let the silence stretch between them. She was asexual, with little interest in romance and no interest at all in physical intimacy, but she knew what it was like to miss someone who wasn't really gone. After the council had branded her parents as rebels and taken everything they owned, her family had been shattered. They stayed together, but to Alys it was like living with phantoms, haunted by the memories of who they used to be. It had taken a long time to get her parents and brother back.

And now her parents were gone again—this time for real.

She swallowed hard against the panic rising in her chest and squeezed the blankets in her fists. If they didn't help the chancellor, what would happen to her parents? If they didn't help Solan, what would happen to the city? She couldn't help but think that neither of them was telling the whole truth and that no choice was the right one. But they still had to choose. What if they chose wrong? What if what if what if—she scrambled out of bed like she was fleeing the thoughts, like her anxiety was something she could run away from. Her hands were shaking as she pulled open her wardrobe, but rifling through her clothes, focusing on something practical and necessary—it helped. Slightly.

"He wanted it too, you know," Cassa said cautiously. "It's not like I broke his heart."

It took Alys a couple of seconds to figure out that Cassa was still talking about Evander. Of course she had no way of knowing that Alys's mind had already spiraled to a new subject.

"I know." She kept her face buried in the wardrobe, but Cassa must have caught the breathiness of her voice, because Alys heard the bed squeak as she straightened.

"Are you okay?"

Alys hated that question. What did it even mean to be okay? She wasn't hyperventilating on the floor of a prison cell, but she wasn't exactly fit to save her parents or the city—especially not both.

"I'm fine." Her stomach growled to remind her that she hadn't had a decent meal in two days, but she ignored it. She pulled some work clothes out of the wardrobe, the sturdy pants and loose shirt she wore when she and her father foraged for mushrooms, herbs, and medicinal roots in Eldrin Wood.

"Liar."

Alys slammed the doors shut.

"And how do you expect me to feel after everything that happened yesterday?"

Cassa shrugged, but it wasn't a casual gesture. Her eyes were steady on Alys, sharp and inscrutable. "We had to come back to the city. We didn't have a choice."

"Why? Because Solan said so? Because the chancellor already knew we were coming?" Alys dressed quickly, hating how vulnerable she felt shivering in her nightgown. Cassa had slid off the bed and wandered back to the window, resting her arms on the ledge. Alys wondered if she was planning on climbing out again—midconversation. She wouldn't put it past her. "You're the one who's always going on about how the prophecies can't control our lives. Either we have a choice or we don't."

"It's not that simple," Cassa said.

"You were singing a different tune on the lake. What happened to all that sentimental tripe about making our own way, about not needing auspicious stars?"

"Fine, we had a choice," Cassa snapped, whirling to face her. "We had a choice, and we chose wrong. Is that what you want to hear?"

"I didn't want to come back." Alys's pulse thrummed in her ears. Why did every conversation with Cassa turn into an argument? "Maybe if we hadn't, my parents would be safe."

She braced herself for a scathing retort, but Cassa's shoulders sagged a bit. She turned back to the window before Alys could decipher her expression.

"I told you, I'm sorry about your parents. I didn't—I should have stopped the chancellor somehow."

Alys shivered again, though she had already pulled on her woolen socks. She remembered the glint of the letter opener as it sped through the air. Such a harmless thing. Such a deadly arc. The look in her brother's eye wasn't something she ever wanted to see again. She'd almost wept at the sound of Newt's voice, because her own had been trapped inside her, stifled by the fear that Evander, in that lethal moment, wouldn't hear her at all.

"There wasn't anything you could have done," she said at last, picking up her hairbrush.

"It doesn't feel that way." Cassa's voice was soft and strange. "It never does."

Once again, Alys didn't know what to say. It didn't feel like a conversation or an argument anymore. It felt like a confession. Cassa hadn't moved away from the window, hadn't even glanced back. Alys finished brushing her hair and tied it back from her face. Then she left without saying anything, shutting the door gently behind her.

twenty-one

Evander

THE Sera house was too dark and quiet for Evander's comfort. He had hung a CLOSED sign on the front door, hoping that there weren't any customers with dire medicinal needs. He knew that even in the dungeons or wherever they were being kept, his parents would be worried about their apothecary shop. Alys would no doubt love to open the doors and pretend it was a normal business day. Keeping busy in the workroom was her way of dealing with almost any problem, but pretending everything was normal wasn't going to help them or their parents.

He met Newt in the kitchen, and together they scrounged enough food to make a passable breakfast. On the table they laid out a couple of loaves of bread, cold cuts of salted ham, and two jars of canned apples. Evander was so hungry that he tore off a hunk of bread and started eating while they laid out some plates.

Newt was patient enough to fetch some butter from the larder and cut the loaves into even slices before taking his first bite. Evander had never figured out where Newt's deliberate patience came from. He'd always been quiet and careful, though Evander had never thought of him as being gentle. There was something about his caution that was razor-sharp, as if he was eternally poised on some kind of precipice, as if he was holding something back.

Alys joined them a few minutes later and filled her plate in silence. Evander tried to catch her eye, but she ignored him. He knew he should apologize for snapping at her last night, but before he could decide on the right words, Cassa wandered down the stairs, her jaw cracking with a yawn. The sudden sight of her in rumpled clothes, hair disheveled, wearing a jacket she'd stolen from his room, made his heart stutter. For a moment, he was transported back to a morning about a year ago. A morning that wasn't so different from dozens of other mornings over the course of their relationship. When the sun had broken through his bedroom window, she'd still been lying against him, her back pressed against his chest, her body fitted to his like a puzzle piece. He remembered that her hair smelled like autumn leaves even though it was the middle of summer. She'd never made a lot of sense to him, but he liked that about her. He liked how brash she was, how reckless, how unapologetic. Back then it felt like something he needed.

Of course, he liked the feel of her too, her skin against his. The urgent way she kissed him, with her fingers wrapped around the back of his neck like he might try to escape. The way that sometimes she would rest her head on his shoulder and close her eyes, and for those moments she was a different person. Younger and softer. He wondered if that's who she would have been all the time if she'd been born into a different life. Somehow, he doubted it.

That morning there hadn't been anything soft about her. He didn't remember what he'd said—something about her needing to pay rent—and she'd elbowed him in the chest and rolled out of bed.

"You're lucky you're gorgeous," she told him as she got dressed.

He scrubbed his hands across his face and dropped back to stare at the ceiling.

"And clever and daring and spectacular in bed," he added.

"Sure." She sat down on the edge of the bed to put on her shoes.

He started to reply, but she twisted around to kiss him. The words died in his throat.

"Passable kisser," she said, her eyes bright with mischief, her warm breath tickling his chin. She'd grabbed his gray canvas jacket from the back of a chair and pulled it on without asking if she could borrow it. Then she'd climbed out his window and was gone before his family woke up.

His memories of those mornings were a pleasant ache inside him. He didn't necessarily want them back, because so much had changed since then, and Cassa's brash, reckless, unapologetic, unwavering determination wasn't what he needed anymore. He wasn't what she needed anymore either. That's why they had ended it. Though some part of Evander knew that Cassa had never really needed him in the first place. She'd only ever needed one thing, for as long as he'd known her.

"You'll be happy to know that I have a brilliant plan," Cassa announced as she plopped down beside Evander with a slice of bread in each hand.

"Are we allowed to finish eating first?" Evander asked, eyeing the hard set of his sister's jaw as she sawed at a piece of ham.

Cassa shot him an unappreciative glance but shrugged and took a bite. They all finished their first helpings without further conversation. The quiet was just starting to make Evander nervous when finally Alys spoke up.

"If we help Solan, what's to stop the chancellor from hurting our parents?"

"Solan will," Cassa said. "He's seen the downfall of the council. He knows how to make it happen."

"What if he's lying?"

"What if the chancellor's lying about letting your parents go free?" Cassa tapped her fork impatiently on the edge of her plate. "What if we do his dirty work for him, and then he just kills us and your family so that there aren't any witnesses?"

Alys pursed her lips together until they were a thin white line.

"Maybe the only way to help our parents is to help Solan," Evander said, and Alys finally met his eye. He told her and Cassa about the prophecy Solan had given him before they left. "He helped us escape the crypts, and even if we didn't understand at the time, he warned us about the chancellor and the danger to our parents too."

"That doesn't mean he's on our side," Alys said.

"No one's on our side," Newt said softly. "It's only us. It always has been."

No one seemed comforted by this idea, but no one disagreed. Evander took a deep breath, wishing briefly, confusingly, for the days before he'd met Cassa and Vesper and Newt, when the rebellion was just a mysterious force at the edge of his existence, when his only purpose every day was to keep his family from starving. It had been so much simpler back then. No choices to make. No motives to decipher. Just survival.

"Alys," he said, then waited for her to look up from her plate. "The last time the council took everything from us, there was nothing we could do to stop them."

"I could have." There was a crack in her voice. "I saw it in the coins."

"You couldn't have," Evander said firmly. He ignored Newt's and Cassa's gazes. For this moment, it was only him and his sister at the table, making this decision together. "They take whatever they want without consequence. They always have. But this time we can do something. For the first time, we can take something *back*."

Alys had been fiddling with a strand of hair, but her hand stilled. There was a stitch in her brow as she studied his face, as if she could find the future there.

"Okay," she said at last, and her voice was steady. She cast a glance around the table at the others. "I guess I wouldn't want to die next to anyone else."

"That's the spirit," said Cassa. "Now who wants to hear my brilliant plan?"

The Day Evander Met the Blacksmith

HE knew only three things about the Blacksmith. The first was that the Blacksmith owed his parents a huge debt. "Your mother saved someone very dear to him once," his father had told him one night in conspiratorial tones. "The physician was at his wit's end, but your mother knew what was necessary. Your mother didn't give up. The Blacksmith told her he would never forget what he owed her."

Evander's mother had told the story differently, when she had finally been persuaded to tell it. "That physician was useless," she'd said flatly. "Even Alys would have known what needed to be done—and she was six at the time."

His mother always looked at every situation with a calculating eye. She didn't tell stories, only facts. While Edric Sera experimented wildly, joyfully, doing his best to turn the world inside out and learn all its secrets, Lenore Sera kept the world outside his head and workroom running in orderly fashion. Alys had always been closer to their father. If given the choice, she would have gladly spent every minute of every day working alongside him. But Evander had always thought she took after their mother. He'd always envied that a little, the way she knew the answer to every problem, the way she could see everything like a diagram in her head, easily picked apart, easily mastered. Even the future was at her fingertips.

All of that, of course, was before the council ruined their lives. Evander didn't know the answer to his family's problem as they slowly starved to death in the worst corner of the lower ward. He experimented. He learned how to smile, what to say, and what trick of the coin he could use to earn money on the street from the wealthy citizens who once would have paid his parents handsomely to treat their most difficult ailments. He told stories about the future that he knew people wanted more than the facts. Slowly, he started to hate his own smile and the words that came out of his mouth. Slowly, he realized that the pittance he was earning could only help his family continue to eke out their miserable existence.

The second thing he knew about the Blacksmith was that you had to bring your own material. Evander stole three spoons from a pawnshop after he overheard the owner boasting to a customer that they were pure silver. It was his first time stealing outright. He knew that if his plan succeeded, it wouldn't be the last. That was okay. He could hate himself if it meant his family would survive.

The final thing he knew about the Blacksmith was where he lived. He left at dusk, letting the shadows chase his heels along the compacted dirt road that wound through the wood. He didn't tell his parents he was going. He didn't tell Alys either. He knew she would have tried to stop him.

The Blacksmith was a bear of a man, with a bushy beard and calloused hands. When Evander told him who he was and why he had come, the Blacksmith stared at him for a painfully long time, as if he could read everything Evander wasn't saying in the hollows of his eyes, in each distinct line of his rib cage that showed through his ratty shirt. The Blacksmith told him it would hurt. Evander said he didn't care. The Blacksmith told him he might die. Evander said he didn't care about that either.

The leather straps cut into his bare arms and chest. The wood was worn and smooth against his back. Overhead, strings of glass orbs twinkled like stars in the lantern light. Evander's nose filled with a harsh, metallic scent as the Blacksmith melted the spoons in a small crucible. The searing sound of the hot metal made his skin crawl as memories of that glowing brand glimmered brightly in the darkness of his mind. The Blacksmith never said a word. Evander thought he heard another set of footsteps enter the room, but before he could look, the Blacksmith was at his side. The blade he held caught the glow of the lantern, then he sliced open a line along Evander's left forearm. Evander bit back the cry of pain. He knew this was nothing. He knew this was only the beginning.

It wasn't until the Blacksmith lifted the smoking crucible with a set of tongs and poured the molten silver along that bleeding line that Evander began to scream. He screamed so long and so hard that he thought for sure his lungs would shrivel up inside him. A distant, unhelpful part of his brain wondered if the reason the Blacksmith lived outside the city was so that no one had to hear the screams. Then he blacked out.

He woke up to another wave of pain crashing into him. All he could see was the blur of the gleaming orbs through his tears. He blacked out again. Woke up again. More pain. It was less like a wave now and more like a fire burning through his blood. He had no idea how long it lasted, the rotating cycle of darkness and agony. Every time the light slipped away, he was afraid he was dying, and every time the pain woke him back up, he wished he was dead.

He lived a hundred lives and died a hundred times on that wooden table. When he woke up the final time, when the pain was only a simmering threat, he could barely remember his own name.

"It will be about six hours before the bloodbond takes effect—assuming it does," the Blacksmith told him as he undid the straps. He helped Evander sit up. "In about an hour, there's going to be more pain while your body tries to reject it. If you can survive that, then you should be all right."

His voice was gruff and clinical, but Evander could feel the concern dripping off him while he checked his pulse. Evander lifted his left arm, blinking until his vision cleared. The skin was red but not burned. The only evidence that remained was a raised silver scar. When the Blacksmith released him, he slid off the table. His legs held him upright, barely.

"You need to stay here until the second phase is over," said the Blacksmith.

Evander shook his head and took a few stumbling steps.

"Home," he croaked. His throat felt like it had been shredded with knives.

The Blacksmith kept talking, trying to convince him, but he didn't move to stop him. Evander grabbed his shirt and kept walking. Some part of him knew he should thank the Blacksmith. Another part of him begged to stay, to be safe. Evander had the capacity to listen only to the part of himself that pushed toward home.

It was dawn. The sky was streaked pink and purple and blue as he trudged back to the city. The gates had just opened for the day, and the Merchants' Bridge was crowded with noise and bodies and odors. Evander was shoved and jostled, but he forced himself forward. He was so parched that he was afraid he would pass out again. When he entered the city, his feet wanted to take him north, to the fourth ward, where his real home had been. With conscious effort he turned west, through the muck and mire to the hovel that was their only refuge. His hands had gone numb, and he couldn't get the door open. Just when he thought he might collapse right there on the stoop, it swung open, and he collapsed into Alys's arms instead.

She dragged him to a pallet in a corner. The one-room tenement was small enough that he could see Alys was the only one there. He found some small relief in that. He didn't want his parents to know what he had done, at least not until he could prove that it was worth it. Alys forced him to drink some water, even though he felt like his throat was closing up. She kept murmuring things, but he couldn't make out what she was saying. When the second wave of pain the Blacksmith had promised hit him, he forgot his name again, forgot where he was, forgot why he'd gone to the Blacksmith in the first place. He lost everything but the searing agony that kept him tethered to his body.

He didn't know how long it lasted. When he came out of it, there was a cool, damp cloth on his forehead and Alys was still beside him, crying softly. And he hated himself just a little bit more.

twenty-two

Vesper

ONLY a few hours after she'd siphoned all her uncle's memories of his past dealings with Solan Tavish and their current plans to rid the city of him, Vesper found herself in the custody of two citadel guards. She'd taken refuge in one of the workrooms set aside for clerks and was copying some notes from old council meetings for her uncle when the men arrived. They offered no explanation as they led her to an interrogation room and locked her inside.

She called through the door after them, but no one replied. Her nerves were fraying, and an itching voice in the back of her head whispered that something was very wrong. She had no choice but to sit and wait it out. It had to be some mistake. Or maybe it was a bizarre attempt by her uncle to ensure some privacy, away from prying ears and eyes.

When the door opened and Crispin Cavar walked in, she lost the sliver of hope she'd been clinging to. He worked for the council, and he always had. He had no loyalty to the chancellor.

"Hello, Vesper," he said, taking the other seat and clasping his hands on the table.

"Hello, Crispin," she said, trying to match his pleasant tone.

"I hope you've been comfortable," he said. He had an effortless geniality about him. She wondered if that helped when he was reading people's faces, if they didn't notice the intrusion as quickly. He was only a few years older than her, young for a council-employed sentient but very talented. What he lacked in wizened solemnity, he made up for with his easy smile and liquid brown eyes. Vesper had known clerks of all genders to swoon after him, though she didn't understand the appeal. He was nice to look at, but she didn't think she could ever be with someone while knowing that everything she'd done and said and sometimes even what she was thinking was written across her face for him to read. How could you ever trust someone that deeply?

"I'll be more comfortable when you tell me why I'm here," she said.

"It's just a precaution, really," he said. "There have been some . . . rumors that worry the council members. They've decided to launch an investigation into anyone who may be involved. With your uncle's blessing, of course."

He said the last with a small flick of his hand and a twinkle in his eye, and Vesper knew very well that her uncle had no idea she was being questioned like this. He'd be furious when he found out, but by then it could very well be too late. The council had their own diviners, and it was only a matter of time before they started catching glimpses of the machinations her uncle had set into motion. The council needed Solan Tavish and his prophecies more than they needed the chancellor. He was technically in charge, but he was outnumbered. If they suspected he was trying to undermine the power they had worked so hard to achieve, they wouldn't hesitate to destroy him.

"You look nervous," Crispin said.

"I'm being treated like a criminal," Vesper said. "Wouldn't you?"

He flashed her an indulgent, somewhat condescending smile.

"You're not a criminal until we prove you committed a crime."

The subtle implication in his choice of words wasn't lost on Vesper. They were expecting to find some proof before she left this room. His eyes were narrowed slightly now, roving over her face as if to memorize it. He was reading her right now. She didn't have long before he knew everything.

She wondered, a little desperately, if there was a way to feed him memories she wanted him to see and keep him from the ones he was looking for. She took a deep breath and tried to envision how her memories—and her uncle's that she still kept—must look inside her. The fantastic tangle of iridescent thread, pulsing with life and feeding one into another. She imagined she was teasing out the thread of one of the many uneventful chapel services she'd attended in her life, not the memorials for the Slain God but the regular services where the citizens sat drowsily in the pews while a priest droned on and on about the responsibilities left to them by the elder seers. Vesper felt sleepy just thinking about it. She shut her eyes and focused on that thread, pretended it was the only one that existed. A single shimmering strand alone in the dark.

Crispin shifted in his chair. Vesper opened her eyes to find him glaring at her.

"Something wrong?" she asked with feigned innocence that he wouldn't believe for a second.

"What are you doing?" he asked.

"Well, I thought I was being interrogated," she said. "Have you found what you're looking for?"

His eyes narrowed again, and this time Vesper could have sworn she felt something. A slight prodding. As if the threads inside of her were being sifted through. The sensation gave her a moment of panic, and she lost her focus. She thought she could feel his eyes on her memories. It was the worst kind of vulnerability. She shut her eyes again and this time envisioned the threads in a whirl of chaos and color. A vibrant, unpredictable storm.

Crispin pushed his chair back a couple of feet. Vesper's eyes sprang open at the sound, and she was a little surprised to find him clutching his head with one hand and gripping the tabletop with the other as if he were dizzy.

It took every bit of willpower she had not to smile.

"You look ill," she said. "Maybe we should take a break."

"They know you're hiding something," he snapped, a crack in his affable demeanor that was oddly satisfying to see.

"I think a sentient of all people would know that everyone is hiding something." Vesper clasped her hands on the table, mirroring his posture from before. Now she let herself smile at him, even though her heart was drumming so violently in her chest, she was afraid he could hear it.

Her uncle was the only person in the citadel who knew she was a rook. She'd never been officially confirmed. She had been twelve when her gift began to manifest—older than most. Her mother and father were at a loss for how to handle it. Her mother had two cousins who were sentients, but Vesper's great-great-grandfather had been the last rook in the family. It had been Uncle Ansel, a councilor then, who'd suggested that they delay her confirmation and keep her gift a secret for a few years at least. He'd spun some story about her needing to hone her abilities before making them public, but Vesper knew now that he'd been worried about her. There was great wealth and comfort to be had by rooks loyal to the council, but any who balked at the council's less honorable demands risked ruination, swift and sure. Back then, her uncle hadn't been ready to stand against his fellow councilors, but that didn't mean he was willing to sacrifice his niece to their agenda.

It was around that time that she met Cassa and started working with the rebellion. After that, she had no desire to receive an official confirmation from the council. If there was one thing the past few years had taught her, it was the value of secrets. Some people, like Crispin, might suspect she was a rook, but he couldn't prove it.

"I'm not interested in everyone's secrets," Crispin said. "Just the treasonous ones."

"I'll be sure to let you know if I come across any." On a hunch, she stood up. "I don't think you have any right to keep me here unless the council announces formal charges against me."

Cassa had told her once that if you did something with confidence, you almost always got away with it. Vesper mustered up every shred of confidence she had and walked to the door. It wasn't locked. Crispin didn't try to stop her.

"I hope you recover soon," she said over her shoulder. "I hear peppermint is good for dizzy spells."

She left the room and walked with what she hoped resembled purpose rather than panic. The guards who had escorted her to the interrogation were posted in the hallway. They eyed her as she passed but didn't move. Her hunch was right. The council was using scare tactics, but they hadn't yet resorted to drastic measures.

That time would come though, if they didn't find the answers they were looking for. Did they suspect her uncle at all? Or did they think she was working with someone else? Did they even know what it was they were looking for?

She left the Central Keep and kept her pace brisk as she turned onto the main road. It was a chilly afternoon, though the air held the first scents of spring. Normally a walk through the citadel would soothe her, but she only felt more on edge with every step she took. She couldn't shake the feeling that someone was following her. She wasn't even sure where she was going. What she really wanted to do was find her uncle and give him back his memories. She wanted to ask him what they were supposed to do next, but he'd given her strict instructions not to return the memories until Solan was dead. Any time before that and the council might learn what he was planning. He was vulnerable against every sentient and rook in the citadel loyal to the council. That was most of them.

Vesper knew the council wasn't through with her yet, but at least she had a line of defense. She wouldn't be able to hold out against Crispin forever, but her thoughts and memories were relatively safe for now. That still didn't help her decide what to do next. Ansel expected her friends to succeed. He couldn't trust any diviners enough to read the outcome, but he'd put all his faith in them—mostly at Vesper's behest. He didn't have a contingency plan. He was like Cassa in that regard.

Her only allies outside the citadel hated her. Her only ally within the citadel didn't even remember what they were trying to accomplish.

Vesper was on her own.

twenty-three

Cassa

CASSA didn't like being alone with Newt. It wasn't that she didn't trust him or that he made her nervous. It was that some subconscious part of her still felt she was supposed to hate him. She knew it wasn't fair to hold his father's cowardice against him. She knew the relationship between Newt and his father was strained, to say the least, that Newt hadn't even been home in months—though he was reticent about the reasons why. She knew that he was as loyal and dedicated as any of them.

But still there was that part of her. The knee-jerk reaction that just kept reacting. His father had cut ties with the rebellion and run to the council with everything he knew—which wasn't much but was still enough to put several lives in danger, including her parents'. She remembered the day they found out about his betrayal, the way her father's laugh lines had twisted with a frown, the way her mother folded up the missive neatly and then flung it into the fireplace. She remembered the way they had both looked at her, and for the first time in her life she had realized that it was possible for her parents to be afraid, for her sake and for all the firebrands.

And for the first time in her life, she was afraid for them.

"Are we going to hide?" she asked.

"You are," her father said, reaching out a hand to her. Cassa took it, amazed at how steady and strong it was, when her own had begun to tremble. "We have to make sure everyone else is safe first, then we'll join you."

"Why can't someone else go?" she asked. At eleven, she knew she was too old, but she crawled into her father's lap anyway. He pressed a warm kiss to the top of her head.

"Because it's our job," her mother had said, as if it were the simplest thing in the world. Their job to lead, their job to protect, their job to keep her safe.

Their job to die.

Her parents were heroes of the rebellion, but it was her mother and father she missed. Warm kisses and the complicated made simple. She couldn't help but think that she would have preferred them to have been cowards if it meant they could be alive, living in a cozy house in the third ward like Newt's father did. Instead, the Valeras were nothing but legends now, and her mother and father were dead.

She didn't hold it against Newt, but sometimes she wanted to.

They'd left the apothecary shop behind and headed west across the lower ward. Now that winter was edging into spring and the mountain passes had begun to clear, traders from the south had started pouring into the city with their wares, congesting the main thoroughfares. There were a few guards scattered across the ward, but mostly they were bored patrols, paying attention to nothing but the most blatant troublemakers.

Cassa and Newt took full advantage of the crowds whenever it was necessary to travel along the streets while sticking mostly to the alleys and back ways. They both knew the city well enough that their progress required no conversation. The last time either of them had spoken was back at the shop, trading last-minute cautions and advice with Alys and Evander, who were leaving the city to convince the Blacksmith to help. She and Newt were tasked with finding the mirasma that Solan needed for the bloodbond. They only needed a small amount, but even a thimbleful of mirasma could sell for nearly one hundred silvers. There weren't many places in the city to get it.

Later they would all meet in Aurelia Valley, at the cave mouth where they had emerged just last night. Then it was only a matter of getting Solan out of the cave and to the Blacksmith. An elegantly simple plan, provided none of them was followed and everyone was successful in their task. And that none of the chancellor's diviners caught on.

"Do we know where we're going?" Newt's voice startled her a little in the relative silence of the alley they were passing through.

"To steal some mirasma," Cassa said, "in what will hopefully be remembered as one of the cleverest and most perfectly executed heists in history."

"And where are we supposed to find it?"

"I happen to know a lowlife degenerate who has some to spare."

Cassa led the way through the rougher side of the lower ward to the Dream Merchant. Gaz Ritter claimed he didn't make much money on his little enterprise, and he kept his shop ramshackle enough for that to be believable. It was the same as it had always been, with a weather-beaten sign dangling by one corner over the door and a square hole cut roughly into the front wall to serve as a window. By all appearances, Gaz lived a humble life.

Cassa knew for a fact he kept a proper house several wards higher, with real windows and a rose garden out front.

"There's a smaller window cut into the back of the shop, behind his desk," Cassa told Newt, when they had stopped at the street corner a hundred yards away. "You should be able to fit through."

"Should?" Newt echoed, but he was already massaging his wrists and rotating his shoulders. It was a strange ritual Cassa had noticed before.

"Why do you do that?" she asked, even though she knew it wasn't the time or the place.

Newt glanced at her in surprise, then ducked his head and rubbed the back of his neck.

"I'm just curious," Cassa said.

"My joints get sore sometimes." He hesitated, still not looking at her. "A lot, actually. And they can pop out of place if I'm not careful."

That must be why he wore the bandages all the time. Cassa had always assumed it was just a precaution. She'd seen him bend his body in fantastic, sometimes unsettling, ways. He could fit in the smallest spaces and maneuver out of the tightest spots. He'd always seemed unbreakable. She'd never considered there might be more to it than that.

"It's not a big deal," Newt said in response to her silence. He was eyeing her now, his expression guarded.

"Okay," Cassa said. "I just didn't know."

Newt had always been tight-lipped about himself in general. She doubted anyone knew—except maybe Evander. But Cassa had a feeling that Evander kept several of Newt's secrets close to the vest. He had been the first to befriend Newt and the first to accept him into their group. He was the one Newt trusted the most. Lately she had begun to guess that there was more than that growing between them. She didn't want to think about it, but it was another knee-jerk reaction. Evander was her first romance, her first kiss, her first everything. Evander was *hers*.

But not anymore. She knew that. She did. They had both been ready to end things. It wasn't just that they were better as friends, as she'd told Alys. It was that the fire inside her burned away everything else. Sometimes when she'd held Evander, it had felt like she was holding the last good part of herself. Goodness couldn't stop the council though, and so it burned with all the rest.

"What am I looking for in the shop?" Newt asked, his attention shifting back down the street.

"Gaz keeps his stash in a wooden chest," Cassa said, holding out her hands to indicate the size. "There should be several doses in there. He's been addicted for as long as I've known him."

"How big is the shop?"

"Only one room, but I'll keep him plenty distracted for you."

Newt nodded and stared at the shop a little longer, gnawing on his bottom lip.

"I heard sometimes he steals people's memories without them knowing, then sells them to the council if they're incriminating."

"If there was a way to collapse the roof on his head without getting caught, I'd do it," Cassa said. "We'll just have to settle for this, for now."

Newt left without another word, headed for the street that ran behind the shop. Cassa started down the road, sidestepping the potholes and piles of refuse. She felt sorry for the desperate souls who had to crawl to Gaz for help. Except Alys. It had never occurred to her to feel sorry for Alys, whose desperation that day four years ago had seemed more like obstinacy. As if she'd never learned how to just give up.

She'd never told Alys that before. She wasn't sure how.

Gaz was lounging in front of his shop window, his filthy boots propped on the sill, his chair rocking back and forth precariously. Cassa considered how easy it would be to knock him off balance, but she resisted. When Gaz saw her, his eyes flashed shock, then suspicion. Then he smiled.

"Well, well, if it isn't the little rebel herself," he said, stretching his arms above his head with exaggerated leisure. His teeth were even more rotten than they had been the last time she'd seen him. She wondered why he didn't put some of his under-the-table earnings toward some dental hygiene.

Cassa stayed several feet away, reasoning that it was best to keep Gaz's attention as far away from Newt as possible. She crossed her arms.

"How have you been, Gaz?"

"How've I been?" he crowed. "Must be a cold day in hell if you're here to swap niceties with me."

"Freezing," Cassa said, keeping her tone as agreeable as she could manage. "I'm here for a favor."

"Don't do favors," Gaz said, but he swung his legs down and leaned forward against the windowsill. "I buy dreams."

"Among other things," Cassa said.

Gaz eyed her for a few seconds, then smiled again. This one was tighter, crueler.

"Among other things," he said.

Behind him, the interior of Gaz's shop was shadowy and still. In her periphery, Cassa thought she could see Newt's fingers grasping the sill of the small, high window cut into the back wall. She couldn't risk a better look without Gaz noticing.

"I'm getting out of the city while I still can," she said. "But I'm a little short of funds."

"Ain't we all."

"I have some memories to sell that I think you'll be interested in buying."

Gaz didn't look surprised. He'd probably already guessed as much. He scratched at the stubble on his chin in thought, never taking his eyes off her.

"I heard you was supposed to be executed a few days back," he said.

"Why else do you think I'm running?"

Some people laughing at the end of the street stole Gaz's attention momentarily, and Cassa used the opportunity to squint into the shop. She could definitely see the shape of Newt's head, and then shoulders, as he pulled himself through the window.

Cassa met Gaz's eye as he looked back at her.

"I don't often consort with criminal types." He flicked some dirt off his collar in what he probably thought was a genteel gesture. It might have been more believable if his entire shirt wasn't stained with sweat and grime.

"And I don't often consort with lowlife street scum," Cassa replied, forgetting her determination to stay civil. Old habits.

Gaz wasn't ruffled by her response. If anything, he was smug. Cassa wondered if he was reading her ire as desperation. That was fine with her. It would help sell what she was going to say next. Newt was in the shop now. There was no going back. Gaz had a knife with him at all times, and if Cassa didn't keep him distracted, Newt was going to be on the wrong end of it.

"I went below the citadel," she said. "I walked through the crypts. I saw the executioner with my own eyes."

Gaz's eyes glinted, and he leaned closer. His forearms were resting on the sill with his fingers intertwined. Cassa could see that they were trembling with excitement. She moved a couple of steps closer.

"You can take all of it—from my arrest all the way to my escape. That includes a route out of the dungeons, which I imagine those criminal types you don't consort with would pay a pretty penny for. And I'll bet some bored nobleman in the upper echelon would just love to know what's under the citadel."

Newt was searching the shop for the chest. His movements were silent and swift, but he wouldn't remain undetected for long.

"What about those friends of yours?" Gaz asked. "You ain't smart enough to break into the citadel on your own."

"Leave them out of it."

"That's not exactly possible." Gaz tapped a finger to the side of his head and grinned. "You runnin' out on them too?"

"They'll make their own way," Cassa said, uncomfortable with the turn in conversation. "Are you interested or not?"

"I'm plenty interested." Gaz stood up. "I'll give you ten coppers for the lot."

He started to turn, but Cassa lunged forward and grabbed his arm.

"I'm not talking coppers, you greedy bastard." She jerked him to face her.

Her caustic tone had the intended effect. He glared at her and wrenched her hand off his arm. Up close, he stank of beer and body odor. Cassa had to fight the urge to step back.

"You'll take what I give you," he said. "Or you can try your luck somewhere else."

"What I have is worth ten silvers at least, and you know it," she said. "I didn't come here to get cheated."

Gaz spit out the window, narrowly missing her left foot.

"And what if I decide you're too much trouble? Maybe I can earn more turning you in for the reward money."

"I think we both know that the council isn't going to pay money for information they can just take from you." Just because he was a rook didn't mean he was immune to sentients—or even other rooks.

Gaz spit again, his smugness twisting into a scowl.

"Fine, but you don't see a single coin until I have all the goods," he said. "I don't intend to get cheated either."

"Deal," Cassa said. "We don't have a lot of time."

The last was meant for Newt. She couldn't drag the conversation out much longer, and there was no way she was letting Gaz Ritter anywhere near her mind. In response, Newt lifted the chest high enough that she could see it over Gaz's head.

"Don't worry, sweetheart, I'm quick," Gaz said with a wink.

There was a joke there she so badly wanted to make, but she was busy ducking away from Gaz's hands as he reached for the sides of her face.

"What now?" he complained.

Newt chose that moment to open the chest. The lid creaked with a terrible squeal. Gaz spun around before Cassa could stop him. Her heart was in her throat, smothering her breath.

But the shop was empty—or looked that way. Cassa's mind caught up, and she realized Newt must have dropped behind the desk. Hidden for now, but not if Gaz decided to take a peek out the back window.

"Sorry," she said, and Gaz turned back to her. "You caught me off guard. I'm ready now."

She stepped even closer to the window, a fly into the web. Gaz's eyes glittered with a dark sort of triumph as he put his fingers against her temples. If Newt didn't hurry, she wasn't sure what was going to happen. She had no doubt that Gaz would try to take far more than the memories she'd offered. And she didn't know if she'd be able to stop him—or pull away once he'd started.

She felt the tug inside her head almost immediately. It was strange and nauseating. Even years into their friendship, she'd never let Vesper near her memories, and Vesper had never asked. This violation of her mind wasn't something Cassa had ever wanted to experience.

She could *feel* him rooting around her head. Her thoughts were a jumbled, tangled mess, and Gaz yanked at the threads indiscriminately, searching for what he wanted. Cassa's mind swam with memories, old and new together. The sound of her mother's laugh. The hard stone of her prison cell. Her father lifting her onto his broad shoulders. Vesper on the Merchants' Bridge, telling her that she couldn't go through with their plan. The blue sheen of the ghost light against ancient crypts. Her first kiss, and the smile on Evander's face before he leaned in to kiss her again. The Seras' cozy kitchen as she laid out her plan to the others.

In the present, Cassa saw Newt disappear out the window. It somehow felt like a distant memory, but a part of her mind registered what it meant. She wanted to pull back from Gaz, but she felt tethered to him. She could feel the memories slipping away, into his greedy hands. It was almost too late.

She head-butted him.

Gaz howled, and Cassa gasped. It didn't hurt as much as she'd expected, but maybe that was because she was too dazed to feel anything. She stumbled backward into the street, her vision reeling. For a horrible moment, she thought she might retch, but then her focus returned, and so did her balance. She didn't wait to see what Gaz would do. She ran.

twenty-four

Evander

WITH the crowds swarming the Merchants' Bridge, it was easier than Evander expected for him and Alys to sneak out of the city and onto the path through the woods that led to the Blacksmith's cottage. He kept stealing glances over his shoulder, certain that citadel guards would appear out of nowhere and give chase, but they were alone in the calm of the forest. The pines and budding oaks were so thick and close that they formed a canopy overhead, blocking out all but a few motes of sunlight.

Once they were a mile outside the city, Evander began to relax, though Alys stayed quiet. He made a few attempts at conversation to pass the time, but she was being purposefully taciturn.

"Okay, I'm sorry," he said finally, stopping to face her.

Alys stopped short and blinked at him in surprise.

"Sorry about what?" she asked.

"About last night. That I yelled at you."

"Do you really think I care about that?" Her eyebrows arched. "I was more upset that you almost got yourself shot."

"But I didn't. I'm fine."

"I know."

"If you're not mad at me, then why are you acting like we're marching to our deaths?"

Her eyes narrowed slightly, and she kept walking.

"I don't know how it's escaped your notice, but we very well might be," she said. "Not to mention the fact that our parents are probably in the dungeons right now, if they're even still alive."

"You know Mother would be the first one to tell you that moping never solved anyone's problems."

Alys slowed but didn't turn around.

"Stop treating it like a joke," she said. "Why do you always have to do that?"

Evander frowned at her back. Her rebuke hit him a little harder than he would have liked to admit. Of course he understood the precariousness of their position. Of course he was terrified that their parents would be killed and it would be his fault for wanting to help Solan.

"Truth or lie?" he asked.

That stopped her. With her back still to him, she took a deep breath. Then she turned.

"Truth." She met his eyes without hesitation.

"Because if I don't take it seriously, I don't have to be afraid of it."

She studied him in silence for a few seconds, thin lines of concentration wrinkling her brow.

"Must be nice," she said at last. She started walking again.

It was baffling to hear that from her. Evander had always thought of his older sister as fearless. She was cautious and calculating, and though sometimes her own mind betrayed her with uncontrollable panic, that had always felt separate from the fact that she was impossibly brave. She'd been the one to start working with the rebellion, even knowing the risk. For months, she had plied the trade that their parents had taught her, keeping the firebrands stocked with medicine. For months, she had brought home ever-increasing sums of money, giving vague answers when their parents asked, giving their family hope before Evander had even considered hope to be possible. She'd been the one to take care of him when he stumbled home after his visit to the Blacksmith. She'd been the one to get them out of the citadel dungeons. Everything he had to deflect with humor, she faced without flinching.

He tried to think of how to tell her that in a way she might believe, but knowing his sister as he did, he had a sinking feeling that she never would.

He caught up with her, and they continued their walk along the rutted dirt road.

"Is the Blacksmith going to remember you?" Alys asked, after almost half an hour of silence. Her tone had lost its reproach, but he could still sense the tension in her.

"Probably," he said. "It's not as if he gets many visitors."

The selection process for bloodbonding was intensive. It had to be. Before the process was in place, dozens of people had died during the bonding—some of them very important members of nobility. Finally, twenty years ago, the council had summoned the Blacksmith to the citadel, and with his help developed a set of criteria for what made someone most likely to survive the gruesome ordeal. A good constitution was vital, but it wasn't everything. The Blacksmith insisted that every minute detail of a person's anatomy affected the process: the thickness of their bones, their blood pressure, the rate of their pulse, their energy levels, and even the size of their tongue. A person's temperament and threshold for pain were also taken into account. Bloodbonding wasn't for the weak-willed.

Evander had heard once that for the final test, the applicant was cut with a knife so deeply that the blade nicked bone. If they cried out, they failed.

He didn't know if that was true, but it made sense. The council had many uses for people bloodbonded with common metals—like Captain Marsh's bond with iron—or even with the rarer gold and silver. They had no use for corpses.

Evander hadn't gone through any of those tests. The Blacksmith hadn't asked about his blood pressure or taken his pulse or measured his tongue. Sometimes Evander wondered if the process hurt less for people who were better suited for it. He didn't think his survival was a testament to his strong constitution—just his luck.

Alys was side-eyeing him, and Evander noticed that a silver coin was in orbit around his head. He hadn't even realized he was doing it. He reached up and plucked it from the air. It was warm in his hand. When he held silver, it didn't even feel separate from his skin. It was a natural part of him now.

The Blacksmith's cottage was a slapdash collection of different materials, as if it had been built over the course of a decade using whatever was on hand. The original house was a squat square with a pitched roof and short chimney, built from crumbling gray bricks. Thrust against its side was a second structure, built from logs and patched with straw in places. From the other side, a newer addition protruded, walled by red bricks and mortar. There were two great wooden doors at the front that stood open.

Evander and Alys stood at the threshold, peering into the dusky interior. It was fairly large—maybe even larger than the entire original cottage. Inside was the same as he remembered it, if a little more cluttered. Alys breathed in sharply at the sight. He'd never talked much about his visit here. She'd probably been expecting cold, hard surfaces and rows of metalworking tools and an angry furnace. But this was less a workshop and more a gallery. There was one long bench at the farthest end of the room that was cluttered with various tools, casts, crucibles, and metal cylinders of different sizes. In the very center of the room was a wooden table, roughly the size of a bed, with leather straps dangling from its sides. Evander remembered that table very well. Just the sight of it sent phantom pain through his arm and into his chest.

The rest of the space was crammed with shelves and smaller tables, all covered with trinkets and ornaments. On one table was a menagerie of animal figurines, cast in different metals, each one perfectly shaped. Beside it was a shelf full of silverware and small brass kettles and six identical tin gravy boats. More prominent than the displayed metalworking was the glass. Strands of delicate glass orbs hung from the ceiling in crisscross patterns, creating a galaxy overhead. Near the door dangled fishing line dotted with little glass teardrops, giving the illusion of rain that had been frozen in time. On other shelves, there were colorful vases blown in the most fantastic shapes and rows of figurines a hundred times more detailed than their metal counterparts.

When he'd come three years ago, it was after dark, the space lit solely by lanterns and candles perched or hung on every empty surface. Then, the spectacle of glass ornaments inside had glowed golden, seeming to amplify the light. Today, with the sun reaching its apex, the room was dim and murky with pale-gray shadows.

"What are you doing here?"

Evander and Alys both whirled at the voice behind them. It was a woman, probably in her thirties, wearing trousers, a faded green shirt, and a leather vest. She was carrying a rifle against her right shoulder. In her other hand she held a lumpy burlap sack.

"We came to see the Blacksmith," Evander said.

The woman didn't react. She was still staring at them, her suspicion unyielding. She was tall and broad-shouldered, with golden skin and a mess of brown hair that was pulled into a loose bun. She reminded Evander of Eldrin Wood itself, all dappled shades of earth and umber, at once restive and still.

"I remember you," she said to Evander. She passed between them and into the workshop, dropping her bag on the ground and setting the gun on the table in the center. "You must be the Sera siblings, then."

She turned to look at them, arms crossed. Amid the delicate finery of the room, she seemed even more stolid. Evander exchanged a glance with Alys, and then they joined her inside.

"I don't remember you," Evander said, which felt rude, but she didn't appear to notice.

"I helped with your bonding," she said. "But we didn't meet beforehand, so I'm not surprised you don't remember."

Evander wasn't surprised either. There was very little he remembered about that night. Mostly it was one long stretch of bright, racking pain. Absently, he rubbed his chest, where one of the leather straps had cut in. Afterward he'd been bruised everywhere the straps had touched.

Alys stepped forward and extended her hand.

"I'm Alys."

The woman eyed her hand strangely for a second, as if it were an unfamiliar sight. Then she shook it.

"Mira," she said.

"It's nice to meet you," Alys said, her tone so consciously polite that Evander wanted to laugh. "We need to speak with the Blacksmith, if he has some time."

"He's gone," Mira said. She waved a hand as if the answer were clouding the air, then she grabbed Evander's left wrist and tugged him closer. "Let's see it then."

She studied the scar on his forearm with the diligence of an artist examining a painting.

"Good, clean line. No excess scarring," she murmured to herself. She squinted at him. "Since the procedure, have you experienced any dizziness? Fainting spells?"

"No," he said, fidgeting in her grip.

"What about trouble swallowing?"

"No."

"Any difficulty getting aroused?"

Heat washed over his face, and he yanked his arm free.

"No!"

Alys was snickering quietly, and he shot her a glare. Mira nodded to herself, unfazed.

"He was a master at his work," she said. She left her sack and gun where they lay and headed for the interior door.

"What do you mean *was*?" Alys asked.

Mira paused with her hand on the door latch. She didn't look back at them.

"My father's dead." Her voice was a little higher than it had been, a little tighter. "It's been three months now."

twenty-five

Newt

NEWT found Cassa five streets over, in the shade of an abandoned factory. It was charred black and gutted, probably a casualty of the devastating fire that had sparked the rebellion so many years ago. Cassa leaned against the wall, massaging her temples. He'd never seen her this pale. Her usually faint freckles contrasted starkly against her bloodless cheeks. The bruise under her eye was a violent purple.

"You could have been a great thief in another life," she said, but her tone was weak.

"Are you okay?" Newt asked.

He knew it was a pointless question. Out of anyone, he was the last person whom Cassa would tell the truth.

"Fine," she said, straightening.

"I'm sorry I wasn't faster." He hesitated. "Did he get any of your memories?"

She shook her head, but he caught the flash of uncertainty in her features. Disquiet crept over him.

"Cassa, if he did—if he saw anything about Solan or our plan—"

"He didn't," she snapped. "I know what's in my own head. He didn't take anything."

Newt wanted to point out that he didn't have to take the memories to catch glimpses of them, but Cassa's expression was dangerous, like she was daring him to disagree with her. He didn't think it was a fight he could win. He wasn't sure there would ever be one, with Cassa.

He fished the stolen bottle of mirasma out of his pocket and weighed it in his palm. The bottle was as slender and long as his hand, though half-empty. Inside was a blue-green liquid, viscous and shimmering like fish scales in the sunlight. He wondered idly what it would feel like to be bloodbonded to something so beautiful—or to anything, for that matter. Evander had told him once it didn't feel like anything in particular. The metal was just an extension of him, as natural and forgettable as his fingers and toes. At the time, Newt had thought that only Evander Sera could sum up the mysterious, incredible power of a bloodbond as feeling like nothing in particular.

"I think you might have broken Gaz's nose," he said. "If we're lucky."

He lifted his eyes and watched as Cassa blinked and smiled. All evidence of her earlier distress drained away until she was herself again, bright-eyed and effervescent.

"I'm nothing if not lucky," she said. Then she faltered, and something more serious slipped into the smile's place. "You were great back there. I—I couldn't have done it without you."

Coming from Cassa Valera, the admission was the highest of compliments, which he never would have expected from her. He'd never believed for a second that she would have accepted him into the group if Evander hadn't spoken for him. Cassa was quick to forgive almost anything, but she never forgave anyone who betrayed the rebellion. He couldn't blame her for that. Bringing down the council meant everything to her, even now that the real rebels were all gone. Too many people had died to just forgive and forget. Her parents had died fighting.

No matter how much distance he put between himself and his father, Newt knew he was guilty by blood. But in that moment, he felt that that unspoken tension between them had thinned. She wasn't looking at him like she was waiting for him to disappoint her or like she wished he was someone else. She was looking at him like she trusted him.

"Thank you," he said. He'd never meant anything more.

The first afternoon bell was sounding when they finally made their way back to the front gates. The crowds weren't as thick as they were before noon, but there were plenty of people milling around and enough traffic on the bridge that they would be able to pass through undetected. When Newt wanted to stay below notice, he slipped through the crowds like an eel through reeds, quick and silent. Cassa was different. She didn't know how to be invisible, so she wielded her visibility like a shield. She moved with deliberate casualness, as if she was out for a stroll with no destination in mind, and she had an uncanny intuition for when and where the guards were looking. She used the passing wagons, horses, and her fellow pedestrians to avoid their lines of sight without seeming the least bit suspicious. Occasionally, she would even exchange friendly hellos.

They stayed close enough to see each other but kept enough distance that if one of them was spotted, they wouldn't both be caught. They made it past the city wall without any trouble, and on the Merchants' Bridge they came together again. Newt's chest loosened with relief. In less than an hour they'd be back with the others and far away from the citadel guard.

He started to say something about the best path through the valley, when Cassa suddenly froze. Someone over her shoulder had caught her attention. Newt looked back, confused. He couldn't see anything but the merchants driving their wagons of goods, the street vendors with their colorful booths set up along the edges of the bridge, and the press of people coming and going. Then there was a brief gap, and he could see straight back to the guardhouse, where Gaz Ritter was talking to two guards, his hand gesturing wildly in their direction.

"Keep moving," Cassa said, grabbing his arm. Their stop was disrupting the flow of people, drawing notice.

They walked quickly, heads down. Newt's heart was pounding in his ears. They had to get off the bridge. If they could make it to the forest or even the valley, then they had a chance. He knew that terrain better than his own name. He knew where they could hide.

"Dammit," Cassa whispered, then louder, "Dammit."

"You said he didn't see anything." Newt didn't mean to sound accusatory, but Cassa shot him a fierce glare.

"He didn't," she said. "He couldn't have."

But even she didn't sound convinced. Newt concentrated on navigating through the crowd. They didn't have much farther to go. They just had to get off the bridge. There was an odd scraping sound behind them, metal on stone. Newt wanted to look, but he didn't dare. He started walking faster, almost a jog.

Cassa stopped again, so abruptly that Newt made it several steps farther before he realized. He whirled around. Cassa's eyes were wide, her lips parted with an unspoken warning. It was an expression he'd never seen on her before. Fear.

She took a step toward him, then another, but she was moving slowly, with visible effort. Her arm was bent behind her back. People had backed away from them instinctively, leaving a wide berth around Newt and Cassa. Their apprehensive stares felt almost tangible.

Cassa had turned her back to him and was struggling with something. Newt still couldn't see what was happening, until Cassa was dragged several feet down the bridge. She yelped with pain as she lost her footing and grated her knees. Her arm was over her head, and an iron shackle was clamped to her wrist. The chain extended straight back, as if an invisible person was holding the other end. Newt ran to Cassa, his eyes following the line of the chain as he ran. It was pointing straight to Captain Marsh, who was a stone amid the turbid confusion of the crowd. He met Newt's gaze evenly, his detached stare raising the hairs on Newt's neck, just as it had the night he'd arrested them in the citadel. Harsh sunlight glinted on the brass buttons of his uniform, the knife at his side, the looped chain hanging from his belt. He hadn't touched his weapons. Newt's head spun as he clutched uselessly at the shackle around Cassa's wrist. Bloodbond. Iron.

"Newt, run," she gasped out, climbing to her feet.

Newt ignored her and dug his fingers into the thin gap between her skin and the iron, as if he could pry the cuff open with willpower alone. Distantly, he registered the other end of the shackle clamping onto his right wrist. Cassa was pulling on the chain with all her strength, heedless of her own panic, but they may as well have been chained to a wall for all the progress she made. The captain was walking toward them now, unhurried. The citizens had all parted before him as if he were a king moving among his subjects.

Cassa grabbed Newt's collar and jerked his face toward her. Newt blinked at her sudden nearness.

"If you don't run right now, I'll break your nose too," she told him.

The chain jerked them both backward a few more feet. Newt barely remained standing. The captain was close now, trailed by other guards. There was only one way out of this, and it was only open to him.

"Now!" Cassa shouted into his ear.

Something clicked in his mind, and his thoughts fell away. He became pure instinct. He popped his thumb out of joint, slid his hand free from the cuff, and started to run. One or two people threw out their arms in a clumsy attempt to stop him. He dodged them easily. *If you're fast enough, nothing can hurt you.* His father's voice in his head. The knife coming down without warning, a flash of steel in a lamplit room, slashing mercilessly across flesh. For a long time Newt wasn't fast enough. He had the scars on his hand to remind him.

But the lesson had been learned. He was faster now.

More shouts behind him. The heavy thump of boots. And Cassa's voice above the din, unyielding, unafraid.

"Come and get me, you spineless shits!"

Newt flew through the crowd. The closer he got to the end of the bridge, the more normal everything seemed. No one had realized yet what was happening farther up. Their curious faces blurred in his vision as he ducked and darted. He could still hear pursuers behind him. Even if he made it off the bridge, he might not be able to lose them now. He was nearing a thick cluster of people. A merchant was trying in vain to drive his wagon through the mass of unconcerned citizens. Some men were arguing loudly with a vendor, and people were gathering around to watch the action. Newt slowed a little and slipped into the thickest part of the crowd. Quick and silent. It was all he knew how to be.

When he reached the side of the wagon, he dropped to his stomach and rolled under it, narrowly missing the wheels as it lurched forward, the way finally open. He reached up and found handholds before it passed over him. He was dragged a short distance before managing to wedge his feet into place. His muscles burned with the effort, but he knew he could sustain it. The guards would realize they'd lost him any second now. They'd probably shut down the bridge, search every wagon, question every passerby. But by then his unwitting savior would be well on his way.

There was a jolting thump as the wagon wheels rolled off the bridge and onto the packed-dirt highway. Newt barely kept his grip. He realized he was holding his breath and forced himself to breathe in and out. He'd have to wait at least a mile before it was safe to drop down and make his way into the cover of the woods. Then he'd have to circle all the way back to the valley to meet Evander and Alys at the cave. After that—he didn't know. Cassa was always the one who figured a way out of these situations, and now she was gone.

twenty-six

Evander

MIRA had left the door open. Evander took a slow breath and followed her, with Alys close behind. The cottage was a wide, undivided space. Against one wall was a potbellied stove and a polished wood countertop stacked neatly with dishes and cookware. A round table with two chairs sat in the middle of the room. In its center was a glass vase holding a bunch of wilting wildflowers. There was a fireplace in another wall, with a rough-hewn oak mantel stacked with worn books. Two armchairs were facing it, both with faded floral patterns and sinking cushions.

Against a third wall was a bed, neatly made with a simple quilt, which Evander registered as strange. If this is where she slept, then what was in the other section of the house? The door leading to it was closed.

Mira was standing at the kitchen counter, scrubbing her hands in the porcelain water basin. She didn't react when they came inside and Alys shut the door.

"Your father is the Blacksmith?" Alys asked.

It seemed like a pointless question, but Evander knew she was just hoping that there had been some confusion. That the hinge of their entire plan wasn't dead and buried. Besides, he'd never heard of the Blacksmith having a daughter. It had never found its way into Eldra's rumor mill—neither, for that matter, had his death.

Mira dried her hands on a towel and didn't respond.

"We never heard about his passing," Evander said tentatively. "I don't think anyone in the city knows."

"Because it's no one else's business, is it," she snapped. She threw down the towel and sank into one of the chairs by the fireplace. "The council knows, if that's what you're worried about."

There was a note of disdain in her voice that was difficult to miss. Evander took that as a good sign.

"My father taught me his trade well," Mira went on, glaring into the hearth even though it held nothing but ash. "All the council wants is a Blacksmith, and they have one still."

It occurred to Evander for perhaps the first time that the Blacksmith had had a name. He'd been a person with ambitions and regrets like the rest of them. A man who sat by his fireside at the end of a long day. A man who blew glass into fairy trinkets, maybe for his young daughter.

In Eldra, the Blacksmith was more idea than person. A vague entity, separate from the world, whose only purpose was to use his strange art to give people preternatural power. He was the first of his kind in the city as far as anyone knew, gifted with a skill that even the alchemists couldn't dissect or define. The story was that he had come to Teruvia from a foreign land that had been desolated by war, its people scattered to the corners of the earth with blood magic as their only birthright.

Evander didn't know how true any of that was. Alys insisted that just because the alchemists couldn't explain the process didn't mean it was magic. She insisted the same thing about the elder seers and her own skill at divination. Evander wasn't sure that the world they lived in could be explained so logically, but he'd also never known Alys to be wrong.

Without letting himself think too hard about it, Evander crossed the room and laid a hand on Mira's arm.

"I'm sorry about your father," he said. "He helped save my family from starving. He was a good man."

Mira glanced down at his hand, then back toward the hearth. Several strands of hair had escaped to rest on her cheeks and neck. Her expression was impossible to read.

"Your mother saved my life a long time ago, when the physician was sure I was going to die. My father owed your family a debt. That's not the same thing as kindness."

"Maybe," Evander said, removing his hand, "but it would have been easy for him to refuse."

"He probably should have," she said with a snort. "You were a fool to come here in the first place. You could have easily died on that table. I'm surprised you didn't."

"Me too."

Mira was quiet for a little while longer, then pushed the hair from her face and stood up.

"So you thieved enough silver to save your family, and now you're back here—for what? The same treatment with gold? Your family needs a bigger house?"

She looked pointedly at Alys, who crossed her arms defensively.

"That's not why we're here," she said. "And Evander doesn't steal anymore."

Mira shrugged.

"Then why are you here?" she asked.

Evander swallowed hard. His mouth was suddenly dry. They'd come all this way, and now he had no idea what he was supposed to say. There was too much riding on this. They had so much to lose.

It was Alys who spoke at last.

"We do need you to bloodbond someone, but it's a little more complicated than that." She hesitated, visibly weighing her words. "There's a man who needs to be bonded with mirasma to . . . save his life."

Mira jerked her head around, toward the closed door leading to the other part of the house, as if she'd heard a sound. Evander hadn't heard anything. Mira's gaze swiveled back to them, her expression showing no trace of the momentary distraction.

"What man?" she asked.

"Someone important," Evander said. "Someone who values his privacy."

They'd decided beforehand that telling the Blacksmith anything more than the barest information was a bad idea. They didn't know anything about Mira's loyalties, about how likely she was to turn them in if she knew what they were really asking.

Mira's eyes narrowed slightly. He could almost see her mind churning. What was she trying to figure out?

"It doesn't matter anyway," she said, waving a hand and slouching in the chair. "I can't bloodbond someone with mirasma. It's impossible."

"It's a pure element," Alys insisted. "Same as silver."

"It's man-made."

"Your father has bonded people with glass before."

Mira cut her a glare. Her lips twitched.

"Do you think arguing with me about the finer points of my own trade is going to change my mind? I have no reason or desire to help you. You should leave."

"What if I told you helping us would hurt the council?" Evander asked.

Alys sucked in a sharp breath. He kept his eyes on Mira. He knew very well what he was risking, but something about the way she'd spoken about the council earlier had stuck with him. Though he hadn't fought in it, he'd grown up during the rebellion. The first skill anyone learned in those times, if they wanted to stay alive, was to recognize who shared their opinions and who didn't. Who was safe and who was dangerous. Ally and enemy.

Mira stared back at him, unflinching.

"I'm not interested in joining a rebellion," she said.

"The rebellion's over," said Evander. "The council won. That doesn't mean we have to be happy about it."

Mira kept his gaze, her expression softening barely.

"I didn't think—" she started, but cut herself off. She shook her head, but it was with resignation rather than refusal. "You'll bring him here?"

Evander nodded.

"I can't promise the bloodbond will work," she told him. "Even if it does, I doubt he'll survive."

"We know the risk," Alys said softly.

And the risk was so much greater than Mira could fathom. She closed her eyes for several long seconds, then sighed and looked at Evander.

"Why do I get the feeling that agreeing to attempt this makes me as big a fool as you were three years ago?" she asked.

Evander flicked his wrist and all three coins in his pocket shot into the air between them, spinning around each other in a hypnotic dance.

"Because it takes a fool to do the impossible," he said.

Mira watched the coins. The corners of her mouth tugged into a small smile.

"I can see why my father liked you," she said.

twenty-seven

Cassa

IT was only the fourth time Cassa had stepped foot in the citadel. The first time had been with her parents when she was seven or eight. From hearing bits and pieces of her parents' conversations, she'd known she was supposed to hate it. But it felt impossible to hate the grand, stone archways, the broad, paved streets, or the castle-like keeps stretching toward the sky. The paths were streaming with ink-stained clerks and frowning alchemists and the small gold badges of diviners and sentients and rooks. Secretly, Cassa had loved the citadel.

The second time, she watched a chapel burn just inside the walls. She'd been too distracted by the chain of events that followed to think much about the citadel or its inhabitants.

The third time was four days ago, when she was carted past the walls in a beer barrel. The trip had been nothing but darkness and sloshing liquid and the pit deep in her stomach. That time, Cassa had secretly feared the citadel.

Today she had the hatred she needed. That scalding, scarring ache inside her. A fire she'd been born with. For centuries, the council had hidden behind these walls, twisting prophecies to their whims and forcing the entire city toward a future seen only by long-dead seers. She knew the history of their mistakes better than her own name. The unfair allotment of resources and the convenient "prophecies" giving them license to seize land and imprison dissenters. The years of protests that were either ignored or violently dispersed. The massacre a century ago that had sparked a rebellion doomed to end in yet another massacre.

Over the years, almost everyone Cassa had ever known or loved gave their lives to that rebellion. She didn't know how to be anything but angry. She didn't know how to do anything but fight. Now she was so close to destroying the chancellor and his council, to ripping everything away from them the way they had ripped everything from her. She had no doubt that Newt would escape and that Alys and Evander would be able to convince the Blacksmith to help them. The plan could still work. She just had to get out of the citadel.

She had been in this room before. She'd sat at this table before with cuffs on her wrists. The ankle shackles were new. She'd kicked a few guards in their tender parts when they subdued her, so she couldn't blame them for the precaution. It was a bare, windowless room, with none of the antique woven rugs and tapestries the nobility was fond of. When the citadel was built, it was probably meant to be a storage room. Now it held nothing but a table and two chairs. There was also a ghost globe suspended overhead casting its eerie light over the proceedings. Lamps would have been cheaper and easier, but the sentient would need as much light as possible if he wanted to find all her deepest, darkest secrets.

He was going to see everything.

Her hatred flared momentarily into panic. She didn't mind it. Panic made her sharp and strong. Panic meant she hadn't given up. She let it roil inside of her, though she kept her expression neutral. It wouldn't fool the sentient, but she wouldn't give anyone else the satisfaction.

The door opened. She didn't recognize the man who entered, except for the golden sentient pin on his lapel. With his hunter-green tie and matching waistcoat, he looked like he was sitting down for a dinner party rather than an interrogation. He also looked irritated, which she couldn't imagine boded well for her. The sentient who'd read her after the first arrest had been a completely different sort of creature, gangly and mumbling and very visibly terrified of messing up what was probably his first real assignment. She'd broken his concentration so many times, he finally had to call in a guard to shut her up.

Somehow she didn't think this sentient would be so easy to fluster. He was young, but there was nothing hesitant about him. He had dark eyes and an impeccable haircut, and he had the look of someone who had never walked into a room without everyone taking notice. Handsome. Dangerous.

He was going to see everything.

"My name is Crispin Cavar," he said brusquely, taking the other seat. "Have you heard of me?"

"Afraid not," she said. Her voice was softer than she'd meant it to be. That was annoying.

"I'm the best sentient in Eldra," he said, "so let's get one thing clear. I don't care who you are or how noble you think your cause is. I'm going to read everything you're hiding, and then I'm going to return to the dinner party that your arrival very inconveniently interrupted."

Cassa wanted to laugh at that, but the panic had coiled around her lungs, and she had to concentrate on breathing. He was staring hard at her, his eyes roving over her face. She never understood how sentience worked, how you could see a person's entire past in their features. Was it like watching their history play out again in your mind's eye? Or was it more like scanning the pages of a book? She'd never known a sentient well enough to ask.

Strange thoughts to be having when everything she'd worked for since the day her parents died was about to be ruined. When her own memories were about to betray the last friends she had in the world. The council wouldn't bother with the death rites this time. They'd just shoot her and be done with it.

Crispin was frowning at her. He must have found what he was looking for. He must have seen . . . Cassa couldn't think of what it was he must have seen. Her head felt light. Her thoughts were flitting, unsettled. Why couldn't she concentrate? Had they drugged her somehow?

"She's not going to get away this time." Crispin's low voice drew her focus. "Not this time."

Cassa opened her mouth to ask what the hell he was talking about, but he stood abruptly and left the room. Cassa stared at the closed door. She moved her manacled hands into her lap. Something was wrong. She just couldn't figure out what.

The minutes ticked past. Cassa kept casting her thoughts back, but her mind felt slippery. It was like having a word on the tip of her tongue that she couldn't quite speak. It was like trying to remember something too important to have ever been forgotten.

Voices in the hall, muffled but pleasant. Soon there was silence again, then the door opened.

It was Vesper. She looked the same as the last time Cassa had seen her, on the bridge the night before they broke into the citadel, in her neat clerk's uniform with her red hair pinned back and her fingertips stained black with ink. Now her eyes were bloodshot, as if she hadn't slept since.

Cassa's panic tightened into something harder and darker.

"What are you doing here?" she asked.

Vesper didn't reply. She rounded the table and pressed her hand against Cassa's head.

"Don't touch me!" Cassa pushed her hand away and scrambled back from her. She made it out of the chair, but her feet got tangled in the shackles, and she fell hard to the ground.

"Cassa, please just listen—"

"No, you listen to me." Cassa twisted so that she was at least sitting up, her back against the cold wall. "You tell the honorable members of the council that if they want to steal my memories, they're going to have to pry them from my corpse."

"I'm not here to take your memories," Vesper said, kneeling down in front of her. "I'm here to give them back."

Cassa's head felt light again, her thoughts slick. Something important on the tip of her tongue, just out of memory's reach.

"What are you talking about?" she whispered.

"Please, it'll be faster if you just let me . . ." Vesper reached out tentatively and put her hand on Cassa's.

Almost immediately her mind began to clear. Spans of time she hadn't known were missing began to fill in. Puzzle pieces of memories were clicking together. Nausea welled, and she clutched her stomach.

"I'm sorry," Vesper said. "It's a lot of memories to give back all at once. It may take you a few minutes to adjust."

"I'm fine," Cassa said through gritted teeth.

Vesper had been here earlier. After they'd first put her in the room, Vesper had slipped in, begging Cassa to listen to reason, to let her help. Cassa hadn't wanted to trust her, but what choice did she have? If the sentient read her memories, he would know everything about their plans, about Solan, about where to find the others. The only way to stop him was to make sure none of those memories were there to read.

"Do you think it worked?" Vesper asked. She produced a key from her pocket and unlocked the shackles. She helped Cassa stand, even though Cassa insisted she didn't need help.

"He seemed pretty upset, so I'd say yes." Cassa paused. "Vesper, I think he knows it was you."

Vesper nodded, her features grim. Cassa realized she had never expected to get away with it. The anger in her chest shifted at the thought. She'd trusted Vesper once, maybe more than anyone, even knowing who her uncle was, even knowing that one day her loyalty might be torn. There was a small part of her, smothered by the anger, that wanted desperately to have that again.

"We have to leave now," Vesper said. "Before he comes back."

"What about the guard outside?"

"I—I took care of him." Vesper ducked her head and went to the door.

"What is that supposed to mean?" Cassa asked in a low voice, as she followed her into the hall.

"It means I sort of . . . made him forget why he was standing there in the first place."

"You took his memory."

"Just a small one."

Cassa bit back the reproach that sprang to her lips. She couldn't exactly take Vesper to task for the very thing that was saving her life. At least not until she was safely out of the citadel.

"Where, exactly, are we going?" she asked instead.

Vesper was leading her through corridors of the Central Keep that Cassa was sure had been forgotten even by the inhabitants. Everything was less grand than she remembered from her first visit to the citadel. Curtains were moth-eaten, rugs were threadbare, and the gaslights lining the halls were cracked and blackened with grease. She felt a small surge of satisfaction that the century of rebellion had drained the council's resources if nothing else.

"Out of the keep," Vesper said. "And then to the old chapel, where we first met."

The chapel that Cassa's parents had gutted with flames. The chapel where Cassa had saved Vesper's life and then Vesper had saved hers. She wondered suddenly if Vesper had seen the note she'd left in her prison cell. *I should have let you burn.* That night she'd meant every word. Now she wasn't sure. Now her fury and distrust were tangled with relief and gratefulness and the realization that if they were caught now, Vesper would be executed alongside her.

Cassa was surprised to find that she actually cared.

"Wait." She grabbed Vesper's arm. She'd finally caught up with what Vesper was thinking. "The door in the wall that led to the upper echelon—it was bricked up years ago. After the fire."

She desperately hoped that Vesper knew something she didn't. Another passage. Another way out. But when Vesper looked back, her face was bleak.

"Are you sure?"

"They were hardly going to leave it open."

A secret door in the wall was obviously of particular interest to the rebellion. When she'd told her parents, it had almost assuaged their anger at her running into a burning building to save a citizen of the citadel. But less than a month later, workmen arrived with stones and mortar, and soon the hidden passage was almost indistinguishable from the rest of the wall.

"I didn't tell anyone," Vesper said. "About you, I mean. About that night. I never told anyone."

There was a line of desperation drawn between her brows, and she searched Cassa's face as if seeking out any doubt. Cassa almost laughed. Vesper had already betrayed her when it mattered the most. Why did she think Cassa cared about a night six years ago?

"Don't worry," Cassa said. "I know you've always been a loyal friend, except for that one time you tried to get us all executed, of course."

"I'm the only reason you *didn't* get executed." The desperation was gone as quickly as it had come. Vesper had never been one to bask in her own vulnerability. It was one of the things that had drawn Cassa to her in the first place.

"My apologies," Cassa said coolly. "I'm sure you can understand why that was hard for us to believe when sentients were digging through our heads and the council was sentencing us to death."

She tried to keep walking. She wasn't sure where she was going, exactly, but she knew she couldn't stay here. Vesper blocked her way.

"Cassa, please," she said, her tone soft again. "I just need you to understand why I had to do it."

"I do understand." Of course she understood. She'd never thought for a moment that Vesper would turn on them because of some latent loyalty to the council. Vesper had seen the corruption firsthand. She wanted change as badly as any of them. That was the reason she'd fed information to the rebellion, the reason she'd sneaked out of the citadel more and more often over the years until she and Cassa were inseparable. There was only one reason she would have backed out. "You didn't trust me to pull it off."

Cassa pushed past her, but Vesper dogged her steps.

"Your plan wasn't going to work. They would have—"

"It *was* going to work," Cassa snapped over her shoulder. "We got caught because you told your uncle everything."

"If we'd gone through with it, we would have been caught and executed. All of us."

"There was nothing wrong with my plan."

"It wasn't going to work."

"You don't know that."

"Yes, I do." Vesper yanked on her arm so forcefully that Cassa almost fell backward. She caught herself and whirled, but Vesper didn't flinch. "I didn't *have* to tell my uncle anything, Cassa. He already knew. His diviners saw it all."

Cassa could feel her heartbeat in her head, a dull, steady ache. She thought about the slaughter in the lower ward almost a century before she was born. She thought about the path it had carved for the generations who followed. She thought about the day her parents didn't come home. Why did she ever think she could make a difference with all of the past and future stacked against her? When all those generations had failed. When her parents had died trying.

"What are you saying?" she asked, even though she already knew. Even though a part of her had always known.

"You were foretold."

It felt more like a death sentence than the one the chancellor had given her. Cassa suddenly felt impossibly tired. She put her hand against the wall and dropped her head, considering what would happen if she just sat down here and never moved again. Surely it didn't matter what she did anymore. Surely her fate was already written in a handful of runes, in the dreams of seers.

I've been waiting for you a long time.

Solan's words tugged at her mind, so gently that she couldn't tell if they were a memory or if he was somehow speaking to her. Cassa straightened up. Vesper was watching her with silent worry.

"There's another way out of the citadel," Cassa said. "We have to go below."

TWENTY-EIGHT

ALYS

ALYS had never expected to be alone in the darkness beneath the citadel. She knew that down the stone corridor behind her, Solan's enclave was glowing golden. Solan was there too, a man disfigured by time and loneliness, surrounded by once-beautiful furniture now ruined by age and elements. The teapot was probably still warm. She knew that she could go back now if she wanted. Nothing was stopping her. Nothing, except that Evander and Newt were probably already long gone. Nothing, except that if she didn't keep going, Cassa would never make it out of the citadel alive.

When Newt had returned with the news of Cassa's capture, they'd stayed with the plan and returned to Solan. If he wanted their help, he was just going to have to help them first. Solan hadn't seemed surprised. In their absence he'd been divining—Alys had seen the ancient bone-shard runes scattered on his coffee table. Diviners had stopped using bones decades ago. It was considered uncouth.

He'd also been scanning memories in the citadel, which Alys hadn't known was possible from such a distance. Sentients had to see people's faces in order to read them. According to Solan, he wasn't reading memories so much as "borrowing" them. Fresh memories were easy to siphon off and return before they were missed. He said that to the people above, it would just feel like a moment of confusion, like walking into a room and forgetting why you'd come.

Throughout the entire exchange, Alys's stomach had turned at the thought of the unsuspecting souls overhead whose memories were being plundered. That didn't stop her from asking him if he knew anything about her parents. He didn't, and though he promised to keep searching, Alys's heart had already plummeted. If Solan couldn't find them, did that mean they were already dead?

She refused to let her mind wander down that road. At the moment, they had to focus on saving Cassa. Thanks to Solan's borrowed memories, they knew what was happening to her above. And that she was headed below.

Alys stood at the head of the strange maze of pathways. The massive chamber was no longer lit by the fires atop the pillars. In the shadows beyond the reach of her ghost globe, the statues of the elder seers were dreaming in their stony slumber. Below her, the channels cut by the paths were so dark that she could almost imagine they ran with ink instead of water. She gripped the rope suspending the globe with aching fingers and took her first uncertain steps.

"Alys, wait."

Her stomach lurched at the voice, and despite her grip, she almost dropped the ghost globe into the water. She turned. The blue light illuminated Evander's features.

"I thought you were already gone," she said, trying to steady her breathing. The fact that her own brother could frighten her so easily did not bode well for the rest of her solo journey through the caverns.

"Newt's waiting for me. I just—I wanted to make sure you were going to be okay."

Alys wasn't sure whether to be touched or insulted. Mostly she just wanted to cry, but that would hardly help the situation.

"I'm fine," she said. "I don't have nearly as far to go as you do."

"You don't have to go alone," Evander said. "I can go with you, or Newt can. It doesn't take two of us to fetch the Blacksmith."

Evander had always had a habit of making things sound less difficult than they really were. As if crossing the valley and the woods to the Blacksmith's house and convincing her that instead of them bringing Solan to her, she should come with them to the dismal cave beneath the citadel was going to be a simple task. That didn't even take into account the citadel guards who were probably on the lookout for them by now, if a sentient had read Cassa's memories.

Solan couldn't tell them much about the current state of the world above, but he had seen one thing very clearly: The guards were going to arrest the Blacksmith at dawn. Alys didn't see how that was possible, since the Blacksmith hadn't done anything to help them yet. Newt was less certain. If Gaz Ritter had seen any of Cassa's memories, then they had to assume he'd seen all of them. They had to assume he knew the entirety of their plan and that he would sell the information to the council as fast as he could. Their only chance was to move faster.

"We don't know what's waiting up there," Alys said. "You have your silver, and Newt knows those woods. You stand a better chance together. All I have to do is take a leisurely stroll through the crypts to find Cassa."

She was pleased at how easy she made her task sound. Evander probably couldn't have done better. He glanced over his shoulder, taking a deep breath. His fingers were drumming erratically against his thighs. When they were growing up, people always assumed that Evander was the anxious one. That his constant movement was a sign of constant nerves. No one ever guessed that he was the unflappable one and that beneath Alys's stillness a maelstrom spun.

"Alys, do you really want to do this?" Evander asked.

Alys fiddled with the rope in her hand, avoiding his eyes.

"Truth or lie?" she asked.

"Truth."

She made herself look at him, to feel the earnestness of his gaze. Maybe he was the unflappable one, but she was still his older sister. He shouldn't have to protect her, not when there was so much hanging in the balance. So she did something she'd never done before. She lied anyway.

"Yes," she said. "It's the best way."

Evander watched her for a few more seconds, and she wondered if maybe she hadn't fooled him. But then he nodded.

"Okay," he said. "I'll see you in a few hours. Try to keep Cassa in one piece."

"No promises."

She wanted to hug him, but she was afraid he would hear the pounding of her heart. She gave a wave and turned, forcing her feet along the path. The longer she walked, the easier it felt. She knew that as long as she didn't look back, she could make it to the other side.

The caverns beyond the chamber of seers seemed different than the first time she'd seen them. Being alone made everything feel emptier and vaster. The echoes of her footsteps fluttered around her, reminding her that the farther she walked, the farther she was from everyone who knew she was here. Cassa had told her once that being alone underground was unlike being alone anywhere else. Down here the isolation was slowly consuming.

Alys felt a pang of pity for Solan. No one should have to live their life like this, cut off from the world with only the long-dead for company.

It didn't take her as long as she'd expected to reach the shore of the lake. The eerie reflection of the ghost light against the clear, still water sent a chill down her spine. The rowboat was where they had left it, with the oars perched neatly against its sides. She set the oars and the ghost globe inside and pushed it toward the water. It was heavier than she expected and scraped grudgingly against the stone. She'd almost gotten the front half past the waterline when she had to pause to catch her breath.

Somewhere beyond the light was a splash. It echoed so tremendously that she had no way to gauge how big the fish might have been. Assuming it was a fish. Her heart was racing painfully, though she couldn't tell if it was from fear or exertion. Probably both. She stared across the lake, thinking how in different circumstances she would have been fascinated by the sheer improbability of it. The lake and these caverns were a lost world ruled by Solan and forgotten by everyone else. In different circumstances she would have loved the uncharted nature of it.

But in current circumstances, the lake was a gaping expanse that she had to cross alone, with only some wood and tar to protect her from whatever creatures lurked in its depths. She didn't know what could survive down here, so far from sunlight. She didn't want to know. Surely the splash had just been a fish.

Her legs felt heavy all of a sudden, and she sat down on the cool ground even as she told herself she couldn't sit, she couldn't waste time, she had to find Cassa. Solan had told them she was descending into the crypts, but he couldn't see any more than that. For all they knew she was being pursued by the guards—or being dragged down here for her execution. The only thing they knew for certain was that if someone didn't take the boat across the lake, she was trapped on the other side.

Alys knew she had to stand up, she had to push the boat into the water, and she had to row across the lake. She also knew that she couldn't stand up, she couldn't push the boat into the water, and she couldn't row across the lake. She was alone down here except for whatever lived in the depths. She was alone down here, beneath the crushing weight of the earth above.

Her breaths were becoming gasps. She pushed her palms against the ground, trying to relieve the sudden tingling in her arms, as if the panic was electricity running through her veins. She was pathetic. A minute ago she had been fine, she had felt fine, everything was fine, and now she couldn't move, couldn't breathe. She felt weightless. Outside herself. A brightness encroached on her vision. She couldn't keep hold of her own whirling thoughts. Pathetic. How could she help Cassa when she couldn't even help herself?

Her chest hurt so badly, she knew she was dying. The maelstrom in her mind felt so familiar, but this time, like every time, she knew she wasn't going to survive it. Everything was faded. Everything was gone. All she had to do was stand up.

But she couldn't do it.

twenty-nine

Cassa

CASSA and Vesper crept through the lowest floor of the Central Keep, listening for the telltale footfalls and creaking weaponry of citadel guards. Everything was quiet for now. Cassa allowed herself to hope that it could stay that way. There was no reason anyone would think to follow them here. Why would an escaped prisoner run straight to the dungeons?

"Cassa, I wish you would just trust me," Vesper said, keeping her voice low. "I know you hate my uncle, but you *can't* help Solan."

Of course she'd seen everything in Cassa's memories. Their entire plan. Cassa couldn't stand the thought of so much being laid bare, but it was too late now. Her only solace was that if all went well, Solan would be free before the chancellor could stop them. She tightened her grip on the lantern they had stolen along the way. She wasn't sure how much oil was left in it. Hopefully enough.

"This may surprise you, but there are precious few people I trust," Cassa said. Three to be exact. Three people in the world. She told herself the tightness in her chest was exhaustion, but she had a feeling it was closer to despair. "And you're not one of them. Not anymore."

She wouldn't let herself think about what it meant that Vesper was here helping her when by all rights she should be running to Chancellor Dane with everything she knew. Vesper was quiet for almost a minute. When she spoke again, her tone was low and rippling with hurt.

"Would you have even listened to me if I'd told you the truth that night on the bridge?"

Cassa paused to peer around a corner. The next corridor was empty, its gaslights on a low burn. Faded portraits of long-dead councilors stared down in silent disapproval. They were nearing the stairwell to the dungeons. She wanted to keep walking, to ignore the conviction in Vesper's question, but she couldn't. She turned around.

"I don't know," Cassa said, "but you should have told me anyway."

Something flickered in Vesper's gaze.

"If I had told you, and you had gone through with your plan anyway, the sentients would have seen everything," she said. "All of us would have been executed—my uncle too."

Cassa wondered if Solan would have still helped them from afar had the chancellor been sent to his execution alongside them. Would it have been worth it to die, knowing that Dane died with her?

"You've seen everything, all my memories from our escape until today on the Merchants' Bridge." Cassa's throat burned with the threat of tears, but she refused to yield. "And you know how much I've lost. Can you honestly tell me you wouldn't do the same thing if you were in my place and had the same chance?"

Vesper opened her mouth as if to reply, then pursed her lips together. Her gaze dropped to her feet. She shook her head.

"I don't know," she said. "But I do know that there's nothing you can do that will bring your parents back."

"I know that." Cassa's voice felt faint, as if she were miles away from her own body. She could never have her parents back. They were nothing but legends now, a story belonging to everyone and no one. She didn't understand the followers of the Slain God and their obsession with death rites to cleanse their minds before passing into oblivion. All she had left of her parents were memories and the fire they had given her. She couldn't imagine ever giving that up, even at death's door. Especially then.

"Then what is it you want?" Vesper asked.

Cassa wanted to keep walking. She wanted to avoid this conversation. She wanted there to be more than three people alive whom she could trust.

"I just want to know that it mattered," she said.

"That what mattered?"

"All of it . . . any of it." There was a lump in her throat that felt suspiciously like a sob, and she fought against it. "All those people—my parents—everyone I cared about is gone, Vesper. And I'm still here. That has to mean something. There has to be something I'm meant to do."

Vesper kept her gaze.

"I think you're the only one who can decide what that is."

Cassa took a shaky breath. Her head ached from keeping the tears at bay.

"Funny, I thought that was the seers' job."

Vesper glanced away, and her face flickered with an expression that Cassa couldn't understand.

"There aren't any seers left," Vesper said.

Silence. For a few heartbeats, Cassa was acutely aware of the stillness all around them, of centuries' worth of the dead just beneath their feet. Then she found her voice.

"What?"

"The last one died two years ago. The council has been scouring the city for years, but there aren't any more." Vesper started walking again, her head ducked under the stares of the portraits. Cassa followed her, trying to wrap her head around what Vesper was saying. What that meant for Eldra. What that meant for her.

"But the prophecies haven't stopped."

"Some of them are old, I think," said Vesper. "Some are probably fake. But most come from Solan."

"That's why the council is so determined to keep him alive."

"Fake and recycled prophecies can only fool people for so long. When they've lost the prophecies, they've lost their power over the city."

Around the next corner was the massive oak door that opened to the steep steps of the dungeon. Vesper's fingers hesitated on the handle. She turned and faced Cassa again. This time her grim expression was easy to decipher.

"Please, just do the right thing." She pulled something from her pocket and opened her hand to Cassa. The vial of poison. She must have retrieved it from wherever the guards had taken it when Cassa was arrested.

Cassa's pulse thrummed. All the rebels were dead, but she was still here. There had to be a reason why. She reached out to take it, but Vesper put her other hand on top of hers. Her fingers were icy.

Something foreign and cold twisted through Cassa's mind, and she reeled. She yanked her hand away, still gripping the vial. A wave of nausea washed over her. She shuddered.

"What did you do?" she whispered, clutching her head.

"I'm sorry," Vesper said, her voice pleading. "I don't know how else to make you understand what's at stake. When my uncle gave me his memories, he—he gave me a secret he's kept for a very long time." She yanked open the door. "Let me go first. I can distract the guards on duty long enough for you to slip past."

"Vesper—"

"Just do the right thing, Cassa."

She disappeared down the steps. Cassa steadied herself against the doorframe, trying to listen for sounds below and behind her while wrestling with the unfamiliar memories that had taken root in her mind. A journey below the citadel that she hadn't taken. A night of agony that wasn't hers. She tried to ignore them, to push them away, but the knowledge was hers now, hopelessly entangled with her own life. The chancellor wasn't the only one who had been lying to them.

Cassa told herself that it didn't change anything. Solan had to be freed, and the council had to be defeated. Nothing else mattered. She had almost convinced herself when she heard Vesper's voice at the base of the stairs, and she crept down slowly.

Vesper was talking to the guard in the alcove about a discrepancy in last year's official records that her uncle had discovered. Cassa dared to peek around the corner just in time to see Vesper pat his hand reassuringly. The man started to say something and then blinked, his eyes wide and dazed. Cassa didn't wait to wonder exactly what Vesper was doing to him. She darted past into the dungeon corridors, gripping her lantern in one hand and the little glass vial in the other.

She heard footsteps and ducked into a side corridor just in time to avoid the patrol guard as he passed. The jeering of the prisoners was loud enough to drown out her unsteady breaths. Once he was out of earshot, she kept running all the way to the far end of the dungeon, where the door leading into the crypts was waiting.

The gently sloping tunnel felt shorter than it had the first time she'd raced through it. It felt like only a couple of minutes before she reached the head of the staircase that spiraled down, down, down. She forced herself forward before she could even catch her breath, before she could change her mind.

Once she reached the crypts, she followed the carved arrows on the walls, thinking about how much easier this journey had been with her friends at her back. When she reached the fork in the path where the arrows ended, she hesitated. The chancellor had talked as if the path to the right led to another maze of tunnels. She thought about the other prisoner he'd mentioned who'd gotten lost and wasted away in the dark. She had a generally high opinion of her own instincts, but she wasn't sure that extended to finding her way through an underground labyrinth alone. And even if she did manage to make it out, what if Vesper decided to tell the chancellor everything after all and he sent a squad of guards to wait for her at the exit?

There wasn't time to risk either scenario. If they didn't manage to bloodbond Solan soon, either the chancellor or the council's diviners would discover the plot, and all would be lost anyway. She went left.

The great archway rose before her, the elegant scrolls of the elder seers' ancient language lending it an air of mystery. The pitiful lantern light barely cut into the gloom beyond, and she fought an instinctual fear that wormed its way through her gut. With a deep breath, she pressed forward and wound her way through the rock formations to the shore of the lake. It was even vaster than she remembered. There was no sign that anything had changed since the last time she was here, except this time there weren't any angry guards in pursuit. She assumed that someone had come down to find the three guards and that they weren't wandering mindlessly around in the dark—assuming they were even alive. She hadn't thought to ask Solan exactly what he'd done to them.

There was also no sign of the boat.

Cassa stared at the empty shore for a long time, pondering her own lack of foresight. Of course there was no boat; they had rowed it to the other side. That was not the sort of thing a halfway intelligent person would forget. She didn't even have a rook to blame for it.

Down here she had no measure of time, but she knew she was running out of it. Vesper wasn't the only one who had been inside her head. If Gaz saw anything about their plan in her memories, then he would no doubt go straight to the council to sell the information. Even if Vesper kept her mouth shut, her friends were still exposed, and the Blacksmith was still at risk. She had to find them before the citadel guards did.

Without letting herself think too hard about her continual bad decision-making, she knelt down and untied her boots. She slipped out of them and stood in her socks. The cool dampness of the ground permeated even through the wool. She couldn't remember exactly how long it had taken them to row across the lake. She hadn't been paying much attention at the time.

She was a fairly strong swimmer, although she had no idea how long she could go. Alys would be aghast at the number of uncertainties she was ignoring, but Cassa couldn't think of another option. She waded knee-deep into the water. It was so cold that she almost reconsidered, but she pushed forward. Soon her feet had left the ground. She struggled to find a good rhythm, keeping the pace easy and steady. Her clothes dragged slightly, but not enough to make her want to pull them off. She did not intend to arrive at Solan's chamber in only her undergarments.

She had no way of keeping track of the time. All she could do was focus on her breathing and her strokes. It wasn't so bad at first. She grew accustomed to the temperature quickly, and the water was much fresher and cleaner than the murky river where she'd learned to swim. Once she'd left behind the last vestiges of the lantern's light, her enthusiasm began to wane.

The darkness felt like an oppressive weight. She lost all sense of direction. For all she knew she was swimming in circles. The thought was chased by a gnawing desperation that made her lose her rhythm. She floundered for a few seconds, choking on a mouthful of water. She gasped in a few ragged breaths, kicking her legs so hard to tread water that they felt weak. Her hands grasped uselessly, as if there were something to grab onto, as if there were anything out here to save her.

She realized with creeping horror that she didn't know which direction she'd been swimming. There was no forward or back. There was only blackness. The dark was so enveloping that she wondered briefly if she'd already died. She couldn't tell the difference between when her eyes were open and when they were closed. She was completely untethered. Completely lost. Completely alone.

Something brushed against her thigh.

She tried to scream but only succeeded in sucking in more water. She paddled wildly, driven only by instinctual panic. She couldn't tell how far she'd swum when she finally had to stop to catch her breath. Her limbs and lungs ached so badly that she couldn't even tread water. She floated on her back to regain some strength, trying to stay perfectly still. She kept her eyes tightly closed, like a child afraid of the monsters beneath the bed.

Something slid along her back. Whatever it was, it was smooth and unhurried. And it was long.

Her eyes were still squeezed shut. A sob burst from her chest. She didn't know what else to do but roll over and keep swimming. She didn't let herself stop, even though her body ached and she hadn't gotten a decent breath in what felt like forever. Occasionally she dipped below the surface, stretching her foot down, begging for it to strike solid ground. It never did. The lake could have been ten feet deep or one hundred; there was no way to know. All she knew for sure was that she wasn't near enough to land to have any hope of surviving this.

She'd heard once that drowning was one of the most painful ways to die. She wondered if maybe whatever was stalking her would kill her first. She wondered if anyone would ever find her body. She wondered if maybe the Slain God was real and if dying without death rites really meant she was doomed to an eternity of reliving all her worst mistakes, all her most painful memories. She wondered if a long time ago, a seer had dreamed of her death here in the darkness, and if it was scribbled somewhere in a book among all the other trivial, useless prophecies. Maybe she was never meant to accomplish anything after all.

She was dipping more and more frequently below the surface, not always on purpose. She was barely kicking anymore, and her strokes were weak and uneven. She kept reaching forward, even though there was nothing to reach for.

Until she opened her eyes and saw light.

THIRTY

VESPER

VESPER had never been summoned before the council before. She knew each of the councilors, some better than others, depending on how long they had held their position, but she had never been escorted into the Judgment Hall by armed guards. She had never stood breathless beneath the intricate ceiling mosaic of the elder seers. She had never pressed her fingertips into her thighs to keep from fidgeting while the collective scrutiny of Eldra's highest power pinned her to the spot. High Chancellor Dane was in the center of the four councilors, all seated behind the long table atop the dais. Overhead, three ghost globes dangled from the ceiling on thin chains. Instead of the usual netting, they were encased in delicately wrought silver whorls, like gemstones hanging from a necklace.

Everything, from the marble floors to the mahogany table to the silver fixtures, was polished and gleaming. The rest of the citadel might be slowly falling into ruin, but the Judgment Hall was pristine.

None of the councilors were in their ceremonial robes, which Vesper took to be a good sign. Maybe the informality meant she wasn't in any trouble. Although, if the guards just behind her were any indication, that was a vain hope. In the past couple of hours, she had foiled their best sentient, stolen one guard's memories, and befuddled another guard enough that he wouldn't remember her or the escaped prisoner sprinting past him in the dungeons. She'd known that helping Cassa escape would eventually end in her standing here, but she didn't have a choice. Solan had to be stopped, and even as precarious as her loyalty was, Cassa was still their best chance. Vesper just hoped she could figure a way out of her current predicament. If the council learned she was a rook, the minute or two of memories she'd stolen from the guard was a death sentence in itself.

"Do you know why you're here, Vesper?" her uncle asked, not unkindly. His thin, gnarled hands were clasped on the tabletop. In his gray jacket and simple blue cravat, he was the least impressive of the bunch.

Vesper shook her head. She didn't trust her voice not to waver. She'd always thought Ansel's gentle dignity was the same as quiet authority, but seeing him now in the middle of the councilors, each of them finely dressed and emanating confidence and control, she wondered if she was wrong. For almost a year now, she had been helping her uncle in his efforts to dispose of Solan—and she knew he had been working on this long before he brought her into the scheme. Even with the power of his position, he had spent all that time in the shadows, hiding from his own councilors. For the first time, it occurred to Vesper that maybe her uncle wasn't cut out for his position. Maybe he wasn't cunning or cutthroat enough to keep the council in hand. Maybe he was a sheep among wolves.

Ansel started to speak again but fell into a coughing fit. On the far left, the youngest of the councilors rolled her eyes and leaned forward.

"One of our prisoners escaped today." Delia Vicaro was dressed in violet satin overlaid with black lace. She wore her dark hair in serpentine braids, with a thin string of pearls inset like a crown. Her pretty face was perpetually drawn in an expression of boredom, though her eyes were sharp. "I don't suppose you know anything about that."

Vesper shook her head again. Her stomach was sinking under the weight of Delia's stare. People who possessed any of the Slain God's gifts were forbidden from serving on the council. It was a means of balancing power that Vesper had always found ironic, given the last century of rebellion. Still, she could have sworn that Delia was reading everything in her face.

"The guard on duty seems to have wandered away from the interrogation room, and now he claims that he doesn't remember ever receiving the order." Grantham Barwick flicked a speck from his sleeve, his golden cuff links flashing. Under the ghost globes, his perfectly coiffed blond hair had taken on a ghastly bluish hue. Her uncle had let slip once that it was a wig. She wondered if the rest of the councilors knew and were content to let him preen. Despite his faint air of ridiculousness, Vesper had still always been wary of him. He wasn't as artful as his peers perhaps, but what he lacked in subtlety he made up for in relentless ambition.

"With all due respect, Councilor," said Vesper, struggling to keep her voice even, "I don't think I can be held responsible for someone else's dereliction of duty."

Delia let out a little sound that may have been a laugh. Grantham scowled. He opened his mouth but was forestalled by his fellow councilor on the other side of the chancellor.

"We are also informed by one of our sentients that the prisoner had a peculiar lack of memory of the past couple of days, as if she'd been in contact with a rook before her interrogation." Tempest Adara was the only councilor that Vesper didn't actively avoid on a day-to-day basis. She had a kind face, with dark freckles and heavy laugh lines around her eyes and mouth. Unlike many members of nobility, she had done nothing to hide the encroaching gray in her short black hair. She'd held her seat since before Vesper was born—a feat of endurance that none of the current councilors could boast. She also cared more about her duty to the city than about amassing wealth and prestige like her counterparts.

"I don't know anything about that." Vesper dared a glance at her uncle. He was watching her with a vague frown. He would have no memory of any of their plans. He'd given her everything—even the earliest memories that birthed his determination to kill Solan. It was possible that at this moment Ansel Dane had no qualms about the executioner who lurked beneath the citadel. It was also possible that he believed his only niece was a traitor.

"Do you know anything about why that same sentient was unable to read *any* of your memories, during your little chat yesterday?" Delia asked.

"Perhaps he's not very good at his job."

Delia definitely laughed this time.

"Oh, I'm sure Crispin will love to hear that."

"Vesper, this is serious," Tempest said, though her irritated glare was aimed at Delia. "We have good reason to believe that you helped Cassandra Valera escape our custody today."

Did they know she was a rook? Had her uncle, unaware of what was at stake, told them her secret?

"Why would I do that?" She hoped her shock sounded genuine. She'd always considered herself a decent liar, but her life had never been on the line before.

"We know she's your friend. Did you really think something like that would escape our notice?" Roth Andras's somber voice surprised her. He was the quietest of the councilors, hiding behind a stony stare and a thick mustache. The only thing she knew about him was that his predecessor had died of a sudden heart attack—at age thirty.

"That was—" Vesper's voice caught in her throat, and she took a deep breath. "That was years ago. I didn't know she was a rebel then. I haven't spoken to her since I found out the truth."

"She's not a rebel." Tempest traced a slow circle on the table with her fingertip. "She is the daughter of rebels. The war is over. Now she's just a criminal."

Vesper wasn't sure what she was supposed to say to that, so she just nodded.

"Surely you can understand the position we're in," said Ansel with a hint of pleading. "You know I've always had the utmost trust in you, but your behavior over the past several days has been . . . suspicious, to say the least."

Suspicious wasn't even the half of it. She was holding years' worth of plotting inside her—most of it not hers—and was standing face-to-face with her coconspirator, who didn't even know that's who he was.

"I love this city." Her voice shook a little. "I would never do anything to hurt it, and I would never betray your trust, Uncle." That, at least, was entirely true.

"Even so," said Tempest, her finger still circling. "We've determined it's best that you remain confined to your room until we can get to the bottom of Valera's escape." Until they could find her, read her memories, and then execute them both.

Vesper wondered if they already knew where Cassa had gone. Surely they already had their diviners scanning the future, piecing together her destination. Depending on how much Gaz Ritter had seen, they might already know everything. That was exactly what her uncle had hoped to prevent. As long as the council's attention was diverted from what was happening below the citadel, there was still a chance at success—assuming Cassa pulled through. Vesper had given her the only two memories that she thought might change her mind about Solan's intentions, but even then she wasn't sure they were enough. She knew how deeply Cassa hated the council. And even though that put Vesper in a difficult position, considering who her uncle was, she'd never been able to blame Cassa before. Ansel Dane, however indirectly, was responsible for the Valeras' deaths. And the deaths of every other rebel who'd died in their final stand against the citadel.

Vesper had hated him for it once, but she knew him better now. She knew why he'd made the decision he made and how much it tormented him, even after all this time. It didn't bring any of those people back, but it did make it harder for Vesper to choose a side. And now there weren't any sides to choose. There was just the executioner beneath the citadel waiting to exact his revenge. There was just the hope, however small, that the last of the firebrands could stop him.

She blinked out of her thoughts when she realized that the guards were taking her by the arms, gently but firmly. She couldn't let them lock her up. The next few hours were too pivotal to leave to chance. Breaking free from the guards was hardly an option—especially in full view of the council—so Vesper did the only thing she could. She started to cry.

It wasn't as hard to summon the tears as she expected, and once she got started, it was easy to escalate into sobbing. She hardly ever cried, and she definitely didn't cry in front of people. Both Tempest and Grantham appeared unsettled and slightly nervous. Roth was still glaring at her, his expression unyielding. Delia rolled her eyes again.

Vesper let her shoulders shake and her breaths devolve into hiccuping gasps.

"I—swear—I—didn't—do—anything," she sputtered between sobs.

The entire exercise was the most humiliating thing she'd ever done in her life, but when her uncle stood up, his face stricken, she knew it was worth it.

"I think it's probably best if I escort my niece to her rooms," he said, taking the dais stairs one painstaking step at a time.

"If you're sure you can make it that far," Delia said sweetly.

Grantham chuckled, and Tempest shot them both a glare. The chancellor ignored them both as he reached Vesper's side and waved the guards away.

"Come," he told her softly, offering her his arm. "I think some hot tea will do you good."

Vesper nodded, still hiccuping wildly. There was something wrong in Ansel's expression, a blankness in his usually canny eyes. Warm tenderness in place of stoicism. He reminded her of the Uncle Ansel she had known as a little girl, when he was just a councilor, when he would come for dinner with his wife and their son and the twins—younger than her but still worthy playmates. That Uncle Ansel was always laughing, always handing out presents and ruffling hair and complaining about how old he was getting, though he could keep up with his grandsons even at their rowdiest.

But that had been a long time ago. The end of the rebellion had granted her uncle ascendancy, but there was always a cost for such power. The Ansel Dane she knew now was different. Everything was different.

Once they left the Judgment Hall behind and were alone in the corridors, Vesper slipped her hand down to grasp Ansel's. His grip was weak and clammy. Though over the past few days, his memories had become harder and harder to distinguish from her own, she still had no trouble finding the right thread inside of her. Without a word, she guided that thread back to him. It was a quicker process to give back memories than to take them. She always imagined that the memories somehow knew where they belonged, that they wanted to return. Her uncle blinked and stopped walking, but he said nothing while she unraveled the last of the memories he'd given her.

When she dropped her hand, he pressed his palms against his forehead and rocked on his feet. She caught him by the arm, but he kept his balance and straightened.

"I'm fine," he said after a few seconds. "I'm fine. Thank you, Vesper."

He was himself again, stoic and canny. She felt a wistful pang for the Ansel of all those years ago, but she didn't let herself dwell on the memories.

"I'm sorry," she said. "I know I was supposed to wait until Solan was dead, but everything is going wrong. I didn't know what else to do."

As they made their way down the corridor, she told him everything in hushed tones, about Crispin's failed interrogation of her and how she'd helped Cassa escape into the crypts. Then, after a second's hesitation, she told him everything she'd seen in Cassa's memories too. She trusted Cassa. She *wanted* to trust Cassa. But she wasn't sure about anything anymore.

"Would a bloodbond really cure Solan from needing the elixir?" Vesper asked, keeping her voice low.

Her uncle shook his head.

"I don't know. I'm no alchemist. He must truly believe it can, or he would never risk the process."

"I should have stopped Cassa somehow." She tried not to think about how a surefire way to stop Cassa would have been to never help her escape in the first place—or how she'd seriously considered it before deciding to help. Maybe Cassa was right not to trust her. Sometimes even Vesper didn't know where her loyalties lay. She'd joined with Cassa and the others because she didn't think the council deserved its power. Then she'd joined with her uncle because she'd seen how much more dangerous Solan was to Eldra. Then she'd betrayed her friends to save their lives. She couldn't be like Cassa, with unquestioning tenacity for a single cause. She could only do what she thought was right, even when it felt like shifting sand.

"From what I know about Cassa, I don't think you could have stopped her if you'd tried," her uncle said dryly. He cast a glance around them, but they were still alone. "You did the best you could. The council wouldn't have wasted any time executing her."

"What are we going to do now?"

"Do you think they'll try to go to the Blacksmith tonight?"

Vesper bit her lip, trying to work out how long it might take Cassa to reach the others and what they would decide to do now that they were compromised. If Cassa was worried that Gaz Ritter had seen too much, she'd want to accelerate the plan. Anyone else would decide to lie low, but not Cassa.

"I think they might."

Her uncle frowned in thought.

"Some rook from the lower ward who calls himself the Dream Merchant has been with one of the council's sentients all day," he said at last. "He claims he saw some memories regarding a planned revolt, and the council is trying to ascertain exactly what he saw."

"They're Cassa's memories," Vesper said. "He's the reason she got caught in the first place. He might have seen everything."

"That's what I'm afraid of." Her uncle hesitated at a corner for a few seconds, then nodded to himself. "Come on."

He started in the direction of the keep's eastern exit, and Vesper followed.

"Before you came," he went on, "I had just gotten word that the council was sending guards to the Blacksmith's cottage to investigate a possible threat. I didn't pay much attention to it at the time, but now that I'm in full possession of my faculties, it makes more sense."

"If Cassa and the others bring Solan there, they'll be arrested," Vesper said. She hadn't known much about the Blacksmith, and his daughter, Mira, was even more of an enigma. Vesper had no idea how loyal she was to the council. She might even help the guards.

The council would execute her friends and put Solan back in his prison, where he'd be more carefully guarded than ever. The council would be free to keep pumping him for prophecies and turning a blind eye as he ripped memories from unsuspecting citizens for boredom or pleasure or whatever his twisted motive was.

"It will take a while to assemble the guards," her uncle said, as they reached the doors leading into the eastern courtyard, where the stables were. "I think we can get there first."

THIRTY-ONE

Newt

AURELIA Valley was beautiful at night. The expanse of tall grass was a dark, rippling ocean. The star-speckled sky felt infinite. In the distance, the tops of Eldrin Wood's towering pines swayed with a rising wind. As Newt and Evander crept across the open field, Newt's mind drifted back to a night only a few months ago. It had been cooler than tonight, and they'd both shivered in their jackets as they sat at the top of the riverbank. The shimmering water flowed below them, catching the bright moonlight in its ripples.

Since well before sunset, Evander had been trying to teach Newt how to roll a coin over his knuckles, which he assured Newt was still possible without a bloodbond to silver. Newt could rely on his fingers to find purchase on brick and stone walls and to slip willingly out of joint when the occasion called for it, but he couldn't coax them into the same fluid motion that Evander had mastered years ago. He probably could have tried harder, but he liked watching Evander demonstrate, his long fingers graceful and sure. He liked those fingers sliding across his as Evander tried to show him the right movement. Every touch was as thrilling and confusing as the first day they'd met, not so far from this very spot.

Evander and Cassa had been broken up for a few months at that point. Evander had claimed it was mutual, but the two of them had been carefully avoiding each other ever since, like they weren't sure how to exist as just friends. Newt didn't like the fissure in their little group, but he also didn't mind how often Evander spent his new free time with him. He wondered if there was a reason for that, or if Evander just found Newt's explorations of the valley and woods more interesting than Alys's work in the apothecary shop. He didn't think now was an appropriate time to ask as they made their way to the edge of the wood, eyes sharp for lantern light, ears straining for any strange sound.

He couldn't help but steal a glance though, just before they passed into the shadows of the trees, while the silvery moon still cast some light. Evander's jaw was clenched, his shoulders tense. His hair was plastered across his forehead. Newt wondered what it said about his own survival instinct that in that moment, when any number of dangers could be lurking just out of sight, all he could think about was that night and the occasional thrill of Evander's touch. He'd never dared hope for anything more than that. Sometimes he could even convince himself that it was enough.

They slipped together into the relative safety of the wood. Out of the open, they took a few minutes to recover and get their bearings. Evander leaned his back against a tree and rested his hands on his knees, though he didn't sound like he was out of breath.

"What's wrong?" Newt asked, keeping his voice just loud enough to be heard over the wind that whistled through the trees. There was a cold bite to it, as if the remnants of winter were chasing its heels.

Evander lifted his head and pushed his hair out of his face.

"I'm worried about Alys."

"Did you talk to her before we left?"

Evander nodded.

"She said she wanted to do it alone—that she was fine." He sighed, a gentle sound almost entirely lost in the breeze. "She was lying."

Newt watched him for a few seconds, unsure what he was supposed to say. Surely he was supposed to say something.

"You could go back."

Evander snorted in what might have been a laugh.

"She'd never forgive me if I did that."

"Then we have to keep going."

Evander was quiet for a while. Newt couldn't see his eyes, but he couldn't shake the feeling that Evander was studying him. Finally, he straightened.

"Right as usual," he said, patting Newt on the back as he passed.

He didn't say anything else for a long time, and Newt found the old deer path that would lead them through the heart of the wood. Even though they hadn't seen signs of any pursuers, it was too dangerous to take the road to the Blacksmith's house. They had to circle through the forest to approach from the south. Newt took the lead on the narrow path, with Evander trailing behind. The wind was less forceful in the thick of the wood, but they could still hear it howling through the treetops overhead. Even though it had been a clear night, there was obviously a storm blowing in.

"Just our luck," Newt said over his shoulder, mostly because he wanted Evander to say something—anything. His uncharacteristic silence made Newt uncomfortable in a strange, nervous, gut-wringing way.

At first there was no reply, and Newt had to convince himself not to stop and turn around. Maybe he hadn't heard. Maybe Newt had said something wrong before. Maybe—

"Funny, I don't remember us ever having any luck to speak of," Evander said, sounding so nonchalant, so much like himself, that Newt had to smile.

"I don't know. I think we've eluded death too often to be considered *un*lucky."

"The unluckiest lucky bastards alive," Evander said a little wistfully.

A laugh escaped Newt before he could stop it. They needed to be quieter for caution's sake, but he couldn't help himself. If he didn't let himself think about it too hard, the night almost felt like any other night before that first fateful foray into the citadel. It almost felt like their lives weren't balanced on a knife's edge, like Solan in his dungeon of crypts was just an old, fading nightmare.

In the clearing around the Blacksmith's cottage, Newt could see that the wind had pushed a blanket of clouds across the sky, all but hiding the stars, though the moonlight still poured through. He'd never been to the cottage before, but Evander didn't hesitate to knock on the door of the central brick section of the house. For a long time there was no answer, even though Newt could see a stream of smoke from the chimney. Evander kept knocking.

When Mira opened the door, her features were set into a scowl. She cracked the door just enough for the light to spill over their faces. She was barefoot, dressed in rough-spun trousers and an overlarge shirt.

"You told me you'd be here tomorrow." She peered past them into the night. "Is he here?"

"No," Evander said. "We've hit a snag."

"A snag?" she echoed dryly. The scowl had faded, though her expression still wasn't exactly welcoming. She eyed Newt suspiciously.

"I'm Newt Dalton," he said.

"I don't really care," she said, though not harshly.

"May we come in?" Evander asked.

"No. Just tell me what you want."

"It's kind of a long story."

"Shorten it."

She reminded Newt so much of Cassa that he had to purse his lips to keep from smiling. They'd either be fast friends or bitter enemies—assuming Evander could talk Mira into coming with them. He spilled the whole story of Gaz Ritter and Cassa's capture with a brevity that Newt had to admire. Mira listened with a bare frown. Every once in a while she would glance over her shoulder into the house, and Newt wondered if she had a kettle boiling.

Then came the hard part. Evander told her the truth—or at least most of it—about the executioner below the citadel, about who he really was, and why he needed the bloodbond with mirasma.

She was frowning deeply by the time Evander finished.

"You want to help the executioner—this rook or seer or whatever he is—escape?"

"He's been the council's prisoner for years," Evander said. "He's been forced to give them prophecies. If we free him, we'll be hitting them where it hurts."

He left out the infallible prophecy and Solan's immortality. Some secrets were better kept close to the chest. Newt wondered at how easily Evander spun the words. He thought about the boy he had been all those years ago, reading false futures in coins, charming the nobility with exactly what they wanted to hear. Evander had learned a few lessons of his own.

Mira didn't look charmed.

"You expect me to follow you into the crypts below the citadel to attempt a bloodbond that is probably impossible to begin with?"

"We can't bring Solan here anymore," Newt said. "If Gaz saw anything about you in Cassa's memories, then you can bet the citadel guards will be here by morning."

"All the more reason for you to come with us," Evander said.

Mira's expression remained flat.

"The council can't hurt me," she said. "They need me."

"The council likes to keep their commodities close at hand," Evander said. "Do you think if they suspect you of *anything*, they'll let you stay out here to live your life in peace?"

He slipped so easily from charm into bitter truth that Newt couldn't help but think of the boy behind all those false smiles. Sharp and starving and ready to risk everything for a chance to save his family.

"They can't make me do anything," Mira said. "I haven't done anything wrong, at least not yet."

"Do you really think that would stop them?" Newt asked quietly.

She eyed him for a moment, her expression more of contemplation than fear.

"You're going to take me directly to him?" she asked. "And all I have to do is try to bond him with mirasma?"

Newt and Evander both nodded.

"I can't be responsible if he dies," she said. "I have no way of knowing if he's strong enough to survive."

"He knows the risks," Evander said. "This is his only chance to be free from that prison."

Mira was quiet for a long time, her eyes cast down toward the ground. She was leaning against the doorframe, her brown hair falling in long, messy curls over her left shoulder. She looked behind her again, at whatever was distracting her inside, then back at them.

"You really think he'll bring down the council?" Her voice was soft now, different.

"He foretold their fall," Evander said. "He might be the only one who can."

Mira regarded them both. Her lips had settled into a firm line.

"I'll go with you," she said finally, "but first you have to tell me something, and you have to tell me the truth."

"Deal," Evander said.

Newt didn't respond. He wasn't about to promise honesty to a question he didn't know yet. Mira didn't notice.

"Why are you doing this?" she asked.

"What do you mean?"

"Why do you hate the council so much? You may have been alive during the last days of the rebellion, but it's not your war. It never was. You've just inherited the aftermath."

Evander didn't have a ready response for that. Mira made no attempt to fill the quiet. She crossed her arms and eyed them expectantly. Newt dropped his gaze.

All I want is for you to make something of yourself. His father's words. He tried not to think about them, but they were his first answer. Maybe the only one. His father couldn't be the man he wanted to be, but maybe Newt could. One day. Or maybe he could die trying and become a legend that would live on like the firebrands who came before him.

"Why does it matter?" Newt asked into the lengthening silence. "Obviously we're committed to this. Why do you care about our reasons?"

"A deal's a deal," she said lightly. Her gaze was on Evander, who stared back at her. Judging from his expression, his thoughts were miles away. A few more seconds passed, then he blinked.

"When I was eight years old, my parents gave medicine to a dying man." His voice was thin and strained. "The man happened to be a rebel, and the council branded them as traitors for it. They took everything from us. Our home, our hope, our future. No one should have that kind of power."

His jaw was quivering, and he clenched it tightly. Newt's chest ached at the sight of him. Slowly, he moved his hand, just enough that his knuckles brushed Evander's. It was the only comfort he could think to give. Evander didn't react, but Newt could have sworn the tension in the corded muscles of his neck loosened barely.

Mira still watched Evander, her features betraying nothing.

"I don't suppose we're very different, you and I," she said at last, but she didn't elaborate. "I need a few minutes to get ready."

"Is there anything we can help with?" Newt asked. Mostly he just wanted out of the dark and the rising wind, if only for a short while. He could smell rain in the air.

"No, wait out here." Mira shut the door. Newt thought he heard a lock slide into place, but he couldn't be sure.

Evander let out a long breath that he must have been holding and took a few steps back. Newt leaned his back against the wall of the house and watched as Evander began to pace. Though clouds were rapidly blocking out the moon, he still saw a glimmer of the silver coins that had begun to circle Evander in wide, opposing arcs.

"All things considered, I think it went well," Newt said.

Evander shot a lingering glance in his direction but didn't slow his pacing. It was the second time tonight that Newt couldn't get a read on his mood. He circled one fingertip absently on the rough brick, keeping his eyes on Evander.

After a minute or two, Evander stopped a few feet away and looked in his direction.

"I wasn't lying," he said abruptly.

"About what?"

"About the reason why I started helping Cassa in the first place. That's really why." He rubbed the back of his neck and dropped his gaze. "I—I don't think I've ever told you before."

Newt frowned and started to disagree, but the more he thought about it, the more he realized Evander was right. He felt he knew Evander and

Alys's reasons for joining Cassa in her unrelenting mission because it seemed as obvious as the scars on their parents' faces, but Evander had never actually told him. And he'd never told Evander his reasons either. It was one conversation that had never been broached. He wondered if Evander had already guessed at his reasons too. If anyone could, it would be him.

Evander moved a couple of steps closer. They were face-to-face now. Newt's breath hitched in his lungs. He hoped it wasn't noticeable. Evander looked distracted. This close, Newt could make out the slight wrinkle in his brow, his pursed lips. His eyes were dark and fathomless. With so little space between them, Newt couldn't bear to look away. He loved every curve and line of Evander's face, the soft brush of his hair across his forehead, the lean strength of his frame. His constant, concentrated energy. His easygoing confidence, so carefully cultivated to appear effortless.

"May I ask you something?" Evander's voice sounded strange. Raw.

"Sure," Newt said. He didn't know what his own voice sounded like. His heartbeat was drowning out the world.

The two coins hovering lazy circles behind Evander dropped to the ground. Then suddenly he was so close that Newt could feel the warmth of his body. His lips were a hairbreadth away, an unspoken question that Newt never thought he'd get the chance to answer. He didn't allow himself any hesitation. He slid his hand behind Evander's head and pulled him in. His lips were soft and cool, but he kissed like there was fire inside him. Newt gripped his hair tighter, wrapping his other hand behind Evander's neck, but Evander didn't need the encouragement. It wasn't

Newt's first kiss, but it was the first one that mattered. His thoughts were deliciously hazy. He was kissing Evander Sera.

Evander Sera was kissing *him*.

Evander was pressed so close now that Newt could feel every crack of the bricks at his back. One of Evander's hands was on the wall beside his head, the other resting featherlight on his hip. Their breaths mingled with their heartbeats. It felt like a dream he'd forgotten, like a memory that wasn't his. It felt like the first time he'd ever been truly happy.

When their lips parted, Newt couldn't tell if it had been seconds or minutes or hours. Evander's forehead rested against his, and at first they just breathed. The wind had stilled for a moment, leaving them with the charged silence before the storm.

"What did you want to ask me?" Newt murmured. His chest was a riot of emotions, not all of them identifiable. Every inch of skin was alive with the thrill of Evander's touch.

Evander grinned.

"Can't remember."

And he kissed him again.

thirty-two

Alys

ALYS'S arms and back ached from rowing, but she didn't mind. The ache kept her anchored. It reminded her that she was alive, that she'd gotten off the ground, pushed the boat into the lake, and started rowing. She might not be impossibly brave like her brother and friends, but she had yet to give up. That had to count for something.

After about ten minutes of rowing, she stopped to rest her arms. The shore behind her had faded out of sight, and the shore ahead was not yet visible. For the moment, she was drifting in a bubble of light. She felt strangely peaceful.

Then something rocked the boat, and she screamed. She fumbled for the oars, not sure if she should try to hit whatever it was or just keep rowing. Something yanked on the left oar, and she nearly lost her grip. She shook it as hard as she could. Hit something solid. And then: "Dammit, Alys!"

All at once she was flooded with relief, confusion, and utter disbelief.

"Cassa, what the hell are you doing?" she demanded, leaning over the edge of the boat.

"Thought I'd go for a swim." Cassa's voice was too weak to carry any bite.

She was treading water, but barely. There was no way she was going to pull herself into the boat.

"Hold on," Alys said.

She secured the oars beneath the seats, then dropped onto her knees on the floor, hoping that would keep it steadier. Cassa was gripping the side now, and it tipped in her direction. Alys grabbed her wrists.

"We have to do it quickly," she said. "Otherwise the boat will flip."

Cassa nodded. Her teeth were chattering, and she was trembling all over. Alys moved her hold down to Cassa's forearms.

"One, two, *three*."

She pulled as hard as she could, trying to keep herself counterbalanced, but Cassa was deadweight. Alys leaned a fraction too far forward and realized it a second too late. The boat tipped over, and Alys plunged into the water headfirst. For a few moments, she was completely disoriented. She had no idea which way was up, and her legs were kicking against Cassa's. She reached out, felt the wood of the boat against her fingertips, and broke the surface. She gulped in a breath. The light of the ghost globe was so bright, it hurt. She realized she was beneath the overturned boat, with the globe floating in front of her. Cassa was already there, clutching the seat overhead with one hand.

"I hate you," Alys gasped out as soon as she had enough breath.

"I know," Cassa said. "We have to flip it over, right now."

"Can I at least catch my breath first?"

"Alys, we have to get back into this boat right now." Despite her visible trembling, Cassa's voice was strangely calm. "There's something in the water with us. Something big."

Panic lurched in Alys's throat. She looked down, expecting there to be a dark shape lurking there. The blue light illuminated the clear water fairly deep, but she saw nothing except her own kicking feet. She forced herself to breathe.

"Alys, stay with me." Cassa's tone was still unnaturally calm.

Alys's panic was replaced momentarily with irritation.

"Oh, for seers' sake, stop patronizing me, and let's flip the damn boat."

Cassa blinked at her. Obviously that had not been the reaction she was expecting, which bolstered Alys even more. After all, she was the one doing the saving here. Not the other way around.

"Are you strong enough to push it with me?" Alys asked. "There's going to be a lot of suction."

She didn't actually know very much about boats, but that was simple physics. Cassa hesitated, then nodded. The hesitation was the answer Alys needed.

"Never mind," she said. "Hold on while I look at something."

She grabbed the ghost globe's rope and ducked under the edge of the boat without waiting for a reply. Panic was still sharp in her chest, but she forced herself to focus on the problem at hand. The sloped sides of the rowboat came to a narrow peak at the bottom, and it sat fairly low in the water. Her legs were already tired from kicking. If she was going to try her idea, she had to do it fast.

She slipped back under the boat.

"Can you tread water on your own for a couple of minutes?" she asked.

"Yes," Cassa said. "What are you thinking?"

"Come on."

Alys swam out again. After a few seconds Cassa surfaced beside her. Alys passed her the ghost globe and eyed the wooden hull for a few seconds. Then she scissor-kicked as hard as she could and launched out of the water, grabbing for the peak. Her hands found a modicum of purchase, and she scrambled for more, dragging herself up until she was flopped over the middle of the boat.

Painstakingly, she crawled forward until she was hanging over the opposite side. The boat sank farther into the water under her weight. She gripped the edge with both hands, held her breath, and threw herself backward with as much force as she could muster. The boat flipped with her. She released the edge and let herself sink into the water before she kicked back to the surface. Cassa had already put the ghost globe in the boat and was hanging on to the side. Alys swam around to the opposite side. She counted off again, and she and Cassa pulled themselves up at the same time. Their weights weren't equal, but Cassa was better at counterbalancing than Alys had been. Alys thought she felt something brush against her ankle right before she pulled it free of the water, but she told herself it was just her imagination. They both collapsed into the bottom of the wobbling boat without capsizing it again. It had a fair amount of water in it, but it was still afloat, and the paddles were still secured under the seats.

Alys handed one to Cassa, though neither of them started rowing. She wouldn't let herself look into the water. She was too afraid of what she might see.

"Is it even worth asking what could have possibly compelled you to try to swim across the mysterious underground lake?" she asked after she'd caught her breath.

"Well, if I'd known you were coming for me, I would've taken a nap instead." Cassa's breathing was still jagged and labored.

Alys resisted the urge to whack her with the paddle.

"Of *course* one of us was coming for you. What, did you think we were just going to sit on our hands until you were executed? For seers' sake, Cassa, a little bit of faith would be nice. I think we've earned that much."

Cassa was still trembling. She rested her paddle across her lap and rubbed her shoulders vigorously. Alys eyed her, expecting a sarcastic retort, but Cassa's features were twisted in a soft frown.

"You're right," she said finally. She met Alys's eyes. "I'm sorry."

Alys was caught off guard by her sudden sincerity. In the moment, it was actually rather discomfiting.

"It's fine," she said. "Let's just get back to shore."

She adjusted her grip on the oar, but Cassa didn't move.

"Alys, you were amazing just now," she said quietly.

"I'm not sure flipping a boat qualifies me for hero status, but thanks."

"I'm serious. You're the only reason we made it out of the dungeons in the first place. You're the only reason I'm alive now. You always know the right thing to do."

"Then why are you always arguing with me?" Alys couldn't bring herself to match Cassa's earnestness.

Cassa didn't rise to the bait. Her tone remained soft and genuine.

"Because I'm afraid that if I'm wrong about one thing, I'm wrong about everything."

Alys stared down at her hands, which had gone numb with cold. She wasn't sure how to deal with what Cassa was saying. Cassandra Valera was an unstoppable force. She never worried, never flinched, never backed down. Alys had never heard Cassa express doubt, and she'd never heard her express admiration for anyone, least of all her.

For a few moments, the only sound was Cassa's shivering breath. Outside their sphere of blue light, the darkness was silent.

"That's the most irrational thing I've ever heard," Alys said at last.

Cassa's frown deepened, but then she coughed out a laugh.

"I thought you would have figured out by now that all I bring to the table is an endless supply of irrationality and sarcasm."

"Trust me, I have." Alys straightened up in her seat and dipped her oar into the water. "Now will you please help me row so that we can get away from this godforsaken lake?"

She wasn't sure if Cassa was strong enough to row, but she knew that Cassa would never agree to rest while she rowed alone. Cassa gripped her paddle and twisted around in her seat.

"I never thanked you for saving me," Cassa said as together they propelled the boat through the quiet water.

"Still haven't."

"Thank you, Alys."

"You're welcome, Cassa. I hope at the very least this situation has prompted you to consider your own mortality."

"Why should it? I'm still alive, aren't I?"

Alys rolled her eyes. She could practically hear Cassa's grin, which meant that things were back to normal. For some reason, that was the biggest relief of all.

THIRTY-THREE

EVANDER

EVANDER was starting to feel like his entire life had been whittled down to darkness and stone. He was hard pressed to find a patch of skin that wasn't scraped or scratched by their journey through the caves or the woods. His legs ached so steadily that he couldn't remember what it felt like to not be in pain. It had gotten to the point where he spent most of his spare energy trying to decide whether it would be better to die below or above. The hope that they might somehow survive this ordeal had long since slipped away.

Maybe that's why he had kissed Newt.

His motivation had been perplexing him ever since they'd left the Blacksmith's cottage. None of them had spoken much on the way back to the valley. Mira was restless and distracted. Newt had been too busy trying to keep them from being ambushed by the citadel guard. Evander had been too busy thinking about Newt.

The truth was, he had kissed Newt because he had wanted to. There hadn't been any thread of conscious decision-making. There was just Newt, who looked so alive in the valley and the forest, who traded secret for secret like they were precious gold, who in spite of appearances was probably the bravest of them all. There was just the sight of him—leaning against the brick in the shadow of the storm, his hair tangled and windblown, his blue eyes catching every ray of moonlight. He'd been somehow entirely inscrutable and entirely open at the same time. And suddenly Evander had never wanted anything more.

Now he couldn't figure out why he'd waited so long. Or what he was supposed to do next.

When they finally made it back to Solan's chamber, Alys and Cassa were waiting for them. Both of them were shivering and damp. Both of them declined to explain why. Evander was too relieved to find both of them alive and whole to care about the specifics of how they'd stayed that way. Solan's enclave was not any less unsettling than the first or second time he'd been here. It had only been a few hours since he'd last seen it, but it still felt like a different world. The golden glow of the lights here gave the cold cavern a warm, homey feel that was at the same time utterly wrong. Not far from where they stood, thousands of dead bodies were decaying silently in their tombs. Above their heads, the citadel slept, hopefully oblivious to the machinations below.

Mira stood a little apart from them, eyeing the chamber with a wary sort of awe.

"You are the Blacksmith?" Solan asked her.

She nodded tersely, not quite meeting his eyes. Evander couldn't blame her. He still hadn't gotten used to Solan's strange, shifting visage.

"I thank you for coming all this way." Solan extended a hand, the very picture of gentility.

Mira took a small step back and ducked her head.

"If it's all the same to everyone here, I'd rather just get this over with," she said quietly.

Evander frowned at her sudden reticence and exchanged a glance with Newt, whose brow was also wrinkled with confusion. Cassa hopped to her feet and clapped her hands together.

"I like you already," she told Mira. "Just getting it over with is my preferred approach to almost everything."

Mira gave another short nod and glanced around the chamber again, this time with an appraising eye.

"This space is too small," she said. "I don't like being crowded while I work."

"The cavern with the statues is much bigger," Alys said. She took up the ghost globe and led the way into the next chamber.

If Mira was impressed by the massive stone seers or the elaborate grid of walkways, she didn't show it. She just looked around for a few moments, then declared it suitable. None of the paths were wide enough for their purposes, but the platform at the feet of the two seers nearest the tunnel gave Mira enough room to work. Since mirasma was already liquid, Mira hadn't brought the crucible or any other equipment with her. Newt handed her the bottle of mirasma, and she knelt down and pulled from her belt the only tool she needed. A knife.

Evander hadn't gotten a good look at the Blacksmith's tools during his own procedure, but he remembered the knife well enough. It was hard to believe that such a life-changing ordeal could be accomplished with one single item.

Something brushed his arm, and he looked to see Solan standing beside him, watching the process with somber intensity.

"It's not so bad," Evander told him. He wasn't sure why he'd said it, except that the agony he'd endured during his own bloodbond wasn't something he would wish on his worst enemy.

Solan smiled barely without looking at him.

"You forget that I've already seen my own pain," he said. "But thank you for trying to comfort me."

"Have you seen whether you'll survive?"

It occurred to Evander that Solan's supposed immortality might also protect him from the rigors of bloodbonding. Nearby, Alys shot him a habitual glare for his rudeness. He ignored her. Solan stared steadily at Mira as she unsheathed the knife.

"I've seen the fall of the council," he said. "This is not how I die."

Evander chewed on the inside of his lip and tried to believe him.

"You'll need to lie on your back," Mira said to Solan. She still hadn't managed to meet his eyes. "The rest of you will have to hold him down."

Evander shivered at the memory of the leather straps on the table in the Blacksmith's workshop. The sole evidence of pain amid the dazzling display of glass and metal creations. Alys and Newt both looked a little sickened by the directive, but Cassa stepped forward.

"We live to serve," she told Mira.

She seemed her usual glib self, but Evander couldn't help but think that she was forcing it somewhat. He wondered exactly what had happened between her capture and her arrival here. He had a feeling she wouldn't tell the full truth even if he asked. Cassa had never been one for heartfelt sharing.

Solan took his place on the ground while Cassa handed Mira the mirasma. Solan's breathing was rapid, but otherwise he showed no signs of distress. Evander had to admire him for that, especially if he'd foretold even half the agony that was in store for him.

Evander knelt down beside Alys at Solan's ankles, while Newt and Cassa each took an arm. Mira picked up the knife, and Evander swallowed down a surge of nausea at the assault of memories. He thought he'd blocked out the entirety of his own bloodbonding, but unwelcome sensations kept flaring in his mind.

Mira looked among the four of them.

"After I make the cut, I have to work quickly," she said. "If you can't keep him still, the bonding will fail. Understand?"

They nodded in unison. A strange expression flashed across Mira's face, and she opened her mouth but shut it again without speaking. Evander couldn't help but notice that she'd been very purposefully not looking at Solan. Maybe it was her way of distancing herself. He wondered how many council-approved applicants had died on her father's table.

Without ceremony, Mira leaned in beside Cassa and slit a long, deep line into the inside of Solan's left arm, a mirror to Evander's own scar. Solan flinched and squeezed his eyes shut but didn't make a sound. Maybe it was the way the light hit his face, but he seemed younger now, free of wrinkles and his usual gravity. He seemed vulnerable. Evander's heart wrenched in his chest.

True to her word, Mira worked quickly. As soon as the cut had been made, she took up the bottle of mirasma and poured it along Solan's arm, tracing the cut. Solan hissed but made no other movement, and for a moment Evander thought that maybe the pain of the bloodbond came from the molten metals rather than the process itself. Then Solan buckled beneath their hands. Evander pressed his full weight onto Solan's ankle as he flailed, his cries primal, guttural sounds. Cassa had one hand on his shoulder and the other on his wrist, barely an inch from the trickling mirasma. Her face was screwed tight with determination.

Mira tossed the bottle aside, her eyes never moving from the shimmering, viscous element mingled now with blood. Solan was gasping, his chest heaving wildly, but Cassa and Newt kept their hold. Mira was lost to the world, her eyes bright, her hands perfectly steady as she held them both over Solan's arm.

For a moment, just a moment, Solan calmed. His gasping receded. Then Mira clenched both hands into fists, and his scream echoed through the cavern. Evander flinched, but Mira never wavered. She loosened her right fist, and her hand drifted up his arm, over his shoulder, across his chest. Then she held her left hand over his chest and moved it down to his leg, while her other hand drew a line to his neck.

She was tracing his arteries, Evander realized, coaxing the element along the pathways of his blood. He looked at Solan's arm and saw that the amount of mirasma had indeed receded. Cassa was noticing the same thing, and she caught Evander's eye with undisguised amazement. Solan was shaking uncontrollably, his limbs straining against their grip. He was no longer making any sound, and that was worse than the screams somehow. His eyes had rolled back in his head, and his eyelids fluttered rapidly.

Mira never stopped her strange motions. Her eyes were shut now, as if she were conducting a symphony only she could hear. A sheen of sweat had risen on her face, and two loose tendrils of hair clung to her cheek. For almost ten minutes, her graceful, silent gesturing and Solan's agonized struggles were the only movements in the cavern. Evander's arms and back and knees ached. His vision had tunneled so that all he could see was Mira's hands. Everything else was the bright blue glare of the ghost light.

Finally, her hands came back together over his left arm. Almost all trace of the mirasma was gone now, though Solan's skin was red with blood. Mira's breathing had quickened. She closed her hands into fists again, but more slowly this time. Her features strained with effort. Evander blinked away sweat that had trickled into his eyes and watched as a thin line of shimmering mirasma rose inside the cut, suturing it closed. A permanent scar. Evander's own arm itched, and he fought the urge to scratch it.

Mira sat back on her heels and wiped her hand across her face. Solan had fallen still. His eyes were closed.

"I don't think he's breathing," Alys whispered.

Evander's stomach was in knots. If Solan was dead, they had lost their advantage over the council. He claimed the prophecy of the council's demise was infallible, but what if it wasn't? The only way to be sure was to have Solan on their side, alive.

"Oh no, you don't," Cassa said. "Not after all we've been through."

And she slammed her fist into Solan's chest, over his heart. She did it twice more, despite Alys's protests that it wouldn't do any good. Then Solan heaved in a massive breath, and his eyes flew open. He floundered briefly, but Newt kept a hold on his shoulder. His face was chaos, a dizzying array of looping time. Impossibly young and impossibly ancient. He'd never looked so inhuman.

He tried to sit up, but Mira put a hand on his shoulder and gestured toward Cassa.

"Don't let him move," she said. "He needs to stay still."

Cassa pressed down again on his arm, keeping him down as he gasped in ragged breaths. Evander could scarcely believe it had worked. If the bloodbond could free Solan from his prison, then maybe the prophecy could come to pass. Maybe Solan really could help save their parents. Maybe the council really would fall. Evander was light-headed with the implications of what they might have just accomplished. Four years ago, a century of rebellion had ended in utter defeat, and now, in the forgotten caverns beneath the citadel, they had salvaged one last chance at victory.

Mira was still staring down at Solan, her expression working its way from disbelief into something sharper and then into something bleaker altogether. Her shoulders were trembling. Before Evander could decide whether it was relief or despair, Mira picked up her knife from the ground. Its edge still gleamed darkly with blood. She pressed it against Solan's throat.

"I've held up my end," she said to him, her voice low and lethal. "Now do as you promised. Give me my father back."

The Day the Chancellor Met the Executioner

THE labyrinthine crypts looked different through the chancellor's eyes. He knew the entire history of this place. He knew from his studies that when the first of the elder seers had been laid to rest, all Teruvia had mourned. He knew that when the last of the elder seers finally passed, only the city of Eldra mourned her death. Teruvia had left the citadel and its dead god behind. He knew from different, dustier tomes that the world beneath the citadel was always supposed to be a place of rest and peace. It was never supposed to be a place of spilled blood and devoured memories, and it was never supposed to become a prison.

All these things permeated the chancellor's memory of the long, lonely walk through the crypts, and so Cassa knew them too. The memory was hers now after all.

Ansel Dane wasn't the chancellor then. Just a council member, listening to reports of the ever-strengthening rebellion with unease until finally he'd made a decision. The then-chancellor and the other three council members never spoke of the man kept locked below the citadel. They provided the mirasma and took the prophecies he gave, but they never spoke of him directly.

Ansel brought only one guard with him, a trembling young man—a boy, really—who nonetheless put on a brave face. At the shore of the lake, Ansel told him to wait. The relief shone clearly in the boy's eyes as he helped launch the boat. Ansel wasn't much younger then, but he was stronger. His muscles didn't shirk from the grind of the oars. He'd never seen the lake before, and he marveled at its beauty, at its strangeness. He knew from his studies that there was something much older and much hungrier than fish lurking in its crystalline depths.

The chamber with the seer statues had been built as a temple to the Slain God. It was there that the first death rites had been performed. The ritual had begun as a way to give seers and rooks peace in their final moments, to strip away all their prophecies and memories, both wonderful and terrible, so that they might meet their end without the weight of the past and future on their weary souls. The maze of pathways was a symbol, an initiation. Acolytes had to learn to navigate the paths by memory alone. Death rites were given in complete darkness, to ease the passage into oblivion.

Ansel tread carefully on the stone. The fires atop the pillars were lit. He wasn't surprised that the executioner knew he was coming, but it still worried him. When he entered the smaller illuminated chamber, Solan Tavish was seated in a chair, his back straight, his hands gripping the armrests as if this was his throne. The moment that Ansel met his eyes, he knew deeply and without doubt that whatever part of this creature had once been Solan Tavish had long since died away.

"Greetings, Chancellor." His voice was charred and crumbling.

"I'm not the chancellor," said Ansel.

The rook only smiled. But he wasn't just a rook. A sentient as well. A diviner. A seer. The workings of his mind must have been laid bare, because Solan's smile widened.

"I already know why you've come," he said.

"Then perhaps you can save us both time and give me your answer."

A laugh, if that's what it could be called. Like sharp rocks crashing from great heights.

"Thanks to your cowardly predecessors, I have nothing but time," said Solan. He leaned forward and rested a forearm on his knee. "I want to hear you ask, Chancellor. I want you to beg."

Some unnamed instinct in Ansel recoiled, but he stood his ground. He had made the decision after all. He had to see it through.

"How can we end this rebellion," he asked, "without tearing Eldra apart?"

"And why should I tell you that?" Solan cocked his head slightly. There was still a ghost of a grin on his preternatural features. "Maybe I want Eldra torn apart. What has Eldra ever done for me?"

"If the council falls, so will you." Ansel's temper flared behind his words.

Solan straightened and raised his hands in a brief, lazy gesture of indifference.

"Perhaps," he said. "Or perhaps I already know how this ends. Perhaps I've already seen the death of everyone you know and love, Chancellor. Perhaps I've already seen your death as well. Would you care to know?"

He was practically crooning now. That same unnamed instinct in Ansel's chest demanded that he take something sharp and drive it through the executioner's heart. It wouldn't kill him though. Nothing would kill him. There were those who had tried before, to their detriment. The mirasma kept Solan tethered, but if they withheld it, he would only become more dangerous as his powerful mind ripped apart at the seams.

"It was your prophecy that began this rebellion in the first place," he said. "I know your wicked appetites have been well-satiated by the executions."

Solan chuckled.

"Wicked appetites," he echoed. "What a strange way of describing the duty that *your* pathetic religion demands of me."

"There has to be a way to end this."

"Of course there is," Solan replied. "But why would I tell you, when—as you just said—it is serving my wicked appetites so well?"

He's toying with me, Ansel realized.

"Very good, Chancellor," murmured Solan. "And what a pleasure it has been."

Ansel's heart thrummed in his ears. He'd known better than to expect help from this quarter, but still a part of him had hoped. He turned to leave.

"Seeing as you're the first councilor in a century who has been brave enough to venture down here, perhaps I will help you after all." Solan's voice had an air of nonchalance, but something in it slithered.

Instinct now begged him to run. Ansel held his breath and turned back to the executioner.

"In exchange for what?" he asked.

"My freedom." Solan's smile was more like a grimace now. "I will tell you what you want to know, and when the rebellion has ended, you will free me from this prison."

"I can't do that."

"You'll find a way. I've paid for my crimes a hundred times over, and I won't be used any longer."

Ansel stared at him. He was dangerous. Too dangerous to Eldra to ever be freed—yet if the war continued much longer, the city would fall to ruin anyway.

"Agreed," he said, though the word hurt to speak.

Solan studied his face closely, and finally he nodded.

"The last stand of the rebels is very near." He steepled his fingertips and stared over them at Ansel. "Soon they will kill your chancellor, and after his death they will amass their forces and strike. That will be your time, Ansel Dane. That will be your only chance."

"My chance to do what?" Ansel's voice hitched in his throat.

Solan shrugged.

"That is up to you. I imagine you'll figure it out when the time comes. A man like you doesn't come into a position like yours without some measure of cunning." He chuckled.

"What's so funny?" Ansel asked, before he could stop himself. His mind was churning over and over a single thought. A seer was calling him *chancellor.*

A grin. Hazy in his shifting face but undeniably lethal.

"Now that you know the future, you must stand back and let your chancellor die. If you don't—if he lives—the rebellion will indeed tear Eldra apart."

Ansel's heart stopped for a moment, and when it started again, its every beat ached with the realization.

"You bastard," he breathed.

"It's time you got your hands dirty." Solan's grin was gone, replaced by a snarl. "Or rather, it's time you understood they were never clean to begin with. You accepted the legacy your predecessors gave you, and now you must count the cost."

"I'm trying to protect the city."

"Yes, that's what they all said." The executioner leaned his head back and closed his eyes. For half a second, his features stilled, and Ansel caught a glimpse of the Solan Tavish who once was. "But believing the lies you tell yourself doesn't make them any truer."

Ansel left without another word and tried to convince himself the whole way back to the lake that he wasn't fleeing. The return trip felt longer and more taxing, and by the time he dragged the boat onto the crushed-shale shore, his muscles burned steadily. At first, there was no sign of the guard who'd accompanied him. Perhaps his nerves had bested him, and he'd retreated back to the citadel.

Then Ansel saw the light from the guard's lantern, gleaming just beyond the rock formations. He called out, but there was no reply. More than just his muscles ached as he walked toward the light. The boy was crumpled on the ground, perfectly still. Without moving any closer, Ansel already knew he was gone.

When you kill all the rebels, I shall be forced to find other means to satisfy my wicked appetites.

Solan's voice in his head was strained and distant, but he heard every word.

That was the last thing that Cassa remembered, except for a single stab of feeling. A shame that was fresher than the memory itself. The chancellor couldn't remember the boy's name.

THIRTY-FOUR

Cassa

CASSA'S head hurt so badly that for a moment she thought she was dying. Then the pain dissipated in aching degrees, and finally she felt capable of opening her eyes. The blue of the ghost light stung her vision, and she immediately squeezed them shut again. Everything was quiet, so quiet. Her mind spun in the silence. The bloodbonding had worked. Solan was alive. Mira had a knife.

Cassa sat up so quickly that her head lurched, and she almost retched onto the stone floor. She blinked rapidly, trying to find her bearings. Mira had held the knife to Solan's throat. She'd said something about her father. And then—then Cassa had blacked out.

There was movement in the corner of her eye, and she whipped her head around. Solan was standing at the tunnel's entrance, the golden glow from his chamber casting him in soft silhouette. Above Cassa, the statue of the elder seer loomed. A few feet away, Evander was lying on the ground, unmoving. Her heart clenched, and she dragged herself on hands and knees to his side.

"He's alive," said Solan, just as Cassa laid her hand on Evander's chest to feel its steady rise and fall. "Your friends are all fine."

Cassa ignored him and crawled to Alys and then Newt. Her chest didn't loosen until she'd checked them both. She stood on shaky legs, and her vision dipped dangerously.

"What did you do?" she asked Solan as she searched the murky shadows for Mira.

"I'm sorry," Solan said. "I was trying to stop the Blacksmith, but my control is shaky after the bloodbonding. They should wake soon."

Now that she could see him more clearly, Solan's weakened state was obvious. Tremors flitted through his body, and his complexion was sickly pale. Evander had told them the bloodbond would take effect in about six hours. After that, Solan would no longer be dependent on the council's elixir—assuming his theory about the bloodbond with mirasma was right. He would be free.

"How does Mira know you?" Cassa asked. "Why did she—"

"Cassandra, we're running out of time. There's something I haven't told you."

There were many things he hadn't told her, judging from the memories Vesper had funneled into her mind. But she didn't want to think about that right now.

"What?" she asked, hugging herself against the chill. The caverns were perpetually mild, but her clothes and boots were still damp.

"The prophecy. Before the council falls, the chancellor must die. Tonight."

"When we know for sure the bloodbond worked, we'll take you up to the surface," Cassa said. "You won't need the mirasma from them anymore. You can—"

"Not me," Solan said. "I've seen the chancellor's death, and it's not at my hand."

He pulled an object from some hidden pocket in his robe and offered it her. The steel of the gun glinted in the light of the ghost globe. The pistol she had left behind.

"Me?" Her voice stuck in the back of her throat.

Solan nodded. Cassa didn't move.

"Isn't this what you wanted?" He took a step forward. Though his face sagged wearily, his eyes were bright.

Of course it was. It was everything she'd wanted. He didn't need to read her face to know that. There were very few infallible prophecies involving individual people—most were natural disasters or wars of grand scale. Cassa had never believed that the prophecies that spoke of people's personal choices could be infallible. People's lives couldn't be dictated by dreams. Her parents had taught her what it meant—what it really meant—to not be foretold. It meant the council couldn't own you. It meant the shadows of a long-dead religion couldn't touch you. It meant everything you did was *yours*.

But what if the prophecy was true? What if all those years ago, Solan had seen her absolute future in a dream? What if she was destined for this and always had been? Maybe she didn't have a choice. Maybe it was better that way. Maybe the past hundred years of loss and pain could finally mean something.

Maybe it didn't matter either way. Maybe she just wanted to kill Chancellor Dane.

With faltering steps, she closed the gap between them. Still she couldn't bring herself to reach out and take the pistol. Her heart slammed an uneven rhythm against her chest.

"You were born of greatness," Solan said, "but there's not really anything great about you, is there?"

There was no malice in his tone. Only gentle certainty. Her entire past was laid bare before him. He knew everything about her. He knew the truth she'd spent so long trying to ignore. She tried to breathe but found no air.

"There can be, Cassandra," he said, taking her hand and pressing the gun's handle into her palm. "There will be."

Finally, a breath. Then another. Her heart began to slow to a calmer pace. She wrapped her fingers around the cool grip and stared down at the weapon.

"He's headed for the Blacksmith's house as we speak," Solan said. "If you leave now, you'll reach him in time."

It took a few seconds for the words to register. She looked up.

"What's he doing at the Blacksmith's house?"

Solan shook his head.

"I haven't seen everything." He gestured toward the gun. "Only this."

"I'm not leaving until my friends wake up," she said.

He shook his head again.

"There isn't time, Cassandra."

"I'm not leaving them here—" She cut herself short. *With you.*

Maybe Solan guessed what she meant, because he studied her face more closely now, his clear eyes ranging over her features. In the midst of his shifting visage, a frown took shape.

"Those memories . . ." He grabbed her chin as she tried to turn her face away, moving so close that she could hear his ragged breaths. "Those memories aren't yours. How did you get them?"

"Can't you see for yourself?" Cassa jerked out of his grip.

"How long have you had them?"

Cassa didn't answer. She knew she didn't have to.

"You let me have the bloodbond," he said softly. "Even knowing what you know now?"

"It doesn't change anything," Cassa said. A lie. It changed everything. How could it not? Vesper had given her those memories for this precise reason, but Cassa had given Solan his freedom anyway. A betrayal for a betrayal. At least she and Vesper were even now.

Solan was quiet for a few long moments.

"Do you think I'm a monster?" His voice was thin and brittle.

"Yes," Cassa said. No hesitation. "But so is he."

Her grip on the gun tightened. Four years ago, the chancellor had taken everything from her. He hadn't been the one to pull the trigger or to burn the bodies, but he was to blame for her parents' deaths—and for all the brave souls who had been cut down that brutal summer day. His order. His choice.

It didn't matter that he claimed to be working against the council now, that he claimed Solan was a danger to the city. The memories Vesper had given her weren't enough to absolve him. Nothing ever could be.

"Go," said Solan. "Your friends will be safe here. You have to finish what they started."

She didn't know who he meant. Her parents and all the people who had died trying to take the citadel or the very first rebels to whisper treason by firelight a century ago? It didn't matter. She was here now. Her future was foretold.

She cast one last glance over her friends' sleeping forms, and then she left.

THIRTY-FIVE

VESPER

IT was almost an hour before Vesper and Chancellor Dane rolled through the citadel gates and into the city. While she waited for the stablemen to prepare the carriage, her uncle went in search of one of his trustworthy diviners to learn what he could about their upcoming journey. Horses would have been faster, but they would have had to stop at every gate in the city to explain themselves. At the sight of the chancellor's carriage, the gates would open at their approach, even at this hour. Vesper hadn't seen any signs of citadel guards other than the usual watchmen, but they might have been leaving out the rear gates and circling through the valley to avoid frightening the citizens.

During the jostling ride, Vesper couldn't help periodically pulling aside the curtain from the little back window to check for pursuers. Her uncle sat in perfect silence the entire trip, lost in his own thoughts. He'd told her the diviner hadn't been able to give him much information, but she couldn't shake the feeling that he was keeping something from her. Ansel Dane was never unprepared. It was how he'd become chancellor in the first place. Four years ago, on the day his predecessor died, he had been the only person on the council who knew what to do next. An advantage he'd gained from Solan Tavish. An advantage he'd paid dearly for in the end.

The history was well-recorded. The rebels had seized the then-chancellor as he returned from a hunt in Eldrin Wood. Ansel said that they probably hadn't intended to hurt him, only to use him as a hostage for negotiations. But the citadel guards fought back, and the chancellor was killed in the melee. Accident or not, it didn't stop the rebels from hanging his body outside the citadel gates as food for flies and scavenging birds, with a piece of paper nailed to his chest. *We are not foretold.*

The next day, they broke through the citadel's outer gates to the inner keeps. It would have taken them only a couple of days more to overrun the Central Keep. They weren't well-armed, but they were many, and they were fierce. Maybe history would have remembered it as a glorious battle won. The oppressed triumphing over their oppressors.

But it never came to that. Despite their battle cry, the rebels had been foretold several years earlier by a captive seer in the decaying sanctuary beneath the citadel.

Ansel had known from the moment the news came of the chancellor's demise that the rebels had forced their own hand. They had been building their forces for a while, trying to muster support among the citizens within the citadel walls. But now they had to attack while the high council was in turmoil, while the people were questioning their own loyalties. They had to strike before a new chancellor could be named and order retaliation.

Her uncle had seen it all plainly, like a child's game of chess, and he ordered half the citadel forces out of the city through the rear gates under cover of night. They circled the entire city and marched up the main highway in the predawn mist. Midmorning, only hours after breaking through the citadel's outer gates, the rebels were attacked from behind by a thousand well-trained, well-armed soldiers. The doors to the five inner keeps swung open, and more soldiers poured out. Pressed on all sides and corralled as they were by the citadel's outer walls, the rebels were broken in the noonday sun. It was a crushing, brutal defeat. No one knew the exact numbers, but Vesper had read estimates as high as three thousand dead. That was the same day that Cassa's parents were killed, fighting alongside their fellow firebrands. There were certain things that didn't bear thinking about too closely.

It wasn't until after his terrible victory, after he was voted the new chancellor, that Ansel began to realize the mistake he'd made in asking Solan Tavish for help. By the time he fully understood the danger Solan posed to Eldra, he also understood that the councilors were willing to sacrifice the city's safety to secure their own power. As chancellor he had hoped to make a difference, to lead the council and serve the city; instead he was forced to work against the council, with only his niece as an ally, searching for a way to rid Eldra of their executioner for good.

By the time they reached the cottage, rain had begun to pelt the carriage seemingly from all angles. Her uncle conversed briefly with the driver, who was the picture of blank disinterest—which is what he was paid for. Ansel told him to take the carriage back up the road, around the bend where the trees grew close enough to form a tangled canopy that would provide the horses a little more shelter. The driver's empty expression did leak some relief when Ansel suggested he wait inside the carriage, out of the rain. Vesper took down one of the carriage's lanterns to carry with them, and the driver guided the horses in a wide circle around the muddy yard and back down the road.

Ansel knocked for a full minute at the front door of the cottage, but there was no reply. No smoke trailed from the chimney, but Vesper could see a thin rim of light around the curtains of the wooden addition to the house. She tapped at the window, shouting for Cassa or Mira or anyone to let them in because they were there to help. No reply.

Ansel called her name, and she looked over to see that he'd gotten one of the big doors at the other end of the house open. As she got closer, she could see that the doors, which swung outward, only had a simple sliding latch to keep them shut. Apparently the Blacksmith hadn't been too worried about strangers accessing his workshop when he'd built it. She supposed he didn't have a reason to be. The Blacksmith was under the council's direct protection.

She held up the lantern and sucked in a short breath at the glistening ornaments all around her. The golden light was refracted by hundreds of pieces of glass, and she felt for a moment that they had stepped into another, lovelier world. Her uncle moved to one of the shelves, heedless of the water dripping from his hair and face, and took up a delicate glass flower.

"He always did love creating beautiful things," he said, turning the flower over gently so that it caught the light.

"You met the Blacksmith?"

"Several times, when I was a councilor. I even met Mira a couple of times. She was a wild little thing back then. Treated the forest like it was her own kingdom."

He sighed and returned the flower to the shelf.

"When she sent news of his death, I wanted to ensure a proper burial, but she refused to let anyone come near. She was devastated."

Vesper watched him in silence, the sad resignation in his features, the wistfulness as he eyed the glass and metal treasures of the workshop. She'd never even laid eyes on the Blacksmith or his daughter, but her heart ached all the same. Ansel shook his head.

"I'm sorry," he said. "I'm wasting time."

Before Vesper could decide on a reply, he'd moved to the door that led into the house. More knocking. Still no reply. He tried the handle, and the door swung open easily. The cottage was dark and quiet. Vesper circled the kitchen table with her lantern, searching for anything amiss. Other than some dishes left in the sink, everything was tidy.

She remembered the light she'd seen from outside and walked in the direction of that window. There was another door beside the hearth. She could see a rim of light spilling onto the floor at its base. Ansel saw it at the same time and went to it. He knocked softly, explaining in urgent tones who he was and why he'd come. Still no reply.

A sick, sinking feeling began to expand in the pit of Vesper's stomach. She stepped closer to her uncle, clutching the lantern with both hands. He turned the knob, but it was locked. He shook it experimentally, but the door was solid oak and didn't even rattle. Vesper eyed the keyhole, thinking it strange that it locked from the outside. Strange and unsettling.

She cast a glance around their immediate surroundings. There was no convenient key dangling from a hook on the wall, and the top edge of the doorframe wasn't wide enough to hold even a small key. Her lantern light glinted off something on the mantel. She retrieved the brass key and handed it wordlessly to Ansel.

"The joys of young eyes and a sharp brain," he remarked.

She couldn't tell if he was trying to compliment her or just lighten the mood. She wasn't feeling particularly proud or lighthearted at the moment, so she said nothing. He turned the key in the lock and opened the door slowly. A golden glow washed over them, and Vesper blinked at the brightness.

"Hello?" Ansel called. When there was no reply, he glanced over his shoulder at her. "Stay here."

Part of Vesper wanted to argue, but the other part of her very much wanted to stay exactly where she was. Her heart thudded in her chest, and the lantern trembled in her grip. Her uncle stepped cautiously into the room. Vesper waited, holding a breath until her lungs burned and she had to release it.

"Vesper," came Ansel's voice finally, shot through with an acute distress she'd never heard from him before.

She wanted to stay where she was. She wanted to be back in that other, lovelier world. She wanted to leave and never come back. She went into the room.

At first, she couldn't understand what had upset her uncle so much. The occupant of the room was a barrel-chested man with golden skin and amber eyes that were deep-set in his wrinkled face. His jet hair and beard were peppered gray. He was seated comfortably in an armchair near a neatly made bed. He was definitely alive. He was definitely whole.

It took her a few seconds to see it. The vacant stare in his eyes, the utterly blank expression of his face. He had yet to acknowledge either of them. He had yet to move at all except to blink.

Ansel stepped closer, hesitantly. Still no movement from the man. He knelt down slowly beside the chair, gripping the arm for support.

"Tor," he said carefully. "Tor, do you recognize me? Ansel Dane. I was on the council the last time we spoke."

The man did not reply.

"What's wrong with him?" Vesper whispered, even though she had a haunting certainty that she already knew.

"His memories have been taken," Ansel said. His tone was sharp and bitter as he made his way to his feet. "All of them."

"How is that possible? We're so far from the citadel!"

"From what I understand, he initially fell ill at the citadel. I was away at the time, so I never saw him. Mira must have convinced the council to let her take him home." He closed his eyes and rubbed his temples. "The council told me he was dead. Maybe they suspected that I had misgivings about Solan, or maybe Mira lied to them."

Ansel let out a sigh, the anger in his expression melting into sorrow.

He placed a gentle hand on the man's shoulder. There was no reaction, not even a flicker in his empty eyes.

"This is what the other victims look like too," Ansel said. "Once they wake up, this is all that's left. Physicians have been able to teach them some simple tasks, like eating and drinking, but none have spoken again or shown any recognition of their loved ones."

Vesper couldn't pull her gaze away from Tor, the first Blacksmith, the legend that had permeated Eldra for nearly half a century.

"Do—do you think that his memories are what gave Solan the idea to try a bloodbond?" she asked. Her voice felt faint. She thought of Mira, alone here and caring for the shell of the man who had once been her father. Did she know it was the executioner who had done this to him? She couldn't have—she never would have agreed to help him. The sick feeling in Vesper's stomach had expanded to every part of her.

"If so, then that means he understands the process as well as Mira. The chance of it actually curing him is much higher than I thought."

If Solan was free from the citadel, then no one was safe. And what would happen to her friends, once he had no more use for them?

"We have to go below the citadel," she said. "We have to stop him somehow."

"I'm not sure that will be possible tonight." Her uncle checked his pocket watch and nodded to himself. He took the lantern from her and went to the front door.

"Your diviners did tell you something, didn't they," Vesper said, as he opened the door and blustering rain howled into the quiet cottage.

"I'm afraid so." He stood motionless in the doorway, heedless of the pelting rain against his face and coat.

Vesper stepped behind him to look over his shoulder and sucked in a sharp breath. Standing in the road in front of the cottage, her hair clinging wetly to her cheeks, the hatred in her eyes burning brightly in the darkness, was Cassa. And she was aiming a gun at Ansel's heart.

THIRTY-SIX

ALYS

WHEN Alys opened her eyes, she saw nothing but darkness. She felt nothing but the stone beneath her, pressed against her cheek, her palms, her stomach. She didn't panic, but only because her head felt too heavy to even form a coherent thought. She felt like she was trapped in the terrible paralysis between waking and sleeping. Slowly, her eyes began to adjust, even though her mind did not. There was light coming from somewhere distant, and she could make out a shape beside her. With excruciating effort, she slid her hand across the rough ground until she touched Newt's hand. His skin was warm. That seemed like a good sign.

Alys tried to lift her head, but her neck wouldn't cooperate. She tried to speak, but she felt stuffed full of cotton, and all that came out was a scratchy moan. There was a stir of movement somewhere near her other shoulder. Then a voice, weak and jagged.

"Shit." Evander.

Alys concentrated all her willpower into her arms and managed to push herself up a few inches. She fell back down, smacking her cheekbone painfully on the ground. The success gave her some strength though. She gathered herself and tried again. This time she made it to her hands and knees. She shook her head slowly, trying to clear the stupor.

Newt still hadn't moved, but Alys could see that his chest was rising and falling with soft breaths. She looked over to find Evander's hip near her left hand. He was on his back, dragging his hands across his face with miserable sluggishness. Alys tried to say his name but ended up coughing instead.

He looked at her for a few seconds, then gradually pushed himself onto his elbows.

"What—" he started but couldn't seem to finish.

Alys shook her head again. It was coming back to her in brief flashes. The poison, Solan's agonized cries, the cut on his arm sealed with a mirasma scar. Then the knife. Mira. Crying. There was something else. Something worse. Alys didn't know if she couldn't remember or if she just didn't want to. Newt began to stir. Alys dragged her gaze around the room. No Cassa.

It took them ten minutes to recover enough to find their feet. No one said anything as they each took stock of themselves and their situation. They were still in the seers' chamber. The only light was from the ghost globe at the base of the statue. Alys's chest tightened as she surveyed the murky shadows.

"Where's Cassa?"

No one replied. Evander's face was pale and pinched with worry as his eyes drifted across the chamber. Alys took a few unsteady steps closer to the ghost globe, straining to see past it. The knife was lying there, still crusted with blood.

Mira had held it to Solan's neck. None of it made sense. She had come down here to help Solan. She knew that he was going to help them destroy the council. None of it made any sense. She'd been crying.

There was something else. Something worse.

Her eyes were drawn to the inkiness beyond the globe. Something much worse. She stumbled forward wordlessly past the knife, past the light. She dropped to her knees beside Mira's supine body. She shook her, but Mira didn't wake. Her hair was tangled across her face. One arm rested on her stomach, the other flung over her head, fingers dangling only inches from the surface of the still waters. She'd been crying, and then she'd told them what Solan had done to her father.

Alys's throat felt tight and raw. She pressed two fingers into Mira's neck, just below her jaw. Evander knelt down beside her. Alys waited for a long time, much longer than was necessary, straining to feel any hint of a pulse. Nothing.

A dry sob she hadn't realized she was holding back burst from her chest. Mira had told them the truth, how three months ago during a visit to the citadel, her father had crumpled to the ground, crying out in pain before falling unconscious. When he awoke, there was nothing of her father left. That same day, a voice—Solan's voice—had crawled into her mind and told her that she could have her father back if she helped the Seras when they came to her door. Nothing else. No details. She convinced herself that her own mind was playing tricks on her, and after a couple of months of trying in vain to awaken any recognition in her father's blank eyes, she convinced herself that it was hopeless. And then Evander and Alys arrived at her doorstep, and she knew that helping them was her only chance to save her father.

She'd begged Solan. She'd threatened him. And then suddenly she collapsed. Solan shoved her limp body away and climbed to his feet. Alys remembered scrambling backward. She remembered the others doing the same. Newt had kicked the ghost globe in his haste. She remembered making it to her feet. She remembered Evander asking him why. And then there was nothing.

"We did this," Evander said from behind her, his voice hoarse. "We brought her here."

"She must have known who he was from the moment we told her what we were going to do." Alys struggled to keep her voice even.

"Do you think Solan ever intended to give her father back his memories?" Newt asked.

She didn't say anything, but Alys couldn't help but think that they should have known. They should have known that it couldn't be this easy. They should have known that bringing Mira here was as good as leading her to her death. They should have known that Solan really was a monster.

If you want to insult me, Alys, have the courtesy to do it to my face.

Alys lurched at the voice in her head, and she looked sharply at her brother.

"Did you hear that?"

"Hear what?"

Alys jumped to her feet. A wave of dizziness almost sent her right back to the ground, but Newt grabbed her arm and kept her steady.

"Solan is still down here," she said, glancing toward the corridor that led to his chamber. "He's waiting for us."

"This is just a suggestion," said Evander, "but maybe we should stay far away from the murderous, immortal executioner who's well on his way to becoming all-powerful?"

"What if Cassa's in there?" Alys demanded.

Evander bit his lip and stared at the golden light that seeped through the tunnel.

"We should at least have a plan first," Newt said quietly. "If we go in there now, we're at his mercy."

Come, or I'll do more than make you sleep.

"I don't think we have a choice." Alys was unable to keep a tremor from her voice. She hated that Solan was in her head. She hated that he could see exactly how scared she was.

"Newt's right," Evander said. "We need a plan."

"Let's head back toward the lake," Newt said. "At least get some distance."

I'll start with him, I think.

"No!" Alys cried. She didn't know if it was directed at Solan or Newt.

The boys looked at her strangely. Evander put a hand on her shoulder and tried to catch her eye.

"What's going on? What's wrong?" he asked.

Would you prefer I start with your brother?

Desperation flared in her chest. Alys decided to try the move that had always worked for Cassa in the past.

"I'm going in there," she said. "You can follow me or not."

She pulled away from Evander and walked quickly toward the corridor. At first, she didn't hear them following. She wondered if when Cassa tried it, she felt the same barbed tangle of emotions in her chest. The certainty that of course they would follow. The creeping fear that maybe this time they wouldn't.

But of course, they followed.

Good girl, Alys.

And the only emotion she had left was fear.

The Night Ansel Betrayed Solan

IT was the middle of the night when he woke. He knew it without looking at a clock, and so, in the memory, Cassa knew it too. Summer. The windows were open, and a faint night breeze brushed the curtains. Yellow curtains. His wife loved the color and only laughed when he complained about their bedroom looking like a giant lemon had exploded in it. She was asleep beside him, her soft gray curls falling over her eyes. A very long time ago, when she was just a milliner's daughter and he was just a farmer's son, her hair had been yellow. Not like a lemon, but like sunlight on wheat fields just before the harvest.

Those years were so far past, they felt like stories someone else had told him. Blurred and unreal. She'd followed him so far, from a lonely, distant village to the citadel itself. It had taken him so much longer to get here than he'd thought it would, back when his dreams were only a poor boy's ambitions. Tomorrow those ambitions would finally mean something. Tomorrow he would take his vows as the high chancellor of Eldra.

You've done well, Chancellor.

The voice, faintly familiar, scraped the back of his mind. He shivered, despite the warmth of the room, and sat up. For a few minutes, all was quiet. Sleep was tugging at his eyelids again.

Surely you haven't forgotten about our bargain.

Ansel leapt out of the bed, nearly tripping over the rug in his haste. His joints creaked and complained until he'd steadied himself against the wardrobe. He gasped and shot a glance at the bed. Nima stirred but didn't wake.

"What do you want?" he whispered, pressing his hands against his head as if he could somehow force the executioner out.

Only what I was promised.

"I—I need more time." He'd never forgotten the deal he'd made for Eldra's survival. He'd also never intended to follow through with it. Solan was too dangerous. His prison beneath the citadel was the only way to ensure the city's safety from his unnatural gifts.

A long moment of silence, and Ansel dared to hope that his excuse might work. Then the voice again, just as soft, just as calm.

I see.

Somewhere in the house, someone began to scream.

Ansel's feet carried him into the hall before his mind had even fully registered what he was hearing. Some sounds called to the deepest of instincts. He ran toward the east wing's guest quarters, where his son was staying with his wife and the twins. Aden. Kira. Reed. Rowen. Their names were a pounding rhythm in his head, in his heart.

If you hurry, maybe I'll let you say good-bye.

The voice was not drowned out by the rising cries of pain. It remained an insistent whisper at the back of his mind, impossible to ignore. Though his bones felt like they were splintering and his lungs felt like they were withering, he ran faster. Aden. Kira. Reed. Rowen.

He could hear the servants stirring downstairs, but they couldn't help him. He rounded the last corner. He could see the open door of the twins' bedroom. A light shone dimly from inside. Aden. Kira. Reed. Rowen.

Abruptly, the screams stopped. For a brief eternity, Ansel's heart did too.

"Please," he whispered. Somehow his pace had slowed to a walk. Each step took him too far and not far enough. The light still shone like a beacon in the corridor, but everything was quiet. So terribly quiet. Even the voice had fallen silent.

When he finally stood in the doorway, it was like standing on the edge of the world's end. He didn't think he was breathing anymore. He couldn't feel his heartbeat. It didn't seem to matter somehow. Kira was on the floor with Reed still clutched in her arms. His hair, yellow like his grandmother's once had been, gleamed in the candlelight. Slumped over one of the beds was Aden, who only hours ago had been laughing at the twins' insistence that surely once Grandpa was the high chancellor, he could do away with bedtime. Wrapped in his arms, as if somehow he could be protected, was Rowen.

Everything was so quiet.

"Please," he said again, into the wretched silence. "Please, I'll do anything. Just bring them back."

More quiet. Aden. Kira. Reed. Rowen. He moved on shaking legs, touched each of their faces with shaking fingers, willing it to not be true. Willing some movement, some hint of life. Willing himself to wake up.

You forget that I can see the future. I'm afraid the time for bargains has passed.

"They're all I have." He swept his hand over Rowen's yellow hair. He looked so peaceful now. But those screams—

On the contrary, Chancellor, you have so much more to lose.

The servants rushed into the room, bleary-eyed, wielding lamps. The entire house had awoken, it seemed.

That was when Ansel realized who was missing.

He pushed past the servants, who were just starting to realize the gruesome truth. He might have been screaming Nima's name, but maybe it was only in his mind. He didn't have any space for conscious thought. Instinct alone drove him. The shadowy corridors were never-ending. The bedroom door was still open, with no light beyond, no sign that Nima had awoken. This time he didn't slow. He plunged straight into the dark.

She was just as he'd left her, on her stomach, hugging the pillow, her face turned toward the window. Moonlight rested gently on her curls. As Ansel pulled himself unsteadily onto the bed, he thought of sunlight on wheat fields just before the harvest. How far away those years were now. The milliner's daughter and the farmer's son. Making plans for a grand, unreachable future.

He lay down beside her and ran his fingers across her cheek, through her hair. She didn't stir. She was already gone. His eyes burned with tears, but his sobs were trapped in his chest, a tangled mass of agony. Aden. Kira. Reed. Rowen. Nima.

Just kill me, he thought. He didn't have strength for speech anymore. *Isn't that what you really want?*

Not yet. We've a new future now, you and I. So much better than the one we had before. Until then, give my regards to the council.

And that was the last thing Cassa remembered.

THIRTY-SEVEN

CASSA

SHE hadn't expected Vesper to be here, but that didn't change anything. If she could hold in her head the memory of the night Chancellor Dane lost everything and still have more hate than pity in her heart, then there was nothing that could change her mind now. Maybe she had become a monster too. Solan was wrong; she could never be great. She could never be even half of what her parents were, but she could at least finish what they'd started.

The rain stung her face and eyes, and she couldn't catch her breath. Her feet—still bare, since her boots were sitting on the lakeshore under the citadel—ached and bled. She'd run almost the entire way here, cutting across the valley to the road that wound through the wood to the Blacksmith's cottage. It would have been wiser to make her way through the forest, safe from any ranging patrols, but there wasn't time for that. If the prophecy was truly infallible, then there was nothing that would stop her from reaching her destination, from standing face-to-face with the chancellor one last time, from pulling the trigger.

She'd seen the chancellor's carriage waiting on the road a short distance from the cottage, but the driver had been too busy fussing with the horses to notice her ducking through the trees. She wasn't sure if the chancellor was in the carriage or not, but something inside nudged her to the cottage. She'd blinked at it through raindrops for a few seconds, and then, as if all of this was scripted—and in a way it was—the front door swung open. Chancellor Dane hadn't looked surprised to see her. He stepped out into the rain without hesitation, his steady gaze never leaving hers, even when she raised the gun. Vesper had been surprised as she stumbled after him, tugging her cape tightly around herself.

"Vesper, get back inside," the chancellor said.

"Like hell," Vesper snapped. "Cassa, what are you doing?"

Cassa couldn't look at her. She kept her eyes on Chancellor Dane, kept her gun leveled at his heart.

"Did it never occur to you that disposing of the current regime would involve disposing of him as well?" Cassa asked, loud enough that her voice carried through the rain. A wind gusted, whipping through her legs and hair, but she kept her stance.

Vesper didn't answer, and Cassa risked a quick look. Water ran down her pale face in rivulets. Light and shadow from the lantern's wavering glow played across her features. Her lips were a thin, uncertain line.

"Or did you never expect to dispose of the current regime at all?" Cassa's voice shook a little with the question. She'd thought betrayal was a single, merciless blow, but really it was a blooming ache, unfurling repeatedly with new pain.

"It's never been as simple for me as it is for you." Vesper's cape flapped in the wind, and she didn't bother to pull it closed again. "You know I hate everything the council has done. You know I want things to change. But I can only do what I think is right—even if that's different now than it was before."

Cassa bit down on her lip until she tasted blood. *Before*. Before they'd been caught trying to infiltrate the citadel. Before she'd hatched her plan to find out what was happening to people's memories. Before her parents' death had changed everything.

Before all of that, when they had just been two sharp minds, two fearless hearts, thrust together by chance and bound together by a single purpose. Maybe Vesper had abandoned that purpose, but it was the only thing Cassa had left.

Some part of her whispered that this wasn't true, and her thoughts drifted back to the cavern beneath the citadel, to the friends she'd left behind.

She shook away that line of thinking. It was too late to go back now. Solan's prophecy had laid her future out for her, but it was up to her to claim it. She had to focus. She jerked her gaze back to Chancellor Dane, who hadn't moved. The trigger was slick beneath her finger. Before she could pull it, Vesper stepped into her line of sight, in front of the chancellor.

"Get out of the way," Cassa ground out through her locked jaw.

"I'm not going anywhere."

"Vesper," the chancellor said quietly, pushing a hand against her shoulder.

Vesper shook him off and crossed her arms, glaring at Cassa. Her hair was soaked by now into a dull auburn. A few tendrils clung to her forehead.

"I'm not moving," she said.

Heat flared in Cassa's chest and filled her lungs.

"Vesper, get out of the way!" she shouted, her voice slicing through the wind and rain.

"No!" Vesper shouted right back. "You listen to me, Cassa Valera. If you want to shoot him, you're going to have to shoot me first."

Cassa's finger twitched on the trigger.

"You think I won't?"

Vesper didn't flinch, didn't drop her eyes from Cassa's.

"I think you won't."

"You didn't think I would help Solan after I saw what he did to your family, but I did anyway." Cassa wasn't sure if she was being cruel to Vesper or the chancellor or herself. "He survived the bloodbond. Soon he'll be free."

Vesper's lips trembled. She pressed them together and said nothing.

"The council deserves to pay for what they've done," Cassa said. "If the only way to destroy them is to set a monster loose, then so be it."

"What about all the innocent people he's hurt?" Vesper asked. "All the people he will hurt while he gets his revenge?"

"There's still the poison," Cassa said. "Once the council is gone, once Eldra is free, I'll kill him myself."

Vesper shook her head slowly.

"This has never been about Eldra, and you know it. This has only ever been about revenge."

Cassa's arm was starting to shake, but she kept the gun level. Aden. Kira. Reed. Rowen. Nima. The names sprang unbidden to her mind, thrumming in time with her heartbeat, as they had ever since Vesper had passed the memory to her. Isn't this what Vesper had wanted? As if knowing Ansel Dane's loss so intimately could somehow alleviate her own. As if what had been taken from him could ever absolve him for what he'd taken from her.

"I've never cared about anything else—not since I lost them," Cassa said. "I've never pretended otherwise."

"You care about Evander and Alys and Newt." Vesper took a small step forward. Her hands were clenched into fists at her sides. "You cared about me."

Cassa dragged the back of her hand across her eyes, telling herself it was the rain and not tears that stung them.

"Not enough," she said. "This has always mattered more. I guess I'm as bad as Solan."

Vesper's mouth twisted slightly, and her eyes flashed.

"You're a stubborn little shit, but you're not heartless, Cassa. You're not a monster."

Cassa laughed. It sounded hollow in her ears.

"Are you sure about that? There's an infallible prophecy that says otherwise." She leaned to the right so that she could catch Dane's eye over Vesper's shoulder. "Chancellor, you've always been so eager to treat prophecies as law. A hundred years ago the council slaughtered thousands because of one seer's dream. Don't tell me you've lost faith in their accuracy now. If the last seer in Eldra tells me that I'm supposed to kill you, do you think I have a choice?"

With an agility that belied his age, the chancellor moved around his niece and forward until the gun was only inches from his chest. He still held the lantern, and Cassa could see that he was shivering. She could see in his eyes that it wasn't from fear. It was so cold that she was having trouble remembering what warmth felt like. Her jaw ached with the effort to keep her teeth from chattering. Her strength sluiced off her with the rain.

Vesper made a noise of protest and stepped forward, but Chancellor Dane raised a hand to stop her. He kept Cassa's gaze. She couldn't stop thinking about what he'd felt all those years ago when facing the executioner for the first time. Fear and disgust and desperation and shame. They all coiled in her chest like they were her own—and they *were*. The memories were hers, as if she'd been the one standing there, as if she'd been the one to wake in the middle of the night and find her world ripping apart at the seams. Boundless fury. Gaping despair. Those were the chancellor's, but they were hers too. Something they shared.

"My hands are not clean in this, and they never have been," said Chancellor Dane, his voice cracking. "I'd hoped that killing the executioner might atone for my sins and the sins of my predecessors, but perhaps it is too late for that. Perhaps it was always too late."

He dropped his gaze, down to the barrel aimed at his heart. He didn't move.

After everything, it all came down to one bullet. So simple. Cassa had spent her whole life refusing to believe that her actions were somehow predetermined, but surely this one was. Surely, she was meant for this moment. Surely this was the reason she was still here, when her parents and almost everyone she had known in her childhood was gone. Surely if it was in a seer's dream, then she had no choice but to pull the trigger.

The fire inside of her burned so bright, so hot. Sixteen years and now it finally meant something. The chancellor had taken her parents from her. He and the council were corrupted, a festering disease at the heart of the city that was slowly infecting everyone. He and the council were everything that was wrong with the world.

The chancellor was, when all was said and done, just an old man, shivering in the rain, waiting to die.

Cassa swallowed hard. Her mouth was so dry, her throat so tight. Her every nerve, her every sinew, burned and burned, but she lowered the pistol.

There's not really anything great about you, is there? A constant, aching refrain. Even before Solan had spoken the words, they had been waiting inside of her, a dark doubt for her darkest nights. Would her mother or father have pulled the trigger? She didn't know. She just knew that she couldn't.

"Why?" the chancellor asked, his eyes still lingering on the gun.

"It wouldn't change anything." Even as she spoke the words, she hated the truth of them. Pulling the trigger wouldn't dissolve that fury and despair. It could only cause more. Nothing was ever so simple.

Her limbs ached. The cold had become a vise on her body, sending shooting pain from her head to her toes. Despite that, she felt strangely detached. Too exhausted to move. Maybe this was what it felt like when you ruined an infallible prophecy. A punishment that the Slain God administered from beyond the grave.

She was so tired that when the thundering of horses' hooves rose beneath the rain and she turned to see a squadron of heavily armed guards surrounding them, she didn't try to run. She couldn't even make herself care. It was too late to escape the citadel's clutches. Maybe it always had been.

THIRTY-EIGHT

Newt

SOLAN'S chamber felt colder somehow. Newt had no idea how long they had been unconscious. Down here there was no way to keep track of time. Hours could have passed. His stomach growled with the realization. Solan was slouched in one of his armchairs, his sleeve still pulled away from the fresh scar. It took Newt a few seconds to figure out what was different about him. The strange shifting of his features had stopped—or, rather, it had slowed down. There was still an unsettling vacillation to his face, but his appearance was easier to pin down. Brown hair. Clear gray eyes. Sallow complexion. A narrow jaw and aquiline nose. He looked to be in his thirties.

Was that how he'd looked the day his alchemical experiment granted him immortality?

"Please," said Solan, gesturing toward the sofa. His voice was strained, as if he was still in some pain. On the small table at his elbow was an elixir bottle, empty except for the shimmering remnants of mirasma streaking the glass. "Have a seat. Would you like some tea?"

None of them answered. Newt didn't even want to sit down. His basest instincts were pulling at his muscles, begging him to flee. Cassa wasn't here, at least not that he could see. Had Solan done something to her? Alys went to the couch first and sat down on the end nearest Solan. Her hands were clenched into tight fists in her lap. Evander sat down hesitantly beside her, his eyes never leaving Solan. Newt sank onto the couch beside Evander, his stomach sinking with him. If Solan wanted them dead, he would have killed them already like he'd killed Mira. But maybe he just wasn't finished with them yet.

"How long were we unconscious?" Evander asked.

"I don't see how that's important."

"How *long?*"

Solan frowned at him. Newt didn't understand Evander's insistence either. It hardly mattered right now.

"Only an hour. I am sorry it had to happen like this. I wanted to keep everything civil," Solan said, steepling his fingers. "I did try."

"You turned Mira's father into a corpse with a pulse," Evander said.

Solan flinched at his tone, then shook his head.

"An accident," he said. "A fortuitous one, as it turned out, since it's how I discovered a bloodbond could deliver me from this prison."

"And what about all the others?" Newt's voice wavered only slightly. "Were they fortuitous accidents as well?"

Solan smiled. Without the usual tumult of his features, it was easier to read his expressions. There was something predatory in that smile. A side of him that he hadn't shown them before. Newt's muscles itched again to flee.

"I learned a long time ago that the more memories I take, the stronger

I become. My reach grows longer, my divinations clearer, and my dreams more vivid. The council wants me to supply them with more and more prophecies. I've only ever heeded their demands."

"That's why they made you the executioner," Alys said, not quite looking at him. "Performing the death rites, eating the memories—it was to make sure you kept dreaming prophecies."

"Very good, Alys," he said. "Although I must say, they weren't very diligent in their supply. There aren't many death sentences to be had in a peaceful, prosperous city. I had to take matters into my own hands with the rebellion. Those hundred years proved to be very fruitful, but as I'm sure you've noticed, all the rebels are gone now."

For a long while, the silence in the room was palpable. Newt could feel Evander tense beside him. His own heartbeat was thudding in his ears.

"How?" Evander asked. His voice was low and trembling, not with fear but with anger. "How did you take matters into your own hands?"

Solan waited a long time before he replied.

"I'm sure the poor wretches in the lower wards would have risen up eventually," he said, dragging a finger absently along the arm of his chair. "I just told the council it was coming sooner rather than later."

The fatal prophecy. The citadel guards arriving in the dead of night. Thousands annihilated with flame and sword. Newt knew the history as well as he knew his own. It was the night that started the rebellion. It was the night that started everything. It was the reason they were sitting here. The reason the Seras were branded traitors. The reason his father was branded a coward. The reason Cassa's parents were dead.

"Bastard," Evander bit off, jumping to his feet.

Solan still traced circles on the faded floral upholstery, unmoved. He didn't even look up.

"I think you should sit down, Evander," he said softly.

"What did you do with Cassa?" Evander demanded.

"I didn't do anything with her."

"Where the hell is she then?"

"I believe I told you to sit." All trace of Solan's calm geniality had vanished. His voice was ice.

For a couple of seconds, no one moved. Newt saw Evander's hand in a tight fist at his side. The silver tea service rattled. Solan kept Evander's gaze with a cool poise that could only be a dare.

Newt grabbed his wrist and tugged gently.

"Evander," he said, trying to sound reasonable and keep the urgency and panic from his voice. "Just sit down. Please."

He could feel Evander's pulse, so rapid, it was a steady thrum. Solan hadn't so much as blinked. The world felt balanced on a razor's edge. Finally, Evander's hand loosened, and slowly he lowered himself back to the couch.

Solan was smiling again.

"Thank you," he said. "There's no need for the theatrics. I'm happy to tell you where your friend is. She's probably reaching the Blacksmith's cottage as we speak."

"Why would she go there?" Alys asked, the skepticism so sharp in her tone that Newt could practically hear the question she didn't ask. *Why would Cassa leave us behind?*

Newt realized that he was still holding Evander's wrist. He started to release it but at the last second changed his mind and slid his hand into Evander's instead. His skin was clammy, but the feel of their interlaced fingers was soothing. Evander's leg, which had been bouncing up and down with frenetic energy, stilled.

"Any minute now," he murmured, so softly that Newt wasn't sure he'd even spoken.

Solan didn't seem to notice.

"To fulfill the first half of the prophecy," he said. "First, she'll kill the chancellor, and then when my bloodbond takes full effect, I'll leave this prison behind and serve the council the justice they so richly deserve."

"And then what?" Evander asked. "A peaceful retirement in the countryside?"

Solan smiled that predatory smile again.

"I think that after all this time, Eldra owes me a few considerations."

How could they have ever trusted him? How could they have ever thought that Solan's appetite for vengeance would be sated with the council's demise? Maybe there had never been a prophecy in the first place.

"Oh, I assure you, the prophecy is quite real."

Newt blinked and realized Solan's eyes were on him, finding the thoughts only moments after he had them. He'd heard that skilled sentients could read so quickly and thoroughly that they might as well be reading someone's mind instead of just their past. His stomach curled at the notion.

"Why else would I have whiled away the years down here?" Solan went on, indicating his surroundings with a disinterested wave. "Perhaps you haven't paid much attention to history, but infallible prophecies must happen the way they are seen. That's the *only* way they can happen. When I dreamed this future, perfect and infallible, I knew that all I needed to do was wait."

"Wait for us to come to you," Alys murmured.

"Precisely." Solan's finger tapped a measured rhythm on his knee. "I needed Cassandra to kill the chancellor. I needed Evander to convince the Blacksmith to come, and I needed Alys because her seer's blood makes it easier to communicate when necessary. And even Newt proved useful, runt that he is."

As much as Newt hated to admit it, the comment stung. Solan hadn't even glanced in his direction, but he could feel the blood rising to his face. Without turning his head away from Solan, Evander squeezed his hand tightly. Newt let out a slow breath. Worse than his words were the implications behind them. They'd been pawns from the start. Had their decision to help Solan even been a choice at all? Cassa had always been adamant that seers and diviners couldn't dictate their future, only guess at it. But Newt wasn't so sure—not anymore.

"What do you want from us now?" Alys asked, her voice admirably even.

Solan's gaze swiveled to her. For a few seconds, he just studied her in silence. Then he leaned back in his chair, with a slight wince.

"I'm glad you ask," he said, cradling his left arm. "I have need of your divination skills."

"What—why?"

Solan huffed out a short breath and looked at the ground. Newt followed his gaze to the bone runes scattered across the rug.

"The infallible prophecy gave me many certainties but not everything. For the rest, I see too many possibilities," he said. "Too much is uncertain. I need a second reading to make things clear."

"Make what clear?" Evander asked.

For a long while, Solan only stared at the runes, his expression distant, his eyes glassy. Newt thought he was going to ignore Evander, but then he shook his head slowly.

"You can't possibly understand everything I've done to get this far. I've been working toward this moment since before you were born. The rebellion was just the start, but even all those memories didn't give me the power I needed to foresee my own escape. Four years ago, I thought Dane might be my salvation—and I suppose in a way he was. After I showed him what happens to those who betray me, it was his family's memories that gave me the strength I needed. My next dream was the infallible prophecy. My true salvation."

Newt shuddered. He couldn't follow everything Solan was saying—he seemed to have drifted momentarily into his own private world—but Newt understood enough.

"I can leave nothing to chance," Solan said, his gaze snapping back to the present. "I must be certain . . . It's the only way I can be free."

"Free to destroy more innocent lives?" Evander spit out the words like an acrid taste in his mouth.

Solan only smiled at him, slow and vicious.

"I'm disappointed in you all. So small-minded. Cassandra may not be anywhere near as useful as you, but at least she understands that sometimes unsavory means are necessary for a satisfying end."

"Even Cassa wouldn't go this far," Evander said, but he didn't meet Solan's eyes.

Solan nodded thoughtfully, a trace of that wicked smile still hovering on his lips.

"Yes, I think the chancellor's little niece probably thought the same thing when she gave Cassandra her uncle's memory of the night I took my revenge. I've carried a lot of other people's suffering in my time, but I imagine Dane's must be particularly unbearable. Losing your wife and son and grandchildren in the same night is a very special sort of punishment." He tapped his fingertips together in a ponderous rhythm. "Yet Cassa has gone to finish the job, and you're all still here with me. Tell me, Evander, how much further does she have to go until she's a monster as well?"

Evander was squeezing Newt's hand so hard it hurt, but he didn't pull away. A thousand thoughts ricocheted in his head, impossible to catch. He tried to tell himself that the Cassa Valera he knew would never do this. She would never help Solan after finding out what he really was. She would never abandon them here for the sake of her own personal revenge.

He tried to tell himself, but part of him suspected that the Cassa Valera he knew absolutely would.

"I think that's enough about my sordid past. Alys." Solan's gaze flicked to her. "If you would kindly read the coins?"

His breathing was becoming more labored. A sheen of sweat had broken on his forehead. Alys glanced at Newt and Evander. If she was hoping for some direction, Newt certainly didn't have any to give her.

"You've been in my head," she said carefully. "You know I'm not any good."

"And yet here we are," snapped Solan, slamming his right hand down on the arm of the chair. The break in his composure was so abrupt that they all jumped. Alys's breath had begun to quicken. "I won't ask you again, Alys."

Newt stared hard at Solan, trying to wrap his mind around the seemingly simple request. He reminded Newt of a dog, bristling and snarling because it was afraid. He wasn't as certain of the future as he had led them to believe. Was he afraid the bloodbonding wouldn't take? There was still a possibility his body would reject it. Or maybe he was afraid that he wouldn't last long enough to find out. Vesper had seen all of Cassa's memories, and so had Gaz Ritter—the chances of the council staying ignorant for much longer were slim. The bloodbond wouldn't be complete for another five hours, which meant he still needed one more dose of elixir. He still needed one last thing from the council before he could take his revenge.

Suddenly, Newt understood.

"Don't do it, Alys," he said, so forcefully that even he was surprised. Everyone was looking at him now. Solan's glare was dagger-sharp. Newt swallowed hard, steeling himself. "He's trying to make sure he doesn't need us anymore before he kills us. It's the only reason we're still alive."

Silence. Newt had never realized before how quiet the caverns were, as if all sounds were swallowed by the earth itself. Evander was the first to speak, of course.

"Rat bastard," he said.

Solan ignored him and leaned forward in his chair, his eyes still on Newt. They roamed all across his face, a careful examination, an unforgiving judgment.

"You know I can choose exactly what memories I take." His voice was low and terrible. "It's the precious memories that taste the richest. The ones you play over and over in your mind, for comfort, for joy. But you don't have many of those, do you?"

Newt said nothing. His jaw was set, but he knew his hands were shaking.

"Leave him alone," Evander said.

"I'm fine," Newt managed, though his voice quavered. "He can bluster all he wants, but if he truly thought we were expendable, we'd already be dead."

Solan's eyes narrowed, and something so dark and hideous flashed across his features that the hair on the back of Newt's neck stood on end. His instincts sang, begging him to run, to fight, to do anything but sit there, gaze locked with Solan's.

"You're right, of course," said Solan, his honeyed voice belying his expression. "I do need you all alive until I'm certain you're no longer useful. But you've so much more to lose than just your life, Newt Dalton."

A memory bubbled to the surface of Newt's mind. His mother, singing on a stormy night. She had a lovely voice, like the rushing of water over smooth stones, like the warmth of the sun on a summer day. Then Newt couldn't remember what he had been thinking about, what had filled his chest with comfort and his eyes with tears.

Solan was smiling.

A memory. His father, red-faced and laughing at the dinner table, slapping his thigh. Newt had said something funny, though he couldn't recall what. His father beamed across the table at his mother, clasped Newt's shoulder.

Then the memory faded, and the sound of his father's laughter was the last thing to go, and Newt realized dimly, desperately, what was happening. He tried to speak, but the words caught in his throat. Somehow he'd lost his grip on Evander's hand. He couldn't see anything through the tears.

A memory. Evander, dripping wet and shirtless, lying on his back in the grass by the river. The sun scorching overhead, glistening against his skin, his silky black hair. He was grinning at nothing, saying something that Newt didn't remember, because it didn't matter, because all that mattered was that he was happy, so happy, so . . .

Solan was siphoning away everything good he had. With every second, Newt could feel more and more slipping away. And with every second, the bad expanded. His mother's coffin. His father's anger. The world-ending hate inside him. Soon there would be nothing else left.

Somewhere far away, he could hear his friends' voices. Panic and fear and fury. He tried to make out what they were saying, but the memories were coming too fast, clouding out the present. For a split second, Newt's vision cleared. Evander was kneeling in front of him. His face was the only thing Newt could see. He was saying something that Newt couldn't make out, but it didn't matter, because he was slipping under again.

And he was back at the Blacksmith's house. The wind whipping at his cheeks. The sky looming with rain. Evander in his arms. Evander's mouth on his. Newt struggled to hold on, but he could already feel it fading, fading . . .

"Stop, dammit, stop it, please!" Evander's voice jolted through him, and he could see the present again. Evander held out a hand toward Alys, silver glinting in his palm. "Take them, Alys. Just do it."

"Evander." Alys's voice was tight with panic. "If I—"

"*Now*." Evander's voice rang across the stone, and Newt didn't know why he'd ever thought the caverns were silent, when every inch of them reverberated with sound.

He dropped his head into his hands, choking on his own tears, trying to catch his breath. His thoughts were torn and scarred. He felt hollowed out. He knew deep in his bones that he'd lost something irreplaceable, but he couldn't remember what.

There was the clatter of coins hitting the ground. And Evander's hands were on his shoulders, his voice soft again.

"Just look at me. Please."

Newt shuddered with a phantom sob but dropped his hands. Evander's face was blurred through the tears. Newt rubbed at his eyes with his sleeve.

"Are you okay?" Evander asked.

The nearness of him felt somehow familiar and somehow not. Newt tried to grasp at what he was sure was a memory, but there was nothing there.

"I don't—I don't know."

Evander's lips were a hard line, and the concern in his eyes was so profound that Newt's chest ached. He knew he was missing something important. It was a shadow at the corner of his mind, impossible to catch.

"I'm not sure what I'm looking for." Alys's voice was strained. She was kneeling on the floor a few feet away, poring over the silver coins. Her messy braid hung over her shoulder, and a loose tendril near her mouth quivered with her breaths.

"Stop stalling and tell me what you see," said Solan.

Newt flinched at the sound of his voice and immediately hated himself for it.

"Any minute now," Evander whispered. He squeezed Newt's shoulders. "We're almost there."

Newt wanted desperately to ask what he meant, but he was too scared. Scared that Solan would hear him. Scared that it was something he was supposed to know but had forgotten.

"I'm trying," Alys said. "I told you, I'm not very good at this."

"Stop making excuses." Solan rose to his feet. "This is your last—" He doubled over, clutching at his stomach. For a few seconds, he just gasped, then a cry of pain tore from his throat. He collapsed back into his chair, his limbs shaking uncontrollably.

"Finally." Evander jumped to his feet, pulling Newt up with him. "Let's get out of here."

"What did you do to him?" Alys scrambled to her feet and backed cautiously away from Solan, who was still writhing insensibly.

"I didn't do anything. There's a second wave of pain to the bloodbond, when your body tries to adjust. It's almost as bad as the first." Evander snatched up the ghost globe that had been deposited in the corner and headed down the corridor toward the seers' chamber. The coins in front of Alys rattled and then darted through the air after him.

Newt stumbled after him as well, more from instinct than from any clear thought. Alys was close behind.

"Wait," she said when they emerged from the tunnel. Evander was already on one of the paths over the water, his globe a sole beacon in the vast darkness. "Evander, for seers' sake, just wait."

Evander stopped and turned, but he didn't come back toward them. In the blue ghost light he seemed half a ghost himself. Somewhere in the shadows nearby, Mira's body was still lying there. Newt knew it was selfish of him, but he was glad there wasn't enough light to see her.

"We need to go the other way," Alys said, panting. "This way leads back to the crypts."

"I know," said Evander. "We're going to the citadel."

"Have you lost your mind?"

"Most definitely. But unless you can think of another way to warn someone about the monster we just unleashed, then we don't really have a choice."

"What about Cassa?" she asked, but Newt could hear in her voice that she already knew the answer.

"She left us here so she could go play executioner," Evander said darkly. "She left us here, unconscious, with *him*."

Newt knew it was the simple reality of the situation, though he hadn't let himself consider it before. Hearing Evander say it, with an undercurrent of heartbreak in his usually carefree voice, made it feel so much worse. So much more like betrayal.

"He might have been lying," Alys said, with no conviction. "Or maybe he didn't give her a choice."

"Maybe," Evander conceded with equal conviction. "It doesn't matter though. When the bloodbond takes full effect in a few hours, Solan won't depend on the elixir anymore, and he'll be free to wreak whatever devastation he wants. We have to warn the citadel."

"What about our parents?" Alys persisted. "If Cassa really went to kill the chancellor, then they're in even more danger than before."

"They'll be in just as much danger if Solan escapes, and so will everyone else in the city. This might be the only way to actually help them now."

Alys hesitated. She glanced back once toward Solan's chamber. Newt wondered how much time they had left—if they'd already lost too much. Even if they made it up to the Central Keep and convinced the council to listen to them, they might still be too late.

"They're going to arrest us the moment we step foot in the keep," Alys said, but resignation underscored her tone.

"We escaped once," Newt said. "We can do it again, if we have to."

Alys offered a mirthless smile, her gaze flitting between Newt and her brother.

"I wouldn't want to die next to anyone else," she said.

And together they headed for the lake.

THIRTY-NINE

CASSA

CASSA was the only one manacled, but she couldn't help but notice that the guards kept Vesper and Chancellor Dane very tightly corralled. They ignored all of the chancellor's quiet inquiries, which Cassa suspected wasn't normal protocol between the high chancellor and his subordinates. She didn't bother asking any questions. She was having a hard time caring what happened next, though she was grateful that they put her in the carriage for the long trip back to the citadel, even if it meant being crammed next to a surly guard. Vesper was in the seat across from her, and Cassa studiously avoided her gaze the entire way.

When they reached the Central Keep, Vesper and Dane were led in a separate direction, probably to someplace warmer and cleaner than where Cassa knew she was headed. The guards pushed her through corridors until they reached the metal-braced oak door that hid the steps into the dungeons. In front of it stood Captain Marsh, his arms crossed. His eyes gleamed in the lantern light. The thin iron chain looped at his belt was somehow more intimidating than the pistols surrounding her. His men saluted him, but Captain Marsh only eyed Cassa with a cool expression.

"If I had my way, you would have been shot on sight," he told her. "But the council wants you to be properly sentenced."

"Wonderful," Cassa said. "It was so much fun the first time." Sarcasm was so habitual that it actually required less effort than staying quiet did.

The guard holding her arm fidgeted as if he wanted to hit her. Or maybe he was expecting the captain to do it. Marsh ignored her and uncrossed his arms.

"Take her down. The others have just been brought in as well."

"Others?" Cassa asked, her heart leaping into her throat.

Marsh ignored her and pulled open the door. Cassa considered the consequences of elbowing the man beside her in the face and charging the captain. Her insouciance was starting to evaporate. Before she could make a move, the guard pushed her forward.

The steps felt steeper and longer than she remembered. The stone, polished smooth after so many years of use, was icy cold under her bare feet. Before they'd reached the alcove, Evander's voice drifted up to meet her.

"For seers' sake, would you just listen to us? The citadel's in danger! Someone has to tell the—"

"Just shut up already," cut in an unfamiliar voice, probably a guard. "You'll get your time in front of the council soon enough."

When Cassa saw her friends at the base of the stairs, handcuffed but very much alive, she was somehow simultaneously dismayed and relieved. They were supposed to be in the caverns, far away from the council's clutches. Why were they here?

Alys and Newt both stared at her, as if she could convey with her eyes the answers to all the questions they weren't asking. Evander wouldn't look at her. The pit of fury and despair in her stomach expanded with a new ache. It took her a few seconds to place the unfamiliar feeling. Guilt.

"Have they been searched?" Captain Marsh asked, his flinty gaze resting on each of them in turn.

"Yes, sir," chimed two guards.

"Do it again," Marsh said. "Thoroughly."

The guard who had been with her since the Blacksmith's cottage started patting her down, much more thoroughly than he had before. Not that there was anything else for him to find. She turned her head, but Evander was still avoiding her gaze. She couldn't see his coins, but she knew he must already be evading the diligent efforts of the guard searching him. At least they would have that small advantage.

No sooner had she thought that than Captain Marsh lunged forward with startling speed. Cassa flinched away, but he wasn't coming for her. He grabbed Evander by the shoulder and threw him face-first into the stone wall, so hard that Cassa's own teeth shook. Evander gasped out in pain, and with a delicate clinking sound, three silver coins dropped to the floor, bouncing and rolling at the feet of the shocked guard. He stared for a few seconds and then hurried to retrieve them and button them into his jacket pocket.

"It's a nice trick." Marsh gave Evander a hard shake. "But sloppy execution."

"Let him go," Alys cried, straining against the guard who held her.

The captain did so but not before slamming Evander into the wall a second time. Cassa jerked instinctively toward him, but her guard grabbed her arm and yanked her back. Captain Marsh pushed Evander back toward the man who'd been searching him. Evander sagged in the man's grip. His teeth were red with blood, and he blinked rapidly, as if he was fighting to stay conscious.

"What are you waiting for?" Marsh snapped at the other guards. "Finish the search."

Cassa's guard had finished his task and dug in his pocket for the item he'd confiscated from her earlier.

"Captain," he said. "I found this on her at the cottage."

He held out the little vial of inky black liquid—the poison that was supposed to be Solan's demise before they'd decided instead to give him new life. Captain Marsh took it and held it up to the light. The lines in his weathered face deepened with suspicion. Cassa could feel the burn of Alys's and Newt's and even Evander's eyes on her. She couldn't bring herself to look at them. What did it matter if they lost the only means of killing Solan? It was too late for that anyway. They'd made their decision. He was free, and there was no going back.

"What is it?" Marsh asked her.

"It's medicinal," she replied. The guard did cuff her this time. Involuntary tears sprung to her eyes, but she blinked them away. Nowhere seemed safe to look, so she kept her gaze steady on the captain, daring him to force the answer out of her. Maybe a part of her hoped he would try. She deserved much worse.

Captain Marsh glared at her for a long time. She could almost see the wheels of his mind turning, but in the end, he just gave a mirthless smile.

"I don't suppose it matters what it is," he said. "You'll all be dead before morning."

She wanted to reply that they'd been assigned that same fate a few days ago and were still alive, but for once she decided not to push her luck. They had some long hours ahead of them. The captain unlocked the cabinet in the corner with new leisure and set the vial inside. He turned back to face them again, giving them each a final once-over.

"Put that one in leg irons too," he said, gesturing toward Newt, "and if he even tries to slip out of the manacles, shoot him."

One of the guards scurried to obey. Cassa braved a glance at Newt. There was a marked weariness in his features, but if the captain's words had frightened him, he wasn't showing it. He met Cassa's eyes, and she looked away quickly. Captain Marsh had advanced on her, his arms crossed again as he studied her.

"I met your parents once," he remarked. "Of course, I didn't know who they were at the time."

Cassa's mouth was suddenly dry. A peculiar tingling rushed up her spine.

"Your mother picked my pocket," he went on. Cassa couldn't be sure, but he seemed on the verge of a smile. "Just for fun, I think. They were both very brave. And very reckless. I was almost sorry to hear about their deaths."

He stared meaningfully at her, and Cassa wondered if he was sizing her up, comparing her to the legend of the incomparable Valeras. *You were born of greatness, but there's not really anything great about you, is there?*

She wanted to say something, but no words would come. Then Captain Marsh shook his head, and the moment passed.

"Get them out of my sight," he said, "and put them in the same cell this time so you can keep a good eye on them."

The guard behind Cassa shoved her forward, and she fumbled for balance as he propelled her down the corridor. She managed to keep her feet until he thrust her into a cell. She landed hard on her hands and knees, the pain jolting through her bones. She twisted around in time to see Alys and then Newt being pushed in after her. She never would have admitted it to herself, but the prospect of being alone again had been torturous. Evander came in last, on his feet but barely. The door slammed shut behind him.

For a few seconds, the darkness felt as absolute as it was in the lake, and Cassa's heart began to pound a little faster. But gradually the light from the corridor filtered in through the eye-level metal grating in the door, and she was able to make out the shapes of her friends. Evander sank to the ground while Alys fussed over him. Newt was stock-still in the corner by the door. Cassa was a little surprised that he'd managed not to lose his footing with the heavy irons around his ankles, though she knew she shouldn't be. She'd never once seen Newt lose his balance.

"I'm fine, Alys," Evander said. There was a dangerous edge to his tone that Cassa knew wasn't aimed at his sister.

Cassa sat down, pressing her back against the cool stone. The cell wasn't any bigger than the last one she'd been in, and they were in close quarters. She could hear Evander's and Alys's breaths—his ragged, hers rapid. Newt, as always, was perfectly silent.

"You'll be lucky if you don't have a concussion," Alys said, but she relented and sat down beside her brother.

"I'm fine," Evander repeated, more softly.

Cassa could tell, even from their shadowy silhouettes, that all three of them were looking at her. She knew she should speak first, try to reassure them, try to explain herself, but she didn't. For a minute that dragged into eternity, no one said anything.

"Cassa, why did you leave?" Evander's voice was low and raw, like it hurt to speak.

Reassurances. Explanations. She had neither.

"To kill the chancellor," she said.

More quiet. In such a small space, it was almost unbearable.

"You just left us there with him," Newt said. He still hadn't moved. "After everything." The way he said it, so simply and resignedly, as if he hadn't expected anything better of her, rankled in Cassa's chest.

"What was the point of *everything*, if I didn't try to end it when I had the chance?" She squeezed her hands into fists and pushed them against her forehead. It was a good question. What was the point of everything they'd given up, now that she'd had the chance to kill the chancellor, and she hadn't been able to pull the trigger?

"Solan killed Mira," Alys said. "He might as well have done the same to her father. He was using her the whole time, just like he was using us. How could you—"

"Mira's dead?" Cassa's stomach twisted. In the cavern she'd checked Evander and Alys and Newt to make sure they were breathing, but Mira . . . She'd never gone to Mira.

"Of course she's dead," Evander bit off. "You saw him kill her."

Cassa shook her head. Mira had pulled the knife. She'd been

crying. She'd said something about her father. And then there was just blackness.

"I don't remember," she said. She didn't remember it because Solan had *taken* it from her. He knew she would never leave her friends with him otherwise.

Or at least she hoped that was true. That fire inside her, that intense need—she wasn't sure there was anything she wouldn't have done to satisfy it. The thought scared her, and she drove it away. She hadn't pulled the trigger. She hadn't killed the chancellor tonight.

But she had abandoned her friends alone with a monster.

"Did—did he—" But she couldn't force out the words.

"It's a little late for you to start caring about us now." Alys hugged her knees to her chest and pressed her forehead against them. Evander's hand moved to her back instinctively.

"I didn't know what he'd done to Mira," Cassa said, well aware that she was pleading now. "I thought you'd be safe."

"How could you possibly have thought that," asked Newt, "when you knew what he'd done to Chancellor Dane's family?"

The words, though spoken in Newt's usual even tone, were a stinging rebuke. Cassa opened her mouth, trying to find a reply, a reason, a vindication—but, of course, there was none. How did they even know about the chancellor's memories?

"You knew before the bloodbond, and you didn't tell us," Evander said, his voice carrying all the accusation that Newt's hadn't. "You just let us go through with it."

"I didn't know what else to do," Cassa said. "He was the only way to stop the council."

No one had a reply, and for a few precious seconds, Cassa thought that they understood, that they realized what it had meant to her in that moment, to make that decision. Even if she hadn't been able to follow through in the end. Then Alys raised her head.

"We could have helped Chancellor Dane." Her voice was strained but calm. "If Solan was dead—"

"Solan's death wouldn't stop them," Cassa said. "Not having their pet seer and executioner might weaken them, but they would still be in power. They would find a way to cover it up. The chancellor never said he wanted to bring down the council—just kill Solan."

Even as she spoke, she doubted the truth of her conviction. Vesper had said all the seers were dead. If Solan really was the last one, then killing him really might be enough to destroy the council. Without any new prophecies, they wouldn't be able to keep their hold on the city for long.

"Does revenge really mean more to you than the fate of the whole city?" Alys asked.

"Solan might be a danger to Eldra, but so is the council," Cassa said, heat building in her chest. "They've slaughtered thousands. Of course I'd do anything to stop them. How can you feel differently—after all they've done to you?"

"Look where we are, Cassa," Evander said sharply. "It doesn't look like killing the chancellor did us any good, did it? As far as I can tell, our parents are still prisoners, the council is still in power, and we'll all be dead by morning. I hope it was worth it."

The flaring anger inside her dimmed. Her chest was so tight, she thought her lungs might collapse at any moment.

"I couldn't do it." The words were barely a whisper. Even now, Solan was recovering, gathering his strength, readying for the revenge that had been centuries in the making. It occurred to Cassa that whatever came next was entirely her fault. Whatever was taken, whatever was lost. She was to blame. Aden. Kira. Reed. Rowen. Nima. Aden. Kira—

"What?" Alys asked. She was looking in her direction, but Cassa could only make a dull outline of her features.

"I couldn't kill him." Admitting it didn't hurt any less the second time. She still wasn't sure she'd done the right thing—back there in the pouring rain with Dane staring down the barrel of her gun, it hadn't even been about right or wrong. It was about pulling the trigger, and she just couldn't.

"Oh, for seers' sake," Evander muttered, leaning his head back against the wall. "I can't believe this is how it ends."

Cassa squeezed her eyes shut. The tightness in her chest was scalding now, burning up the back of her throat. She'd stopped breathing, and she couldn't remember how to start again. She tried to fully understand her own guilt. Tried to wrap herself in it, to drown in it. But it didn't feel real. What felt real, even after all this time, was being told that her parents were dead. That their bodies had been burned. That there would be no good-byes. What felt real was the crushing weight of her own failure. Solan had been right. There was nothing great about her after all.

She kept her eyes closed, kept her hands choked into fists until they went numb. She thought she'd already lost everything, but it turned out there had been more to lose. She knew without opening her eyes, without seeing their faces, that she'd lost the last people in the world that she loved. A sob was building inside her, but she forced it down. No one said anything more.

FORTY

VESPER

VESPER listened to the muted ringing of the eleventh bell and tried to keep her mind from wandering to the fond, distant memory of her bed. The past couple of hours had been a study in the art of focus. Whenever she let her guard down, even for a moment, Crispin would find his way to another memory. She refused to give him anything, even though that refusal was more on principle than anything else. He would have already read her uncle's memories before coming to her. The council had to know she wasn't an unwitting pawn in her uncle's schemes, but apparently they wanted her confession. They had always been precise about matters like these. They were ruthless with dissenters but clever enough to keep every judgment seemingly aboveboard. If their corruption ever came to light, it wouldn't be because of their own carelessness.

Now that Vesper could barely keep her eyes open, she was having a hard time remembering why she was resisting—especially when Crispin looked as fresh-faced as when they had begun, sipping the tea he'd had a guard bring him and making polite conversation as if they were two old friends having a chat. The council was going to execute her anyway. She just wanted some sleep.

But she couldn't. There was one thing they couldn't have learned from her uncle's memories. One crucial fact that she had to keep from the council as long as possible if there was any hope of seeing this thing through. They still had the poison. They still had a chance.

"Vesper, I assure you, I find this as tiring as you do." Crispin set his cup on the saucer with a tiny *plink*.

"Unlikely," Vesper said, straining with effort as she felt the invisible fingers tugging at the threads of her mind. He was very subtle, and he was very good. She wasn't going to be able to hold out much longer.

"You know I'll get to the memories eventually," he murmured.

She didn't know if he had caught a glimpse of something that betrayed her hopelessness or if he was just stating the obvious. She said nothing. He was rooting around again, his solemn eyes roving across her features. With a burst of defiance, she concentrated on spinning her memories into the roiling storm that had made him dizzy during their last encounter. The results were equally satisfying this time around.

Crispin squeezed his eyes shut and turned his head. He wasn't fast enough to hide his nauseated expression. Vesper allowed herself a small, private smile.

"I know you took those memories from Cassandra Valera to hide them from me," he said, once he'd regained some equilibrium. He didn't look at her. "And I know you've been doing the same with your uncle."

"You don't have any proof of that."

"We don't—" He stopped himself short and frowned.

We don't need proof.

She wondered if the frown was at his near slip of the truth or at the implication behind it. The councilors liked to have all their papers in order, but at the end of the day they would rid themselves of anyone they deemed a threat. What was legality but semantics, anyway?

"They don't want you dead," Crispin said, after a few moments of tense silence. "For seers' sake, you're just a kid."

Vesper bristled but held her tongue. It wasn't as if he was much older than her. And she carried more inside her now than most people would in a lifetime. The memory of every memory she'd ever taken was entangled with her own. Other people's childhoods, other people's nightmares, other people's plans and dreams and regrets, knotted up inside her head. She always gave memories back, but the imprints remained, much the way a bright landscape stayed seared on her eyelids for just a moment when she closed her eyes. Other people might be able to forget, but she never could.

It occurred to her that if anyone could understand that, it would be Crispin. Didn't he see the echoes of people's pasts in their every expression, their every gesture? Didn't he know what it was like to be an intruder in other people's minds?

"If the council really doesn't want me dead," she said, "then stop interrogating me so that I can get some sleep."

To her surprise, Crispin stood up. He walked out of the room without another word, and for a few seconds Vesper just stared at the closed door in confusion. Minutes passed. She let herself bask in the hope that he was actually going to leave her alone. They had very generously left her uncuffed, so she buried her face in her arms and shut her eyes with hazy relief.

The bliss lasted a couple of minutes more, until the door opened again. Vesper didn't move. Let Crispin try to read something from the top of her head if he was so desperate for answers.

"Vesper."

She shot up at her uncle's voice. Ansel stood just inside the room with Crispin at his shoulder. Behind them a guard loomed in the corridor. Her uncle looked dead on his feet, but he was still standing at least.

"Have a seat, Chancellor," said Crispin, moving the teacup aside.

Vesper glared at Crispin as Ansel slowly lowered himself into the chair, using the tabletop for support. If he thought that bringing her uncle into this was going to damage her focus, he was going to be sorely disappointed. Crispin's eyes weren't on her though. He was watching Ansel, his expression unreadable.

"Are you all right?" her uncle asked her, folding his hands in front of him on the table. He was somehow older than the last time she'd seen him—only hours ago. The wrinkles folded into his features were starker. His usually bright eyes were dim and sunken. Vesper could see every vein on the backs of his mottled, tremulous hands. Even his attire seemed wilted. His shirt collar, which had been so impeccably starched at the beginning of the evening, drooped to his shoulders. His maroon silk tie was loosened almost to the point of slipping off his neck entirely. The sleeves of his jacket were speckled with mud.

"I'm fine," Vesper managed. "Are you—"

He lifted one hand in a vague, dismissive gesture, and she bit down on her words. Even as weary and bedraggled as he was, the chancellor could command a room with ease.

"Listen to me very closely, Vesper." He reached across the table to cup both her hands in his own. His skin was icy cold. "The council is offering you amnesty if you'll give Crispin access to your memories. They just want to make sure there aren't any more threats."

Vesper swallowed hard, trying to find in his gaze what he wasn't saying. Surely there was something he wasn't saying. Surely he didn't intend for her to give up now. The councilors had made it abundantly clear that they didn't care how many innocent lives Solan ruined with his far-reaching rook abilities as long as he kept providing them with the prophecies that kept them in power. They would do anything to keep him alive and under their thumb—even execute the high chancellor.

But there was one thing Crispin couldn't have gleaned from Ansel's memories. Ansel didn't know where the vial of poison was right now. She never told him she'd given it to Cassa, and even Vesper didn't know what had happened to it after that. Maybe it was still safe. A small hope. Vesper couldn't give up their last chance—however slim—of stopping Solan.

"I—I can't," she said, aware of Crispin's eyes on her now. He wasn't trying to read her though, not yet. "What about you?"

"I want you to take the deal," her uncle said. "Just take it, Vesper."

He squeezed her hands, his gaze never leaving hers. Then she understood.

The memory he offered was waiting for her the moment she reached for it. The thread, invisible to everyone but her, snaked across their linked hands. Vesper let it dissolve into her, become her own. She saw the councilors at their table, gauzy and dreamlike beneath the ghost globes. The seat at the center of the table was empty. She listened to Councilor Adara make the offer, and it was just as he'd said. Vesper's life in exchange for her memories. *We don't want any more bloodshed*, said Adara. *But we have to protect our interests. You know we do.*

On its surface, that's all the memory was. An offer of mercy in exchange for security. But because Vesper was seeing it through Ansel's eyes, she saw so much more.

The twitch of disdain in Councilor Barwick's lips. He'd always been at odds with the chancellor. He'd tried to block Ansel's accession from the beginning—secretly, of course. The fascination with which Councilor Vicaro studied him, twisting a strand of hair around her finger. The way Councilor Andras stared at the table for the entire conversation.

The way Adara's mouth closed over her words as something like regret slid across her face. She wasn't happy, but her hands were tied by her fellow councilors. *You know we do.*

The council was lying.

Vesper knew she shouldn't be surprised, but the knowledge still burned in her chest as she gave the memory back to her uncle. Maybe that twinge of betrayal was actually his. She glanced at Crispin, who was eyeing them with marked suspicion. Any second now he would read the exchange in Ansel's face.

"Tell me, Crispin," she said, hoping to stall his attention a little longer—until she or her uncle could figure out what to do next. "Did you grow up wanting to be a lackey for a corrupt government, or was that a more recent ambition once you figured out how much it pays?"

His hand flew to the gold pin that designated his status as a sentient. Vesper wished that she could read his face as easily as he could read everyone else's, because his expression wasn't the contempt she'd expected or the shame she'd hoped for. It was something more twisting, more complex, and then it was gone. He stared back at her with cool indifference.

"An amusing question, coming from one of the most privileged girls in Eldra."

She felt the sting he'd intended but kept it off her face. She glanced in her uncle's direction, wondering if he was going to say something, but then the door opened.

"Not now," Crispin snapped at the guard who entered.

The guard didn't reply. Vesper saw his grip on the doorknob, knuckles white. With his other hand, he clutched his head. His lips were moving, but no sound came out. He was so pale that when he doubled over, Vesper thought he was going to retch all over the floor. Two seconds later he collapsed into a heap. He didn't move again.

Crispin moved toward him but stopped suddenly and grabbed the edge of the table to steady himself. He let out a gasp, color draining from his face, wide eyes fixed on nothing.

"Something's wrong." Now Ansel was cradling his head in both hands. She couldn't see his face. "It's the—it's—"

It was Solan. Vesper felt the tug in her mind a moment later, as if someone had gathered up a handful of threads and was pulling. She gritted her teeth and yanked the memories back out of his reach. A few of the threads snapped, splintering those memories, but they were still hers.

That was what mattered. Solan might be powerful, but he wasn't going to steal from her that easily.

She lunged across the table to grab one of Ansel's hands. She didn't know what she was doing. She didn't know if it could possibly work. She just knew she had to try. The tangle and whorl of her uncle's memories felt familiar to her now. As soon as she touched him, she could see the shimmering lengths of them, a thousand tiny strands, all flowing downward. Experimentally, she twined a bunch of them around her hand and pulled. They jerked free from the force that summoned them downward. Solan hadn't been expecting that.

She allowed herself a tiny smile and kept working. She couldn't just return them to her uncle for Solan to take again, so she let them coil up her arm. Once she started the process, the rest of the gleaming threads followed. The natural state of memories was to be connected, intertwined. That made it easier for her. Solan was still trying to take hold. She could feel his efforts reverberating through the strands, but she had the better connection.

Movement to her left caught her eye, and she remembered Crispin. He was still barely conscious, on his knees, head bowed, fingers still digging into the tabletop. Vesper watched him for a couple of seconds, then cursed. She reached out with her free hand to grab his. Instantly his own memories lit up around him, clearer and brighter than Ansel's. They flowed downward with less speed, probably because Solan was focusing his efforts on the chancellor now. Vesper wasn't sure if she could stand the split focus, but she took a deep breath and tried anyway.

Crispin's memories were less eager to her touch. She had to wind several different threads around her fingers before they finally reversed their direction, snaking up her wrist and arm. Her uncle's memories had crept all the way to her chest now, and soon Crispin's were lacing through, weaving an intricate pattern. Vesper had never held so much of another person before. Her focus was starting to fray. Her heart was hammering in her ears. She could feel the executioner, somewhere far below, begin to pull again, this time from her.

She couldn't keep her own memories in place while holding the threads of Ansel's and Crispin's on the surface. Her past was siphoning away, and while she scrambled to close herself off from Solan, the threads surrounding her began to unravel. She was going to lose everything.

She didn't know what else to do. She cut the strands connecting her to Ansel and Crispin. Immediately they both fell limp, and all their memories became hers.

Her mind was a prism of light, blinding and fractured. There were two other lifetimes tangled inside her. She remembered the smell of the farm on a summer morning—manure and hay and pungent green grass. That was her uncle's. She remembered the raking claws of hunger in her stomach and the haunting sight of her sister's eyes, dark and sunken in her skeletal face. That was Crispin's.

She felt a sharp tug, frighteningly strong. In a panic, she tugged back as hard as she could. Instantly the prism flashed with new light, somehow blinding and black at the same time. She remembered weeping in the darkness of a cavern, feeling the true weight of what it meant to be forgotten.

That was Solan's.

She realized, dimly, that when she pulled back her own memories, some of Solan's consciousness must have come with them. They were just shreds, fragments of threads that no longer gleamed.

A pearl-white alchemical solution, glittering in a crystal glass. Utter failure or eternal life—there was only one way to know.

A quicksilver dream of the council's demise. Of the chancellor's death. One gun, one bullet. So simple.

Blood turned to agony and the Blacksmith's daughter overhead, coaxing that agony deeper, deeper.

Then she was underground, in a bizarre sanctuary of civilization. The rest of the caverns felt far away and fading, and the world above hadn't felt real for a long time. Was that her own mind playing tricks, or was there something in the air down here? Finally, because she couldn't think of any other options, she moved to sit gingerly in one of the armchairs.

But that was one of Cassa's memories that she had borrowed, not Solan's. The threads in her mind were a tangled, thorny core, expanding slowly, threatening to choke out every other part of her being. She searched desperately for a memory that was her own—the smell of her mother's perfume or the day she'd realized she was a rook or the night she'd met Cassa for the first time. They were so thin and strained, she thought they might snap.

You can't hold on forever, came the voice in her head. She recognized it from memories that weren't her own, but this wasn't a memory. Solan was speaking to her. *I'll get what I want eventually.*

You'll have to get in line, she shot back. And then she drew into herself every bead of focus and every ounce of strength she possessed, and she took that tangled, thorny core, and she forced it to expand with obliterating speed, until it had filled every corner of her, until there wasn't room for anything else—even Solan.

For the length of a heartbeat, Vesper knew what it was to not exist. To be unmade. To forget.

Then she threaded herself through the memories, finding the cracks and filling the creases, and slowly, slowly, she untangled the knot. She returned Crispin's memories first, because his were the easiest to distinguish, utterly foreign as they were. Separating her uncle's took a bit more care. Many of them had been traded back and forth so often that the telltale gleam had almost worn off, as if even the memories weren't sure whom they belonged to anymore.

Only when she'd finished, only when Crispin and her uncle were beginning to stir and she felt reasonably certain that Solan wouldn't have the energy to try again for a little while at least—only then did she let herself fall unconscious.

FORTY-ONE

Evander

EVEN after all the time he'd spent underground the past few days, Evander still hated the dark. Somehow being surrounded by his sister and friends didn't make it any better. They were so close, but in the cloaking shadows they might as well be miles away. Newt was sitting against the wall opposite Evander, one knee hugged to his chest, the other leg outstretched. His foot was inches from Evander's ankle. He didn't seem to notice, but Evander couldn't stop thinking about how vast a distance those few inches felt. They hadn't touched since those agonizing minutes in Solan's chamber. Evander couldn't escape the image of Newt shaking, crying, looking like some part of his soul was being ripped away. In that moment, seeing Newt in so much pain, Evander was sure he would have done anything Solan wanted. Anything.

It scared him a little, to realize that. And it scared him to know that whatever Solan had taken from Newt, he hadn't given it back. The change was subtle and indefinable, but Evander could see it, could *feel* it. He didn't think there was anything he could do about it. He didn't even know how to broach the subject—assuming they had a chance to talk before their imminent execution.

He hadn't looked in Cassa's direction in almost half an hour. The tension in the small space was palpable and suffocating. When Solan had told them why she was gone, why she had left them behind, Evander had believed him. He knew Cassa too well. He'd always known that even when he would have given up anything for her, she wouldn't do the same for him. For them.

An untapped fury welled inside him. Evander didn't often move past mild exasperation. During his relationship with Cassa, he'd edged into full-blown annoyance a few times, because that was inevitable, but he'd never been *angry* at her before. She was foolhardy, but she'd never taken risks at their expense. He'd never once considered that maybe they would have been better off without her. Now he couldn't get that thought out of his head. It was a wicked, barbed thing, tangled as it was with the image of Newt. Shaking. Crying. Pieces of him being ripped away.

Alys nudged his shoulder with her own, and Evander blinked out of his reverie. She was watching him, her head tilted to the side, though he knew she couldn't see him any better than he could see her.

"How's your head?" Her voice barely audible, as if there were any chance of privacy in their cramped quarters.

"Still fine." It was the truth, mostly. He had a glaring headache, but his chest and ribs had taken the brunt of the damage. He didn't think anything was broken. There would definitely be bruises, but those were the least of his problems.

Alys shifted, and she seemed about to say something else. A shadow passing over the grate forestalled her. A key jolted in the lock, and the door swung open. Evander squinted up at the guard silhouetted in the doorway. He had his pistol drawn at his side, finger poised on the trigger.

"You," he said, gesturing toward Evander with his gun hand, which wasn't a particularly pleasant way to be summoned. "Come on."

Evander eyed the gun and didn't move.

"If it's all the same to you," he said, "I'd rather not climb all those stairs just to die at the top. Much less effort for everyone if you shoot me right here."

Newt made a startled noise and kicked his shin, although Evander couldn't tell if it was by accident or not. At the same time, Alys elbowed him in the ribs, which hurt worse than she'd probably intended. He felt a little guilty for rattling them, but he couldn't help it. To take any of this seriously was to admit he was afraid. He knew Cassa would be amused, but he wasn't about to look to her for camaraderie.

The guard was still staring at him, definitely not amused. His trigger finger was twitching. Evander let out a sigh and stood up, his vision lurching momentarily with the sudden movement. His head was pounding, but his ribs actually hurt less when he was standing. The guard stepped aside to let him through the doorway and slammed it shut behind him. Panic bubbled in Evander's chest as he realized he might have just seen the three of them for the last time. He started to turn, trying to think of something—anything—to say, but the guard grabbed his arm and yanked him down the corridor. It was the same man who had taken his coins. Evander could feel the silver that was securely buttoned in his jacket pocket. He curled his fingers, tugging experimentally on the coins.

The guard's hand flew to his pocket, his expression flickering between confusion and alarm. Evander had the thought that now was his chance to run, but of course there was nowhere to go. And there was the small matter of the gun. The guard caught on, and he grabbed the front of Evander's shirt and pushed him against the wall—thankfully with much less force than the captain had.

"Try that foreign magic again, and I *will* kill you now." He tapped the barrel of the gun against Evander's collarbone.

A laugh escaped Evander before he could stop it. More alarm and confusion on the guard's face. His death threats probably didn't get that reaction very often.

"Sorry," Evander said. "I was just imagining my sister's face if she heard you call bloodbonding magic."

The guard frowned but didn't reply. He grabbed Evander's arm and propelled him toward the stairs. Another guard waited for them at the top, lounging against the wall and picking his cuticles.

"What took so long?" he complained.

The first guard said nothing, just gave Evander a little shove. The three of them walked in silence through the Central Keep. Evander tried to find a clock, but there weren't any in the dim hallways they passed through. He thought they must be somewhere around the fourth bell. Time underground felt more like a hazy notion than a steady stream though. He couldn't be sure.

He recognized the route they were taking, the faded blue carpet, the series of tapestries depicting infallible prophecies. He lost count at twenty-seven, but he didn't think all fifty were represented. Would someone someday stitch a new tapestry if Solan's prophecy came to pass? These were the same halls he'd walked a few days ago. They were headed to the Judgment Hall.

The four councilors were seated when he entered through the grand double doors. Their hands were folded, expressions blank. The doors creaked shut behind him. The last time he'd been here, he'd had two silver coins in hand. He'd known exactly where he stood. He'd known the council was corrupt and the chancellor was a powermonger, and he'd never once imagined the truth of the executioner who lurked in the caverns beneath their feet.

The last time he'd been here, everything had made sense.

"Evander Sera," said one of the councilors, a woman with a broad, open face and curly hair shot through with gray. Her voice was low and oddly soothing. She had to be Tempest Adara, the oldest member of the council aside from the chancellor himself. There was a lit candle in front of her, casting her features in a warm, flickering glow so different from the ghost globes ensconced in silver that were suspended overhead.

"Where's the chancellor?" Evander asked, aware that he was interrupting what would probably be a very well-rehearsed summary of his crimes.

The councilors exchanged glances among themselves. It occurred to Evander that this was only the second time he'd seen them face-to-face, these people he'd been working against for so long. They had always been a vague, collective enemy. More a personification of hundreds of years of secrecy and corruption than four living, breathing human beings.

"Only a majority vote of the council is necessary to pass judgment," said one of the men, as if that were any sort of answer. He had a head of thick blond hair that looked entirely fake, and there were crumbs stuck to the front of his ceremonial robe. Presumably Grantham Barwick. Junior or Senior—Evander couldn't remember. Some Barwick or another had held a seat on the council since before the rebellion.

Councilor Adara opened her mouth to continue the recitation of his crimes, but Evander forestalled her again.

"Did you kill the chancellor?"

A satisfyingly awkward silence. None of the council members looked at each other this time. Maybe when Cassa couldn't do the deed, the councilors had done it themselves. There had to be a reason that Chancellor Dane had kept his plans for Solan a secret from them.

"The chancellor no longer presides over this council," said the other man, Roth Andras. His black hair was slicked back, and he sported an impressive mustache.

"A coup?"

"Nothing so dramatic." Delia Vicaro, the fourth councilor, wore a crown of tiny pink rosebuds in her dark hair. She looked like she might be wearing a ball gown under her robes. Probably she had been called away from some fete or another. "He has served the city well, but he's a very old man, ready to retire from the burdens of public life."

Evander wondered if he was really dead. And if so, what did that mean for his parents? He couldn't bring himself to ask, in case the council didn't know about them already. Besides, it wasn't as if they would tell him the truth. The council's unwavering dedication to their version of events, even when they knew he would be dead before he could tell anyone the truth, was impressive. Maybe the councilors over the years had preserved their power for so long not through wiles but rather simple diligence.

Once again Councilor Adara tried to continue his sentencing, and once again Evander interrupted her.

"We know all about your pet executioner," he said. "Not a very pleasant fellow, as it turns out."

Adara's annoyance was in danger of leaking past her careful, impassive mask. Evander didn't need coins to make a nuisance of himself.

"It might interest you to know," he went on, "that he now has a bloodbond with mirasma. Soon he'll no longer need your elixir, which means he'll no longer need any of you."

He'd hoped to unsettle them with that information, but if the councilors were surprised, they didn't show it.

"Your concern for our safety is touching," said Councilor Vicaro, her pouting pink lips thinning into a smirk. "But we have the matter well in hand."

"If you had the matter in hand, he wouldn't be divesting innocent people of their entire consciousness on a whim," Evander shot back. Then, seeing the councilors' expressions, he added, "Or maybe you don't care about the damage as long as your precious prophecies keep coming."

He knew his words had finally struck a nerve. Vicaro scowled at him. Barwick harrumphed and became suddenly engrossed in dusting the crumbs from his robes. Andras and Adara both dropped their gazes.

"Solan Tavish can be made to see reason," Councilor Adara said, her words painstakingly precise. She picked up a stick of black wax in front of her and held it over the candle's flame. "Unfortunately, as you've proved time and time again, you and your friends cannot."

Evander stared at the softening wax, mesmerized as she rotated it slowly. He couldn't help but think of his mother melting the wax they used to seal bottles of medicine. He couldn't help but think of home, and how he was never going to see it again. Would his parents be executed too? Were they even still alive? He had to blink himself free of the thought.

"Yes, we're a real danger to the city," he said. "Unlike the monster your predecessors created who's been devouring memories at his leisure."

The sarcasm took more out of him than usual. He was very tired now. The manacles felt so much heavier than they had a minute ago. Distantly he registered the chiming of the midnight bell.

Councilor Adara didn't rise to his remark. She only dribbled a small pool of wax onto the paper in front of her. Maybe she'd decided not to waste any more time with a recitation of his crimes. There had to be a lot of them piled up by now.

"It is the duty of this council to sentence you once more to death, to be served without the customary rites." Adara stamped the wax with the seal of the citadel. It felt more final than it had during his first sentencing.

Councilor Barwick gestured to the guards, betraying his eagerness for the proceedings to be complete. As they took Evander's arms to lead him away, Councilor Adara looked up from his sealed fate. Her eyes were sharp despite the wrinkled age in her papery brown skin. She considered him for a few seconds, and then right as his escorts turned him toward the door, she spoke.

"Do you believe in the Slain God, Evander?"

He looked over his shoulder at her, taking a moment to wonder what she was really asking. Her fellow councilors were eyeing her warily. The room was quiet except for the creaking of the guards' leather holsters as they shifted their weight uncomfortably beside him. And his own uneven breaths. His own thudding heart.

"Sometimes," he said.

"Then sometimes, perhaps, you understand that everything we do is in service to his memory. To preserve the precious gifts he gave us in death. Divine blood runs in our veins. That is not a responsibility to be taken lightly."

Councilor Adara looked as if she truly believed every word she was saying. Evander wanted to point out that since diviners, sentients, rooks, and seers weren't allowed to sit on the council, none of the councilors actually had any divine blood in their veins. As he looked across their self-satisfied faces, he understood for a brief moment the loathing that Cassa wore like a second skin. The council was meant to carry the burdens of the city, to protect and to serve. Instead, they sat here beneath a mosaic of a distant past, shielded by tradition, and fighting only to preserve their own significance in a world that had long ago left Eldra to decay. The responsibility that had driven him here wasn't to a dead god but to the city full of people who had been left behind.

But it hadn't been enough, and he was so tired. Maybe the councilors had preserved their power for so long merely by outlasting everyone else. There wasn't anything he could say that would make a difference here, so he said nothing and let the guards lead him away.

Once in the corridor, he heard the familiar cadence of Cassa's voice as she came around the corner, cuffed and flanked by a pair of guards. Whatever mocking comment she was making died on her lips when she met his gaze. Her hair had fallen across one eye, and for a split second she was that younger, softer version of herself—that person she might have been in a different life. Some forgotten part of himself ached. He knew he ought to say something, but no words came, and his escorts propelled him in the opposite direction. The council really wasn't wasting any time with this second sentencing. Alys would be mollified by the efficiency at least.

He thought the guards would take him back to the dungeons to await his execution, but they were headed through unfamiliar corridors. When they reached a barred wooden door, Evander's heart skipped a beat. Fear burned through his veins, and for a moment his exhaustion was forgotten, drowned in the certainty of what awaited beyond that door.

The night air was damp with a recent rain, and he splashed through a few puddles pooled in the cobblestones before one of the guards jerked him to a stop. The clouds had cleared enough that moonlight shone through. Once his eyes adjusted, Evander could see that they were in the middle of a small, empty courtyard. The walls were high, but a cool wind dipped in, pricking his exposed skin. The night was the same as it had been a few hours ago. This was the same wind that had whipped through the valley as he and Newt crossed to the wood. This was the same moon that had glinted off the roof of the Blacksmith's cottage. Not so long ago, he'd kissed Newt in the shadow of that cottage, swept by the wind and surrounded by silver.

That was what he tried to think about now. That, and none of the rest. Not the executioner beneath the citadel or the council in their Judgment

Hall. Not his parents, somewhere alone in captivity because he hadn't been able to save them. Not the weight of the iron around his wrists or the bite of stone as the guards pushed him to his knees. Not the click of the pistol's hammer behind his head. Not the painful breath he drew in that would be his last.

FORTY-TWO

ALYS

ALYS had lost track of time, but she knew that Evander and Cassa should have been back by now. Even taking into account their penchant for back talk, how long could it possibly take for the council to pronounce a sentence they'd already decided on? She tried not to let her mind run through the possibilities, but it ran anyway, circling around and around them until she was dizzy and exhausted. Her chest started to constrict, and she could feel the panic creeping from her brain into her body. *Not again, not again, not again.*

She'd been on the verge of losing control after the guard came for Evander, and then when a different guard showed up shortly thereafter to take Cassa, the maelstrom spun wild. She didn't want the council to decide her death or her parents' deaths. She didn't want to die. But more than anything, she didn't want to watch her brother and her friends die *first*. They were in this together, they had always been in this together, they couldn't leave her alone, they couldn't—

Dimly, she had recognized that Cassa was kneeling in front of her, despite the guard hovering impatiently at the threshold. It was Cassa's fault they were down here in the first place. If only she'd told them the truth. If only she hadn't left them behind.

Cassa took both Alys's hands in hers. Alys hadn't realized she was driving her fingernails into her palms, but they burned as Cassa's fingertips slid across them.

"Let's go," the guard said. His voice felt so far away. Her vision was growing hazy and bright at the edges as her thoughts roiled and raged.

"Hold on," Cassa told him. She tilted her head to look Alys in the eye. "Alys."

If only she'd told them the truth. If only she hadn't left them behind. Alys ignored her. It wasn't difficult, with the world falling away piece by piece. Soon it wouldn't exist at all. Soon she would be alone.

"Alys," Cassa repeated, giving her hands a squeeze. "Remember that time you fished me out of an underground lake just before a creature with probably very sharp teeth dragged me down to my death?"

"I said, let's *go*." The guard rapped his pistol against the door.

"And I said hold on," Cassa shot back, her eyes never leaving Alys's.

Alys managed a short breath. Then another. Though he hadn't made a sound, she knew that Newt was staring at them both with marked concern. Cassa was going to get herself shot right here in their prison cell. So typical.

"What about it?" Alys asked, surprised at how steady the sound of her own voice was despite everything.

Cassa's lips twitched into a smile.

"Nothing," she said with a shrug. "It's just a great story. The bards are going to love it."

Then she stood up and turned toward the guard. Alys watched her, realizing belatedly that the maelstrom had slowed, her vision was clearing, and Cassa had just given her something small and simple but so important.

"Doesn't matter how many times I save your life," Alys called after her. "You're still not immortal."

Cassa threw her and Newt a backward glance. Silhouetted by the lantern light, chin high, heedless of the gun at her chest, she really did look like someone the bards would sing about in the centuries to come.

"I dare anyone to prove it," Cassa said with a grin. Then the guard slammed the door shut.

That had been a long time ago. Too long. Alys had kept the panic at bay for a while, but it was circling back, ever closer, ever hungrier. She raised her eyes to meet Newt's, thinking that if he wasn't worried, she could let herself breathe. But if he was trying to put on a brave face for her, he didn't do a very good job. Even in the shadows she could see the apprehension in every line of his features. She felt sick.

The voice of the guard on duty yanked her out of the downward spiral. His words were indistinct, but not so much that she couldn't make out what he was saying.

"What are you doing down here?" he asked.

Alys climbed to her feet and pressed her ear against the metal grating. The reply was softer, lost in the corridor of stone. The guard coughed uncomfortably.

"I don't think that—"

Quiet. A faint, muffled thump. More quiet. And then:

"Cassa? Alys?"

Behind her, Alys could hear the rattle of iron as Newt jumped to his feet as well. That meant she wasn't imagining it. It really was Vesper.

"Here," she called out and banged the iron of her cuff on the grating.

A few moments later, Vesper's face appeared. Her face glistened with sweat, and she was panting like she was either exhausted or in pain. She turned the key in the lock and yanked the door open. Alys had the urge to hug her but stopped short at how strangely fragile she looked. She wavered slightly on her feet. Her hair was falling from its pins in frizzy tendrils, and she was ghostly pale.

"Are you hurt?" Alys asked as Vesper inserted a smaller key into her cuffs.

"No. Just not feeling quite myself at the moment." She flashed a mirthless smile and ducked her head over Newt's cuffs. "Where're Evander and Cassa?"

"The guards took Evander maybe half an hour ago," Newt said. "And Cassa pretty soon after."

Vesper's lips flattened into a grim line, but she didn't say anything.

"We have to find them," Alys said.

"We've got to find a way to get through the citadel undetected first," said Newt.

Vesper led the way toward the alcove. She was shaking her head.

"There was an . . . incident in the interrogation room. A guard is dead. One of the council's sentients and the chancellor have gone missing. The alarm will be raised any minute now. Soon every corridor will be crawling with guards."

"What happened?" Newt asked.

"I think the less you know the better," Vesper said. "But the rook is getting stronger. And bolder."

"No, I mean here." Newt nudged the unconscious guard with his foot. "Did you hit him with something?"

"Something like that," Vesper muttered, tugging nervously on her sleeve.

"We can't leave here without Evander," Alys said. "Cassa too. I don't care how many guards are up there."

"I might have an idea," Newt said, scooping something up from the table.

"What?" Alys asked.

Newt turned and extended his hand, palm up. He uncurled his fingers to reveal the rook's bone runes.

"You could guide us to them," he said.

Alys's heart stuttered, and she pushed Newt's hand away.

"I can't read those," she said.

"I thought diviners could read anything," Vesper said.

"Maybe some diviners, but I can barely read coins." She shot a glare at Newt. "You know that."

He didn't say anything, just watched her in that composed, careful way of his. She couldn't believe he was putting her in this position. Putting the weight of Evander and Cassa's lives on her shoulders, knowing that Alys always cracked under pressure. It was true that she'd read the coins in the crypts when they'd had no other choice. That she'd rowed alone across that silent lake to save Cassa. That a long time ago, she had followed the daughter of the city's most notorious rebels toward a new, fiery purpose, changing her life irrevocably in the process.

Why did every challenge have to feel like the first she'd ever faced, when Cassa and Evander and Newt always grew sharper, stronger, braver? Why, then, was it never any easier?

Her lungs were aching, and the edge of her vision was bright and blurry. Her head whirled in the maelstrom, uncontrollable, unstoppable, incurable. Sharper, stronger, braver. She could never be any of those things. She could never be. She could never. She could.

Alys took the runes from Newt and spilled them onto the tabletop. He and Vesper stepped back to give her space, and she leaned closer to the runes. At first, she saw nothing. Just a handful of old bones and forgotten symbols of a bygone era. Nothing here could help them. The corners of her vision were still painfully bright, and the panic still lurched in her chest, but she wouldn't let it control her. Nothing. There was nothing.

Then she saw too much. A spasm of futures. Too many to differentiate. Some of them blindingly tragic and others comfortingly sweet.

She blinked, reminding herself what her mother had taught her. How the variations of the future were like hundreds of pieces of paper, held up to the light. Sometimes the images overlapped, sometimes they didn't. Alys just had to find the boldest images, the ones that repeated the most.

Two guards in front of a moonlit chapel. Meaningless. And not what she was looking for.

A cold hand wrapped around a colder vial. Still not what she needed.

Evander. She seized on the image, letting everything else fall away.

From there it was easier to work backward, expanding her focus until she could see a whole picture, until she could see what they had to do and what would happen if they didn't. Bile rose in her throat at the last image, and for a moment she was more terrified than she'd ever been in her life.

It didn't have to happen that way though. There was time to stop it.

"We have to hurry," she said, sweeping the runes into her hand and shoving them into her pocket. "They're going to execute him."

She led the way up the stairs. She hadn't seen Cassa, but if she was in trouble too, she was going to have to hold her own for a while. Evander's future was too precarious, too immediate for Alys to possibly ignore. Cassa would understand.

Their path was laid out in her mind's eye like a map. She didn't know the layout of the citadel, but she knew the way to Evander. Every turn, every detour, every corner to pause at while waiting for guards to pass, every doorway to hurry through while avoiding watchful eyes.

When they reached the wooden door, it was unbarred, and Alys knew they still had a chance. She didn't warn the others what to expect. She didn't even slow down. She yanked open the door and threw her shoulder into the back of the man she knew would be standing there. A shot rang out, echoing across stone, but it went wide.

The man spun around, and Alys stared down the black barrel of his gun for a heartbeat. Then Evander found his feet and tackled the guard to the ground with much more success than she'd had. A second guard emerged from the shadows, pointing his pistol but unable to fire while Evander and his partner were locked together in struggle. Alys opened her mouth to shout a warning—for whom, she didn't know—but in the next instant Newt was at the man's back, one arm tight against his throat. The man flailed, firing wildly. Alys could have sworn she felt the heat of the bullet on her arm.

Vesper stepped out of the doorway and placed her hand on the man's cheek. He tried to jerk away from her, but Newt held him in place. A few seconds later the man slumped to the ground, unconscious or dead—Alys didn't know. Vesper swayed on her feet, gripping her head, and Newt caught her by the elbow. At Alys's feet, Evander had managed to knock the gun from the guard's hand. Alys kicked it away, and it skittered across the cobblestones into shadow. She was trying to decide if she should try kicking the guard too, but Evander got a hold of the back of his head and slammed his forehead into the ground. The man fell limp.

For a few seconds, the courtyard was deathly still. Then Alys's mind caught up with what had just happened, with what had *almost* just happened, and she choked back a sob.

"Are you hurt?" she asked, trying to help Evander disentangle himself from the unconscious man.

Newt was there too, and together they got Evander onto his feet. He was gasping for breath and looking between the two of them like he was looking at ghosts, like he didn't believe they could possibly be standing there.

"I've been worse," he managed.

Newt still had a hold on Evander's arm. From the look on his face, he was either about to laugh or cry or pass out. Maybe all three. The unmistakable heat between them, which had been simmering for a couple of months now, wasn't something that Alys had ever experienced, but that didn't mean she was oblivious to it. She decided now was a good time to check on Vesper, who was leaning against the wall of the citadel.

"I'm fine," Vesper said, before she could ask anything. She didn't meet Alys's eyes.

Alys looked down at the guard. She could see now that his chest was moving with slow breaths.

"I didn't take anything from him," Vesper said quietly. "Memories are delicate. If you twist them around enough, the mind shuts down to protect them. It's not permanent."

"Thank you," Alys said. "We'd be dead if it weren't for you."

Vesper looked up at her, her eyebrows raised. If she'd been expecting some sort of fear or rebuke, Alys wasn't going to be the one to give it to her. It was true that the council and Solan had made a habit of taking advantage of people with the gifts at their disposal, but Vesper wasn't like them.

"You're welcome," Vesper said, still hesitant.

"I don't just mean for tonight," Alys said. "Telling your uncle about Cassa's plan was the best decision. I think Cassa must see that too, even if she'll never admit it."

The corners of Vesper's lips curled up in a small, sad smile. The boys came over before she could reply.

"Can I get a little help here?" Evander extended his manacled wrists.

Vesper dug the key out of her pocket and freed him.

"Where do we go next?" Newt glanced at Alys.

"I guess we should find Cassa," Alys said. A tiny part of her wanted to just let Cassa lie in the bed she'd made—isn't that what Cassa herself would tell them to do? But just like the first time they'd escaped the dungeons, leaving Cassa behind was never an option. Not really.

"She must still be in the Judgment Hall," Evander said. "I saw her before—"

He cut himself off at the sound of the bell ringing the quarter hour. For a few seconds, no one said anything. They were all thinking the same thing. With every passing minute, Solan was closer to being free.

"There's still time to stop Solan," Vesper said. "His next dose of mirasma is at the first morning bell, and I know where they deliver the elixir."

"We have to help Cassa," Alys said. "And we have to find our parents too."

"Your parents are safe," Vesper said. "They're in a house in the upper echelon. No one can hurt them there."

"Except your uncle." Evander's eyes flashed darkly.

Vesper shook her head.

"I tried to convince him not to take them, but he was afraid you wouldn't agree to help otherwise. He never would have hurt them though. I swear, they're safe."

Alys studied Vesper's face, wishing she were a sentient instead of a diviner, wishing that trust wasn't always such a risk. Things couldn't be that simple though.

"I believe you," Alys said. "But we still have to save Cassa."

"And we have to stop Solan too." Evander pushed a shaky hand through his hair and squinted toward the sky as if it might have a suggestion.

"The vial of poison is still in the dungeon," Newt said.

"We can't go back there," Vesper said. "We'll be walking right into the guards' arms."

"If that's the only way to kill Solan," Alys said, "I'm not sure we have a choice."

"I can do it." Newt's quiet confidence was, as always, a relief. "I can get in and out without being seen."

Evander frowned at him.

"You can't go alone. It's too dangerous."

"Alone is the only way I won't be seen," Newt replied, pushing his sweat-damp curls out of his eyes. "And besides, it's not any more dangerous than going after Cassa alone, which is exactly what you were about to volunteer to do."

Evander blinked at him, and Newt's thin lips twitched with a smile. His pale skin was flushed, but with exertion and not embarrassment. Alys couldn't help but think he looked a little older than he had when all this had begun. Sharper, stronger, braver. And the last time Evander had looked at anyone the way he was looking at Newt right now was four years ago, when he'd first met Cassa.

Despite everything, Alys felt her own lips curving into a smile.

"We have to split up. It's our only option," Vesper said. "I have to get something from my uncle's study."

"I think the chancellor's errands can wait until after our heroic escapades are over," Evander said.

"Not this one." Vesper gnawed briefly on her lip, like she was deciding something. "He told me where to find your pardons, signed and sealed. If we—if we survive this, they might be enough to keep you all safe."

If she was honest with herself, Alys was surprised that the chancellor intended to keep their bargain after all that had happened. Surprised but grateful. Even if it was a useless gesture.

"The council's not just going to grant us pardons and be done with it," she said.

"Executions require a majority vote, but pardons need only the chancellor's seal," Vesper said. "If the council insists on abiding by one law, then they are bound by the other as well."

Evander snorted in disbelief. Even Newt was shaking his head. Alys agreed with them—the council members would find a way around any law to get what they wanted. They'd probably invent some prophecy to lend themselves credibility.

Then again, the council could have ordered the guards to kill them in the crypts, instead of insisting on a proper sentencing. Even though the chancellor had obviously fallen out of favor, he was still the chancellor. Maybe a pardon from him could make a difference.

"Fine," she said. "If you're sure you want to risk it."

Vesper nodded. "I could use your help divining a route though," she said. "His study is in the southeast tower, on the other side of the keep."

Alys's heart clenched at the thought. Another challenge. Never any easier, but maybe she was getting used to that, because her breathing stayed even.

"I'll go with you," she said.

Evander went to the nearby unconscious guard and stooped down to unbutton his jacket pocket. The silver coins rolled free and up his arm as if they were eager to be home.

"Keep them," Alys said, when Evander offered them to her. She pulled the runes out of her pocket. "These work just as well."

Evander's eyebrows arched at that, but he didn't say anything. The coins flew neatly into his hip pocket.

"Meet at the chapel on the eastern wall of the citadel," Vesper said. "The one they rebuilt a few years ago. Do you know it?"

In her mind's eye, Alys saw two guards in front of a moonlit chapel. Her heart began to beat just a little faster. Newt and Evander nodded.

"We have less than an hour," Alys said, "so don't get sidetracked."

"What, no final words to inspire us?" Evander asked, wrapping his arm around her shoulders and pulling her into a side hug.

She looked up at him, remembering the morning, when he'd told her that he didn't take things seriously so that he didn't have to be afraid. Maybe that was something she'd come to depend on. Maybe bravery was contagious.

"How about, 'if you die, I'll never speak to you again'?" she replied.

"Or, 'failing is better than not trying at all'," Vesper said, "because either way, you're dead."

"'If you believe you can succeed, then maybe you'll be too distracted to notice when you don't,'" said Newt.

"All right, all right." Evander raised his hands in mock surrender. "Consider me inspired. Let's just save our backstabbing fearless leader and get this over with."

FORTY-THREE

Cassa

ON the way to the Judgment Hall, Cassa wondered why so many of the threadbare tapestries and faded rugs looked identical in the citadel—endless iterations of the same corridors. She might as well have never left the crypts. It made her miss the city. The realization came with a pang in her chest. She missed the crooked streets and bright chipped paint, the way the hand-carved signs creaked in the wind, and the ease with which she could blend in or stand out, depending on her needs. Maybe more than anything, she missed the way the city was *hers*, every curve and corner of it. The firebrands had laid claim to Eldra a long time ago. Even though the citadel had never fallen and the rebellion was dead, the city would always belong to the people, not the council—no matter what they chose to believe, hidden here behind their stone walls.

The city was the only inheritance she had from her parents: the city and the responsibility to somehow protect it. She was pretty sure she'd failed, considering she was moments away from being sentenced to death. This time the sentence would probably stick.

When she finally stood before the great double doors of the Judgment Hall, her hands were shaking. One of the guards yanked open a door while the other shoved her inside. She stumbled forward a few steps and heard the door shut with a thud. The guards took their places on either side of her, a few steps behind. The councilors' murmured conversations fell silent as they looked at her.

It was so different than before. The first time she had been in this room, the future felt bright and infinite and entirely hers. Now she couldn't help but think that in breaking away from Solan's infallible prophecy, she'd given up her future too. Maybe there was no place for her in the world anymore, since she hadn't done the one thing she was meant to do.

"Cassandra Valera." Councilor Adara clasped her hands over the document she'd been perusing.

"Cassa," she replied automatically. She cast a glance over all of them. Their faces were only passingly familiar, but still she knew them each by name, by history, by crime—just as her parents had. Her father was adamant that they always know their enemies just as well as their friends. Maybe that was the real reason he'd made her memorize the fifty infallible prophecies. All that knowledge was useless now.

"Can you please just seal the order and be done with it?" Delia Vicaro yawned and rolled her neck before shooting a pointed glare at Adara. "It's obvious that these brats care as much about your precious protocols as we do."

She cut Cassa a look, as if expecting some kind of affirmation. Adara very deliberately ignored her and continued.

"You stand here before the high council faced with charges of high treason."

"Among other things," Grantham Barwick muttered. He was pushing a pen around the table with one finger, every bit as bored as his fellow councilor.

Cassa fought the urge to roll her eyes. Standing here before them, seeing them as they truly were, didn't make her hate them any less. But it did make them less sinister and more ridiculous. Councilor Adara did roll her eyes.

"We're in the middle of an unprecedented crisis right now," she said. "Surely it's not too much to ask for a little decorum?"

"Is it true," Councilor Vicaro asked, ignoring Adara, "that you tried to kill Chancellor Dane tonight?"

Cassa blinked at the unexpected directness.

"Why do you ask?" she said carefully. "Are you disappointed that I didn't succeed?"

"I'm just trying to figure out whose side you're actually on." Councilor Vicaro leaned forward on her elbows, twirling the emerald ring on her finger around and around. "You tout the ideals of the rebellion, but we know you made a deal with the chancellor after you escaped. And tonight we've learned that you somehow managed to bloodbond Solan Tavish to mirasma in an attempt to free him. Surely you can understand our confusion."

Cassa ground her teeth, hating that she had to stand here while they reveled in their supposed moral superiority. Hating that she didn't even know whose side she was on anymore. She'd always been on her parents' side, but now they were gone. For a while she had her friends, but then she'd betrayed them for a chance at revenge. Now what did she have?

I can only do what I think is right, Vesper had said. Would it have been right to kill the chancellor as payment for his crimes? Or were crimes only crimes when you were on the wrong side of the citadel walls? The chancellor had agreed that his hands weren't clean in any of this, but neither were the councilors' or Solan's. Neither were hers.

At least when she was following the prophecy, she didn't have to worry about right or wrong—just what had been foretold. Maybe that's why the Slain God's religion had lasted all this time. No one remembered how to decide for themselves anymore. No one wanted to believe that their mistakes were preventable. If your future was foretold, then you weren't accountable for it. All your decisions and mistakes belonged to a seer's dream, a diviner's runes.

If they own your future, then they own you, her mother had told her years ago. Cassa could still feel the faint caress of soft fingers in her hair. *Never let that happen.*

"The rebellion was only ever trying to protect the city," she said. It wasn't really an answer, but it was all she had. "I know that may be a foreign concept to you."

Councilor Adara straightened in her seat and pressed her palms against the tabletop. Her wrinkled hands showed none of the telltale trembling of age.

"Everything we've ever done is for Eldra," she said, "to keep it from falling to ruin while the rest of the world forgets what once made it great."

And for a moment—just a moment—Cassa believed her.

Then her attention was drawn to the ghost globes suspended over the council's heads. They had begun to sway. Only slightly, in a phantom breeze. There was enough light in the room that the shadows shifted minimally, and none of the councilors had glanced up. If the guards behind her had noticed, they weren't saying anything.

Cassa's gaze slid back to the councilors.

"If you really want to do what's best for Eldra, then you will let me and my friends go so that we can stop Solan Tavish before the entire city is at his mercy."

"We have our reasons for keeping him alive," said Councilor Barwick, crossing his arms.

Their power was all that mattered to them. It was all that had ever mattered. Maybe the right thing to do would be to just accept her death and let Solan wreak his revenge on the council. For a heartbeat, the thought was actually tempting, but then she noticed that the ghost globes had picked up momentum. They now swung from side to side. Perfectly synchronized pendulums. She considered the delicate silverwork encasing the globes and what she knew about the swirling Alchemist's Fire within. She looked back at Councilor Adara.

"Last chance," Cassa said.

A definite frown had carved its way into Adara's features. She shook her head. "The council has already passed its judgment. The sentence for treason is death."

The globe on the left stopped swinging, while the other two continued their arc to the right, reached their apex, and hung there for just a moment too long to be natural.

“Then I guess I’ll see you all in hell,” Cassa said, squeezing her eyes shut.

The crash of glass against glass and a flash that seared white-hot against her eyelids came a second later. Cries of pain. She told herself to move. She had to move. She had to—

Someone grabbed her arm and yanked her backward. She pivoted, throwing back her elbow before she opened her eyes. She missed and almost lost her balance, but the hand on her arm kept her upright. Evander. He winced at her and tugged her arm again. This time she followed him through the open door. One of the guards lunged as if to grab her but, judging from how easily she avoided him, he still hadn’t recovered his full vision.

“Hurry.” Evander pushed the door shut with his back and took hold of her wrist. He was holding a key.

Once she was free from the manacles, Evander helped her hold the door shut—the guards were fighting to open it—while she looped the chain through the two handles and then interlocked the cuffs. Crude, but it would hold. Evander pocketed the keys, and they ran.

FORTY-FOUR

Newt

HIS father had told him once that in any situation the right choice usually didn't feel like a choice at all. Newt hated the way that even now the guiding voice in his head was his father's. Had defecting from the rebellion felt like a choice? Or had his father felt the way Newt did right now as he crept through the corridors? Like this was the only thing worth doing. Like every hard-learned lesson was to ready him. Like somehow his whole life had been leading up to this.

Evander was alive.

That fact still glowed in his chest, a steady, comforting light. Alongside it was the dark and jagged fear of how close they'd come to the alternative. The devastating terror of that first gunshot would no doubt haunt his nightmares for years to come. That bullet had been meant for the back of Evander's head. If they'd arrived even a moment later—he couldn't let himself dwell on that, not when there was still so much distance and so many guards between him and the dungeons.

When Alys had led them, they had been guided by the runes, but now Newt had only his senses to aid him. If he was honest with himself, he preferred it this way. Just him and the whisper-soft fall of his feet on the cracking marble floors, the brush of the old tapestries beneath his fingertips as he passed, the sounds of the citadel all around him. Between the tromping and talking of the guards and the occasional banging of doors, maneuvering the halls unseen was almost easy for someone who knew how to listen. He did have a few close calls, a few heart-stopping moments when he spun around a corner with only seconds to spare. He could hold his own well enough in a brawl, but he wasn't fool enough to think he'd stand a chance with a citadel guard in a fair fight. Their blades were too sharp, their pistols too quick. It was easier to remain invisible—it always had been.

When he reached the door leading down to the dungeons, he knew his luck was likely to run out. Even assuming the sentry was still unconscious, there were bound to be guards on patrol. As Newt slipped into the stairwell and eased the door shut behind him, he kept his ears trained on the sounds below. Muffled coughs and curses—the prisoners. No telltale footfalls, at least not yet. He descended the steps as slowly as he dared. He was afraid a guard would enter from above and spot him before he'd even reached the base.

His breath hitched at the thought that he might not ever make it back up. Even if there were guards in the alcove, he couldn't turn back without the poison. He wouldn't. If Solan was allowed to leave the crypts, he could bring the citadel to its knees in a few hours, Newt had no doubt. The city would be next. They would trade in a corrupt council for an older sort of evil. One that had been left to fester and grow in the black bowels of the earth for hundreds of years.

Before the alcove came into view, Newt had to pause to collect himself. He didn't know how to be ready to face whatever lay below; he just knew he didn't have a choice. If he died tonight, would they tell his father the whole story? Or just that his son was dead, a traitor to the citadel? Newt wondered if coming this far would be enough for the man. Newt was a rebel who had slipped from the council's clutches too many times to count, who had lost a part of himself to a rook so powerful, even the chancellor feared him. And he'd survived. Would his father rest easy in the knowledge that his son had made something of himself in the end?

It was a useless thought. Newt knew that it wouldn't be enough for his father. He'd known for a long time now that nothing he did ever would be.

But it wasn't enough for Newt either. There was more that he wanted, even though he had always been too afraid to admit how much. He'd almost lost Evander tonight. Only a moment later, and all he would have had left would be memories. They'd had only a few short years, and they were not enough. He could tell things had changed between them after Solan got into his head. Evander kept looking at him askance, as if he were waiting for something. And there was more, a glimmer of a thought at the edge of Newt's memories, a ghost of a sensation, a flicker of emotion that he couldn't place. All he knew for sure was that Solan was to blame, and that burning anger was what drove him down the rest of the steps into the alcove, ready to face whatever fate waited for him there.

It was empty.

For a few seconds, Newt could only stare while his heart pounded uselessly with excess energy, prepared for a fight that wasn't coming. Then he stopped questioning the impossibility of his luck and ran for the cabinet. The padlock was heavy and iron, but the hinges on the doors were old and rusted. Newt glanced wildly around the alcove, searching for anything that might be heavy enough to break them off. Nothing. He looked back at the cabinet, unable to believe that he had come this far only to be thwarted by a single lock.

"I had a feeling you'd be back."

Newt whirled at the voice.

"I was hoping to catch more of you," Captain Marsh went on in an unhurried tone, crossing his arms. "But one at a time or all together—it doesn't matter. None of you are leaving the citadel alive."

He was standing on the other side of the table, equidistant from the stairwell and the corridor of cells, cutting Newt off from both of them. He took stock of the captain, who wore a sheathed knife at one hip and a looped iron chain at the other. No pistol at least. Newt's heart was pounding again, but his energy reserves were already wasted. His knees wobbled and his jaw trembled. Newt crossed his arms too, so Marsh at least wouldn't see how his hands shook.

"The others are already gone," he said. A useless lie, but he was still trying to think of a way out of this. He took in the room instinctively, every object, every possible advantage he could take. Nothing. Nothing. Nothing.

"Then I guess there won't be anyone coming to help you," the captain replied.

The chain lashed out from his side so fast that Newt barely even saw it. His movement was simple reflex, and he dropped to the floor just before the chain would have caught him across the neck. He rolled under the table and kicked the chair toward the captain. It hit him, but not with the force Newt had hoped. Still on his knees, he ducked out from under the table before the chain could fly back but was met with a searing pain in his left shoulder. He looked down to see the knife protruding from his arm, buried almost to the hilt, which glinted iron in the lantern light.

His vision dimmed, and he fell forward, catching himself with his right hand. Slowly, sickeningly, the knife slid free from his flesh, guided by the invisible hand of Marsh's bloodbond. It was slick with blood, and for a second that darkly luminous red was the only thing Newt could see. A sound met his ears. He realized dimly it was his own cries of pain.

The blade was coming for his heart next. He knew it in the part of his brain that was pure animal instinct. *If you're fast enough, nothing can hurt you.*

A lesson. A lie. Maybe that's all his father had ever given him in the end. Or maybe he just wasn't fast enough.

The knife lanced toward him again, and Newt twisted to the side. The blade sliced across his chest, cutting a long, stinging line, but at least it wasn't buried in his heart. He rolled under the table again and pushed upward, his shoulder screaming in protest. The table toppled. A split second later there was a thump as the blade slid between two slats of wood, stopped at the hilt—and an inch from Newt's eye.

He pushed off from the table and charged the captain, before his mind could catch up and protest the terrible idea. There wasn't much distance to cover between them, but Marsh was fast. Faster than him. Dimly, Newt heard the scrape of steel against wood. He was only a few feet from the captain. At the last second he dove to the left. He tried to roll with the impact, but his body refused to cooperate, and he ended up on his back just inside the corridor. He looked up in time to see—with no little satisfaction—that Marsh had only barely stopped the knife from driving into his own chest.

The satisfaction was fleeting. Captain Marsh plucked the knife from the air and turned a glare on Newt that might have melted steel. Newt's instincts sang. He scrambled to his feet and started to run down the corridor. He wasn't sure where he was going, but he did know he had to run. Maybe he could be fast enough. Maybe he could—

The iron chain whipped around his ankles, and he flew face-first into the floor. His ears rang, his shoulder throbbed, and his chest ached. He tried to move, to at least pull himself to his hands and knees, but his muscles wouldn't respond. His knee felt odd, and he realized it had popped out of joint. Prisoners had caught on that something was happening and were shouting and banging on their cell doors. The floor was rough and cool against his cheek, and he could feel the dampness of his own blood pooling beneath him.

He expected the knife, but it never came. Instead, the chain slithered from beneath his legs, hissing along the ground. With one last flash of clarity, Newt managed to slip his hand under the chain just as it tightened around his neck. He pushed against it with all his dwindling strength, keeping it from crushing his throat, but still he could drag in only short, painful breaths. His other arm was useless. He couldn't push himself off the floor, could only press his forehead into the stone, press his hand against the iron. Not enough.

"I wish you kids had left the city when you'd had the chance," came the captain's voice, but it was very far away.

Newt's eyes were blurred with tears. The world had shrunk into a single moment of bright, unending pain. He tried to gasp in more air, tried to stay conscious. Not enough.

A thump.

The chain loosened slightly, and Newt sucked in a desperate breath. Another thump. The chain fell slack. He flung it away from himself, blinking at the spots dancing in his vision. With groaning effort, he rolled onto his back, propped on his good arm.

The captain was prone on the floor, not moving. Over him stood Vesper, her hand outstretched and trembling. Beside her was Alys, clutching a cracked lantern, staring wordlessly at Newt with wide eyes. For a second, even the prisoners were silent.

"Good timing," Newt said. It was more like a croak.

That jolted Alys into action, and she ran forward.

"Not that good," she murmured, dropping to her knees beside him. Her hands hovered over his shoulder and chest, like she knew she needed to check his wounds but didn't know where to start. "I caught a glimpse in the runes when we were leaving the chancellor's study—I should have seen it sooner—I'm so sorry."

Her words were tumbling and her voice torn. Newt frowned in confusion at the misery etched into her features. He thought of her parents, ripped from their beds, branded as traitors. Maybe the trouble with seeing the future was that everything felt preventable, even the things that weren't. Wincing at the stab of pain, Newt managed to raise his left hand to take hers. It was wet with blood, but Alys didn't flinch away.

"You're here," he told her. "You saw it in time."

Alys's lips quivered. The jagged regret in her face smoothed the slightest bit. She squeezed his hand, and he thought he saw the ghost of a smile before she was suddenly herself again, all business.

"Vesper, come help me," she said. "We'll need to bandage these wounds before going anywhere."

"We'll have to do it fast." Vesper glanced over her shoulder. Her cheeks were drained of all color, and she swayed on her feet as she walked, as if the floor was the deck of a storm-tossed boat. "There will be other guards soon."

"Can you stand if we help you?" Alys asked Newt.

He nodded. Alys helped him sit up the rest of way, but when he moved his legs, a sharp pain radiated from his knee.

"Wait." He gritted his teeth and took hold of his kneecap. He jerked his leg straight, guiding the joint back into alignment. He gasped out a breath, but the pain was already dissipating. Or, rather, it was overwhelmed by the pain in his shoulder.

Alys's eyebrows twitched a little in either concern or curiosity, but she said nothing. She and Vesper supported most of his weight as he climbed to his feet. His vision tilted and darkened, but he stayed conscious. His legs were working at least.

"The captain has the key to the cabinet," he said, not entirely sure that he was talking out loud. "The poison."

"We'll get it." Alys left him propped on Vesper while she righted the chair. “First you need to sit down so I can take a look at the damage. Evander would never forgive me if I let you bleed out on the dungeon floor.”

Newt wanted to ask exactly what she meant by that last part, but he couldn’t quite form the words. Instead, he did as he was told and sat down.

FORTY-FIVE

EVANDER

HE and Cassa stopped running when they reached an abandoned corridor, dark enough that maybe no one would be coming this way anytime soon. After a few seconds to catch his breath, Evander studied Cassa from the corner of his eye. She looked the same as he'd seen her last. Gaunt and bedraggled. Her hair was limp and stringy, her features wan. The bruise under her eye was a faint greenish purple. He was a little surprised she hadn't jumped onto the table and tried to strangle the councilors with her own manacles. But then he was also surprised that she hadn't killed the chancellor when she had the chance.

Chancellor Dane was the reason her parents were dead. In a way, he was the reason for everything Cassa had ever done since that day four years ago.

He wanted to press her for more details of exactly what had happened when she went after the chancellor, but they were too exposed here, in the middle of the citadel. Also he could see in the faint light that her jaw was quivering. He wasn't sure what to make of that.

"Let's go," he said. "We're meeting the others at the chapel by the western wall."

Cassa frowned and fell into step beside him.

"Why there?"

"That's where they lower the elixir." He hesitated. Only a few hours ago Cassa had deserted them at Solan's word. "It's the last dose he needs before the bloodbond takes effect. This is our last chance to poison it."

If Cassa's thoughts were whirring, there was no evidence on her face. He wasn't sure what he expected from her. He only hoped it wasn't dissent.

"I've been at that chapel before," she said at last. "The night I met Vesper."

A strange sort of relief washed over Evander.

"You mean the night you almost burned her alive?" he asked.

"'Almost' hardly counts."

He snorted but didn't say more. For a while they concentrated on making their way through the Central Keep in silence. Evading the patrolling guards was a matter of good timing and quick instincts, waiting for the right moment to sprint down corridors and duck around corners. They had to backtrack several times to avoid being seen, but between the two of them, they managed to find a way out of the keep and into the inky night.

Evander blinked in the chilly air as the clock chimed the half hour. His near brush with death in that forsaken courtyard felt like it had been a lifetime ago, but it had been barely half an hour. He hadn't let himself think about it too closely. About those raging, breathless seconds, locked in struggle with the guard who only a moment earlier had been ready to kill him. Evander wasn't sure he'd ever escaped that moment. A part of him was still there, cold iron on his wrists, cold stone beneath his knees, waiting for the bullet that would end everything.

Cassa led the way as they crept past brick buildings and shops. Everything was quiet out here and shrouded in a misty fog. It was too early even for the shopkeepers to be stirring. Evander had never imagined the citadel to be a place that slept. In his head, it was always a roiling hive of political machinations and society affairs. As they circled the enormous structure that had to be the Mirror Keep, Cassa glanced over her shoulder at him and slowed just enough to fall into step beside him. In the murk, she was only a silhouette, unreadable and untouchable.

"I'm glad you're not dead," she said, her voice low and halting.

No thanks to you, he wanted to say.

"Me too," he said.

Her steps faltered, but she kept moving. Her head was ducked now, her hands fists at her sides. He could hear her shortened breath punctuating her footfalls. He stayed beside her. He waited.

"I need—" she began, but faltered again. A few more steps in silence. When her voice came, it was so strained, he thought it might break. "I need you to understand why I did it. Why I had to do it."

Despite the anger that still seethed in his chest, he wanted to understand. He really did. He wanted there to be a way that her abandonment wasn't a betrayal. He wanted there to be a way to forgive her.

"You didn't *have* to do anything," he said, keeping his voice at a murmur.

"I didn't know what else to do. Solan's infallible prophecy—he said I was the one who killed the chancellor. I was the one who *had* to kill him. I couldn't give that up. After everything we'd done, after everything we'd lost, I couldn't just let our one chance slip away."

Her breathing was faster now, uneven. There was familiar fire in her words, but beneath that, something new. Desperation. Evander swallowed against the lump in his throat.

"Did you even consider that he might be lying? That he wanted to separate us? That he needed you to kill the chancellor because he couldn't do it himself?"

Cassa stared ahead, her lips a grim line. Then she shook her head.

"I think he really dreamed an infallible prophecy—or thought he did. Otherwise why would he have waited all this time? He had all the knowledge of the citadel at his disposal, whenever he felt like taking it. He could have found another way out. I don't think he was lying."

"He's a murderer!" The words flew out much louder than he'd intended, echoing for a heartbeat. He bit down hard on his lip, tried to ease his own frustration. Cassa didn't reply, and he continued in a forced whisper. "For seers' sake, have you forgotten that Mira is dead down there in the dark?"

"No, I haven't," she bit off. "I also haven't forgotten the thousands of people who died in these streets while the council waited safely behind their walls for the slaughter to be over."

She'd stopped walking, her gaze sweeping across the night, as if she could see the evidence of that slaughter, lurking in the fog, imprinted forever in the stone and shadows. Evander could remember it vividly—

the last battle of the rebellion—though he'd been miles away, warm and safe with his family. The sounds had carried though. And after, the carrion birds had swarmed for days, a dismal cloud over the citadel. It had never occurred to Evander to ask Cassa where she'd been on that day. Wherever she'd been, it wouldn't have been warm or safe, not with her parents in the thick of it all.

He turned to face her. His eyes were adjusting, but her features were still obscured.

"You had your chance to kill the chancellor," he said softly. "Why didn't you take it?"

She looked down at the ground, then at the empty, dying night around them. She wouldn't look at him.

"It would have just been one more person dead." Her voice was feather-light and fragile. "It wouldn't have changed anything—not really. I didn't know what else to do."

It wouldn't have brought her parents back. Wouldn't have filled the gouging holes that the rebellion left behind. There would have just been another chancellor to take Dane's place. The citadel would carry on, as it always had and perhaps always would. Maybe Solan had foreseen the council's fall, but there was nothing that could undo the damage that had already been done. The world they had inherited was broken, and they were fools to think they could somehow piece it back together.

"I just wish you had waited for us to wake up," he said, with a weariness that he suspected was actually forgiveness.

Cassa flung her arms around him so abruptly that he fell back a step. He let out an involuntary gasp at the pain in his ribs, but once he recovered, he returned the embrace. For a few seconds, while he held her, the citadel faded away. A year ago, being this close to her had felt as natural as silver in his hands. The weight of her against him, the murmur of her heartbeat answering his own, the way her head rested so easily on his shoulder. It was all still there, lingering in memory, but things were different between them now. Not better, not worse. Just different. There was still comfort to be had though. Warmth and safety. He knew that was all she wanted. It was all he wanted too.

"We should go," she said at last, but she didn't move.

"I thought I'd wait for you to stop crying first."

She pulled away from him immediately, her scowl visible even in shadow.

"I'd be careful if I were you," she said. "Concussion or no, I'll still knock you upside the head."

He lifted his hands in surrender, and she started walking. He couldn't help but notice that though her stride was as purposeful as ever, she did swipe her sleeve across her eyes.

Once they were away from the Mirror Keep, the possibility of running into guards dwindled, and they picked up their pace. They neared the chapel before the next chime of the bell, though Evander had a feeling it would come soon. The stars had begun to fade behind clouds. The fog felt thicker here, at the edge of the citadel. When the chapel came into view at the end of the street, his heart shuddered. Built of the same stone as the wall, it looked more like a massive tomb than a place for the reverent to gather. The Alchemist's Fire above the door was swirling and hypnotic. A memorial to the Slain God. A summoning of his children.

He saw the two guards at the cross street ahead of them at the same time Cassa did. She swore under her breath and yanked him to the side, into the narrow passage between two buildings.

"Did they see us?" she asked, her back pressed against the wall.

Evander laid his hands against the cool brick and peered around the corner, just enough to catch a glimpse of the guards' backs as they approached the chapel. He eased back behind the wall.

"I don't think so. They're headed for the chapel."

"They're early," Cassa said. The clock rang out as if in response. A quarter till the first morning bell.

"Or we're late." He chanced another look. One of the guards was disappearing inside, while his partner remained in front of the doors. "We're going to need a distraction."

"We need the poison."

"Newt will get it. They'll be here."

He didn't need to look at Cassa to know she wasn't convinced. Newt wouldn't fail though. Evander knew that like he knew his own name. His heart skipped a beat. They would probably come down the same street he and Cassa had. If the guard was paying any attention all, he wouldn't miss three people, no matter how much shadow and fog they had protecting them.

"I'm going out there," he said.

Maybe Cassa had been thinking the same thing he had, because she didn't seem surprised. She did shake her head. They were elbow to elbow, their backs against the brick, their breaths short bursts into the fog.

"No," she said. "I'll go. You have to wait for the others and figure out a way to poison the elixir before it's lowered to Solan."

"I'm faster than you."

"I'm more stubborn."

Possibly the truest thing she'd ever said. Evander could feel his pulse throughout his whole body, a thundering rhythm. Whoever went out there might not make it back alive. Another moment suspended in time. He wondered how many of those there could be in a life. How many moments could carry the weight of everything before finally something shattered?

"When we were kids, were you just trying to impress me that day you climbed the bell tower?" Evander stared at the brick wall in front of them and tried to breathe.

"What are you talking about?" Cassa paused for a heartbeat. "Did Vesper tell you that?"

"Maybe."

Cassa was quiet. Evander couldn't bring himself to look at her. He was waiting for a sarcastic retort, but when Cassa spoke, her voice was soft with honesty.

"I was. Did it work?"

A smile tugged at his mouth, and he squeezed his eyes shut for a second, just a second.

"Yes." He leaned over to kiss her cheek, to speak into her ear. "My turn."

He spun out from the passage before she could stop him and ran full tilt toward the chapel. He had to lead the guard down the cross street, away from the others. The man saw him immediately and almost cut him off, his shouts echoing through the night. Evander turned onto the street just in time to avoid him. He couldn't see anything in the murk. He didn't know if any second now he'd have a bullet in his back. He just kept running, farther away from the chapel and its eternal flame, farther into the night.

FORTY-SIX

CASSA

IF Cassa could have run down Evander and killed him herself, she would have. All he had to do was wait here for the others. Between the four of them, they could have easily managed to subdue the remaining guard and poison the vial. Simple and safe—or as safe as anything could be in the citadel. She should have been the one running through the dark with death on her heels. It was the least she could do for them.

None of it would matter anyway if the others didn't get here in time. How long would it take the guard inside the chapel to finish his task? Surely not much longer. Maybe it was already too late.

A figure passed by the alley, and even in darkness Cassa caught a glimpse of burnished red hair. Her hand shot out and grasped Vesper's sleeve, pulling her into the passage. Vesper swore and elbowed her in the ribs before realizing who she was.

"Sorry," she whispered as Cassa rubbed her side. "You shouldn't go around grabbing people like that."

"Noted," Cassa said, but before she could say more, Vesper pushed something into her hand. The vial.

"I came ahead to give you this," Vesper said. "We're running out of time, and I already know you're going to insist on taking it yourself."

Cassa nodded and shoved it into her pocket. The least she could do. Her fingers were shaking, but she told herself it was the chilly air.

"Where are Alys and Newt?" She peered down the foggy street, but it was empty. When Cassa looked back at Vesper, she was swaying on her feet. She propped her right hand against the wall and rubbed her temple with her left.

"What's wrong?" Cassa asked, but Vesper said nothing, only stared at her with a strange concentration. Cassa's heart pounded so fast, her chest ached. She couldn't catch her breath suddenly.

"Vesper, what's wrong? Where are the others?" she demanded.

"They're fine." Vesper shook her head sharply, as if shaking herself out of a trance. "Sorry, they're right behind me. Newt's hurt, but he's okay. Alys is helping him. That's why I came ahead."

Cassa forced herself to inhale and tried to steady her heart. They were fine. She had the poison. Maybe there was still time.

"I have to go now." She slipped past Vesper. "Before it's too late."

"Wait," Vesper tugged on her sleeve, but before she could say anything more, Evander rounded the corner, stopping just short of careening into them.

He was panting heavily, hands on his knees, head bowed. Cassa's mind spun.

"Evander, what are you—"

He lurched suddenly to the side, throwing out his arm to catch himself on the wall.

"Something's wrong," he gasped out. He leaned against the wall but only managed to stay upright for a few more seconds before sliding to the ground.

Cassa dropped down beside him, her stomach hurtling into her throat as she searched for an injury, but she couldn't see anything. No blood. Nothing looked broken.

"What is it?" Her voice was as tight as her chest. He was clutching his head now, shaking all over.

Nearby, somewhere along the street, came a sharp cry. Evander's eyes flew open, and he lunged forward with some kind of mindless instinct. Cassa barely caught him before he face-planted into the ground, shaking too hard to even hold himself upright.

"Alys," he whispered, before crying out with another surge of pain.

Cassa lowered him gently to the cobblestones and jumped to her feet. "Stay with him," she ordered Vesper and ran toward the sound.

Alys was only a few yards down the street, a stark, staggering figure against the gray mist. She held Newt against her, desperately trying to keep him on his feet. He was holding his head in both his hands, his jaw locked, trembling all over. When she saw Cassa, she looked ready to sob in relief.

"I don't know—he just—" She stumbled uselessly over the words as she helped Cassa drag him the rest of the way to the alley.

Between them, Newt managed a few steps on his own, but mostly he was deadweight. He sounded like he was trying to say something. Short, strangled whimpers came from his mouth, but no words formed. By the time they'd reached Vesper and Evander, he'd fallen unconscious. Vesper looked up at them from where she knelt over Evander—he had gone still as well.

Alys let out a hiccuping sob—at the sight of her brother, Cassa assumed, but then she also collapsed to her knees. Cassa's own knees buckled at the sudden shift of weight, and she lost her balance, cracking her head so hard on the wall that tears sprang to her eyes. She let Newt's body slump the rest of the way to the ground but fought to keep her feet. Too fast. Everything was happening too fast.

Alys was rocking back and forth on her knees, cradling her head in her hands. She sucked in a wild breath and found Cassa's gaze.

"It's Solan." The words sounded as if they were being torn out of her. "He says—he says he's waiting for you."

No sooner had she spoken than she slid to the ground, unmoving. Cassa tried to remember to breathe. She crouched down and let her hand rest on Newt's chest. It rose up and down in steady rhythm. He was still alive. So was Evander. So was Alys.

"What do we do?" Her voice was so thin that she wasn't even sure she'd spoken aloud.

No reply. Her eyes shot to Vesper, who was sitting back against the wall, both palms pressed against her forehead.

"Dammit." She clambered over Evander to kneel in front of Vesper. "Please, Vesper, please don't—" *Please don't leave me here alone.*

Vesper was rocking back and forth. In that moment, she seemed so far away, so deep inside herself, that Cassa was sure she wouldn't come back. But then she gasped in a ragged breath and dropped her hands.

"It is Solan, but I can keep him away from my mind for a while at least." Her eyes roved across their three unconscious friends, and she pressed her lips into a hard line. "I'm sorry, I could have tried to help them—I didn't realize in time."

"What did he do to them?"

Vesper's brow wrinkled as she considered. She reached out and grabbed Evander's limp hand, searching out those invisible threads that only she could see.

"He took their memories," she said, pulling away with a shudder. "All of them. When they wake up—if they wake up—there won't be anything of them left."

She dropped her head into her hands again. "I'm sorry," she whispered. "I should have known. I should have—we were so close."

Cassa stood up.

"He said he was waiting for me. I don't know what he wants, but maybe I can convince him to give them back their memories."

Vesper peeled her hands from her face and stared up at her.

"You can't go down there alone."

"I can't leave them alone either. Not again." She gestured at her friends' prone bodies. In the eerie night, slumped as they were across the cobblestones, they didn't look like they were sleeping. They looked dead. It struck a chord in her that reverberated through every part of her being. The fire she'd been tamping down sprang back to life, heat licking up the back of her throat. "Stay with them. Let me deal with Solan."

Vesper grabbed her arm and hauled herself up.

"Cassa, if you go down there, you—" But she couldn't finish the thought.

You won't come back.

Cassa forced her lips into a smile, though she knew it was a small, ghastly thing.

"The least I can do." She reached into her pocket and closed her fingers around the vial of poison. "He must have gotten the elixir by now, but if I leave this with you, maybe there will be another chance, some other way."

Vesper grasped her wrist before she could withdraw the vial.

"No," she said firmly. "Keep it. If anyone can find another way, it will be you."

Something flitted through the back of Cassa's mind, a thought she couldn't quite catch, a memory she couldn't quite reach, but she shook away the sensation. She wanted to ask how Vesper expected her to find another way, when Solan knew her every thought just by looking at her, could steal her every thought without even seeing her. Maybe he didn't intend to meet with her at all. Maybe he just wanted to lure her into the dark so that she died alone down there, among the ancient bones. Maybe she deserved as much. Hadn't she lured Mira to her death in the same manner, however unwittingly?

"Okay," was all she said. She left the vial where it was.

Vesper followed her to the mouth of the alley, and Cassa paused in the street, steeling herself, calculating her route. She would have to go back through the citadel, back down those long steps dropping into blackness, back across the silky surface of the lake and whatever monsters lurked below.

"Here." Vesper touched her own temple and then pressed her fingers to Cassa's. Suddenly Cassa had a very vivid memory of the citadel's corridors, the path to the great oak door that opened to the dank air of the dungeons. It was as if she'd walked that way a hundred times.

"I thought you couldn't remove your own memories," she said, once she'd adjusted to the odd sensation of a familiarity that wasn't hers.

"I took it from one of the guards," Vesper said. "Just in case."

She'd always been able to think three steps ahead, whereas Cassa could only ever stumble from moment to moment, reacting to each problem as it came. They'd become friends for a reason.

Vesper's fingers still lingered at Cassa's temple. Their eyes met.

"Do you want me to take back my uncle's memories that I gave you?" Vesper asked softly.

Cassa nodded, swallowing hard. Vesper pulled her hand back slowly. Rapidly the memories rose to the surface of her mind. The bargain with Solan, the dead guard whose name she—the chancellor—couldn't remember, the night he lost almost everyone he loved. Then suddenly they were gone. The only thing she remembered with any clarity was that in a strange and terrible way, she and Chancellor Dane weren't very different at all. Vesper was still staring at her, eyes solemn.

"I understand why you did it," Cassa said. "Why you told your uncle everything."

Vesper had been three steps ahead and pulling Cassa along, trying to keep her alive. Cassa couldn't bring herself to thank her for it, but she couldn't hate her for it either. Vesper hugged herself and sighed.

"And I understand why you tried to help Solan," she said.

"Don't worry, I never make the same mistake twice." Cassa flashed a smile that she didn't feel. She glanced back toward the alley, where her friends were only indistinct shapes. The last people she had left to love. "If—*when*—they wake up, tell them I—I don't know. Tell them I said whatever it is I'm meant to say in a situation like this."

Vesper only stared at her. In the mist she was a pale wraith, almost a stranger but not quite.

"You're not meant to say anything," she said at last. "You're meant to come back."

"Okay." Cassa backed away, before she could change her mind, before she could think of a reason to stay. Soon Vesper was shrouded in fog, and Cassa turned to run toward the citadel. Toward the crypts. Toward Solan Tavish.

The Night Vesper Betrayed Cassa

THE Merchants' Bridge was entirely empty. Other than the whispering flow of the river and the occasional flapping of a tarp covering a market stall, the night was quiet and still. There were no stars visible overhead, but the moon broke through the clouds at intervals, glinting on the water below. Vesper and Cassa were near the center, facing the eastern slopes of Aurelia Valley. They sat, legs dangling, on the stone wall that was supposed to keep people from falling into the river.

"I don't understand." Cassa's fingers curled over the edge of the stone on either side of her hips. Her eyes on Vesper were sharp and demanding. Vesper couldn't hold her gaze.

"I'm sorry," Vesper said. "I just—I just can't."

"We have to find out what's happening to these people who keep disappearing."

"I know, but you four can do it without me. You don't need me."

"What happened? Did your uncle find out?"

"No," Vesper snapped, maybe too forcefully to be believable. Fortunately, Cassa was too distraught and confused to be paying close attention. She also probably didn't suspect that Vesper would ever lie to her.

Cassa stared over the water, her jaw set. Vesper took a few deep breaths.

"You trust me, don't you?" The question felt more like a betrayal than anything else she'd done tonight.

After a few long seconds, Cassa nodded.

"And you wouldn't push me off this bridge, would you?" Vesper asked.

Cassa's eyebrows quirked, and she looked at Vesper.

"That depends," she said slowly, "on what you are about to say."

"I think maybe you should call off the plan. Or at least postpone it. I'm not sure it's a good idea anymore."

Cassa narrowed her eyes, and for a moment Vesper really did think she might push her off the bridge. She'd known the suggestion was a vain hope, but she had to at least try. If she could convince Cassa to call off the plan to infiltrate the citadel, then maybe she could also convince her and the others to help Ansel kill Solan. No deceit, no blackmail.

But that had always been a vain hope.

"We've been planning this for months," Cassa said. "First you want to back out—with no explanation—and now you don't want us to go through with it at all?"

Vesper bit her lip and looked down at her hands in her lap. When her uncle had confronted her earlier that evening, she'd thought for sure that all of them were going to end up in chains. Ansel's diviners had seen everything in their runes and cards and tea leaves. Cassa's entire plan. Vesper's entire involvement. She'd never seen her uncle as weary as he'd been that night, sitting in the armchair across from her in his study.

He hadn't threatened to expose them. Instead, he had asked for her help. There was a monster beneath the citadel, and it had to be stopped.

The council was watching him though, waiting for him to show some sign of disloyalty. He couldn't risk asking for her friends' help until he knew for sure they would help him.

Vesper knew that Ansel always played the long game, that he was always thinking further ahead than everyone else, but even she was surprised when he pulled the four signed and sealed pardons from his desk drawer. One for each of her friends. He already knew they were going to go through with their foolhardy plan and that they would get caught. He already knew they were going to find a way to escape and that without those pardons they would spend the rest of their lives on the run.

Vesper wasn't sure what the right thing to do was. She did know she had to help her friends earn those pardons. She did know the monster had to be killed.

She hadn't known how hard it would be to sit there beside Cassa and lie to her.

"I'm just worried about you," Vesper said, keeping her eyes averted. "No one has ever infiltrated the Central Keep and lived."

A moment of quiet.

"You don't think my plan will work?" Cassa's voice was soft, too soft.

Vesper looked up, but now it was Cassa's gaze that was averted. The hard line of her jaw had begun to quiver.

"I think . . ." Vesper's heart ached more and more with every beat. Guilt dug its claws into her stomach, wrenching at her insides. "I think if anyone can make it work, you and the others can." That was the truth, but it didn't hurt any less than the lies.

She expected Cassa to smile or shoot off a cocky remark, but she just kept staring across the river. The clouds peeled away from the moon long enough for her face to be illuminated. Vesper studied her profile, thinking that she didn't look like either of her parents but rather a perfect blend of them both. Cassa could very well be the last Valera, but their name wouldn't be forgotten for a long time.

"I have to try," Cassa said into the open air. "You understand that, don't you?"

"Yes," said Vesper.

"I'm not stupid," Cassa said. "I know we aren't going to bring down the council tomorrow. I know I'll never be able to accomplish half of what my parents did. But I have to keep fighting. That's all I have left."

"That's not true," Vesper said.

Cassa didn't reply. She just stared across the river and the valley, into the inscrutable night, until finally they had to return to the city.

FORTY-SEVEN

CASSA

CASSA ran all the way to the crypts, stopping to walk only when the stitch in her side made it impossible to breathe. She'd given up trying to be stealthy. The first guard who'd caught sight of her had collapsed immediately to the ground. It seemed Solan was as determined as she was that she would make it to his lair. She had no idea what he wanted with her, but she knew she'd do anything to bring her friends back. Despite all the uncertainty, that alone was enough to keep her moving forward.

With the new familiarity Vesper had given her, the journey to the lake went quickly, though passing by those endless rows of tombs still cast a shiver down her spine. She'd taken a ghost globe from the citadel, but the shadows felt more grasping, more enveloping, now that she was alone. Her heart pounded mercilessly the whole way across the lake, giving her a pulsing headache to rival the pain in her shoulders and back. The chamber of seer statues was as dark as they'd left it, and once she'd crossed the raised path, Cassa forced herself to stop.

Even though her chest clenched at the very thought, she walked to the feet of the statue where Mira's body was splayed on the ground. In the blue light, she was impossibly pale. She didn't look like herself anymore. With shaking hands, Cassa set down the globe. Gently, painstakingly, she positioned Mira on her back, her arms crossed. There was no color in her cheeks, and her skin was cool as Cassa pushed the hair away from her face. She deserved a little dignity, and that was all Cassa could give her. She combed her mind uselessly for the words to the death rites, but it was far too late for that anyway. Maybe Mira didn't even believe in the Slain God. Maybe she had gone somewhere kinder than oblivion.

Achingly, Cassa climbed to her feet and retrieved the ghost globe. Solan was so close, she imagined she could feel his malignant power, leeching at her resolve. She didn't let herself think as her footsteps led her into the warmly lit chamber. Vesper might always be three steps ahead, but Cassa had run out of moves a long time ago. Solan probably knew that. It's probably why he had chosen her for whatever final task or torment he had in mind. The others had their wits and charm and speed and bravery to fall back on. But without her friends at her back, Cassa had nothing.

Solan was seated in his usual armchair. He was healthier than she'd seen him last, though his features still shifted unsettlingly. Did that mean the bloodbond hadn't taken effect yet? Not that it mattered. He had the elixir to get him through the final hours. She could see the clear corked bottle on the table near his elbow. The blue-green liquid, shimmering with a silver sheen, was strangely mesmerizing. That one dose of mirasma was the last thing between Solan and centuries' worth of vengeance.

“Hello, Cassandra,” he said, elegant as ever. He gestured toward the sofa. “Thank you for joining me.”

“It wasn’t exactly an invitation.” She didn’t sit, didn’t move any closer to him. “What do you want?”

“You know what I want.” He cast a glance toward the elixir. There was an undercurrent of impatience in his tone. “I want what I’ve always wanted. What *you’ve* always wanted. To see the council and the chancellor fall.”

“So what’s stopping you?”

He cocked his head slightly, considering her. Even now, was he reading her memories? Turning over every mistake, every doubt and fear and pang of regret?

“What stopped you,” he asked, “when you had the chance?”

She shrugged with forced nonchalance.

“I don’t like prophecies telling me what to do.”

He just stared at her, unmoving. His visage was fluctuating so tumultuously now that it made her dizzy to look at him. Only his eyes were still bright and constant, piercing her with a frustration that was almost visceral. Something occurred to her.

“Shouldn’t you have taken your medicine by now?” she asked, looking pointedly at the mirasma. “It must be getting hard to hold yourself together without it.”

Even as she spoke, she observed the truth of her words, the hard set of his jaw, the sweat gleaming on his brow, the shudders that ran through him periodically. That frustration in his eyes was sharpening into something fiercer. Deadlier.

"I will," he said. There was something dark and slithering in his tone that felt faintly familiar to Cassa, like a nightmare she'd forgotten. "But only once I'm sure."

Sure of what? Between his divination and his sentience, he had to know that they had failed to poison the elixir. He had to know that freedom was finally in his reach.

Or did he?

Cassa smiled, and there was venom in it.

"Must be hard to read the future without your runes." She clasped her hands behind her back and began to meander casually around the room, pretending to admire the decor. "I would have thought a diviner as skilled as you could read the tea leaves or even a handful of pebbles, but maybe you're having trouble staying focused."

She paused to look at him. He was barely containing his anger now. Her smile broadened.

"And I suppose stealing all those memories must really take its toll—even on someone as powerful as you. Maybe your sentience isn't as accurate as you'd like?" She stopped to face him directly, daring him to contradict her, to read something in her features.

His lip curled in disdain, and he said nothing.

"Down here, so far from the rest of us, I suppose it would be impossible to know anything for certain. Like why I let the chancellor live. Or whether your bloodbond is going to work. Or whether we managed to poison your last elixir."

The silence between them was thick and tangible, shot through with his rising fury. She couldn't blame him. How awful it must be to go from borderline omniscience to miserable uncertainty, right at the crux of all his plans. Solan remained still, though his emotions emanated so visibly that Cassa had an idea of what being a sentient was like.

"You don't know anything, you worthless girl," he spit out. His whole body was as taut as a bowstring.

"Maybe a nap would help," Cassa suggested.

He snapped and lunged to his feet. Cassa stumbled back at his approach. She could feel his claws digging into her mind, ripping at her, and she struggled to stay conscious, stay standing. Then, just as suddenly as he'd attacked, he staggered back into his chair. The claws retracted. Her memories were still whole, still hers.

He glared at her through his feeble trembling. She wondered what would happen if he went much longer without the elixir. Would he be just as weak when he lost control of his senses, or would his powers surge once his mind flew apart? Solan himself had said that if he lost control, he didn't know how much damage he might do. Considering that his power could reach the entire citadel, she was willing to bet a lot. Solan wasn't an ailing man in need of medicine. He was a dense, burning star, waiting to explode.

"You're going to help me," he said.

"I'm not afraid of you."

He laughed. A low, creeping sound.

"I don't need to read your thoughts to know that's not true. Of course you're afraid of me. I'm the one holding your friends' lives in my hands." He tapped his right temple. "Or should I say, my mind."

Cassa's hands tightened into fists. No matter how weak he was, no matter what information she managed to glean, she'd never be a threat to him. He held all the cards, just as he always had.

"If I tell you what you want to know, will you return their memories?" She hated the raw vulnerability in her voice.

"I don't harbor any ill will toward you or your friends," he said. "I quite admire you, in fact. You're the only ones in a city of thousands who kept fighting the council, even after the last rebel was dead."

She wasn't sure if she believed him, but did she have a choice? Did it even matter in the end? Once he'd destroyed the council, would there be any limit to his malice? The councilors weren't the only ones complicit in his imprisonment. There were many more in the citadel who were culpable. She knew from experience that when it came to revenge, there was always one more person to blame.

"Do you swear?" Her breath hitched. If she told him the truth, he would drink the elixir, and it would be over. There would be no going back.

In reply, he closed his eyes. For a long while, he sat unmoving, a furrow in his brow.

"It's done," he said at last. "Giving back memories is much easier than taking them."

He could be lying. Probably was. But she didn't have a choice. She was three steps behind, struggling to keep up.

"We didn't get the chance." She almost pulled out the vial to prove it to him, but something stopped her. An inkling of an idea. "I was about to go into the chapel when you sent your little invitation."

Solan studied her. Maybe he was trying to read her past. That was fine. He would only see the truth.

"I'm afraid I can't trust you, Cassandra," he said, a little sadly. "And I have to know for sure."

Panic charged up her spine. Would he hurt her friends again?

"Why would I lie?" she demanded. "I have everything to lose."

"You've already proved yourself to be . . . unpredictable." He gestured toward the sofa. "Please sit down."

There was no ignoring the order in his tone. This time, she obeyed. Gently, Solan picked up the bottle of elixir and offered it to her.

"Just a sip," he said. "It will be quite harmless to you, assuming you're telling the truth."

That easy. She knew it wasn't poisoned. One sip, and she could leave this place. He would wreak his revenge, but maybe there would be another way to stop him later.

Or maybe there was one more possibility.

She took the bottle from him with her right hand. The poison was in her left pocket. If she was careful, and if he was distracted, she could ease out the vial. She wasn't as quick with her fingers as Evander, but she might be able to pull it off. Just one sip. Then all she had to do was pour in the poison and hand it back. So simple.

She popped off the cork, and the iridescent liquid sizzled softly, like it was reacting to the air.

"It doesn't taste as good as it looks, unfortunately," said Solan. He spoke casually, but she could see the eagerness in his eyes. He was ready to down the mirasma the second she took a drink. His entire body must have been craving it by now, straining at the seams.

She took a whiff, and though she'd been prepared for the acrid scent, she faked a racking cough into her right arm. With her left, without looking down, she slipped the poison free, wrapping the cold vial in her colder hand. Just one sip, then she could figure out what to do next.

"Surely there's still a small part of you that wants them dead," Solan said coaxingly, misconstruing her hesitation. "The council took so much from you. They'll probably never understand how much."

He was right, of course. She might as well have died that day, when the news about her parents came. She'd lost the most important part of herself. It had burned with her parents on an anonymous pyre. And from the ashes sparked something both debilitating and empowering. She'd lost her parents, but she gained her purpose.

She opened her hand and glanced down at the vial, just for a second. The rest of the world tilted away. Again she felt that strange sensation, as if her mind was reaching back for a memory that had never existed. Her heart thudded so loudly that surely Solan could hear it. It couldn't have all been for nothing. All those years, all that pain, all that rage. It had to mean something. With Evander and Alys and Newt and even Vesper, she had defied the citadel itself. And now, in the darkness beneath it, she understood what she was meant to do. She hadn't been able to pull the trigger, but Solan wouldn't hesitate to wipe out the council and Chancellor Dane. Before he could do that, she had a choice to make—except it wasn't really a choice at all, was it?

They would never forgive her.

She left the vial where it was and took a drink before she could change her mind. The metallic, bitter taste assaulted her senses, and she handed the bottle to Solan. Her hand was trembling so hard, she almost dropped it. Solan drank the elixir down in four gulps and sank back in his chair.

Too late to go back now.

"You made the right decision, Cassandra," he said, wiping his mouth. "I promise I will finish what you started."

Cassa said nothing. Solan sprang to his feet, energized by the mirasma. He paced around the room as if he could no longer harness his excitement.

"Now I can leave this filthy dungeon behind, and the council will pay. The council and everyone else who let me rot down here while they used my prophecies to fill their coffers."

Cassa watched him as he moved, practically giddy with his victory.

"Cassa," she said suddenly.

He paused and looked at her.

"What?"

"My name is Cassa," she said. "You always call me Cassandra, but that's not my name."

He raised an eyebrow, and she could see him struggling to tamp down his elation and plans of glorious revenge to figure out why something as insignificant as a nickname could matter to her right now.

"Cassandra is the name your parents gave you, is it not?"

"My parents called me Cassa." It was entirely unimportant, and yet somehow, in this moment, it was the most important thing in the world.

He frowned at her in confusion. He started to say something else but winced and clutched his chest. He grabbed at the table and then his chair, managing to sit down before his legs gave out. He was gasping.

Cassa's own chest had constricted so much that she thought it would crush her lungs. She sucked in a few short breaths, each one hurting more than the last. Solan clawed at his sleeve until he'd exposed his forearm. His eyes widened at what he saw there. Cassa raised her own arms, palms up, to examine them in the light. Her veins were turning black. Black as ink. Black as night. Black as poison.

"Look at that," she managed to cough. "I guess neither of us is immortal after all."

What Cassa Forgot

"I came ahead to give you this," Vesper said. "We're running out of time, and I already know you're going to insist on taking it yourself."

Cassa nodded and shoved it into her pocket. The least she could do. Her fingers were shaking, but she told herself it was the chilly air.

"Where are Alys and Newt?"

"They're coming. Newt is hurt, but not bad. Alys is helping him."

Cassa nodded and peered around the corner. The street in front of the chapel was still empty.

"I have to go," she said. "Evander is distracting the guard who was on watch. He'll probably come back here once he's lost him."

"Wait." Vesper put a hand on her shoulder. "Do you even know where you're going?"

Cassa raised an eyebrow and glanced back at her.

"Are you accusing me of running in with no idea what I'm doing?"

Vesper just stared meaningfully. Cassa let out a short laugh.

"The locked room in the tunnel, the night we escaped," she said. "That's where they lower the mirasma to Solan, isn't it?"

"Impressive memory."

"Not all of us can be rooks."

"Be careful, Cassa."

Cassa darted into the street and ran for the front doors of the chapel. Some caution might have been prudent, but she knew they were running out of time. If the guard managed to lower the elixir before she'd poisoned it, then all was lost. She paused at the entrance of the chapel long enough to pluck a stone from the garden plot. There wasn't time for hesitation. She had to move quickly or she'd miss her chance.

She slipped into the chapel and strode up the main aisle. Everything inside was clean and new, at least relative to everything else in the citadel. The council had had to rebuild it quickly after the fire, lest word spread too far about how easily the rebels had infiltrated the wall. Behind the altar, an oak door stood open. The colorful tapestry that had been hiding it was tucked behind the door. If it was open, then the guard was still inside. No hesitation.

She ran for the altar, barely slowing down as she flung the stone into the nearest window. It shattered with satisfying volume. She ducked behind the door, and not a moment too soon. The guard ran out, his hand on his holster, searching for the source of the sound. She slipped into the tunnel as soon as he'd cleared the steps and ran to the left. Warm light spilled toward her. She ducked through the low doorway, taking stock of the room. It was tiny and bare, with a circular stack of bricks in the center that looked like a chimney—or a well. There were ropes dangling from a crossbeam overhead, looped around a wheel attached to a wooden crank. On the bricks perched a wooden tray, its four corners attached to the ropes. The swirl of the mirasma was the most beautiful thing she'd ever seen. She'd made it in time.

Beside the tray was an open flask, and she grinned as she wrenched the vial of poison out of her pocket. The guard's private vice had bought them just enough time. She emptied the poison into the elixir. For a moment the liquid clouded blackish, and her heart stuttered, but then it cleared to its mesmeric blue-green shine. She shoved the vial back into her pocket, corked it, and sprinted the way she'd come. Instead of exiting into the apse, she passed the doorway and stopped short in the shadows beyond, halfway down the opposite tunnel with the exit that had been bricked up years ago. She pressed herself against the wall, just in case, and watched as the guard entered the tunnel, scratching the back of his head. He walked back toward the room, his silhouette stark against the golden light.

Cassa waited until he was inside the threshold before stepping carefully back into the chapel. She kept her footsteps as quiet as possible until she'd reached the carpeted aisle, then she ran the length of the chapel and out the front door. She ran as fast as she could, more to ease the frenetic nerves in her muscles than anything. She rounded the corner into the alley where Vesper still waited, just as the clock tower signaled the first bell. She smiled at the melodic ringing echoing across the citadel.

"It's done?" Vesper asked. Cassa nodded, and she let out a sigh of relief. "I can't believe it." She leaned her back against the wall and stared upward at the sliver of sky.

"Thanks for the vote of confidence," Cassa said, but she couldn't believe it either. Any minute now Solan would drink the elixir that would be his last. Any minute now it would all be over.

Vesper straightened up suddenly and faced her.

"Cassa, I think I need to take the memories. If he suspects anything, Solan might still be able to steal them from you. I can keep them safe."

Cassa balked at the suggestion, even though she knew Vesper was right to worry. Just the thought of losing that strand of time, no matter how short, pained her. She could still remember the confusion from the last time Vesper had taken memories from her, the way her mind had grasped emptily for something it didn't even know it was missing.

"I'll give them back," Vesper promised. "As soon as it's all over. It's such a short stretch, you probably won't even notice the gap."

Cassa bit her lip and nodded.

"Just the past few minutes," she said. "No rooting around for embarrassing secrets."

She was kidding, but Vesper's eyes were solemn as she rested her fingertips on the side of Cassa's face.

"You know I would never," she said quietly.

Cassa felt a gentle tugging, like her mind was a ball of string being slowly, carefully unraveled. She blinked as Vesper stepped back.

Her fingers were shaking, but she told herself it was the chilly air.

"Where are Alys and Newt?"

FORTY-EIGHT

Cassa

MAYBE Solan managed to read something in her face, because he lunged at her suddenly, landing on his knees in front of the sofa. He pushed her roughly aside, his hands shaking violently as he searched. He held up the vial between them. Empty. It was already empty when she entered the crypts, though it had been full when Vesper had given it to her in the alley. The moment she'd taken it out of her pocket and seen that it was empty, she realized what had happened. A gap in time. A memory beyond her reach, beyond Solan's reach. Three steps ahead. Vesper.

"You knew it was poisoned?" Solan demanded. "And you drank it anyway?"

"Of course I knew. And you made it very clear that you wouldn't drink it unless I did too." The tightness in her lungs was easing, but only because the pain was traveling rapidly toward her heart. "Did you really think I'd let you loose on the world?"

"You were going to," he said desperately, as if convincing her could somehow turn back time. "You helped me get the bloodbond."

"Yes, well." Cassa slouched down on the sofa, closing her eyes and leaning back her head. She felt very heavy all of a sudden. And sleepy. "I never make the same mistake twice."

His raspy breathing was the only sound for a long while. Then the sofa creaked and shifted as he pulled himself up. He dropped onto the cushion next to her. She frowned but didn't open her eyes. She didn't particularly want to die with him beside her, but she didn't have the energy to move. She also didn't want to die down here, in the bowels of the earth, so far from everyone who loved her. But it was too late to do anything about that.

"So after everything," said Solan, his voice low and slurred, "this is how you want it to end. With the council free to go on as they always have. Free to quash more rebellions. Free to twist the prophecies to suit their purposes."

"With my friends alive." Her heart was slowing, even as primal panic gripped her. "Free to tell the truth about the prophecies. Free to do everything I couldn't."

"No death rites," he murmured. "Nothing to ease your passage, ensure your comfort in oblivion."

"I wouldn't want any." The last spark of fire in her chased the words. "I want to take it all with me. Every memory, every mistake, every perfect moment. It's all mine. It's all *me*."

For a few moments, all was quiet. Then he spoke again, so softly, she might have imagined it.

"I think I was wrong about you . . ." His voice trailed into nothing. His labored breathing had stilled. It was bad luck to witness someone's last breath. But she didn't believe in that sort of thing.

Cassa kept her eyes closed. She didn't want to see this prison that had housed centuries of suffering and bitterness. She wanted to see her friends, her parents, her city. She wanted to see all her memories, everything she was taking with her. Her lungs ached for air that she didn't have the strength to breathe, but she wasn't panicked anymore. She felt fine. She felt sleepy. Vaguely, she counted the slowing beats of her heart, until finally it stopped.

FORTY-NINE

ALYS

ALYS didn't know how to grieve. She knew how to mix a tincture for pain and a salve for burns and a potion that made people fall unconscious just from contact. She knew how to solve problems and make contingency plans. She knew how to flip a capsized boat and how to read the near future in almost anything.

What she didn't know was how to live in a world where Cassa Valera was dead.

Alys couldn't bring herself to believe it. Cassa wasn't immortal, but she was *supposed* to be. Never once had Alys actually believed her own admonitions. Never once had Alys thought that Cassa wouldn't outlive them all.

She also didn't know how to grieve. Newt bore it in silence, as she would have expected. His exterior calm was unbreakable as always, but sorrow was etched into every line of his face, into every look and every movement. Vesper cried. Trembling, muffled sobs that she kept rigidly restrained as if they might otherwise rip her apart. And Evander—well, Evander was gone again. He stayed with them the whole time, but Alys could see in his eyes that he wasn't really there. She'd seen it before in the boy who sold his wit and charm for pennies on the street, in the boy who was ready to die in agony on the Blacksmith's table if it meant a chance at saving his family.

Alys was scared that her brother wouldn't come back this time. She was angry that she and the people she loved had to pay for sins that weren't theirs, sins that had been thrust on them by generations past. She was frustrated that even after everything, the council was still the council, and nothing had changed at all.

She was furious at Cassa for finding a way to die like a hero while the rest of them had to go on.

She hated herself for being scared and angry and frustrated and furious, but not sad. How could she not be sad? Maybe she really was broken.

Just as Vesper has promised, her parents were in a house in the upper echelon. Seeing them again, exhausted from worry but very much alive, filled Alys with a relief that was almost painful in its intensity. The chancellor offered apologies that no one accepted and assured them that the council had no choice but to honor the pardons he had issued. Alys didn't have the energy to doubt him.

Her parents were okay, but nothing else was.

They held Cassa's funeral pyre in Aurelia Valley in the dead of night so that the flames might be bright enough for the whole city to witness the passing of Eldra's last firebrand. Alys, Evander, Newt, and Vesper were the only ones in attendance. The chancellor had asked to pay his respects, but they refused him. Alys appreciated Dane's consideration. She was certain that Cassa wouldn't.

None of them knew what to say when the time came. Normally, even if someone died without death rites, a priest would be on hand to talk about how every person's greatest honor is to join the Slain God in blissful oblivion. Candles would be lit and doused at intervals. Sometimes someone would sing a verse from the Slain God's requiem. There was a way these things were done.

They didn't do any of those things. In the end, they didn't even say anything. Evander and Vesper lit the pyre. Vesper's eyes glistened in the firelight with brimming tears, but only a few spilled. Alys couldn't see anything in her brother's face, even as he stood too close and watched as the flames rose higher and higher. Soon Cassa was gone, lost in the bright, billowing fire. Alys's eyes stung with smoke as she sat down on the cool grass. Their vigil would last until only embers remained.

After a couple of hours had passed, when there were only a few licking flames across the smoldering heap, Alys realized that Newt and Vesper had both fallen asleep. It was still pitch-dark, but the pyre gave off some light, and her eyes were adjusted well enough. On her other side, Evander was stretched out on his back, eyes closed, but she knew he was awake.

"Evander?"

A beat.

"Yeah."

"It wasn't your fault. There wasn't anything any of us could have done." She pressed her fingers into the grass in front of her until she reached the crumbling soil below. "You know that, right?"

He frowned without opening his eyes.

"Are you trying to use logic to convince me not to be sad?"

A particularly sharp stalk of grass jammed under her fingernail, and she flinched.

"No." She wiped her hand on her knee. "Maybe. Not on purpose."

After a few seconds he huffed something resembling a laugh and propped himself onto his elbows to look at her.

"Logically speaking," he said, "there was a lot we could have done differently. A lot of ways we could have changed the course of the night. Do you really believe there wasn't?"

His voice held a challenge. A dare.

"Truth or lie?" she asked.

Evander raised an eyebrow, studying her face. He was more still than she'd ever remembered him being. No twitching fingers. No orbiting coins.

"Truth." His voice was quiet, the challenge lost.

"Logically speaking," she said, "Cassa never once in her entire life did something other than exactly what she pleased. She wouldn't even let an infallible prophecy tell her what to do, so no, I don't think we could have changed a single thing."

Evander stared at her. The shadows played heavily on his face, and she couldn't decide if he looked younger or older. He always just looked like Evander.

"I don't like when you're right," he said at last. "It's annoying."

"I'm always right."

"And you're always annoying."

Alys swatted his arm and dropped down beside him in the grass. Smoke drifted overhead, reaching lazily toward the stars. Chill bumps rose on her arms as a cold night breeze stirred the air around them.

"Alys?" Evander plucked a blade of grass and let the breeze carry it from his fingers.

"Yes?"

"She really cared about you, you know." Another blade of grass whirled away into the darkness. "She thought you were smug and condescending, but she always used to talk about the day you two met, at the Dream Merchant's shop. She told me you were fearless."

"I was terrified."

"She said no one with any decent sense would have followed her that day, but you did, and that's what she liked about you."

Alys thought about the two of them, dripping wet and gasping in a boat in the middle of a forgotten lake. *You always know the right thing to do.* An unfamiliar ache bloomed in her chest. She knew what loss felt like. She'd once lost everything she owned to the same regime that Cassa had just died saving. This was different. This was deeper and hungrier, a gaping pit inside her that she hadn't felt until now.

"It's not fair." Each word came out a jagged shard.

"What?"

"The council took everything from her. She hated them so much, but she died for them anyway—and for what? They'll never admit to what they did or what they let Solan do. They'll never acknowledge what she did for them. We're the only ones who will ever know, and it's not fair. It's not right."

Her impassioned speech, which had risen in volume with every word, had woken Vesper and Newt, though neither of them said anything. For a long time the only sound in the world was the crackling embers of Cassa's funeral pyre.

"She didn't do it for them." Evander's voice was as soft as the breeze. "She did it for us."

The sky above blurred with her tears, but Alys didn't wipe them away. She let them fall while she let herself feel the new hollowness inside her. A gaping hole, filled only with fear and anger and frustration and fury. As the last of the pyre crumbled into charred wood and ash, Alys closed her eyes and grieved.

FIFTY

VESPER

IT had been almost three months since Vesper set foot in a chapel of the Slain God. It had been almost as long since she last set foot in the citadel. She'd been staying with her family in the upper echelon, playing parlor games with her younger siblings, putting on a fake smile for her parents, and pretending everything was fine, everything was normal. Other than the letter asking her to meet him here today, Uncle Ansel hadn't contacted her. He hadn't mentioned that since she was still being paid as a clerk, she had no right to just vanish for months. He hadn't mentioned that he could really use her help navigating the treacherous waters stirred up by Solan's death. He hadn't mentioned that the rest of Eldra still didn't know what had been sacrificed that early morning three months ago, and if the council had its way, they never would.

He didn't have to mention any of those things, because Vesper already knew. Still she stayed away. Until the letter. *I need you*, he'd written. Vesper didn't know how to ignore that. She didn't think she could.

She came early to sit through a service for the Slain God. The priest recited the usual string of litanies and exhortations. The young acolytes tripped up and down the steps to the altar in their overlong robes, lighting and dousing ceremonial candles. The gentlemen and ladies in attendance hid jaw-cracking yawns behind fans and hats. Yet when the final recitation was complete—an admonition to serve the memory of the Slain God with respect and humility—and the last candle was doused, Vesper burst into tears.

Her whole body shook with the sobs. She knew everyone in the tiny chapel could hear her. Since she was near the front, most of them could see her as well. She didn't *want* to make a spectacle of herself, but she couldn't stop. No one tried to comfort her, and slowly the chapel emptied. The priest stayed the longest, hovering awkwardly at her periphery before finally murmuring a benediction and slipping away. At that, her tears gave way to hiccuping laughter. She could almost hear Cassa's wry tone. *What's the point of a benediction if the divinity you're invoking is dead?*

When her breathless laughter finally dwindled, she felt better. Not fine. Not normal. But better. She dried her eyes on her sleeve and waited for her uncle to arrive. After a few minutes, the door creaked open. Vesper twisted in her seat. It wasn't her uncle coming down the main aisle but Evander. He was only slightly less haggard than the last time she'd seen him. He peered around the chapel's interior with a cross between suspicion and amusement. Alys was right behind him, wearing the frown she reserved for when her brother said something exasperating. Newt came last. He gazed around the nave with more reverence than Evander, though no less suspicion.

Vesper stared past them at the closed door. She realized with a pang that some part of her was waiting for Cassa to stride in behind them with some inappropriate remark or another. When she met Evander's eye, she wondered if he knew what she was feeling, because his mouth twisted into a grim half smile.

"What are you doing here?" Vesper stood and stepped into the aisle to meet them.

"We were hoping you'd be able to tell us that," Alys said. She picked nervously at the end of her braid.

"We tried to politely decline the chancellor's invitation." Evander shoved his hands into his pockets and wandered toward the altar. "But then his carriage showed up right in the middle of the lower ward, and we didn't really have a choice."

Vesper watched his back, trying to figure out what was different about him, other than his neatly pressed shirt and trousers, which were nicer than the lower ward's typical everyday attire. Newt and Alys were dressed in similar fashion, though the sleeves of Alys's green frock were stained in several places. Casualties of her father's workshop, no doubt. Vesper felt a strange twinge of envy. The ink stains on her own fingers, which had once been a constant part of her fine, normal life, had faded a long time ago.

"I don't know," Vesper said. "He asked me to meet him here today. He didn't say why."

"We haven't seen you in a while." Newt was watching her in his steady, careful way. "How are you doing?"

Vesper had an odd urge to hug him. She hadn't realized how much she'd missed his gentle sincerity. She hadn't realized how much she'd missed all of them. One absence had eclipsed everything else for the past months, and she had focused all her energy on ignoring it.

“I’m fine,” she said.

Evander snorted, turning to face them again.

“Right,” he said. “So are we.”

The coins. That’s what was different about him. She couldn’t remember the last time she’d seen him without at least one silver coin in sight, either flipping over his knuckles or defying the laws of physics. He was stiller than she remembered too. No fidgeting, no excess energy. He just stood there, hands in his pockets, regarding her with a slightly arched eyebrow.

She glanced at Alys, who was looking at her brother, a softer frown marring her features. Vesper opened her mouth to say something—she wasn’t sure what—when the door opened again. This time it was her uncle, wearing his ceremonial robes over his trim black suit and black tie. He found Vesper’s eyes first and gave her a small, warm smile before directing his attention to the others.

“Thank you for coming,” he said. “I realize sending the carriage was presumptuous of me after you refused my first invitation, but I didn’t feel it right to let you miss this monthly council session. There are certain . . . matters to be discussed that I think will interest you all greatly.”

“Is this the part where we’re lauded as heroes and granted wealth and fame in exchange for all our dedicated service?” Evander asked.

Ansel smiled again but shook his head.

“I’m afraid not,” he said. “The council doesn’t know that you’ll be there, but your pardons remain valid, and you will be under my direct protection.”

“Comforting,” Evander noted dryly, but he didn’t say anything further.

Ansel led the way out of the chapel, still spry despite all the evidence of his weariness. Vesper exchanged looks with the others. They didn't look particularly thrilled, but none of them objected as they followed the chancellor.

By the time they reached the Central Keep, most of the citizens had already taken their seats. By law, anyone was allowed in the monthly council session, but usually the majority of those in attendance were nobility from the upper echelons. Seating was crowded and limited, and the citizens from lower tiers who did come were relegated to standing around the edges of the chamber. Like the Judgment Hall, this room bore a ceiling mosaic depicting the elder seers in various states of dreaming. There was a dais at the front with an ornately carved lectern where the chancellor and the councilors would stand to speak. Off to the side of the dais, five equally ornate chairs sat in a row. Four were already filled by the councilors, each in their ceremonial robes, each wearing a practiced expression of blank disinterest.

Those expressions crumbled when they caught sight of the chancellor making his way to the dais with his guests in tow. The weight of all the stares in the room was overwhelming. There were four chairs in the front row that had been reserved. Newt, Evander, and Alys filed in and sat, and Vesper followed suit.

Chancellor Dane climbed the steps to the dais and went straight to the lectern. He hadn't even bothered to fasten his robes over his suit. The room hushed.

"Thank you for coming." His voice carried, though not without visible effort on his part. "Today's session will be a short one, I'm afraid. There are only two items of any import to discuss."

The councilors were exchanging glances and shifting uneasily in their seats—well, most of them. Tempest Adara sat perfectly still, with her hands folded neatly and her full attention on the chancellor.

"First," Ansel went on, "I am announcing my retirement. Today will be my last day serving as your high chancellor. I am grateful for the honor of your trust these past four years, but it is time for me to step down."

A buzz of whispers rose in the crowd. Vesper blinked at her uncle. She knew the rigors of his office had been wearing on him, but how could he possibly retire now, when they had just succeeded in crippling the council? She looked at her friends, but they were staring right back at her with wide eyes. She shook her head helplessly.

"My successor is someone far more qualified than I." Ansel looked toward the council, his face holding nothing but gentle benevolence. "Tempest Adara has served on the council for many, many years with distinction, and I'm sure she will serve you just as well as high chancellor."

More whispers. Again, Tempest was the only councilor who showed no reaction to Ansel's words, other than a bare smile. Andras was glaring at her with silent, restrained fury. Delia's fury was less noticeable, but the iciness in her eyes was fatal. Grantham Barwick was turning a startling shade of purple, with veins bulging in his neck and temple. Vesper wasn't sure if the rest of the crowd could understand what was happening here—she barely understood herself. They did seem to realize that whatever it was, it was momentous. Historic.

She sneaked another look at her friends. Alys was frowning in thought, and Newt seemed equally bemused. Evander was grinning at the councilors' disturbed reactions. His fingers tapped a wild rhythm on his knee.

Ansel cleared his throat a few times, and finally the dull roar of the crowd quieted.

"The second order of business is a difficult one. It will raise many questions and doubts and fears, but I ask that you remember that Eldra was here long before any of us were born, and it will be here long after all of us are gone. I take comfort in this knowledge, and I hope you will too."

The silence in the room was almost absolute now. Ansel sighed deeply.

"We have reached the end of an era. Three months ago, the last seer in Eldra died. There are no prophecies left. I'm afraid the distant future is no longer ours to know."

A heartbeat more of silence. Then the room erupted. People shouted questions, disbelief, dismay. The councilors' anger at Tempest had shifted into shock at what the chancellor had just done.

He'd told the truth. Vesper couldn't believe it. After so many years of secrecy, after all the council's desperate attempts to hold on to their power, to keep the city from seeing the decline of the elder seers' bloodline—after everything, Eldra would know the truth.

Cassa would have given anything to see this, Vesper thought. And then, with a hollow ache in her chest, she realized that Cassa had given everything for this.

Heat was building behind her eyes, and she wondered miserably if she was about to make another spectacle of herself. Alys grasped her hand, smiling tightly. Vesper could see that her eyes were also shining with unshed tears. Vesper squeezed her hand and returned the smile.

The chancellor held up both his arms in a plea for quiet. It took several minutes, but finally the crowd settled enough for him to continue speaking.

"As I said, I know you will have many questions. They will all be answered in time. In the past, the council's main duty has been to interpret and preserve the prophecies for the good of the city. Obviously that purpose has now become obsolete." On the last word he shot a glance toward the council that even the dullest citizen couldn't misinterpret. "As such, when Chancellor Adara has sworn her vows, the present council will be dissolved. A new council will be elected with a representative from every ward of the city."

He had more to say, but the room was in an uproar once more. Tempest kept her seat, but the other councilors had jumped to their feet, their angry demands drowned out by the crowd. The citadel guards who normally stood watch unobtrusively around the edges of the room made themselves a little more visible, though no weapons were drawn. The citizens who had been whipping themselves into a frenzy quieted perceptively. Many were already leaving, no doubt to spread the news. Vesper saw that the guards Grantham and Delia were ordering to arrest the chancellor were ignoring them completely. This was more than the end of an era. This was a coup, orchestrated from within the council's own ranks.

Ansel and Tempest must have struck a bargain. He would reveal the truth to the city and dissolve the current council, and she would carry the city into its unknowable future as the high chancellor. Tempest wasn't perfect, but she was driven by duty rather than greed. With the other councilors out of the picture, she might be able to build something good.

Vesper couldn't help but smile. Maybe Ansel wasn't as ruthless or relentless as the councilors, but he knew how to play the long game. He always had. This didn't change everything, but it changed enough. Her part in the game would probably never be known to the city. Neither would Alys's or Newt's or Evander's. Neither would Cassa's. History would remember Chancellor Ansel Dane, who had ended a century-long rebellion, and Chancellor Tempest Adara, who would usher in a new, unforetold era. History would remember Caris and Luc Valera, the legendary rebels who raised up a city and nearly brought the citadel to its knees.

The rest would be forgotten in time. People died, and their secrets died with them. Gods perished. Memories faded. The world moved on.

Maybe it wasn't fair, but Vesper didn't think it mattered much in the end. Even when their futures were foretold, people could still make their own choices. Even when their pasts were forgotten, people's lives still meant something. Cassa might not live forever, even in memory, but she had lived, and she had mattered. Vesper couldn't help but think that was legacy enough, even for Cassa Valera.

FIFTY-ONE

Newt

NEWT hadn't expected to ever stand across the street from his father's house again, to see the scattered, fading rose petals in the garden, the pristine white door with the polished brass knocker. He'd left it behind more than six months ago, when he'd finally realized he could survive on his own. When he'd finally realized that there were no more lessons to learn. Even now, with only the empty street and a decorative iron gate between him and the house, he couldn't bring himself to move closer.

Newt knew his father was home, though he hadn't seen him. Where else did he have to go? The ghosts of Luc and Caris Valera still haunted him, tethering him to the house he had paid for with the trust of his fellow rebels. Newt thought wryly that Cassa would love to join her parents in that task, and then he wondered if thinking that was irreverent. Cassa probably wouldn't think so. Cassa would have laughed. A smile teased his lips, accompanied by a dull ache in his chest.

Alys had written his father a letter from the citadel while a physician was hemming and hawing over Newt's wounds, but there had been no reply. Newt still didn't know if he was relieved or disappointed. He'd been staying in the lower ward. Without much discussion, the Seras had opened up their spare bedroom for him once more. The apothecary shop didn't really feel like home, but it was the closest he'd had for a long time.

A curtain at one of the front windows fluttered, and Newt's stomach clenched. He stared at the front door, wishing it would open, wishing it wouldn't.

It didn't.

In moments like this, he could still feel Solan's presence twining through his memories, suffocating all the good that Newt had left. There was world-ending hate buried somewhere deep inside him, and sometimes he was afraid it would find a way out. Sometimes he was afraid that he didn't remember how to be happy. Maybe Solan had taken that from him too.

Something brushed his elbow, and Newt jumped. He blinked to find Evander standing next to him, raising an eyebrow at his reaction. Newt wasn't normally caught by surprise. Normally he was sharply aware of his surroundings, of every exit, every object, every possible advantage he could take. Another lesson that had long since been learned.

"What are you doing here?" he asked.

"I was just in the neighborhood," Evander said with a shrug. He eyed the house across the street, taking in its subtle affluence. "Nice house."

Newt wondered if the house that the council had taken from the Seras had been anything like this one. He studied Evander's profile for a second. The sun glinted on his jet hair, and Newt found himself habitually searching for the telltale flash of silver. No coins though. There hadn't been any since that night in the citadel. The dull ache throbbed again in his chest.

"It's too small," he said. He didn't bother explaining what he meant or whose house it was. Evander would know. Evander knew more about him than anyone, though not everything. There were certain parts of himself that Newt couldn't share, not even in the intimacy of warm summer days when the valley hummed around them and Evander was listening like there was nothing else worth hearing. Sometimes he wanted to though. Sometimes he even thought that one day he could.

"You spend so much time in the valley, I think any four walls would be too small for you." Evander's manner was relaxed, but his features held no hint of a smile. Those had vanished almost as entirely as the coins.

"Maybe so." Newt managed a halfhearted grin. "The third ward is a strange place for a casual morning stroll."

Evander shrugged again.

"I like it up here. There aren't any murderous executioners or trigger-happy guards."

"Even so," said Newt, "I hear there are wayward children in these parts that'll charm the silver right out of your pocket while they pretend to tell your future."

Something glittered in Evander's eyes.

"Sounds like a genius enterprise. Probably pays well."

"Better than the chancellor pays anyway."

Evander's laugh escaped him, sudden and rich. His eyes widened as if he was surprised by the sound. The smile lingered on his lips as he straightened and clapped an arm around Newt's shoulders.

"Come on," he said, his voice lilting with the laughter. "Let's go home."

Newt let Evander lead him away from the decorative iron gate, the dying rose garden, the pristine white door. The knot in his chest loosened with every step. He did cast one last glance over his shoulder. The curtains were still now. The Valeras weren't the only ghosts haunting that house. Maybe one day he would return. Maybe one day he would look inside himself to find that the world-ending hate had faded. He was bent, but he wasn't broken. That was enough, for now.

FIFTY-TWO

EVANDER

THE weeks crept by with aching slowness, but somehow Evander didn't realize summer had come until one day the last rain of spring evaporated from the earth and the sun was so bright that it drowned out the blue of the sky. In Aurelia Valley, the heather was in bloom, painting the gentle slopes a vibrant purple. The waist-high grasses rippled in the warm breeze like a shimmering ocean of gold. On a day like this, when everything was stark colors and swaying motion, he could understand why Newt loved the valley so much.

When Newt had invited him to come that morning, Evander had agreed only because the house felt more stifling than it ever had before. Even the city no longer felt like a haven. The streets were shadowed in memories of Cassa, and the statues of the elder seers were monuments to everything he wanted to forget. At least the nightmares had eased. For the first couple of months, he'd awoken in a cold sweat every night. His sleep was a cell with no door, a cavern with no exit. A bottomless pit into which he always, always fell. Even when he'd started sleeping through the night again, he couldn't bring himself to douse the lamp. He wasn't scared of the dark, but it suffocated him all the same. If his parents had noticed the waste of lamp oil, they hadn't mentioned it.

Today was different though. Today the sun was so bright overhead that night felt like a distant dream. He was on his back in a patch of thick green grass, close enough to the river that he could hear its murmuring flow but far enough from the city that even the bustling noise of Merchants' Bridge didn't reach them. Beside him, Newt was so still that Evander stole periodic glances to reassure himself that he was breathing. He could understand Newt's love of the valley, but he had never understood the ritual of stillness. Newt had tried to explain it to him before. Something about fading into the landscape. Something about escape. But for Evander stillness was a prison as suffocating as the dark. Movement was the only way he could reassure himself he was free.

He'd first met Newt on a day like today. He wondered if Newt remembered. His chest tightened with the thought, because it was very possible Newt *didn't* remember. Evander wasn't sure how much Solan took from him. He'd never figured out how to broach the subject. He didn't even know if Newt would want to talk about it. Something had changed between them that night. Something indefinable but impossible to ignore.

"Why are you staring at me?" Newt asked without opening his eyes.

"I'm not," Evander said. He realized that he was and turned his head to gaze again at the halcyon sky.

Newt, who hadn't so much as twitched, didn't reply. Evander fidgeted. The grass was prickly against his bare arms, and sweat was soaking the back of his shirt. He wanted to sit up, but he was afraid that if he couldn't maintain some semblance of the ritual, Newt might not invite him next time. Evander liked coming to the valley. He liked the brightness and the landscape's subtle movement and the earthy scent of summer. He liked being here with Newt.

He just didn't like being still.

He thrummed his fingers in the grass by his thigh, and one of the silver coins in his pocket jumped with the motion. He'd forgotten he had them. Putting them in his pocket every day was so habitual that he didn't even notice anymore, but he hadn't used them in months. For a few seconds, he didn't move. He could hear his own heartbeat and wondered if somehow Newt could too. Then, painstakingly, he eased one coin from its hiding place. The scar on his arm burned a little with the effort. The bloodbond was like a muscle that atrophied with disuse. He'd never had that problem before.

He redoubled his focus, and the coin leapt into the air over his chest and hovered there. The longer he concentrated, the easier it felt. The tension that had been building in his body began to unwind. When he summoned the other two coins into orbit around their brother, a delicious relief spread through him. It was like letting himself breathe for the first time since that terrible night. Devastation still echoed deep inside him, but out here those echoes were easy to ignore, just for now.

The coins danced lazily through spiraling patterns, and Evander let out a long, slow breath. He reached up and caught them in one swipe. Fading into the landscape wasn't exactly possible with silver coins flying overhead.

"Don't stop."

Evander jumped at Newt's voice, quiet though it was. He turned his head to find himself looking straight into Newt's solemn eyes. Evander hadn't noticed before how close he actually was. Without breaking from his gaze, Evander uncurled his fingers and let the coins rise between them. Sunlight sparkled on the whirling silver. Newt watched them with a content smile curving his lips.

"It's been a while," he said.

"I know." Evander was having difficulty focusing, because he was acutely aware of how close his hand was to Newt's in the grass. The first time they'd held hands was the same night they'd first kissed. The same night Solan had ripped memories from Newt's mind. The same night Cassa had—but he didn't want to think about that now. There was plenty of time for devastation in the dark. Right now, the sun was warm, and the silver was gleaming, and Newt's hand was barely an inch away.

Evander could hear his heartbeat again, strumming steadily. He slid his hand over Newt's. Newt jerked at his touch, and Evander yanked his hand away. The coins fell to the grass.

"Sorry," Newt said breathlessly. "I didn't—I wasn't—"

He swallowed his words and fell silent. Evander stared at the sky without seeing it. He wiped his hand across his damp face and sat up. His common sense told him to leave before he made things worse, but he didn't move. On the horizon, the trees of Eldrin Wood were a blur of emerald and shadow. A hawk soared from the east, its silhouette black against the sky.

"You don't remember, do you," he said softly.

Newt sat up too. He'd taken one of the coins and was fiddling with it. "Remember what?"

Evander shook his head. Suddenly he was in that courtyard in the Central Keep again. He couldn't stop thinking about the feel of wet cobblestones under his knees. The weight of iron on his wrists. The sound of the pistol hammer clicking just behind his head. The memory of their kiss outside the Blacksmith's cottage was the only memory he'd wanted to relive as he died. He didn't know how he could explain that to Newt. He wasn't even sure he understood it himself.

Not that it mattered anyway. If Newt didn't remember it, then it might as well have not happened. Evander closed his eyes. A breeze had picked up but did nothing to relieve the summer heat. He was just about to listen to his common sense and stand when Newt's fingers slid under his hand, interlacing with his. His eyes sprang open, and for a second all he could do was stare at their hands together in the grass. Newt's was much paler and much more calloused than his. He could feel the silver of the coin pressed between their palms.

"You could remind me, if you want," Newt said.

Evander met his eyes. Newt was biting his lip, and the tousled curls across his forehead ruffled in the breeze. He looked so sincere and so golden that Evander's heart somersaulted. He was certain now that Newt could hear his heartbeat as he leaned in slowly. Their lips brushed, hesitantly at first, but then Newt leaned in, and Evander lost himself in the breathless sensation of it, the tangle of Newt's tongue with his, the weight of him as he pressed closer and closer.

Suddenly Newt pulled away. Evander's head spun with the abruptness of it, and he sucked in a short breath. Newt was staring at the ground, panting.

"I'm sorry." He slid his hand free from Evander's. The coin dropped into the grass again. "It's just—Cassa."

He spoke her name with visible effort and scrubbed his hands across his face. Evander closed his eyes, trying to bring himself back from the mindless bliss of seconds before. It wasn't as if he'd forgotten about her. Cassa had meant too much to him for too long for that to ever be possible. He knew that even when the devastation eventually faded, his memories of her—every wonderful, irritating, eye-rolling, impossible, legendary memory—would remain.

He lay back down in the grass and opened his eyes to the sky. The first time Cassa had kissed him had been on a dare from Vesper. He'd even known it at the time, but he hadn't cared. The last time they'd kissed was the night before they decided they each wanted something different. He still remembered the way the cloudy morning had cast his bedroom in a sleepy gray. They'd stayed up the whole night talking. He remembered the way she'd rested her hand on his chest before she said good-bye, like she was trying to connect to his heartbeat one last time.

"I love her," Evander said. "I always have and I always will. But it's different now. After we split up, I never felt that way about her again."

"What way?" Newt was on his side, his head propped on his hand.

Evander looked at him.

"The way I feel about you."

He watched his words sink in. A new light flickered in Newt's eyes, and Evander's breath caught in his throat, when suddenly their lips were locked again. The kiss was slower this time, savoring and deliberate. Every inch of his body was alive with it. He could feel each blade of grass that scraped against his skin. The ripple of the breeze through his hair. The pressure of Newt's fingers splayed across his rib cage.

This time when Newt broke away, he stayed close, his arm resting on Evander's chest, his lips close enough that Evander could reach them again if he pushed himself up just slightly. He was considering it, but Newt was wearing a strange expression that gave him pause.

"What?" he asked.

"Nothing." Newt's breath tickled his cheek. "I just . . . never expected this to be real."

"What do you mean?"

"When we first met, you were with Cassa," he said, a thin frown creasing his forehead. "And then even after it ended—I don't know. She was *the* Cassa Valera. And I'm just . . . me."

Evander frowned too. He'd never considered how Newt might have felt about him when they first met. He felt oddly guilty, though he knew he hadn't done anything wrong. He also felt fidgety again, but he didn't want Newt to move. He flicked his fingers, and all three coins shot into the air, wheeling freely above them.

"She was never *the* Cassa Valera to me. She was just Cassa," Evander said, struggling to focus as Newt's index finger traced absently along Evander's collarbone. "And I like that you're just you. I wouldn't want you to be anyone else."

He'd barely gotten the words out when Newt moved to capture his mouth again. The coins plummeted onto them. Newt gave a surprised laugh that vibrated in Evander's chest. And all around them the grass swayed and the valley hummed, a symphony of motion and life.

FIFTY-THREE

ALYS

ALYS wasn't sure how long Vesper had been hovering in the doorway when she startled Alys with a pointed cough. Alys had been hunched over her father's workbench grinding some garlic powder with a mortar and pestle.

"Your parents said I could come back." Vesper still lingered uncertainly on the threshold as if she were afraid Alys would deny her entry. She was in her black, silver-stitched clerk's uniform. Alys couldn't understand how Vesper still lived and worked in the citadel, how she walked those streets knowing that beneath her feet were a maze of silent crypts, a fathomless lake, a chamber guarded by stone seers, and the centuries-old prison where Cassa had died to save them.

"I wasn't expecting you," Alys said, cutting off that line of thought.

"I need your help." There was a gravity in Vesper's tone that made Alys nervous.

"With what?"

"Something that's probably impossible, but I have to at least try." Vesper moved closer until she was right across the workbench from

Alys. In this room cluttered with books and tools of the trade, where Alys had spent so much of her life hiding, Vesper was a stark intrusion, a ghost from a life that Alys had never expected to live. "I think there might be a way to reverse the loss of memories. I think we might be able to bring back at least some of what Solan stole from people like the Blacksmith."

Alys frowned, thinking through everything she knew about rooks.

"How? When a rook takes a memory, it becomes theirs, unless they give it back or give it to someone else."

"But rooks don't forget." Vesper tapped her temple with an ink-stained finger. "That's why mirasma was created in the first place. Rooks don't forget memories they give away. I've been thinking about it a lot. What if that ability—that imprinting of memories—could be re-created somehow in other people? Or what if people already *have* that ability, and they just need a way to strengthen it? The alchemists made a substance that can suppress a rook's memories, so why not this?"

Vesper was pacing now, talking with her hands, talking so fast that she had to gulp down a breath with the last word. Alys stared down at the workbench, mentally tracing the logic.

"You want to formulate something that has the opposite effect of mirasma."

"Basically, yes." Vesper paused and studied her reaction. "I told you it was probably impossible."

Alys tightened her grip on her pestle as the rush of a new challenge washed over her, leaving the familiar barbs of panic in its wake. It would mean going back into the citadel. They would need an alchemist's help—or at least an understanding of the mirasma process. Staying here, in the seclusion of her parents' workroom, would be easier and safer.

Is that what she wanted?

"We've managed the impossible before." Alys took a deep breath. She pressed her hands into the tabletop like an anchor. The maelstrom still churned at the back of her mind, but it was gradually slowing.

A grin spread across Vesper's face.

"I was hoping you'd say that. I think between the two of us, we might just stand a chance."

We meant together. *We* meant friends. A phantom ache resounded in Alys's chest. She doubted Vesper realized the parallel to her words four years ago, on the day they'd first met. *Between the two of us, we might just manage to keep Cassa alive.* A bitter laugh rose in her throat but stuck there. Vesper must have seen something shift in Alys's expression, because her grin faded.

"What's wrong?"

Alys shook her head.

"Nothing, just . . . Cassa." She didn't think she could explain it. She didn't think she would have to.

A shadow passed over Vesper's face, and she sighed.

"I think about her a lot too. She's—" Vesper cut short, rubbing the back of her neck. She swallowed hard and began again. "There's still a part of her in my head. I guess it will always be there. The memory I took, when she poisoned the mirasma."

Alys set down the pestle, untied her apron, and rounded the table. She pulled herself up to sit on the edge, and Vesper followed suit. For a long while they just sat there, shoulder to shoulder, feet dangling.

"What's it like?" Alys asked.

Vesper stared into the middle distance. The sunlight streaming in through the windows behind them warmed Alys's back and burnished Vesper's hair a brilliant copper.

"It depends on the day," Vesper replied softly. "Most of the time I like it. I like knowing that even such a small part of her lives on. She told me that all she wanted was for the things she'd done, and the things her parents and all the rebels before them had done, to matter. I think I understand that better now. I never cared much about the prophecies, but now that there aren't any more . . . I don't know. I guess I always felt like the prophecies meant we mattered somehow. Like everyone in Eldra was born to see them fulfilled. Like the future belonged to us."

Alys wasn't sure what to say. She looked at the floor, thinking that it needed to be swept—a strange thing to notice at a time like this.

"I suppose eventually there won't be any more rooks or sentients or diviners either," Vesper said into the silence. "One day we'll all just be an obscure metaphor in poetry and songs, and then the world will forget about us completely."

A flash of a memory. Blue light, rippling water, and the unknown waiting for them on a distant shore.

"Auspicious stars," Alys said musingly.

"What?"

"Cassa didn't think we needed auspicious stars or seers for our lives to matter. What we do is what we'll be remembered for."

Vesper considered for a second. Her lips twitched.

"I know." Alys hopped down from the table. "It's a load of sentimental tripe, but it'll sound very poetic in a song one day."

Vesper laughed and jumped down beside Alys.

"Let's go confound some alchemists then," she said.

"Seems like a good start."

Acknowledgments

I owe the existence of this book and everything else I've ever written to my mom and dad, who have always believed in me, trusted me, and encouraged me. Without you, I never would've had the audacity to think that someone else might want to read my words, and I love you both more than words could ever capture.

My whole family has been incredibly supportive throughout this journey. I know you may not support everything in these pages, but I do know that you'll always be there for me. Thank you.

A million thanks to Mark O'Brien, Quincy Drinker, and all of my other sensitivity readers for their thoughtful insight and critique. My eternal gratitude to Taylor, my superstar agent, and Anne, my amazing editor. And thank you to Siobhán Gallagher, Josh Berlowitz, and everyone else at Amulet Books for all your hard work. Special thanks to Erin Radziwon and Logan Jones for your generous help.

Puffin, I'm glad that we're sisters-in-arms in the publishing trenches. Remember to stay sexy and don't get murdered. Badger, thank you for continuing to be my number one fangirl, even when you can't make it out of the tunnels. Soup, thank you for continuing to answer all my creepy late-night questions and for being there whenever I need to nerd out about something. Mackenzi, without our regular venting sessions, I don't think I ever would have survived the dreaded sophomore slump. We hate Richard Peele.

Lots of love to my majaoes, the best critique group (and friends) a writer could ask for. Katie, Kara, Clare, Emily, Jesi, and Nöel: You're all goddesses. And shout-out to Lana, who wrote the music of my heart.

Cleh, your DM magic is both inspiration and much-needed stress relief. Thank you for keeping all my secrets.

Emily, I can't thank you enough for all the time and energy you put into this one. You guided me through revision hell, and I still can't believe you aren't sick of me yet.

Kara, you dragged me through the slump and dealt with all my whining, self-doubt, and complete breakdowns. Thanks for sticking with me through the highs and the lows and everything in between. Don't tell anyone, but you're my favorite.